PRAISE FOR DEAN KOONTZ
THE No. 1 BESTSELLING AUTHOR

COLD FIRE
'His most enjoyable book to date'   *The Times*

THE BAD PLACE
'He combines rich, evocative prose, some of the warmest – and also some of the most despicable – characters to be found in fiction, technical speculations that seem to come directly from today's headlines and a sense of on-the-edge-of-the-seat pacing to create thrillers that are not just convincing, but thought-provoking as well'   *Mystery Scene*

MIDNIGHT
'A masterly novel a remarkable thriller. Koontz is a predictable writer in only one sense: the action in his novels never ceases'   *Fear*

SHADOWFIRES
'A roller-coaster of a thriller'   *Mystery Scene*

THE SERVANTS OF TWILIGHT
'Dean Koontz is the best writer of the macabre working today'   *Cult Magazine*

LIGHTNING
'[It] sizzles . . . Wow! It's a mix to tingle any reader's fancy'   *New York Daily News*

SHATTERED
'Catches you by the throat and won't let go'
Chicago Sun Times

THE VISION
'Kept me glued to my chair . . . sinister and spine-tingling. Page-turning excitement' *Spectator*

THE VOICE OF THE NIGHT
'Like the best of the genre, it enjoys the horror form, plays with it and even manages to exact some humour' *Independent*

CHASE
'This superb book is more than a novel of suspense. It is a brutally realistic portrait of the role of violence in our society' *Saturday Review*

Also by Dean Koontz

Hideaway
Cold Fire
The Funhouse
Shadowfires
The Servants of Twilight
The Door to December
The Eyes of Darkness
The Key to Midnight
The Bad Place
Midnight
Lightning
Watchers
The Mask
The Face of Fear
Phantoms
Whispers
Shattered
Chase
Twilight Eyes
The Voice of the Night
Strangers
Darkness Comes
The Vision
Night Chills

The House of Thunder

Dean Koontz

Previously published as
The House of Thunder
by Leigh Nichols

First published in the USA in 1982
by Pocket Books

First published in Great Britain in 1983
by Fontana Paperbacks,
a division of HarperCollins Publishers

Reprinted in hardback in 1992
by HEADLINE BOOK PUBLISHING PLC

Reprinted in paperback in 1992
by HEADLINE BOOK PUBLISHING PLC

A HEADLINE FEATURE Paperback

10 9 8 7 6 5 4

ISBN 0 7472 3661 5

Printed and bound in Great Britain by
HarperCollins Manufacturing, Glasgow

HEADLINE BOOK PUBLISHING
A division of Hodder Headline PLC
338 Euston Road
London NW1 3BH

This book is for Gerda,
as it surely should have been
from the start.

PART ONE

Fear Comes Quietly . . .

The year was 1980 – an ancient time, so long ago and far away . . .

1

When she woke, she thought she was blind. She opened her eyes and could see only purple darkness, ominous and shapeless shadows stirring within other shadows. Before she could panic, that gloom gave way to a pale haze, and the haze resolved into a white, acoustic-tile ceiling.

She smelled fresh bed linens. Antiseptics. Disinfectants. Rubbing alcohol.

She turned her head, and pain flashed the length of her forehead, as if an electric shock had snapped through her skull from temple to temple. Her eyes immediately swam out of focus. When her vision cleared again, she saw that she was in a hospital room.

She could not remember being admitted to a hospital. She didn't even know the name of it or in what city it was located.

What's wrong with me?

She raised one dismayingly weak arm, put a hand to her brow, and discovered a bandage over half of her forehead. Her hair was quite short, too.

Hadn't she worn it long and full?

She had insufficient strength to keep her arm raised; she let it drop back to the mattress.

She couldn't raise her left arm at all, for it was taped to a heavy board and pierced by a needle. She was being fed intravenously: the chrome IV rack, with its dangling bottle of glucose, stood beside the bed.

For a moment she closed her eyes, certain that she was only dreaming. When she looked again, however, the room was still there, unchanged: white ceiling, white walls, a green tile floor, pale yellow drapes drawn back at the sides of the large window. Beyond the glass, there were tall evergreens of some kind and a cloudy sky with only a few small patches of blue. There was another bed, but it was empty; she had no roommate.

The side rails on her own bed were raised to prevent her from falling to the floor. She felt as helpless as a baby in a crib.

She realized she didn't know her name. Or her age. Or anything else about herself.

She strained against the blank wall in her mind, attempting to topple it and release the memories imprisoned on the other side, but she had no success; the wall stood, inviolate. Like a blossom of frost, fear opened icy petals in the pit of her stomach. She tried harder to remember, but she had no success.

Amnesia. Brain damage.

Those dreaded words landed with the force of

4

hammer blows in her mind. Evidently, she had been in an accident and had sustained a serious head injury. She considered the grim prospect of permanent mental disorientation, and she shuddered.

Suddenly, however, unexpected and unsought, her name came to her. Susan. Susan Thorton. She was thirty-two years old.

The anticipated flood of recollections turned out to be just a trickle. She could recall nothing more than her name and age. Although she probed insistently at the darkness in her mind, she couldn't remember where she lived. How did she earn her living? Was she married? Did she have any children? Where had she been born? Where had she gone to school? What foods did she like? What was her favorite kind of music? She could find no answers to either important or trivial questions.

Amnesia. Brain damage.

Fear quickened her heartbeat. Then, mercifully, she remembered that she had been on vacation in Oregon. She didn't know where she had come from; she didn't know what job she would return to once her vacation came to an end; but at least she knew where she was. Somewhere in Oregon. The last thing she could recall was a beautiful mountain highway. An image of that landscape came to her in vivid detail. She had been driving through a pine forest, not far from the sea, listening to the radio, enjoying a clear blue morning. She drove through a sleepy village of stone and clapboard houses, then passed a couple of slow-moving logging trucks, then had the road all to herself for a few miles, and then . . . then . . .

Nothing. After that, she had awakened, confused and blurry-eyed, in the hospital.

'Well, well. Hello there.'

Susan turned her head, searching for the person who had spoken. Her eyes slipped out of focus again, and a new dull pain pulsed at the base of her skull.

'How are you feeling? You *do* look pale, but after what you've been through, that's certainly to be expected, isn't it? Of course it is. Of course.'

The voice belonged to a nurse who was approaching the bed from the direction of the open door. She was a pleasantly plump, gray-haired woman with warm brown eyes and a wide smile. She wore a pair of white-framed glasses on a beaded chain around her neck; at the moment, the glasses hung unused on her matronly bosom.

Susan tried to speak. Couldn't.

Even the meager effort of straining for words made her so light-headed that she thought she might pass out. Her extreme weakness scared her.

The nurse reached the bed and smiled reassuringly. 'I knew you'd come out of it, honey. I just knew it. Some people around here weren't so sure as I was. But I knew you had moxie.' She pushed the call button on the headboard of the bed.

Susan tried to speak again, and this time she managed to make a sound, though it was only a low and meaningless gurgle in the back of her throat. Suddenly she wondered if she would ever speak again. Perhaps she would be condemned to making grunting, gibbering animal noises for the rest of her life. Sometimes, brain damage resulted in a loss of speech, didn't it? *Didn't it?*

A drum was booming loudly and relentlessly in her head. She seemed to be turning on a carousel, faster and faster, and she wished she could put a stop to the room's nauseating movement.

The nurse must have seen the panic in Susan's eyes, for she said, 'Easy now. Easy, kid. Everything'll be all right.' She checked the IV drip, then lifted Susan's right wrist to time her pulse.

My God, Susan thought, if I can't speak, maybe I can't *walk*, either.

She tried to move her legs under the sheets. She didn't seem to have any feeling in them; they were even more numb and leaden than her arms.

The nurse let go of her wrist, but Susan clutched at the sleeve of the woman's white uniform and tried desperately to speak.

'Take your time,' the nurse said gently.

But Susan knew she didn't have much time. She was teetering on the edge of unconsciousness again. The pounding pain in her head was accompanied by a steadily encroaching ring of darkness that spread inward from the edges of her vision.

A doctor in a white lab coat entered the room, apparently in answer to the call button that the nurse had pushed. He was a husky, dour-faced

7

man, about fifty, with thick black hair combed straight back from his deeply lined face.

Susan looked beseechingly at him as he approached the bed, and she said, *Are my legs paralyzed?*

For an instant she thought she had actually spoken those words aloud, but then she realized she still hadn't regained her voice. Before she could try again, the rapidly expanding darkness reduced her vision to a small spot, a mere dot, then a pinpoint.

Darkness.

She dreamed. It was a bad dream, very bad, a nightmare.

For at least the two-hundredth time, she dreamed that she was in the House of Thunder again, lying in a pool of warm blood.

2

When Susan woke again, her headache was gone. Her vision was clear, and she was no longer dizzy.

Night had fallen. Her room was softly lighted, but only featureless blackness lay beyond the window.

The IV rack had been taken away. Her needle-marked, discolored arm looked pathetically thin against the white sheet.

She turned her head and saw the husky, dour-faced man in the white lab coat. He was standing beside the bed, staring down at her. His brown eyes possessed a peculiar, disturbing power; they seemed to be looking *into* her rather than at her, as if he were carefully examining her innermost secrets, yet they were eyes that revealed nothing whatsoever of his own feelings; they were as flat as painted glass.

'What's . . . happened . . . to me?' Susan asked.

She could speak. Her voice was faint, raspy, and rather difficult to understand, but she was not reduced to a mute existence by a stroke or by some other severe brain injury, which was what she had feared at first.

She was still weak, however. Her meager resources were noticeably depleted even by the act of speaking a few words at a whisper.

'Where . . . am I?' she asked, voice cracking. Her throat burned with the passage of each rough syllable.

The doctor didn't respond to her questions right away. He picked up the bed's power control switch, which dangled on a cord that was wrapped around the side rail, and he pushed one of the four buttons. The upper end of the bed rose, tilting Susan into a sitting position. He put down the controls and half filled a glass with cold water from a metal carafe that stood on a yellow plastic tray on the night-stand.

'Sip it slowly,' he said. 'It's been a while since you've taken any food or liquid other than intra-venously.'

She accepted the water. It was indescribably delicious. It soothed her irritated throat.

When she had finished drinking, he took the glass from her and returned it to the nightstand. He unclipped a penlight from the breast pocket of his lab coat, leaned close, and examined her eyes. His own eyes remained flat and unreadable beneath bushy eyebrows that were knit together in what seemed to be a perpetual frown.

While she waited for him to finish the examination, she tried to move her legs under the covers.

10

They were weak and rubbery and still somewhat numb, but they moved at her command. She wasn't paralyzed after all.

When the doctor finished examining her eyes, he held his right hand up in front of her face, just a few inches away from her. 'Can you see my hand?'

'Sure,' she said. Her voice was faint and quaverous, but at least it was no longer raspy or difficult to understand.

His voice was deep, colored by a vague gutteral accent that Susan could not quite identify. He said, 'How many fingers am I holding up?'

'Three,' she said, aware that he was testing her for signs of concussion.

'And now – how many?'

'Two.'

'And now?'

'Four.'

He nodded approval, and the sharp creases in his forehead softened a bit. His gaze still probed at her with an intensity that made her uncomfortable. 'Do you know your name?'

'Yes. I'm Susan Thorton.'

'That's right. Middle name?'

'Kathleen.'

'Good. How old are you?'

'Thirty-two.'

'Good. Very good. You seem clear-headed.'

Her voice had become dry and scratchy again. She cleared her throat and said, 'But that's about *all* I'm able to remember.'

He hadn't entirely relinquished his frown, and the lines in his broad, square face became sharply etched once more. 'What do you mean?'

'Well, I can't remember where I live . . . or what kind of work I do . . . or whether I'm married . . .'

He studied her for a moment, then said, 'You live in Newport Beach, California.'

As soon as he mentioned the town, she could see her house: a cozy Spanish-style place with a red tile roof, white stucco walls, mullioned windows, tucked in among several tall palms. But no matter how hard she thought about it, the name of the street and the number of the house eluded her.

'You work for the Milestone Corporation in Newport,' the doctor said.

'Milestone?' Susan said. She sensed a distant glimmer of memory in her mental fog.

The doctor looked down at her intensely.

'What's wrong?' she asked shakily. 'Why are you staring like that?'

He blinked in surprise, then smiled somewhat sheepishly. Clearly, smiles did not come easily to him, and this one was strained. 'Well . . . I'm concerned about you, of course. And I want to know what we're up against here. Temporary amnesia is to be expected in a case like this, and it can be easily treated. But if you're suffering from more than temporary amnesia, we'll have to change our entire approach. So you see, it's important for me to know whether the name Milestone means anything to you.'

12

'Milestone,' she said thoughtfully. 'Yes, it's familiar. *Vaguely* familiar.'

'You're a physicist at Milestone. You earned your doctorate at UCLA a few years ago, and you went to work at Milestone immediately thereafter.'

'Ah,' she said as the glimmer of memory grew brighter.

'We've learned a few things about you from the people at Milestone,' he said. 'You have no children. You aren't married; you never have been.' He watched her as she tried to assimilate what he'd told her. 'Is it starting to fall into place now?'

Susan sighed with relief. 'Yes. To an extent, it is. Some of it's coming back to me . . . but not everything. Just random bits and pieces.'

'It'll take time,' he assured her. 'After an injury like yours, you can't expect to recuperate overnight.'

She had a lot of questions to ask him, but her curiosity was equaled by her bone-deep weariness and exceeded by her thirst. She slumped back against the pillows to catch her breath, and she asked for more water.

He poured only a third of a glass this time. As before, he warned her to take small sips.

She didn't need to be warned. Already, after having consumed nothing more than a few ounces of water, she felt slightly bloated, as if she'd eaten a full-course dinner.

When she had finished drinking, she said. 'I don't know your name.'

'Oh. I'm sorry. It's Viteski. Dr. Leon Viteski.'

'I've been wondering about your accent,' she said. 'I do detect one, don't I? Viteski . . . Is your heritage Polish?'

He looked uncomfortable, and his eyes slid away from hers. 'Yes. I was a war orphan. I came to this country in 1946, when I was seventeen. My uncle took me in.' The spontaneity had gone out of his voice; he sounded as if he were reciting a carefully memorized speech. 'I've lost most of my Polish accent, but I suppose I'll never shake it entirely.'

Apparently, she had touched a sore spot. The mere mention of his accent made him strangely defensive.

He hurried on, speaking faster than he had spoken before, as if he was eager to change the subject. 'I'm chief physician here, head of the medical staff. By the way . . . do you have any idea where "here" is?'

'Well, I remember that I was on vacation in Oregon, though I can't remember exactly where I was going. So this must be somewhere in Oregon, right?'

'Yes. The town's Willawauk. About eight thousand people live here. It's the county seat. Willawauk County is mostly rural, and this is its only hospital. Not a huge facility. It's just four floors, two hundred and twenty beds. But we're good.

14

In fact I like to think we're better than a lot of sophisticated big-city hospitals because we're able to give more personal attention to patients here. And personal attention often makes an enormous difference in the rate of recovery.'

His voice contained no trace of pride or enthusiasm, as it ought to have considering what he was saying. It was almost as flat and monotonous as the voice of a machine.

Or is it just me? she wondered. Is it just that my perceptions are out of whack?

In spite of her weariness and in spite of the hammering that had started up again inside her skull, she raised her head from the pillow and said, 'Doctor, why am I here? What happened to me?'

'You don't recall anything about the accident?'

'No.'

'Your car's brakes failed. It was on an extremely twisty stretch of road two miles south of the Viewtop turnoff.'

'Viewtop?'

'That's where you were headed. You had a confirmation of your reservation in your purse.'

'It's a hotel?'

'Yes. The Viewtop Inn. A resort. A big, rambling old place. It was built fifty or sixty years ago, and I'd guess it's more popular now than it was then. A real get-away-from-it-all hotel.'

As Dr. Viteski spoke, Susan slowly remembered. She closed her eyes and could see the resort in a series of colorful photographs that had illustrated

15

an article in *Travel* magazine last February. She'd booked a room as part of her vacation as soon as she'd read about the place, for she had been charmed by the pictures of the inn's wide verandas, many-gabled roofline, pillared lobby, and extensive gardens.

'Anyway,' Viteski said, 'your brakes failed, and you lost control of your car. You went over the edge of a steep embankment, rolled twice, and slammed up against a couple of trees.'

'Good God!'

'Your car was a mess.' He shook his head. 'It's a miracle you weren't killed.'

She gingerly touched the bandage that covered half her forehead. 'How bad is this?'

Viteski's thick, dark eyebrows drew together again, and it suddenly seemed to Susan that his expression was theatrical, not genuine.

'It isn't too serious,' he said. 'A wide gash. You bled heavily, and it healed rather slowly at first. But the stitches are scheduled to come out tomorrow or the day after, and I really don't believe there'll be any permanent scarring. We took considerable care to make sure the wound was neatly sewn.'

'Concussion?' she asked.

'Yes. But only a mild one, certainly nothing severe enough to explain why you were in a coma.'

She had been growing more tired and headachy by the minute. Now she was abruptly alert again. 'Coma?'

Viteski nodded. 'We did a brain scan, of course,

but we didn't find any indication of an embolism. There wasn't any swelling of brain tissue, either. And there was no buildup of fluid in the skull, no signs whatsoever of cranial pressure. You did take a hard knock on the head, which surely had *something* to do with the coma, but we can't be much more specific than that, I'm afraid. Contrary to what the television medical dramas would have you believe, modern medicine doesn't always have an answer for everything. What's important is that you've come out of the coma with no apparent long-term effects. I know those holes in your memory are frustrating, even frightening, but I'm confident that, given sufficient time, they'll heal over, too.'

He still sounds as if he's reciting well-rehearsed lines from a script, Susan thought uneasily.

But she didn't dwell on that thought, for this time Viteski's odd manner of speech was less interesting than what he had said. *Coma*. That word chilled her. *Coma*.

'How long was I unconscious?' she asked.

'Twenty-two days.'

She stared at him, *gaped* at him in disbelief.

'It's true,' he said.

She shook her head. 'No. It can't be true.'

She had always been firmly in control of her life. She was a meticulous planner who tried to prepare for every eventuality. Her private life was conducted with much the same scientific methodology that had made it possible for her to earn her doctor-

17

ate in particle physics more than a year ahead of other students who were her age. She disliked surprises, and she disliked having to depend on anyone but herself, and she was virtually terrified of being helpless. Now Viteski was telling her that she had spent twenty-two days in a state of utter helplessness, totally dependent on others, and that realization deeply disturbed her.

What if she had never come out of the coma?

Or worse yet – what if she had awakened to find herself paralyzed from the neck down, condemned to a life of utter dependency? What if she'd had to be fed and dressed and taken to the bathroom by paid attendants for the rest of her life?

She shivered.

'No,' she told Viteski. 'I can't have lost that much time. I *can't* have. There must be some mistake.'

'Surely you've noticed how thin you are,' Viteski said. 'You've dropped fifteen pounds or more.'

She held up her arms. Like two sticks. Earlier, she had realized how frightfully thin they looked, but she hadn't wanted to think about what that meant.

'You've been getting fluids intravenously, of course,' Dr. Viteski said. 'Otherwise, you'd have died of dehydration long ago. There's been some nourishment in the fluids you've gotten, primarily glucose. But you've had no real food – no solid food, that is – in more than three weeks.'

Susan was five-foot-five, and her ideal weight

18

(considering her delicate bone structure) was about a hundred and ten pounds. At the moment she weighed between ninety and ninety-five, and the effect of the loss was dramatic. She put her hands on the blanket, and even through the covers she could feel how sharp and bony her hips were.

'Twenty-two days,' she said wonderingly.

At last, reluctantly, she accepted the unacceptable.

When she stopped resisting the truth, her headache and her extreme weariness returned. As limp as a bundle of wet straw, she fell back against the pillows.

'That's enough for now,' Viteski said. 'I think I've let you talk too much. You've tired yourself unnecessarily. Right now you need plenty of rest.'

'Rest?' she said. 'No. For God's sake, I've *been* resting for twenty-two days!'

'There's no genuine rest when you're in a coma,' Viteski said. 'It isn't the same thing as normal sleep. Rebuilding your strength and stamina is going to take a while.'

He picked up the control switch, pushed one of the four buttons, and lowered the head of the bed.

'No,' Susan said, suddenly panicky. 'Wait. Please, wait a minute.'

He ignored her protests and put the bed all the way down.

She hooked her hands around the rails and tried to pull herself into a sitting position, but for the moment she was too exhausted to lift herself.

'You don't expect me to go to sleep, do you?' she asked, although she couldn't deny that she needed sleep. Her eyes were grainy, hot, and tired. Her eyelids felt as heavy as lead.

'Sleep is precisely what you need most,' he assured her.

'But I *can't*.'

'You look as if you can,' he said. 'You're plainly worn out. And no wonder.'

'No, no. I mean, I don't *dare* go to sleep. What if I don't wake up?'

'Of course you will.'

'What if I slip into another coma?'

'You won't.'

Frustrated by his inability to understand her fear, Susan gritted her teeth and said, 'But what if I *do*?'

'Listen, you can't go through life being afraid to sleep,' Viteski said slowly, patiently, as if he were reasoning with a small child. 'Just relax. You're out of the coma. You're going to be fine. Now, it's quite late, and I need a bite of dinner and some sleep myself. Just relax. All right? Relax.'

If this is his best bedside manner, Susan thought, then what is he like when he isn't *trying* to be nice?

He went to the door.

She wanted to cry out: *Don't leave me alone!* But her strong streak of self-reliance would not permit her to behave like a frightened child. She didn't want to lean on Dr. Viteski or on anyone else.

20

'Get your rest,' he said. 'Everything'll look better in the morning.'

He turned out the overhead light.

Shadows sprang up as if they were living creatures that had been hiding under the furniture and behind the baseboard. Although Susan couldn't remember ever having been afraid of the dark, she was uneasy now; her heartbeat accelerated.

The only illumination was the cold, shimmering fluorescence that came through the open door from the hospital corridor, and the soft glow from a small lamp that stood on a table in one corner of the room.

Standing in the doorway, Viteski was starkly silhouetted by the hall light. His face was no longer visible; he looked like a black paper cutout. 'Good night,' he said.

He closed the door behind him, shutting out the corridor light altogether.

There was only one lamp now, no more than a single fifteen-watt bulb. The darkness crowded closer to Susan, laid long fingers across the bed.

She was alone.

She looked at the other bed, which was shrouded in shadows like banners of black crepe; it reminded her of a funeral bier. She wished ardently for a roommate.

This isn't right, she thought. I shouldn't be left alone like this. Not after I've just come out of a coma. Surely there ought to be somebody in attendance – a nurse, an orderly, *somebody*.

21

Her eyes were heavy, incredibly heavy.

No, she told herself angrily. I mustn't fall asleep. Not until I'm absolutely sure that my nice little nap won't turn into another twenty-two-day coma.

For a few minutes Susan struggled against the ever-tightening embrace of sleep, clenching her fists so that her fingernails dug painfully into her palms. But her eyes burned and ached, and at last she decided that it wouldn't hurt to close them for just a minute, just long enough to rest them. She was sure she could close her eyes without going to sleep. Of course she could. No problem.

She fell over the edge of sleep as if she were a stone dropping into a bottomless well.

She dreamed.

In the dream, she was lying on a hard, damp floor in a vast, dark, cold place. She wasn't alone. *They* were with her. She ran, staggering blindly across the lightless room, down narrow corridors of stone, fleeing from a nightmare that was, in fact, a memory of a real place, a real time, a real horror that she had lived through when she was nineteen.

The House of Thunder.

3

The following morning, a few minutes after Susan woke, the plump, gray-haired nurse appeared. As before, her glasses were suspended from a beaded chain around her neck, and they bobbled on her motherly bosom with each step she took. She slipped a thermometer under Susan's tongue, took hold of Susan's wrist, timed the pulse, then put on her glasses to read the thermometer. As she worked, she kept up a steady line of chatter. Her name was Thelma Baker. She said she'd always known that Susan would pull through eventually. She had been a nurse for thirty-five years, first in San Francisco and then here in Oregon, and she had seldom been wrong about a patient's prospects for recovery. She said she was such a natural-born nurse that she sometimes wondered if she was the reincarnation of a woman who had been a first-rate nurse in a previous life. 'Of course, I'm not much good at anything *else*,' she said with a hearty laugh. 'I'm sure as the devil not much of a housekeeper!' She said she wasn't very good at managing money, either; to hear her tell it, just balancing the check-book every month was a Herculean task. Wasn't much good at marriage, she said. Two husbands, two divorces, no children. Couldn't cook very well, either. Hated to sew; *loathed* it. 'But I'm a darned good nurse and proud of it,' she said emphatically, more than once, always with that charming smile that involved her brown eyes as well as her mouth, a smile that showed how much she truly did enjoy her work.

Susan liked the woman. Ordinarily, she had little or no patience with nonstop talkers. But Mrs. Baker's chatter was amusing, frequently self-deprecating, and oddly soothing.

'Hungry?' Mrs. Baker asked.

'Starved.' She had awakened with a ravenous appetite.

'You'll start taking solid food today,' Mrs. Baker said. 'A soft diet, of course.'

Even as the nurse spoke, a young, blond, male orderly arrived with breakfast: cherry-flavored Jell-O, unbuttered toast with a single spoonful of grape jelly, and a thin, chalky-looking tapioca. To Susan, no other meal had ever been so appealing. But she was disappointed by the size of the portions, and she said as much.

'It doesn't look like a lot,' Mrs. Baker said, 'but believe me, honey, you'll be stuffed before you've eaten half of it. Remember, you haven't taken solid food in three weeks. Your stomach's all shrunk up. It'll be a while before you'll have a normal appetite.'

Mrs. Baker left to attend to other patients, and before long Susan realized that the nurse was right. Although there wasn't a great deal of food on the tray, and although even this simple fare tasted like ambrosia, it was more than she could eat.

As she ate, she thought about Dr. Viteski. She still felt that he had been wrong to let her alone, unattended. In spite of Mrs. Baker's sprightly manner, the hospital still seemed cold, unfriendly.

When she could eat no more, she wiped her mouth with the paper napkin, pushed the rolling bed table out of her way – and suddenly had the feeling she was being watched. She glanced up.

He was standing in the open door: a tall, elegant man of about thirty-eight. He was wearing dark shoes, dark trousers, a white lab coat, a white shirt, and a green tie, and he was holding a clipboard in his left hand. His face was arresting, sensitive; his superbly balanced features looked as if they had been carefully chiseled from stone by a gifted sculptor. His blue eyes were as bright as polished gems, and they provided an intriguing contrast to his lustrous black hair, which he wore full and combed straight back from his face and forehead.

'Miss Thorton,' he said, 'I'm delighted to see you sitting up, awake and aware.' He came to the bed. His smile was even nicer than Thelma Baker's. 'I'm your physician. Doctor McGee. Dr. Jeffrey McGee.'

He extended his hand to her, and she took it. It was a dry, hard, strong hand, but his touch was light and gentle.

25

'I thought Dr. Viteski was my physician.'

'He's chief of the hospital medical staff,' McGee said, 'but I'm in charge of your case.' His voice had a reassuringly masculine timbre, yet it was pleasingly soft and soothing. 'I was the admitting physician when you were brought into the emergency room.'

'But yesterday, Dr. Viteski – '

'Yesterday was my day off,' McGee said. 'I take two days off from my private practice every week, but only one day off from my hospital rounds – only *one* day, mind you – so of course you chose that day. After you laid there like a stone for twenty-two days, after you worried me sick for twenty-two days, you had to come out of your coma when I wasn't here.' He shook his head, pretending to be both astonished and hurt. 'I didn't even find out about it until this morning.' He frowned at her with mock disapproval. 'Now, Miss Thorton,' he teased, 'if there are going to be any medical miracles involving my patients, I insist on being present when they occur, so that I can take the credit and bask in the glory. Understood?'

Susan smiled up at him, surprised by his light-hearted manner. 'Yes, Dr. McGee. I understand.'

'Good. Very good. I'm glad we got that straightened out.' He grinned. 'How are you feeling this morning?'

'Better,' she said.

'Ready for an evening of dancing and bar-hopping?'

'Maybe tomorrow.'

'It's a date.' He glanced at her breakfast tray. 'I see you've got an appetite.'

'I tried to eat everything, but I couldn't.'

'That's what Orson Welles said.'

Susan laughed.

'You did pretty well,' he said, indicating the tray. 'You've got to start off with small, frequent meals; that's to be expected. Don't worry too much about regaining your strength. Before you know it, you'll be making a pig of yourself, and you'll be well along the road to recovery. Feeling headachy this morning? Drowsy?'

'No. Neither.'

'Let me take your pulse,' he said, reaching for her hand.

'Mrs. Baker took it just before breakfast.'

'I know. This is just an excuse to hold hands with you.'

Susan laughed again. 'You're different from most doctors.'

'Do you think a physician should be businesslike, distant, somber, humorless?'

'Not necessarily.'

'Do you think I should try to be more like Dr. Viteski?'

'Definitely not.'

'He iz an *egg*-cellent doktor,' McGee said, doing a perfect imitation of Viteski's accented voice.

'I'm sure he is. But I suspect you're even better.'

'Thank you. The compliment is duly noted and has earned you a small discount off my final bill.'

He was still holding her hand. He finally looked at his watch and took her pulse.

'Will I live?' she asked when he finished.

'No doubt about it. You're bouncing back fast.' He continued to hold her hand as he said, 'Seriously now, I think a little humor between doctor and patient is a good thing. I believe it helps the patient maintain a positive attitude, and a positive attitude speeds healing. But some people don't *want* a cheerful doctor. They want someone who acts as if the weight of the world is on his shoulders; it makes them feel more secure. So if my joking bothers you, I can tone it down or turn it off. The important thing is that you feel comfortable and confident about the care you're getting.'

'You go right ahead and be as cheerful as you want,' Susan said. 'My spirits need lifting.'

'There's no reason to be glum. The worst is behind you now.'

He squeezed her hand gently before finally letting go of it.

To her surprise, Susan felt a tug of regret that he had released her hand so soon.

'Dr. Viteski tells me there are lapses in your memory,' he said.

She frowned. 'Fewer than there were yesterday. I guess it'll all come back to me sooner or later. But there are still a lot of holes.'

'I want to talk with you about that. But first I've got to make my rounds. I'll come back in a couple of hours, and I'll help you prod your memory – if that's all right with you.'

'Sure,' she said.

'You rest.'

'What else is there to do?'

'No tennis until further notice.'

'Darn! I had a match scheduled with Mrs. Baker.'

'You'll just have to cancel it.'

'Yes, Dr. McGee.'

Smiling, she watched him leave. He moved with self-assurance and with considerable natural grace.

He'd already had a positive influence on her. A simmering paranoia had been heating up slowly within her, but now she realized that her uneasiness had been entirely subjective in origin, a result of her weakness and disorientation; there was no rational justification for it. Dr. Viteski's odd behavior no longer seemed important, and the hospital no longer seemed the least bit threatening.

* * *

Half an hour later, when Mrs. Baker looked in on her again, Susan asked for a mirror, then wished she hadn't. Her reflection revealed a pale, gaunt face. Her gray-green eyes were bloodshot and circled by dark, puffy flesh. In order to facilitate the treatment and bandaging of her gashed forehead, an emergency room orderly had clipped her long blond hair; he had hacked at it with no regard for her appearance. The result was a shaggy mess. Furthermore, after twenty-two days of neglect, her hair was greasy and tangled.

'My God, I look terrible!' she said.

'Of course you don't,' Mrs. Baker said. 'Just a bit washed out. There's no permanent damage. As soon as you gain back the weight you lost, your cheeks will fill in, and those bags under your eyes will go away.'

'I've got to wash my hair.'

'You wouldn't be able to walk into the bathroom and stand at the sink. Your legs would feel like rubber. Besides, you can't wash your hair until the bandages come off your head, and that won't be until at least tomorrow.'

'No. Today. Now. My hair's oily, and my head itches. It's making me miserable, and that's not conducive to recuperation.'

'This isn't a debate, honey. You can't win, so save your breath. All I can do is see that you get a dry wash.'

'Dry wash? What's that?'

'Sprinkle some powder in your hair, let it soak up some of the oil, then brush it out,' Mrs. Baker said. 'That's what we did for you twice a week while you were in a coma.'

Susan put one hand to her lank hair. 'Will it help?'

'A little.'

'Okay, I'll do it.'

Mrs. Baker brought a can of powder and a brush.

'The luggage I had with me in the car,' Susan said. 'Did any of it survive the crash?'

'Sure. It's right over there, in the closet.'

'Would you bring me my makeup case?'

Mrs. Baker grinned. 'He *is* a handsome devil, isn't he? And so nice, too.' She winked as she said, 'He isn't married, either.'

Susan blushed. 'I don't know what you mean.'

Mrs. Baker laughed gently and patted Susan's hand. 'Don't be embarrassed, kid. I've never seen one of Dr. McGee's female patients who *didn't* try to look her best. Teenage girls get all fluttery when he's around. Young ladies like you get a certain unmistakable glint in their eyes. Even white-haired grannies, half crippled with arthritis, twenty years older than me – *forty* years older than the doctor – they all make themselves look nice for him, and looking nice makes them feel better, so it's all sort of therapeutic.'

* * *

Shortly before noon, Dr. McGee returned, pushing a stainless-steel cafeteria cart that held two trays. 'I thought we'd have lunch together while we talk about your memory problems.'

'A doctor having lunch with his patient?' she asked, amazed.

'We tend to be less formal here than in your city hospitals.'

'Who pays for lunch?'

'You do, of course. We aren't *that* informal.'

She grinned. 'What's for lunch?'

'For me, a chicken salad sandwich and apple pie.

31

For you, unbuttered toast and tapioca and – '

'Already, this is getting monotonous.'

'Ah, but this time there's something more exotic than cherry Jell-O,' he said. '*Lime* Jell-O.'

'I don't think my heart can stand it.'

'And a small dish of canned peaches. Truly a gourmet spread.' He pulled up a chair, then lowered her bed as far as it would go, so that they could talk comfortably while they ate.

As he put her tray on the bed table and lifted the plastic cover from it, he blinked at her and said, 'You look nice and fresh.'

'I look like death warmed over,' she said.

'Not at all.'

'Yes, I do.'

'Your *tapioca* looks like death warmed over, but *you* look nice and fresh. Remember, I'm the doctor, and you're the patient, and the patient must never, never, never disagree with the doctor. Don't you know your medical etiquette? If I say you look nice and fresh, then, by God, you look nice and fresh!'

Susan smiled and played along with him. 'I see. How could I have been so gauche?'

'You look nice and fresh, Susan.'

'Why, thank you, Dr. McGee.'

'That's much better.'

She had 'washed' her hair with talcum powder, had lightly applied some makeup, and had put on lipstick. Thanks to a few drops of Murine, her eyes were no longer bloodshot, though a yellowish tint of sickness colored the whites of them. She had also changed from her hospital gown into a pair of blue silk pajamas that had been in her luggage. She knew she looked far less than her best; however, she looked at least a little better, and looking a little better made her feel a *lot* better, just as Mrs. Baker had said it would.

While they ate lunch, they talked about the blank spot in Susan's memory, trying to fill in the holes, which had been numerous and huge only yesterday, but which were fewer and far smaller today. Upon waking this morning, she had found that she could remember most things without effort.

She had been born and raised in suburban Philadelphia, in a pleasant, white, two-story house on a maple-lined street of similar houses. Green lawns. Porch swings. A block party every Fourth of July. Carolers at Christmas. An Ozzie and Harriet neighborhood.

'Sounds like an ideal childhood,' McGee said.

Susan swallowed a bit of lime Jell-O, then said, 'It was an ideal *setting* for an ideal childhood, but unfortunately it didn't turn out that way. I was a very lonely kid.'

'When you were first admitted here,' McGee said, 'we tried to contact your family, but we couldn't find anyone to contact.'

She told him about her parents, partly because she wanted to be absolutely sure that there were no holes in those memories, and partly because McGee was easy to talk to, and partly because she felt a strong need to talk after twenty-two days of silence and darkness. Her mother, Regina, had been killed in a traffic accident when Susan was only seven years old. The driver of a beer delivery truck had suffered a heart attack at the wheel, and the truck had run a red light, and Regina's Chevy had been in the middle of the intersection. Susan couldn't remember a great deal about her mother, but that lapse had nothing whatsoever to do with her own recent accident and amnesia. After all, she had known her mother for only seven years, and twenty-five years had passed since the beer truck had flattened the Chevy; sadly but inevitably, Regina had faded from Susan's memory in much the same way that an image fades from an old photograph that has been left too long in bright sunlight. However, she could remember her father clearly. Frank Thorton had been a tall, somewhat portly man who had owned a moderately successful men's clothing store, and Susan had loved him. She always knew that he loved her, too, even though he never told her that he did. He was quiet, soft-spoken, rather shy, a completely self-contained man who was happiest when he was alone in his den with just a good book and his pipe. Perhaps he would have been more forthcoming with a son than he had been with his daughter. He always was more at ease with men than with women, and raising a girl was undoubtedly an awkward proposition for him. He died of cancer ten years after Regina's passing, the summer after Susan graduated from high school. And so she had entered adulthood even more alone than she had been before.

Dr. McGee finished his chicken salad sandwich, wiped his mouth with a paper napkin, and said, 'No aunts, no uncles?'

'One aunt, one uncle. Both of them were strangers to me. No living grandparents. But you know something – having such a lonely childhood wasn't *entirely* a bad thing. I learned to be *very* self-reliant, and that's paid off over the years.'

As McGee ate his apple pie, and as Susan nibbled at her canned peaches, they talked about her university years. She had done her undergraduate work at Briarstead College in Pennsylvania, then had gone to California and had earned both her master's and doctorate at UCLA. She recalled those years with perfect clarity, although she actually would have preferred to forget some of what happened during her sophomore year at Briarstead.

'Is something wrong?' McGee asked, putting down a forkful of apple pie that had been halfway to his mouth.

She blinked. 'Huh?'

'Your expression . . .' He frowned. 'For a moment there, you looked as if you'd seen a ghost.'

'Yeah. In a way I did.' Suddenly she was not hungry any more. She put down her spoon and pushed the bed table aside.

'Want to talk about it?'

'It was just a bad memory,' she said. 'Something I wish to God I *could* forget.'

McGee put his own tray aside, leaving the pie unfinished. 'Tell me about it.'

'Oh, it's nothing I should burden you with.'

'Burden me.'

'It's a dreary story.'

'If it's bothering you, tell me about it. Now and then, I like a good, dreary story.'

She didn't smile. Not even McGee could make the House of Thunder amusing. 'Well . . . in my sophomore year at Briarstead, I was dating a guy named Jerry Stein. He was sweet. I liked him. I liked him a lot. In fact, we were even beginning to talk about getting married after we graduated. Then he was killed.'

'I'm sorry,' McGee said. 'How did it happen?'

'He was pledging a fraternity.'

'Oh, Christ!' McGee said, anticipating her.

'The hazing . . . got out of hand.'

'That's such a rotten, stupid way to die.'

'Jerry had so much potential,' she said softly. 'He was bright, sensitive, a hard worker . . .'

'One night, when I was an intern on emergency room duty, they brought in a kid who'd been severely burned in a college hazing ritual. They told us it was a test by fire, some macho thing like that, some *childish* damned thing like that, and it got out of hand. He was burned over eighty percent of his body. He died two days later.'

'It wasn't fire that killed Jerry Stein,' Susan said. 'It was hate.'

She shuddered, remembering.

'Hate?' McGee asked. 'What do you mean?'

She was silent for a moment, her thoughts turning

36

back thirteen years. Although the hospital room was comfortably warm, Susan felt cold, as bitterly cold as she had been in the House of Thunder.

McGee waited patiently, leaning forward slightly in his chair.

At last she shook her head and said, 'I don't feel like going into the details. It's just too depressing.'

'There were an unusual number of deaths in your life before you were even twenty-one.'

'Yeah. At times it seemed as if I were cursed or something. Everyone I really cared about died on me.'

'Your mother, your father, then your fiancé.'

'Well, he wasn't actually my fiancé. Not quite.'

'But he was the next thing to it.'

'Everything but the ring,' Susan said.

'All right. So maybe you need to talk about his death in order to finally get it out of your system.'

'No,' she said.

'Don't dismiss it so quickly. I mean, if he's still haunting you thirteen years later – '

She interrupted him. 'But you see, no matter how much I talk about it, I'll *never* get it out of my system. It was just too awful to be forgotten. Besides, you told me that a positive mental attitude will speed up the healing process. Remember?'

He smiled. 'I remember.'

'So I shouldn't talk about things that just depress me.'

He stared at her for a long moment. His eyes

were incredibly blue, and they were so expressive that she had no doubt about the depth of his concern for her well-being.

He sighed and said, 'Okay. Let's get back to the matter at hand – your amnesia. It seems like you remember nearly everything. What holes haven't filled in yet?'

Before she answered him, she reached for the bed controls and raised the upper end of the mattress a bit more, forcing herself to sit straighter than she had been sitting. Her back ached dully, not from an injury but from being immobilized in bed for more than three weeks. When she felt more comfortable, she put down the controls and said, 'I still can't recall the accident. I remember driving along a twisty section of two-lane blacktop. I was about two miles south of the turn off to the Viewtop Inn. I was looking forward to getting there and having dinner. Then, well, it's as if somebody just turned the lights out.'

'It wouldn't be unusual if you *never* regained any memory of the accident itself,' McGee assured her. 'In cases like this, even when the patient eventually recalls all the other details of his life, he seldom remembers the incident or the impact that was the cause of the amnesia. That's the one blank spot that often remains.'

'I suspected as much,' she said. 'And I'm not really upset about that. But there's one other thing I can't recall, and *that's* driving me nuts. My job. Dammit, I can't remember even the most minor

38

thing about it, not even one little detail. I mean, I know I'm a physicist. I remember getting the degrees at UCLA, and all that sophisticated, specialized knowledge is still intact. I could start to work today without having to take a refresher course. But *who* was I working for? And what was I doing – *exactly*? Who was my boss? Who were my co-workers? Did I have an office? a laboratory? I must have worked in a lab, don't you think? But I can't remember what it looked like, how it was equipped, or where on earth it was!'

'You're employed by the Milestone Corporation in Newport Beach, California,' McGee said.

'That's what Dr. Viteski told me. But that name doesn't mean a thing to me.'

'All the rest of it has come back to you. This will, too. Just give it time.'

'No,' she said, shaking her head. 'This is different somehow. The other blank spots were like mists . . . like banks of heavy fog. Even when I couldn't remember something, I could at least sense that there *were* memories stirring in the mists. And eventually the mist evaporated; everything cleared up. But when I try to recall what my job was, it's not like those misty blank spots. Instead, it's dark . . . very dark . . . black, just a perfectly black and empty hole that goes down and down forever. There's something . . . frightening about it.'

McGee slid forward, sitting on the edge of his chair. His brow was knitted. 'You were carrying a Milestone ID card in your wallet when you were brought into the emergency room,' he said. 'Maybe that'll refresh your memory.'

'Maybe,' she said doubtfully. 'I'd sure like to see it.'

Her wallet was in the bottom drawer of the nightstand. He got it for her.

She opened the wallet and found the card. It was laminated and bore a small photograph of her. At the top of the card, in blue letters against a white background, there were three words: THE MILESTONE CORPORATION. Under that heading, her name was printed in bold black letters, and below her name was a physical description of her, including information about her age, height, weight, hair color, and eye color. At the bottom of the card, an employee identification number was printed in red ink. Nothing else.

Dr. McGee stood beside the bed, looking down at her as she examined the card. 'Does it help?'

'No,' she said.

'Not just a little bit?'

'I can't remember seeing this before.'

She turned the card over and over in her hands, straining to make a connection, trying hard to switch on the current of memory. She couldn't possibly have been more amazed by the card if it had been an artifact from a nonhuman civilization and had just that very minute been brought back from the planet Mars; it could not have been more *alien*.

'It's all so weird,' she said. 'I've tried to remember back to when I last went to work, the day before I started my vacation. I can recall some of it. Parts of the day are crystal clear. I remember getting up that morning, having breakfast, glancing at the newspaper. That's all as fresh in my mind as the memory of the lunch I just ate. I recall going into the garage that morning, getting in the car, starting the engine . . .' She let her voice trail off as she stared down at the card. She fingered that small rectangle as if she were a clairvoyant feeling for some sort of psychic residue on the plastic. 'I remember backing the car out of my driveway that morning . . . and the next thing I remember is . . . coming home again at the end of the day. In between, there's nothing but blackness, emptiness. And that's the way it is with *all* my memories of work, not just that day but *every* day. No matter how I try to sneak up on them, they elude me. They aren't there in the mist. Those memories simply don't exist any more.'

Still standing beside the bed, McGee spoke to her in a soft, encouraging voice. 'Of course they exist, Susan. Nudge your subconscious a little bit. Think about sitting behind the wheel of your car that morning.'

'I have thought about it.'

'Think about it again.'

She closed her eyes.

'It was probably a typical August day in Southern California,' he said, helping her set the scene in her mind. 'Hot, blue, maybe a little smoggy.'

'Hot and blue,' she said, 'but there wasn't any

smog that day. Not even a single cloud, either.'

'You got in the car and backed out of the drive-way. Now think about the route you drove to work.'

She was silent for almost a minute. Then she said, 'It's no use. I can't remember.'

He persisted gently. 'What were the names of the streets you used?'

'I don't know.'

'Sure you do. Give me the name of just one street. Just *one* to start the ball rolling.'

She tried hard to snatch at least a single meager scrap of memory out of the void – a face, a room, a voice, *anything* – but she failed.

'Sorry,' she said. 'I can't come up with the name of even one street.'

'You told me that you remembered backing down your driveway that morning. All right. If you remember that, then surely you remember which way you went when you pulled *out* of your drive-way. Did you turn left, or did you turn right?'

Her eyes still closed, Susan considered his question until her head began to ache. Finally she opened her eyes, looked up at McGee, and shrugged. 'I just don't know.'

'Philip Gomez,' McGee said.

'What?'

'Philip Gomez.'

'Who's that? Somebody I should know?'

'The name doesn't mean anything to you?'

'No.'

42

'He's your boss at Milestone.'

'Really?' She tried to picture Philip Gomez. She couldn't summon up an image of his face. She couldn't recall anything whatsoever about the man. 'My boss? Philip Gomez? Are you sure about that?'

McGee put his hands in the pockets of his lab coat. 'After you were admitted to the hospital, we tried to locate your family. Of course, we discovered you didn't *have* a family, no close relatives at all. So we called your employer. I've talked to Phil Gomez myself. According to him, you've worked at Milestone for more than four years. He was extremely concerned about you. In fact he's called here, asking about you, four or five times since the accident.'

'Can we call him now?' Susan asked. 'If I hear his voice, maybe something will click into place for me. It might help me remember.'

'Well, I don't have his home number,' McGee said, 'and we can't call him at work until tomorrow.'

'Why not?'

'Today's Sunday.'

'Oh,' she said.

She hadn't even known what day of the week it was, and that realization left her feeling somewhat disoriented again.

'We'll definitely call tomorrow,' McGee said.

'What if I talk to him and still can't remember anything about my work?'

'You will.'

'No, listen, please don't be glib. Be straight with me. Okay? There's a chance I'll never remember anything about my job, isn't there?'

'That's not likely.'

'But possible?'

'Well . . . anything's possible.'

She slumped back against her pillows, suddenly exhausted, depressed, and worried.

'Listen,' McGee said, 'even if you never remember anything about Milestone, that doesn't mean you can't go back to work there. After all, you haven't forgotten what you know about physics; you're still a competent scientist. You've lost none of your education, none of your knowledge. Now, if you were suffering from global amnesia, which is the worst kind, you'd have forgotten nearly everything you ever learned, including how to read and write. But you don't have global amnesia, and that's *something* to be thankful for. Anyway, given time, you'll remember all of it. I'm sure of that.'

Susan hoped he was correct. Her carefully structured, orderly life was in temporary disarray, and she found her condition to be enormously distressing. If that disarray were to become a permanent feature of her existence, she would find life almost unbearable. She had always been in control of her life; she *needed* to be in control.

McGee took his hands out of his pockets and looked at his watch. 'I've got to be going. I'll stop by again for a couple of minutes before I go home for the day. Meanwhile, you relax, eat more of

44

your lunch if you can, and don't worry. You'll remember all about Milestone when the time is right.'

Suddenly, as she listened to McGee, Susan sensed – without understanding why or how she sensed it – that she would be better off if she never remembered anything about Milestone. She was seized by an arctic-cold, iron-hard fear for which she could find no explanation.

* * *

She slept for two hours. She didn't dream this time – or if she did dream, she didn't remember it.

When she woke, she was slightly clammy. Her hair was tangled; she combed it, wincing as she pulled out the knots.

Susan was just putting the comb back on the nightstand when Mrs. Baker entered the room, pushing a wheelchair ahead of her. 'It's time for you to do a bit of traveling, kid.'

'Where are we going?'

'Oh, we'll explore the hallways and byways of the exotic second floor of mysterious, romantic, colorful Willawauk County Hospital,' Mrs. Baker said. 'The trip of a lifetime. It'll be loads of fun. Besides, the doctor wants you to start getting some exercise.'

'It's not going to be much exercise if I'm sitting in a wheelchair.'

'You'll be surprised. Just sitting up, holding on, and gawking at the other patients will be enough to tire you out. You're not exactly in the same physical condition as an Olympic track and field star, you know.'

'But I'm sure I can walk,' Susan said. 'I might need a little assistance, but if I could just lean on your arm at first, then I'm positive I could – '

'Tomorrow, you can try walking a few steps,' Mrs. Baker said as she put down the side rail on the bed. 'But today you're going to ride, and I'm going to play chauffeur.'

Susan frowned. 'I hate being an invalid.'

'Oh, for heaven's sake, you're not an invalid. You're just temporarily incapacitated.'

'I hate that, too.'

Mrs. Baker positioned the wheelchair beside the bed. 'First, I want you to sit up on the edge of the bed and swing your legs back and forth for a minute or two.'

'Why?'

'It flexes the muscles.'

Sitting up, without the bed raised to support her back, Susan felt woozy and weak. She clutched the edge of the mattress because she thought she was going to tumble off the bed.

'Are you all right?' Mrs. Baker asked.

'Perfect,' Susan lied, and forced a smile.

'Swing your legs, kid.'

Susan moved her legs back and forth from the knees down. They felt as if they were made of lead.

Finally, Mrs. Baker said, 'Okay. That's enough.'

Susan was dismayed to find that she was already perspiring. She was shaky, too.

Nevertheless, she said, 'I *know* I can walk.'

'Tomorrow,' Mrs. Baker said.

'Really, I feel fine.'

Mrs. Baker went to the closet and got the robe that matched Susan's blue pajamas. While Susan put on the robe, the nurse located a pair of slippers in one of the suitcases and put them on Susan's dangling feet.

'Okay, honey. Now, just slide off the bed nice and easy, lean your weight against me, and I'll help lower you into the chair.'

As she came off the bed, Susan intended to disobey the nurse, intended to stand up straight all by herself and prove that she wasn't an invalid. However, as her feet touched the floor, she knew instantly that her legs would not support her if she dared to put all of her weight on them; a moment ago, they seemed to be made of lead, but now they were composed of knotted rags. Rather than collapse in a heap and be humiliated, she clutched Mrs. Baker and allowed herself to be settled into the wheelchair almost as if she were a baby being put into a stroller.

Mrs. Baker winked at her. 'Still think you can run the mile?'

Susan was both amused and embarrassed by her own stubbornness. Smiling, blushing, she said, 'Tomorrow. I'll do so much walking tomorrow that

I'll wear big holes in my slippers. You just wait and see.'

'Well, kid, I don't know if you have a whole lot of common sense or not, but you've sure as the devil got more than your share of spunk, and I've always admired spunkiness.'

Mrs. Baker stepped behind the wheelchair and pushed it out of the room. Initially, the rolling motion caused Susan's stomach to flop and twist, but after several seconds she got control of herself.

The hospital was T-shaped, and Susan's room was at the end of the short, right-hand wing at the top of the T. Mrs. Baker took her out to the junction of the corridors and wheeled her into the longest wing, heading toward the bottom of the T.

Just being out of bed and out of her room made Susan feel better, fresher. The halls had dark green vinyl-tile floors, and the walls were painted a matching shade up to the height of three feet, after which they were a pale yellow, as was the pebbly, acoustic-tile ceiling; the effect of this – darkness below, light above – was to lift one's eyes upward, giving the hall a soaring, airy quality. The corridors were as spotlessly clean as Susan's room. She remembered the big, Philadelphia hospital in which her father had finally succumbed to cancer; that place had been ancient, dreary, in need of paint, with dust thick on the windowsills, with years of grime pressed deep into its cracked tile floors. She supposed she ought to be thankful that she had wound up in Willawauk County Hospital.

48

The doctors, nurses, and orderlies here were also different from those in the hospital where her father had died. All of these people smiled at her. And they seemed genuinely concerned about the patients. As Susan was wheeled through the halls many staff members paused in their tasks to have a word with her; every one of them expressed pleasure at seeing her awake, alert, and on the way to a full recovery.

Mrs. Baker pushed her to the end of the long main hallway, then turned and started back. Although Susan was already beginning to tire, she was nevertheless in relatively high spirits. She felt better today than she had felt yesterday, better this afternoon than this morning. The future seemed sure to grow brighter, day by day.

When the mood changed, it changed with the frightening abruptness of a shotgun blast.

As they passed between the elevators and the nurses' station – which faced each other midpoint in the corridor – one set of elevator doors opened, and a man stepped out directly in front of the wheelchair. He was a patient in blue- and white-striped pajamas, a dark brown robe, and brown slippers. Mrs. Baker stopped the wheelchair in order to let him pass. When Susan saw who he was, she nearly screamed. She *wanted* to scream but couldn't. Chest-tightening, throat-constricting fear had stricken her dumb.

His name was Ernest Harch. He was a squarely built man with a square face, squared-off features, and gray eyes the shade of dirty ice.

When she had testified against him in court, he had fixed her with those chilling eyes and hadn't glanced away from her for even the briefest moment. She had clearly read the message in his intimidating stare: *You're going to be sorry you ever took the witness stand.*

But that had been thirteen years ago. In the meantime, she had taken precautions to be sure he would not find her when he got out of prison. She had long ago stopped looking over her shoulder.

And now here he was.

He looked down at her as she sat helpless in the wheelchair, and she saw recognition flicker in his wintry eyes. In spite of the years that had passed, in spite of the emaciation that had altered her appearance in the last three weeks, he knew who she was.

She wanted to bolt out of the chair and run. She was rigid with fear; she couldn't move.

Only a second or two had passed since the elevator doors had opened, yet it seemed as if she had been confronting Harch for at least a quarter of an hour. The usual flow of time had slowed to a sludgelike crawl.

Harch smiled at her. To anyone but Susan, that smile might have appeared innocent, even friendly. But she saw hatred and menace in it.

Ernest Harch had been the pledge master in the fraternity that Jerry Stein had wanted to join. Ernest Harch had killed Jerry. Not by accident.

Deliberately. In cold blood. In the House of Thunder.

Now, still smiling, he winked at Susan.

The fear-induced paralysis relaxed its tight grip on her, and somehow she found the strength to push up from the wheelchair, onto her feet. She took one step, trying to turn away from Harch, trying desperately to run, and she heard Mrs. Baker call out in surprise. She took a second step, feeling as if she were walking underwater, and then her legs buckled, and she started to fall, and someone caught her just in time.

As everything began to spin and wobble and grow dark, she realized that Ernest Harch was the one who had caught her. She was in his arms. She looked up into his face, which was as big as the moon.

Then for a while there was only darkness.

4

'In danger?' McGee said, looking puzzled.

At the foot of the bed, Mrs. Baker frowned.

Susan was trying hard to remain calm and convincing. She possessed sufficient presence of mind to know that a hysterical woman was never taken seriously – especially not a hysterical woman recuperating from a head injury. There was a very real danger that she would appear to be confused or suffering from delusions. It was vital that Jeffrey McGee believe what she was going to tell him.

She had awakened in bed, in her hospital room, only a few minutes after fainting in the corridor. When she came to, McGee was taking her blood pressure. She had patiently allowed him to examine her before she had told him that she was in danger.

Now he stood beside the bed, one hand on the side rail, leaning forward a bit, a stethoscope dangling from his neck. 'In danger from what?'

'That man,' Susan said.

'What man?'

'The man who stepped out of the elevator.'

McGee glanced at Mrs. Baker.

The nurse said, 'He's a patient here.'

'And you think he's somehow dangerous?' McGee asked Susan, still clearly perplexed.

Nervously fingering the collar of her pajama top, Susan said, 'Dr. McGee, do you remember what I told you about an old boyfriend of mine named Jerry Stein?'

'Of course I remember. He was the one you were almost engaged to.'

Susan nodded.

'The one who died in a fraternity hazing,' McGee said.

'Ah, no,' Mrs. Baker said sympathetically. This was the first that she had heard about Jerry. 'That's a terrible thing.'

Susan's mouth was dry. She swallowed a few times, then said, 'It was what the fraternity called a "humiliation ritual." The pledge had to withstand intense humiliation in front of a girl, preferably his steady date, without responding to his tormentors. They took Jerry and me to a limestone cavern a couple of miles from the Briarstead campus. It was a favorite place for hazing rituals; they were fond of dramatic settings for their damned silly games. Anyway, I didn't want to go. Right from the start, I didn't want to be a part of it. Not that there was anything threatening about it. The mood was light-hearted at first, playful. Jerry was actually looking forward to it. But I suppose, on some deep subliminal level, I sensed an undercurrent of . . . malice.

Besides, I suspected the fraternity brothers in charge of the hazing had been drinking. They had two cars, and I didn't want to get into either one, not if a drunk was driving. But they reassured me, and finally I went with them because Jerry wanted in the fraternity so badly; I didn't want to be a spoiler.'

She looked out the window at the lowering September sky. A wind had risen, stirring the branches of the tall pines.

She hated talking about Jerry's death. But she had to tell McGee and Mrs. Baker everything, so that they would understand why Ernest Harch posed a very real, very serious threat to her.

She said, 'The limestone caverns near Briarstead College are extensive. Eight or ten underground rooms. Maybe more. Some of them are huge. It's a damp, musty, moldy place, though I suppose it's paradise to a spelunker.'

Gently urging her on, McGee said, 'Caverns that large must be a tourist attraction, but I don't think I've ever heard of them.'

'Oh, no, they haven't been developed for tourism,' Susan said. 'They're not like the Carlsbad Caverns or the Luray Caverns or anything like that. They're not pretty. They're all gray limestone, dreary as Hell. They're big, that's all. The largest cave is about the size of a cathedral. The Shawnee Indians gave that one a name: "House of Thunder." '

'Thunder?' McGee asked. 'Why?'

'A subterranean stream enters the cave high in one corner and tumbles down a series of ledges. The sound of the falling water echoes off the limestone, so there's a continuous rumbling in the place.'

The memory was still far too vivid for her to speak of it without feeling the cold, clammy air of the cavern. She shivered and pulled the blankets across her outstretched legs.

McGee's gaze met hers. In his eyes there was understanding and compassion. She could see that he knew how painful it was for her to talk about Jerry Stein.

The same expression was in Mrs. Baker's eyes. The nurse looked as if she might rush around to the side of the bed and give Susan a motherly hug.

Again, McGee gently encouraged her to continue her story. 'The humiliation ritual was held in the House of Thunder?'

'Yeah. It was night. We were led into the cavern with flashlights, and then several candles were lit and placed on the rocks around us. There were just Jerry, me, and four of the fraternity brothers. I'll never forget their names or what they looked like. Never. Carl Jellicoe, Herbert Parker, Randy Lee Quince . . . and Ernest Harch. Harch was the fraternity's pledge master that year.'

Outside, the day was rapidly growing darker under a shroud of thunderheads. Inside, the blue-gray shadows crawled out of the corners and threatened to take full possession of the hospital room.

As Susan talked, Dr. McGee switched on the bedside lamp.

'As soon as we were in the caverns, as soon as the candles had been lit, Harch and the other three guys pulled out flasks of whiskey. They *had* been drinking earlier. I was right about that. And they continued to drink all through the hazing. The more they drank, the uglier the whole scene got. At first they subjected Jerry to some funny, pretty much innocent teasing. In fact, everyone was laughing at first, even Jerry and me. Gradually, however, their taunting became nastier . . . meaner. A lot of it was obscene, too. Worse than obscene. *Filthy.* I was embarrassed and uneasy. I wanted to leave, and Jerry wanted me to get out of there, too, but Harch and the others refused to let me have a flashlight or a candle. I couldn't find my way out of the caverns in pitch blackness, so I had to stay. When they started needling Jerry about his being Jewish, there wasn't any humor in them at all, and that was when I knew for sure there was going to be trouble, bad trouble. They were all obviously drunk by then. But it wasn't just the whiskey talking. Oh, no. Not the whiskey alone. You could see that the prejudice – the *hatred* – wasn't just an act. Harch and the others – but especially Ernest Harch – had a streak of anti-Semitism as thick as sludge in a sewer.

'Briarstead wasn't a particularly sophisticated

place,' Susan continued. 'There wasn't the usual cultural mix. There weren't many Jews on campus, and there weren't any in the fraternity that Jerry wanted to join. Not that the fraternity had a policy against admitting Jews or anyone else. There had been a couple of Jewish members in the past, though none for the last several years. Most of the brothers wanted Jerry in. It was only Harch and his three cronies who were determined to keep him out. They planned to make Hazing Month so rough for him, so utterly intolerable, that he would withdraw his application before the month was over. The humiliation ritual in the House of Thunder was to be the start of it. They didn't really intend to kill Jerry. Not in the beginning, not when they took us to the cavern, not when they were at least half sober. They just wanted to make him feel like dirt. They wanted to rough him up a little bit, scare him, let him know in no uncertain terms that he wasn't welcome. The verbal abuse escalated to physical abuse. They stood in a circle around him, shoving him back and forth, keeping him off balance. Jerry wasn't a fool; he realized this wasn't any ordinary hazing ritual. He wasn't a wimp, either. He couldn't be intimidated easily. When they shoved him too hard, he shoved back – which only made them more aggressive, of course. When they wouldn't stop shoving, Jerry hit Harch in the mouth and split the bastard's lip.'

'And that was the trigger,' McGee said.

'Yes. Then all hell broke loose.'

58

Thunder grumbled again, and the hospital lights flickered briefly, and Susan had the strange, disquieting notion that some supernatural force was trying to carry her back in time, back to the waterfall roar and the darkness of the cavern.

She said, 'Something about the mood of that place – the bone-deep chill, the dampness, the darkness, the steady roar of the waterfall, the sense of isolation – made it easier for the savage in them to come out. They beat Jerry . . . beat him to the floor and kept on beating him.'

She trembled. The trembling became a more violent quivering; the quivering grew into a shudder of revulsion and of remembered terror.

'It was as if they were wild dogs, turning on an interloper from a strange pack,' she said shakily. 'I . . . I screamed at them . . . but I couldn't stop them. Finally, Carl Jellicoe seemed to realize that he'd gone too far, and he backed away. Then Quince, then Parker. Harch was the last to get control of himself, and he was the first to realize they were all going to wind up in prison. Jerry was unconscious. He was . . .'

Her voice cracked, faltered.

It didn't seem like thirteen years; it seemed almost like yesterday.

'Go on,' McGee said quietly.

'He was . . . bleeding from the nose . . . the mouth . . . and from one ear. He'd been very badly hurt. Although he was unconscious, he kept twitching uncontrollably. It looked like there might have

59

been nerve or brain damage. I tried to . . .'

'Go on, Susan.'

'I tried to get to Jerry, but Harch pushed me out of the way, knocked me down. He told the others that they were all going to go to prison if they didn't do something drastic to save themselves. He said that their futures had been destroyed, that they had no real future at all . . . unless they covered up what they'd done. He tried to convince them that they had to finish Jerry off and then kill me, too, and dump our bodies down one of the deep holes in the cavern floor. Jellicoe, Parker, and Quince were half sobered up by the shock of what they'd done, but they were still half drunk, too, and confused and scared. At first they argued with Harch, then agreed with him, then had second thoughts and argued again. They were afraid to commit murder, yet they were afraid *not* to. Harch was furious with them for being so wishy-washy, and he suddenly decided to *force* them to do what he wanted by simply giving them no other choice. He turned to Jerry and he . . . he . . .'

She felt sick, remembering.

McGee held her hand.

Susan said, 'He kicked Jerry . . . in the head . . . three times . . . and caved in one side of his skull.'

Mrs. Baker gasped.

'Killed him,' Susan said.

Outside, lightning slashed open the sky, and thunder roared through the resultant wound. The first fat droplets of rain struck the window.

60

McGee squeezed Susan's hand.

'I grabbed one of the flashlights and ran,' she said. 'Their attention was focused so completely on Jerry's body that I managed to get a bit of a head start on them. Not much but enough. They expected me to try to leave the caverns, but I didn't head toward the exit because I knew they'd catch me if I went that way, so I gained a few more seconds before they realized where I'd gone. I went deeper into the caves, through a twisty stone corridor, down a slope of loose rocks, into another underground room, then into another beyond that one. Eventually, I switched off the flashlight, so they wouldn't be able to follow the glow of it, and I went on as far as I could in complete darkness, feeling my way, inch by inch, stumbling, until I found a niche in the wall, a crawl hole, nothing more than that, hidden behind a limestone stalagmite. I slithered into it, as far back into it as I could possibly go, and then I was very, very quiet. Harch and the others spent hours searching for me before they finally decided I'd somehow gotten out of the caverns. I waited another six or eight hours, afraid to come out of hiding. I finally left the caverns when I couldn't deal with my thirst and claustrophobia any longer.'

Rain pattered on the window, blurring the wind-tossed trees and the black-bellied clouds.

'Jesus,' Mrs. Baker said, her face ashen. 'You poor kid.'

'They were put on trial?' McGee asked.

'Yes. The district attorney didn't think he could win if he charged them with first- or second-degree murder. Too many extenuating circumstances, including the whiskey and the fact that Jerry had actually struck the first blow when he'd busted Harch's lip. Anyway, Harch was convicted of manslaughter and got a five-year term in the state penitentiary.'

'Just five years?' Mrs. Baker asked.

'I thought he should have been put away forever,' Susan said, as bitter now as she had been the day she'd heard the judge hand down the sentence.

'What about the other three?' McGee asked.

'They were convicted of assault and of being accomplices to Harch, but because they'd had no previous run-ins with the law and were from good families, and because none of them actually struck the killing blows, they were all given suspended sentences and put on probation.'

'Outrageous!' Mrs. Baker said.

McGee continued to hold Susan's hand; and she was glad that he did.

'Of course,' she said, 'all four of them were immediately expelled from Briarstead. And in a strange way, fate took a hand in punishing Parker and Jellicoe. They were taking the pre-med course at Briarstead, and they managed to finish their last year at another university, but after that they quickly discovered that no top-of-the-line medical school would accept students with serious criminal records. They hustled for another year, submitting applications everywhere, and they finally managed to squeeze into the medical program at a distinctly second-rate university. The night they were notified of their acceptance, they went drinking to celebrate, got stinking drunk, and were both killed when Parker lost control of the car and rolled it over twice. Maybe I should be ashamed to say this, but I was relieved and grateful when I heard what had happened to them.'

'Of course you were,' Mrs. Baker said. 'That's only natural. Nothing to be ashamed of at all.'

'What about Randy Lee Quince?' McGee asked.

'I never heard what happened to him,' Susan said. 'And I don't care . . . just as long as he suffered.'

Two closely spaced explosions of lightning and thunder shook the world outside, and for a moment Susan and McGee and Mrs. Baker stared at the window, where the rain struck with greater force than before.

Then Mrs. Baker said, 'It's a horrible story, just horrible. But I'm not sure I understand exactly what it has to do with your fainting spell in the hall a while ago.'

Before Susan could respond, McGee said, 'Apparently, the man who stepped out of the elevator, in front of Susan's wheelchair, was one of those fraternity brothers from Briarstead.'

'Yes,' Susan said.

'Either Harch or Quince.'

'Ernest Harch,' Susan said.

'An incredible coincidence,' McGee said, giving her hand one last, gentle squeeze before letting go of it. 'Thirteen years after the fact – and a whole continent away from where the two of you last saw each other.'

Mrs. Baker frowned. 'But you must be mistaken.'

'Oh, no,' Susan said, shaking her head vigorously. 'I'll never forget that face. Never.'

'But his name's not Harch,' Mrs. Baker said.

'Yes, it is.'

'No. It's Richmond. Bill Richmond.'

'Then he's changed his name since I knew him.'

'I wouldn't think a convicted criminal would be allowed to change his name,' Mrs. Baker said.

'I didn't mean he changed it legally, in court, or anything like that,' Susan said, frustrated by the nurse's reluctance to accept the truth. The man *was* Harch.

'What's he here for?' McGee asked Thelma Baker.

'He's having surgery tomorrow,' the nurse said. 'Dr. Viteski's going to remove two rather large cysts from his lower back.'

'Not spinal cysts?'

'No. Fatty tissue cysts. But they're large ones.'

'Benign?' McGee asked.

'Yes. But I guess they're deeply rooted, and they're causing him some discomfort.'

'Admitted this morning?'

'That's right.'

64

'And his name's Richmond. You're sure of that?'

'Yes.'

'But it used to be *Harch*,' Susan insisted.

Mrs. Baker took off her glasses and let them dangle on the beaded chain around her neck. She scratched the bridge of her nose, looked quizzically at Susan, and said, 'How old was this Harch when he killed Jerry Stein?'

'He was a senior at Briarstead that year,' Susan said. 'Twenty-one years old.'

'That settles it, then,' the nurse said.

'Why?' McGee asked.

Mrs. Baker put her glasses on again and said, 'Bill Richmond is only in his early twenties.'

'He can't be,' Susan said.

'In fact I'm pretty sure he's just twenty-one himself. He'd have been about eight years old when Jerry Stein was killed.'

'He's not twenty-one,' Susan said anxiously. 'He's thirty-four by now.'

'Well, he certainly doesn't *look* any older than twenty-one,' Mrs. Baker said. 'In fact he looks younger than that. A good deal younger than that. He's hardly more than a kid. If he was lying about it one way or the other, I'd think he was actually adding on a few years, not taking them off.'

As the lights flickered again, and as thunder rolled across the hollow, sheet-metal sky, Dr. McGee looked at Susan and said, 'How old did he look to you when he stepped out of the elevator?'

She thought about it for a moment, and she got a

sinking feeling in her stomach. 'Well . . . he looked *exactly* like Ernest Harch.'

'Exactly like Harch looked back then?'

'Uh . . . yeah.'

'Like a twenty-one-year-old college man?'

Susan nodded reluctantly.

McGee pressed the point. 'Then you mean that he didn't look thirty-four to you?'

'No. But maybe he's aged well. Some thirty-four-year-olds could pass for ten years younger.' She was confused about the apparent age discrepancy, but she was not the least bit confused about the man's identity: 'He *is* Harch.'

'Perhaps it's just a strong resemblance,' Mrs. Baker said.

'*No*,' Susan insisted. 'It's him, all right. I recognized him, and I saw him recognize me, too. And I don't feel safe. It was my testimony that sent him to prison. If you'd seen the way he glared at me in that courtroom . . .'

McGee and Mrs. Baker stared at her, and there was something in their eyes that made her feel as if this were a courtroom, too, as if she were standing before a jury, awaiting judgment. She stared back at them for a moment, but then she lowered her eyes because she was made miserable by the doubt she saw in theirs.

'Listen,' McGee said, 'I'll go take a look at this guy's records. Maybe I'll even have a word or two with him. We'll see if we can straighten this out.'

'Sure,' Susan said, knowing it was hopeless.

66

'If he's really Harch, we'll make sure he doesn't get anywhere near you. And if he *isn't* Harch, you'll be able to rest easy.'

It's him, dammit!

But she didn't say anything; she merely nodded.

'I'll be back in a few minutes,' McGee said.

Susan stared down at her pale, interlocked hands.

'Will you be okay?' McGee asked.

'Yeah. Sure.'

She sensed a meaningful look and an unspoken message passing between the doctor and the nurse, but she didn't look up.

McGee left the room.

'We'll get this straightened out real quick, honey,' Mrs. Baker assured her.

Outside, thunder fell out of the sky with the sound of an avalanche.

* * *

Night would come early. Already, the storm had torn apart the autumn afternoon and had blown it away. The twilight had been swept in ahead of schedule.

'His name's definitely Bill Richmond,' McGee said when he returned a few minutes later.

Susan sat stiffly in bed, still disbelieving.

The two of them were alone in the room. The nurses had changed shifts, and Mrs. Baker had gone home for the day.

McGee toyed with the stethoscope around his

67

neck. 'And he's definitely just twenty-one years old.'

'But you weren't gone nearly long enough to've checked out his background,' Susan said. 'If all you did was read through his medical records, then nothing has really been proved. He could have lied to his doctor, you know.'

'Well, it turns out that Leon – Dr. Viteski, that is – has known Bill's parents, Grace and Harry Richmond, for twenty-five years. Viteski says he delivered all three of the Richmond babies himself, right here in this very hospital.'

Doubt nibbled at Susan's solid conviction.

McGee said, 'Leon treated all of Bill Richmond's childhood illnesses and injuries. He knows for an absolute fact that the kid was only eight years old, living in Pine Wells, just doing what eight-year-olds do, when Ernest Harch killed Jerry Stein, thirteen years ago, back there in Pennsylvania.'

'Three thousand miles away.'

'Exactly.'

Susan sagged under a heavy burden of weariness and anxiety. 'But he looked just like Harch. When he stepped out of the elevator this afternoon, when I looked up and saw that face, those damned gray eyes, I could have sworn . . .'

'Oh, I'm certain you didn't panic without good reason,' he said placatingly. 'I'm sure there's a resemblance.'

Although she had come to like McGee a lot in just one day, Susan was angry with him for letting

68

even a vaguely patronizing tone enter his voice. Her anger rejuvenated her a bit, and she sat up straighter in bed, her hands fisted at her sides. 'Not just a resemblance,' she said sharply. 'He looked *exactly* like Harch.'

'Well, of course, you've got to keep in mind that it's been a long time since you've seen Harch.'

'So?'

'You may not remember him quite as well as you think you do,' McGee said.

'Oh, I remember. Perfectly. This Richmond is the same height as Harch, the same weight, the same build.'

'It's a fairly common body type.'

'He has the same blond hair, the same square features, the same *eyes*. Such light gray eyes, almost transparent. How many people have eyes like that? Not many. Feature by feature, this Bill Richmond and Ernest Harch are duplicates. It's not just a simple resemblance. It's a lot stranger than that. It's downright uncanny.'

'Okay, okay,' McGee said, holding up one hand to stop her. 'Perhaps they are remarkably alike, virtually identical. If that's the case, then it's an incredible coincidence that you've encountered both of them, thirteen years apart, at opposite ends of the country; but that's all it is – a coincidence.'

Her hands were cold. Freezing. She rubbed them together, trying to generate heat.

She said, 'When it comes to the subject of coincidences, I agree with Philip Marlowe.'

'Who?'

'Marlowe. He's a private detective in those novels by Raymond Chandler. *The Lady in the Lake, The Big Sleep, The Long Goodbye . . .* '

'Of course. Marlowe. Okay, so what did he have to say about coincidences?'

'He said, "Show me a coincidence, and when I open it up for you, I'll show you at least two people inside, plotting some sort of mischief." '

McGee frowned and shook his head. 'That philosophy might be suitable for a character in a detective story. But out here in the real world, it's a little paranoid, don't you think?'

He was right, and she couldn't sustain her anger with him. As her fury faded, so did her strength, and she sank back against the pillows once more. 'Could two people really look so much alike?'

'I've heard it said that everyone has an unrelated twin somewhere in the world, what some people call a "doppelgänger." '

'Maybe,' Susan said, unconvinced. 'But this was . . . different. It was weird. I'd swear he recognized me, too. He smiled so strangely. And he – *winked* at me!'

For the first time since he had returned to her room, McGee smiled. 'Winked at you? Well, there's certainly nothing strange or uncanny about that, dear lady.' His intensely blue eyes sparkled with amusement. 'In case you didn't know it, men frequently wink at attractive women. Now don't tell me you've never been winked at before. Don't tell me you've spent your life in a nunnery or on a desert island.' He grinned.

'There's nothing attractive about me at the moment,' she insisted.

'Nonsense.'

'My hair needs a real washing, not just brushed with powder. I'm emaciated, and I've got bags under my eyes. I hardly think I inspire romantic thoughts in my present condition.'

'You're being too hard on yourself. Emaciated? No. You've just got a haunting Audrey Hepburn quality.'

Susan resisted his charm, which wasn't easy. But she was determined to say everything that was on her mind. 'Besides, it wasn't that kind of wink.'

'Ahhhh,' he said. 'So now you admit you've been winked at in the past. Suddenly you're an *expert* on winking.'

She refused to be coaxed and kidded into forgetting the man who had stepped out of the elevator.

'What kind of wink was it, exactly?' he asked, a teasing tone still in his voice.

'It was a smartass wink. Smug. There wasn't anything at all flirtatious about it, either. It wasn't warm and friendly, like a wink ought to be. It was cold. Cold and smug and nasty and . . . somehow threatening,' she said, but even as she spoke she realized how ludicrous it sounded to give such an exhaustively detailed interpretation to something as simple as a wink.

'It's a good thing I didn't ask you to interpret

his entire facial expression,' McGee said. 'We'd have been here until tomorrow morning!'

Susan finally succumbed: She smiled. 'I guess it does sound pretty silly, huh?'

'Especially since we know for a fact that his name's Bill Richmond and that he's only twenty-one.'

'So the wink was just a wink, and the threat was all in my head?'

'Don't you figure that's probably the case?' he asked diplomatically.

She sighed. 'Yeah, I guess I do. And I suppose I should apologize for causing so much trouble about this.'

'It wasn't any trouble,' he said graciously.

'I'm awfully tired, weak, and my perceptions aren't as sharp as they should be. Last night, I dreamed about Harch, and when I saw that man step out of the elevator, looking *so* much like Harch, I just . . . lost my head. I panicked.'

That was a difficult admission for her to make. Other people might act like Chicken Little at the slightest provocation, but Susan Kathleen Thorton expected herself to remain – and previously always *had* remained – calm and collected through any crisis that fate threw at her. She had been that way since she was just a little girl, for the circumstances of her lonely childhood had required her to be totally self-reliant. She hadn't even panicked in the House of Thunder, when Ernest Harch had kicked in Jerry's skull; she had run, had hidden, had survived – all because she had kept her wits about her at a time when most people, if thrust into the same situation, would surely have lost theirs. But now she had panicked; worse, she had let others see her lose control. She felt embarrassed and humbled by her behavior.

'I'll be a model patient from now on,' she told Dr. McGee. 'I'll take my medicine without argument. I'll eat real well, so I'll regain my strength just as quickly as possible. I'll exercise when I'm told to and only as much as I'm told to. By the time I'm ready to be discharged, you'll have forgotten all about the scene I caused today. In fact you'll wish that all of your patients were like me. That's a promise.'

'I *already* wish all of my patients were exactly like you,' he said. 'Believe me, it's much more pleasant treating a pretty young woman than it is treating cranky old men with heart conditions.'

After McGee had gone for the day, Susan arranged with one of the orderlies to have a rental television installed in her room. As afternoon faded into evening, she watched the last half of an old episode of 'The Rockford Files,' then the umpteenth rerun of an episode of 'The Mary Tyler Moore Show.' In spite of frequent bursts of storm-caused static, she watched the five o'clock news on a Seattle station, and she was dismayed to discover that the current international crises were pretty much the same as the international crises that had been at the top of the news reports more than three

...ks ago, before she had fallen into a coma.

Later, she ate all the food on her dinner tray. Later still, she rang for one of the second-shift nurses and asked for a snack. A pert blonde named Marcia Edmonds brought her a dish of sherbet with sliced peaches. Susan ate all of that, too.

She tried not to think about Bill Richmond, the Harch look-alike. She tried not to think about the House of Thunder, or about the precious days she had lost in a coma, or about the remaining gaps in her memory, or about her current state of helplessness, or about anything else that might upset her. She concentrated on being a good patient and developing a positive attitude, for she was eager to get well again.

Nevertheless, an unspecific but chilling presentiment of danger disturbed her thoughts from time to time. A shapeless portent of evil.

Each time that her thoughts turned into that dark pathway, she forced herself to think only of pleasing things. Mostly, she thought about Dr. Jeffrey McGee: the grace with which he moved; the ear-pleasing timbre of his voice; the sensitivity and the intriguing scintillation of his exceptionally blue eyes; his strong, well-formed, long-fingered hands.

Near bedtime, after she had taken the sedative that McGee had prescribed for her, but before she had begun to get drowsy, the rain stopped falling. The wind, however, did not die down. It continued to press insistently against the window. It murmured, growled, hissed. It sniffed all around the window frame and thumped its paws of air against the glass, as if it were a big dog searching diligently for a way to get inside.

Perhaps because of the sound of the wind, Susan dreamed of dogs that night. Dogs and then jackals. Jackals and then wolves. Werewolves. They changed fluidly from lupine to human form, then into wolves again, then back into men, always pursuing her or leaping at her or waiting in the darkness ahead to pounce on her. When they took the form of men, she recognized them: Jellicoe, Parker, Quince, and Harch. Once, as she was fleeing through a dark forest, she came upon a moonlit clearing in which the four beasts, in wolf form, were crouched over the corpse of Jerry Stein, tearing the flesh from its bones. They looked up at her and grinned malevolently. Blood and ragged pieces of raw flesh drooled from their white teeth and vicious jowls. Sometimes she dreamed they were chasing her through the caverns, between thrusting limestone stalagmites and stalactites, along narrow corridors of rock and earth. Sometimes they chased her across a vast field of delicate black flowers; sometimes they prowled deserted city streets, following her scent, forcing her to flee from a series of hiding places, snapping relentlessly at her heels. Once, she even dreamed that one of the creatures had slunk into her hospital room; it was a crouching wolf-thing, swathed in shadows, visible only in murky silhouette, watching her from the foot of the bed, one wild eye gleaming. Then it moved into weak amber glow of the night light, and she saw that it had undergone another metamorphosis, changing from wolf to man this time. It was Ernest Harch. He was wearing pajamas and a bathrobe—

(*This isn't part of the dream!* she thought as icy shards of fear thrilled through her.)

—and he came around to the side of the bed. He bent down to look more closely at her. She tried to cry out; couldn't. She could not move, either. His face began to blur in front of her, and she struggled to keep it in focus, but she sensed that she was slipping back to the field of black flowers—

(*I've got to shake this off. Wake up. All the way. It was supposed to be a mild sedative. Just a mild one, dammit!*)

—and Harch's features ran together in one gray smear. The hospital room dissolved completely, and again she was plunging across a field of strange black flowers, with a pack of wolves baying behind her. The moon was full; oddly, however, it provided little light. She couldn't see where she was going, and she tripped over something, fell into the flowers, and discovered that she had stumbled over Jerry Stein's mutilated, half-eaten cadaver. The wolf appeared, loomed over her, snarling, leering, pushing its slavering muzzle down at her, down and down, until its cold nose touched her cheek. The beast's hateful face blurred and reformed into an even more hateful countenance: that of Ernest Harch. It wasn't a wolf's nose touching her cheek

76

any longer; it was now Harch's blunt finger. She flinched, and her heart began pounding so forcefully that she wondered why it didn't tear loose of her. Harch pulled his hand away from her and smiled. The field of black flowers was gone. She was dreaming that she was in her hospital room again—

(*Except it's not a dream. It's real. Harch is here, and he's going to kill me.*)

—and she tried to sit up in bed but was unable to move. She reached for the call button that would summon a nurse or an orderly, and although the button was only a few inches away, it suddenly seemed light-years beyond her reach. She strained toward it, and her arm appeared to stretch and stretch magically, until it was bizarrely elongated; her flesh and bones seemed to be possessed of an impossible elasticity. Still, her questing finger fell short of the button. She felt as if she were Alice, as if she had just stepped through the looking glass. She was now in that part of Wonderland in which the usual laws of perspective did not apply. Here, little was big, and big was little; near was far; far was near; there was no difference whatsoever between up and down, in and out, over and under. This sleep-induced, drug-induced confusion made her nauseous; she tasted bile in the back of her throat. Could she taste something like that if she were dreaming? She wasn't sure. She wished fervently that she could at least be certain whether she was awake or still fast asleep. 'Long time no

77

,' Harch said. Susan blinked at him, trying to keep him in focus, but he kept fading in and out. Sometimes, for just a second or two, he had the shining eyes of a wolf. 'Did you think you could hide from me forever?' he asked, speaking in a whisper, leaning even closer, until his face was nearly touching hers. His breath was foul, and she wondered if her ability to smell was an indication that she was awake, that Harch was real. 'Did you think you could hide from me forever?' Harch demanded again. She could not respond to him; her voice was frozen in her throat, a cold lump that she could neither spit out nor swallow. 'You rotten bitch,' Harch said, and his smile became a broad grin. 'You stinking, rotten, smug little bitch. How do you feel now? Huh? Are you sorry you testified against me? Hmmm? Yeah. I'll bet you're real sorry now.' He laughed softly, and for a moment the laughter became the low growling of a wolf, but then it turned into laughter again. 'You know what I'm going to do to you?' he asked. His face began to blur. 'Do you know what I'm going to do to you?' She was in a cavern. There were black flowers growing out of the stone floor. She was running from baying wolves. She turned a corner, and the cavern opened onto a shadowy city street. A wolf stood on the sidewalk, under a lamppost, and it said, 'Do you know what I'm going to do to you?' Susan ran and kept on running through a long, frightening, amorphous night.

Monday, shortly after dawn, she woke, groggy

and damp with sweat. She remembered dreaming about wolves and about Ernest Harch. In the flat, hard, gray light of the cloudy morning, it seemed ridiculous for her to entertain the thought that Harch actually had been in her room last night. She was still alive, uninjured, utterly unmarked. It had all been a nightmare. All of it. Just a terrible nightmare.

5

Not long after Susan woke, she took a sponge bath with the help of a nurse. Refreshed, she changed into her spare pajamas, a green pair with yellow piping. A nurse's aide took the soiled blue silk pajamas into the bathroom, rinsed them in the sink, and hung them to dry on a hook behind the door.

Breakfast was larger this morning than it had been yesterday. Susan ate every bite of it and was still hungry.

A few minutes after Mrs. Baker came on duty with the morning shift, she came to Susan's room with Dr. McGee, who was making his morning rounds before attending to his private practice at his offices in Willawauk. Together, McGee and Mrs. Baker removed the bandages from Susan's forehead. There was no pain, just a prickle or two when the sutures were snipped and tugged loose.

McGee cupped her chin in his hand and turned her head from side to side, studying the healed wound. 'It's a neat bit of tailoring, even if I do say so myself.'

Mrs. Baker got the long-handled mirror from the nightstand and gave it to Susan.

She was pleasantly surprised to find that the scar was not nearly as bad as she had feared it would be. It was four inches long, an unexpectedly narrow line of pink, shiny, somewhat swollen skin, bracketed by small red spots where the stitches had been.

'The suture marks will fade away completely in ten days or so,' McGee assured her.

'I thought it was a huge, bloody gash,' Susan said, raising one hand to touch the new, smooth skin.

'Not huge,' McGee said. 'But it bled like a faucet gushing water when you were first brought in here. And it resisted healing for a while, probably because you frowned a lot while you were comatose, and the frowning wrinkled your forehead. There wasn't much we could do about that. Blue Cross wouldn't pay for an around-the-clock comedian in your room.' He smiled. 'Anyway, after the suture marks have faded, the scar tissue itself will just about vanish, too. It won't look as wide as it looks now, and, of course, it won't be discolored. When it's fully healed, if you think it's still too prominent, a good plastic surgeon can use derm-abrasion techniques to scour away some of the scar tissue.'

'Oh, I'm sure that won't be necessary,' Susan said. 'I'm sure it'll be almost invisible. I'm just relieved that I don't look like Frankenstein's monster.'

Mrs. Baker laughed. 'As if that were ever a possibility, what with your good looks. Goodness gracious, kid, it's a crime the way you underrate yourself!'

Susan blushed.

McGee was amused.

Shaking her head, Mrs. Baker picked up the scissors and the used bandages, and she left the room.

'Now,' McGee said, 'ready to talk to your boss at Milestone?'

'Phil Gomez,' she said, repeating the name McGee had given her yesterday. 'I still can't remember a thing about him.'

'You will.' McGee looked at his wristwatch. 'It's a bit early, but not much. He might be in his office now.'

He used the phone on the nightstand and asked the hospital operator to dial the Milestone number in Newport Beach, California. Gomez was already at work, and he took the call.

For a couple of minutes, Susan listened to one side of the conversation. McGee told Phil Gomez that she was out of her coma, and he explained about the temporary spottiness of her memory, always stressing the word 'temporary.' Finally, he passed the receiver to her.

Susan took it as if she were being handed a snake. She wasn't sure how she felt about making contact with Milestone. On one hand, she didn't want to go through the rest of her life with a gaping hole in her memory. On the other hand, however, she remembered how she had felt yesterday when the subject of Milestone had come up during her talk with McGee: She'd had the disquieting feeling that she might be better off if she never found out what her job had been. A worm of fear had coiled up inside of her yesterday. Now, again, she felt that same inexplicable fear, squirming.

'Hello?'

'Susan? Is that really you?'

'Yes. It's me.'

Gomez had a high, quick, puppy-friendly voice. His words bumped into one another. 'Susan, thank God, how good to hear from you, how very good indeed, really, I mean it, but of course you know I mean it. We've all been so concerned about you, worried half to death. Even Breckenridge was worried sick about you, and who would ever have thought *he* had any human compassion? So how are you? How are you feeling?'

The sound of his voice kindled no memories in Susan. It was the voice of an utter stranger.

They talked for about ten minutes, and Gomez tried hard to help her recall her work. He said that the Milestone Corporation was an independent, private-industry think tank working on contracts with ITT, IBM, Exxon, and other major corporations. That meant nothing to Susan; she had no idea what an independent, private-industry think tank *was*. Gomez told her that she was – or, rather, *had been* – working on a wide variety of laser applications for the communications industry. She couldn't remember a thing about that. He described her office at Milestone; it sounded like no place she had ever been. He talked about her friends and co-workers there: Eddie Gilroy, Ella Haversby, Tom Kavinsky, Anson Breckenridge, and others. Not one of the names was even slightly familiar to her. By the end of the conversation, Gomez's disappointment and concern were evident in his voice. He urged her to call him again, any time, if she thought it would help, and he suggested that she call some of the others at Milestone, too.

'And listen,' he said, 'no matter how long it takes you to recuperate, your job will be waiting for you here.'

'Thank you,' she said, touched by his generous spirit and by the depth of his concern for her.

'No need to thank me,' he said. 'You're one of the best we have here, and we don't want to lose you. If you weren't nearly a thousand miles away, we'd be there, camping out in your hospital room, doing our best to cheer you up and speed along the healing process.'

A minute later, when Susan finally said goodbye to Gomez and hung up, McGee said, 'Well? Any luck?'

'None. I still can't remember a thing about my job. But Phil Gomez seemed like a sweet man.'

In fact Gomez seemed so nice, seemed to care about her so much, that she wondered how she could have forgotten him so completely.

And then she wondered why a dark dread had

85

grown in her like a malignant tumor during the entire conversation. In spite of Phil Gomez, even the thought of the Milestone Corporation made her uneasy. Worse than uneasy. She was . . . afraid of Milestone. But she didn't know *why*.

* * *

Later Monday morning, she sat up on the edge of her bed and swung her legs back and forth for a while, exercising them.

Mrs. Baker helped her into a wheelchair and said, 'This time I think you ought to make the trip yourself. Once around the entire second floor. If your arms get too tired, just ask any nurse to bring you back here.'

'I feel great,' Susan said. 'I won't get tired. Actually I think maybe I'll try to make at least two trips around the halls.'

'I knew that's what you'd say,' Mrs. Baker told her. 'You just set your mind to getting around once, and that'll be enough for now. Don't try to make a marathon out of it. After lunch and a nap, *then* you can do the second lap.'

'You're pampering me too much. I'm a lot stronger than you think I am.'

'I knew you'd say that, too. Kiddo, you're incorrigible.'

Remembering yesterday's humiliation – when she had insisted she could walk but then hadn't even been able to lower herself into the wheelchair without Mrs. Baker's assistance – Susan blushed.

'Okay. Once around. But after lunch and a nap, I'm going to make two *more* laps. And yesterday you said I might try walking a few steps today, and I intend to hold you to that, too.'

'Incorrigible,' Mrs. Baker repeated, but she was smiling.

'First,' Susan said, 'I want to have a better look out of this window.'

She wheeled herself away from her own bed, past the other bed, which was still empty, and she stopped alongside the window through which she had been able to see (from her bed) only the sky and the upper portions of a few trees. The window-sill was high, and from the wheelchair she had to crane her neck to see outside.

She discovered that the hospital stood atop a hill, one of a circle of hills that ringed a small valley. Some of the slopes were heavily forested with pines, fir, spruce, and a variety of other trees, while some slopes were covered with emerald-green meadows. A town occupied the floor of the valley and extended some of its neighborhoods into the lower reaches of the hills. Its brick, stone, and wood-sided buildings were tucked in among other trees, facing out on neatly squared-off streets. Although the day was drab and gray, and although ugly storm clouds churned across the sky, threatening rain, the town nonetheless looked serene and quite beautiful.

'It's lovely,' Susan said.

'Isn't it?' Mrs. Baker said. 'I'll never regret

moving out of the city.' She sighed. 'Well, I've got work to do. Once you've made your circuit of the halls, call me so that I can help you get back into bed.' She shook one plump finger at Susan. 'And don't you dare try climbing out of that chair and into bed yourself. Regardless of what you think, you're still weak and shaky. You call for me.'

'I will,' Susan said, although she thought she might just carefully try getting into bed under her own steam, depending on how she felt after taking her wheelchair constitutional.

Mrs. Baker left the room, and Susan sat by the window for a while, enjoying the view.

After a couple of minutes, however, she realized that it was not the view that was delaying her. She hesitated to leave the room because she was afraid. Afraid of meeting Bill Richmond, the Harch look-alike. Afraid that he would smile that hard smile, turn those moonlight-pale eyes on her, wink slyly at her, and perhaps ask her how good old Jerry Stein was getting along these days.

Hell's bell's, that's just plain ridiculous! she thought, angry with herself.

She shook herself, as if trying to throw off the irrational fear that clung to her.

He's not Ernest Harch. He's not the boogeyman, for God's sake, she told herself severely. He's thirteen years too young to be Harch. His name's Richmond, Bill Richmond, and he comes from Pine Wells, and he doesn't know me. So why the devil am I sitting here, immobilized by the fear of encountering him out there in the corridor? What's *wrong* with me?

She shamed herself into motion. She put her hands to the chair's wheels and rolled out of the room, into the hallway.

She was surprised when her arms began to ache before she had gone even a fifth of the distance that she had planned to cover. By the time she traveled both of the short halls, across the top of the hospital's T-shaped floor plan, her muscles began to ache. She stopped the chair for a moment and massaged her arms and shoulders. Her fingers told her what she had wanted to forget: that she was terribly thin, wasted, far from being her old self.

She gritted her teeth and went on, turning the wheelchair into the long main hall. The effort to move and maneuver the chair was sufficiently demanding to require concentration on the task; therefore, it was amazing that she even saw the man at the nurses' station. But she *did* see him, and she stopped her wheelchair only fifteen feet from him. She gaped at him, stunned. Then she closed her eyes, counted slowly to three, opened them – and he was still there, leaning against the counter, chatting with a nurse.

He was tall, about six feet two, with brown hair and brown eyes. His face was long, and so were his features, as if someone had accidentally stretched the putty he was made from before God had had an opportunity to pop him into the kiln to dry. He had a long forehead, a long nose with long, narrow nostrils, and a chin that came to a sharp point. He was wearing white pajamas and a wine-red robe, just as if he were an ordinary patient. But as far as Susan was concerned, there wasn't anything ordinary about him.

She had half expected to encounter Bill Richmond, the Harch look-alike, somewhere in the halls. She had prepared herself for that, had steeled herself for it. But she hadn't expected *this*.

The man was Randy Lee Quince.

Another of the four fraternity men.

She stared at him in shock, in disbelief, in fear, willing him to vanish, praying that he was nothing more than an apparition or a figment of her fevered imagination. But he refused to do the gentlemanly thing and disappear; he remained – unwavering, solid, real.

As she was deciding whether to confront him or flee, he left the nurses' station, turning his back on Susan without glancing at her. He walked away and entered the fifth room past the elevators, on the left side of the hall.

Susan realized she'd been holding her breath. She gasped, and the air she drew into her lungs seemed as sharp and cold as a February night in the High Sierras, where she sometimes went skiing.

For a moment she didn't think she'd ever move again. She felt brittle, icy, as if she had crystallized.

A nurse walked by, her rubber-soled shoes squeaking slightly on the highly polished floor.

The squeak made Susan think of bats.

Her skin broke out in gooseflesh.

There had been bats in the House of Thunder. Bats rustling secretly, disturbed by the flashlights and the candles. Bats chittering nervously during the beating that the fraternity men had administered to poor Jerry. Bats cartwheeling through the pitch blackness, fluttering frantically against her as she doused her stolen flashlight and fled from Harch and the others.

The nurse at the counter, the one to whom Quince had been talking, noticed Susan and must have seen the fright on her face. 'Are you all right?'

Susan breathed out. The expelled air was warm on her teeth and lips. Thawed, she nodded to the nurse.

The sound of squealing bats became distant, then swooped away into silence.

She rolled her wheelchair to the counter and looked up at the nurse, a thin brunette whose name she didn't know. 'The man you were just talking to . . .'

The nurse leaned over the counter, looked down at her, and said, 'The fellow who went into two-sixteen?'

'Yes, him.'

'What about him?'

'I think I know him. Or *knew* him. A long time ago.' She glanced nervously toward the room into which Quince had gone, then back at the nurse again. 'But if he isn't who I think he is, I don't

91

want to burst in on him and make a fool of myself. Do you know his name?'

'Yes, of course. He's Peter Johnson. Nice enough guy, if a little bit on the talky side. He's always coming out here to chat, and I'm beginning to fall behind on my record-keeping because of it.'

Susan blinked. 'Peter Johnson? Are you sure of that? Are you sure his name's not Randy Lee Quince?'

The nurse frowned. 'Quince? No. It's Peter Johnson, all right. I'm sure of that.'

Talking to herself as much as to the nurse, Susan said, 'Thirteen years ago . . . back in Pennsylvania . . . I knew a young man who looked exactly like that.'

'Thirteen years ago?' the nurse said. 'Well, then for sure it wasn't this guy. Peter's only nineteen or twenty. Thirteen years ago, he'd have been a little boy.'

Startled, but only for a moment, Susan quickly realized that this man *had* been young. Hardly more than a kid. He looked just like Randy Quince *had* looked, but not as Quince would look today. The only way he could be Randy Lee Quince was if Quince had spent the past thirteen years in suspended animation.

* * *

For lunch, she was given fewer soft foods than before, more solid fare. It was a welcome change of diet, and she cleaned her plate. She was eager to regain her strength and get out of the hospital.

To please Mrs. Baker, Susan lowered her bed, curled on her side, and pretended to nap. Of course, sleep was impossible. She couldn't stop thinking about Bill Richmond and Peter Johnson.

Two look-alikes? Dead ringers, both showing up in the same place, within one day of each other?

What were the odds on that? Astronomical. It wasn't merely unlikely; it was impossible.

Yet not impossible. Because they were here, dammit. She had seen them.

Rather than the chance arrival of two dead ringers, it seemed at least marginally more likely that the real Harch and the real Quince had, by chance, checked into the same hospital that she had checked into. She spent some time considering the possibility that they weren't merely look-alikes, that they were the genuine articles, but she couldn't make much of a case for that notion. They might both have changed their names and assumed entirely new identities after their individual periods of probation had expired, after they could quietly slip away without alerting probation officers. They might have stayed in touch during the years Harch was in prison, and later on they might have moved together to the same town in Oregon. There wasn't really any coincidence involved in that part of the scenario; after all, they had been close friends. They might even both have become ill at the same time and might have gone to the same hospital on the same day; that *would* be a coincidence, all right, but not a particularly incredible one. Where it didn't hold up, where the whole house of cards collapsed, was when you considered their miraculously youthful appearance. Perhaps one of them might have passed thirteen years without noticeably aging; perhaps *one* of them might have been fortunate enough to inherit Methuselah's genes. But surely *both* men wouldn't have remained utterly untouched by the passing of so many years. No, that was simply too much to accept.

So where does that leave me? she wondered. With two look-alikes? The old doppelgänger theory again? If they are just a couple of doubles for Harch and Quince, were they cast up here by chance? Or is there a purpose to their arrival in this place, at this particular time? What sort of purpose? Is someone out to get me? And isn't *that* a crazy thought, for God's sake!

She opened her eyes and stared through the bed railing, across the adjacent bed, at the iron-gray sky beyond the window. Chilled, she pulled the covers tighter around her.

She considered other explanations.

Maybe they didn't look as much like Harch and Quince as she thought they did. McGee had suggested that her memory-pictures of their faces were certain to have grown cloudy over the years, whether or not she recognized that fact. He could be right. If you rounded up the real Harch and the real Quince, and if you stood them beside Richmond and Johnson, there might be only a mild resemblance. This dead ringer stuff could be mostly in her head.

But she didn't think so.

Was there a chance that the two men here in the hospital were the sons of Harch and Quince? No. That was a ridiculous theory. While they were too young to be Harch and Quince, these look-alikes were too old to be the children of those men. Neither Harch nor Quince would even have reached puberty by the year in which Richmond and Johnson were born; they couldn't possibly have sired children that long ago.

But now that the concept of blood relationships had arisen, she wondered if these two might be brothers of Harch and Quince. She didn't know if Harch had a brother or not. At the trial, his family had been there to offer him their support. However, there had only been his parents and a younger sister, no brother. Susan vaguely recalled that Randy Quince's brother had shown up at the trial. In fact, now that she thought hard about it, she remembered that the two Quince brothers had looked somewhat alike. But not *exactly* alike. Besides, the brother had been several years *older* than Randy. Of course, there might have been a younger Quince brother at home, one who had been too young to come to the trial. Brothers . . . She couldn't rule it out altogether. These men *could* conceivably be brothers to those who had terrorized her in the House of Thunder.

But, again, she didn't think so.

That left only one explanation: insanity. Maybe she was losing her mind. Suffering from delusions. Hallucinations. Perhaps she was taking the most innocent ingredients and cooking up bizarre paranoid fantasies.

No. She refused to give much consideration to that possibility. Oh, maybe she was too serious about life; *that* was an accusation she would be willing to consider. Sometimes she thought that she was almost too well balanced, too much in control of herself; she envied other people the ability to do silly, spur-of-the-moment, irrational, *exciting* things. If she were more able to let herself go now and then, more able to let her hair down, she wouldn't have missed out on quite so much fun over the years. Too sober, too serious, too much of an ant and not enough of a grasshopper? Yes. But insane, out of her mind? Definitely not.

And now she had run out of answers to the doppelgänger puzzle. Those were the only solutions that had thus far presented themselves, but none of them satisfied her.

She decided not to mention Peter Johnson to either Mrs. Baker or Dr. McGee. She was afraid she'd sound . . . flighty.

She huddled under the covers, watching the churning, sooty sky, wondering if she should simply shrug off the look-alikes, just forget all about them. Wondering if she should merely be amazed by them – or frightened of them. Wondering . . .

* * *

That afternoon, without asking for help, she got out of bed and into the wheelchair. Her legs almost failed to support her even for the two or three seconds she needed to stand on them; they felt as if the bones had been extracted from them. She became dizzy, and sweat popped out on her brow, but she made it into the chair all by herself.

Mrs. Baker entered the room only a moment later and scowled at her. 'Did you get out of bed alone?'

'Yep. I told you I was stronger than you thought.'

'That was a reckless thing to do.'

'Oh, no. It was easy.'

'Is that so?'

'Easy as cake.'

'Then why did you break out in a sweat?'

Susan sheepishly wiped a hand across her damp brow. 'I must be going through the change of life.'

'Now don't you try to make me laugh,' Mrs. Baker said. 'You deserve to be scolded, and I'm just the grouch to do it. You're a stubborn one, aren't you?'

'Me? Stubborn?' Susan asked, pretending to be amazed by the very notion. 'Not at all. I just know my own mind, if that's what you mean.'

Mrs. Baker grimaced. 'Stubborn is what I said, and stubborn is what I mean. Why, for heaven's sake, you might have slipped and fallen.'

'But I didn't.'

'You might have broken an arm or fractured a hip or something, and that would've set your recovery back *weeks*! I swear, if you were twenty years younger, I'd turn you over my knee and give you a good spanking.'

Susan burst out laughing.

After a moment in which she was startled by her own statement, Mrs. Baker laughed, too. She leaned against the foot of the bed, shaking with laughter.

Just when Susan thought she had control of herself, her eyes met the nurse's eyes, and they grinned at each other, and then the laughter started all over again.

At last, as her laughing subsided to giggling, Mrs. Baker wiped tears from her eyes and said, 'I can't believe I really said that!'

'Turn me over your knee, would you?'

'I guess you must bring out the mothering instincts in me.'

'Well, it sure doesn't sound like standard nursing procedure,' Susan said.

'I'm just glad you weren't insulted.'

'And *I'm* just glad I'm not twenty years younger,' Susan said, and they both started laughing again.

A couple of minutes later, when Susan wheeled herself into the hall to get some exercise, she felt in better spirits than she had been at any time since waking from her coma. The spontaneous, uncontrollable fit of laughter with Mrs. Baker had been wonderfully therapeutic. That shared moment, that unexpected but welcome intimacy, made Susan feel less alone and made the hospital seem considerably less cold and less gloomy than it had seemed only a short while ago.

Her arms still ached from the morning's tour in the wheelchair, but in spite of the soreness in her muscles, she was determined to make at least one more circuit of the second floor.

She wasn't worried about encountering Richmond and Johnson. She felt that she could handle such an encounter now. In fact she rather hoped she did meet them again. If she talked with them and took a closer look at them, their amazing resemblance to Harch and Quince might prove to be less remarkable than she had first thought. She didn't believe that would be the case, but she was willing to keep an open mind. And once she'd taken a second look at them, if they were *still* dead ringers for Harch and Quince, perhaps talking to them and getting to know them a bit would make them seem less threatening. In spite of what Philip Marlowe, that inimitable detective, had said, Susan very much wanted to believe that this was all just an incredible coincidence, for the alternatives to coincidence were bizarre and frightening.

By the time she had wheeled around the halls to room 216, she hadn't seen either of the look-alikes. She paused outside Peter Johnson's open door, finally worked up sufficient courage for the task at hand, and propelled herself inside. Going through the doorway, she put an unfelt smile on her face. She had a carefully rehearsed line ready: *I saw you in the hall this morning, and you look so much like an old friend of mine that I just had to stop by and find out if . . .*

But Peter Johnson wasn't there.

It was a semiprivate room, like her own, and the man in the other bed said, 'Pete? He's downstairs in radiology. They had some tests they wanted to put him through.'

'Oh,' she said. 'Well, maybe I'll stop by later.'

'Any message for him?'

'No. It wasn't anything important.'

In the hall again, she considered asking one of the nurses for Bill Richmond's room number. Then she remembered that he'd just had surgery today and probably wouldn't be feeling too well. This was the wrong time to pay him a visit.

When Susan got back to her own room, Mrs. Baker was pulling shut the privacy curtain that completely enclosed the second bed. 'Brought you a roommate,' she said, turning away from the closed curtain.

'Oh, good,' Susan said. 'A little company will make the time go a lot faster.'

'Unfortunately, she won't be much company,' Mrs. Baker said. 'She'll probably spend most of her time sleeping. She's sedated right now, in fact.'

'What's her name?'

'Jessica Seiffert.'

'Is she very ill?'

Mrs. Baker sighed and nodded. 'Terminal cancer, I'm afraid.'

'Oh, I'm sorry.'

'Well, I don't suppose she's got many regrets. Jessie's seventy-eight years old, after all, and she's led a pretty full life,' Mrs. Baker said.

'You know her?'

'She lives here in Willawauk. And now, what about you? Do you feel up to taking a couple of steps, exercising those legs a little?'

'Absolutely.'

The nurse pushed the wheelchair close to Susan's bed. 'When you get up, hold on to the railing with your right hand, and hold on to me with your left hand. I'll walk you around nice and slow to the other side.'

Susan was shaky and hesitant at first, but with each step, she gained self-assurance and moved faster. She wasn't ready to challenge anyone to a footrace – not even poor Jessica Seiffert – but she could feel the muscles flexing in her legs, and she had a pleasant, animal sense of being whole and functional. She was confident that she would spring back to health faster than McGee thought and would be discharged from the hospital well ahead of schedule.

When they reached the other side of the bed, Mrs. Baker said, 'Okay, now up and in with you.'

'Wait. Let me rest a second, and then let's go back around to the other side.'

'Don't tax yourself.'

'I can handle it. It's no strain.'

'You're sure?'

'I wouldn't lie to you, would I? You might spank me.'

The nurse grinned. 'Keep that in mind.'

As they stood there between the beds, letting Susan gather her strength for the return trip, both of them let their gazes travel to the curtain that was drawn tightly around the second bed, only two or three feet away.

'Does she have any family?' Susan asked.

'Not really. Nobody close.'

'That would be awful,' Susan whispered.

'What?'

'To die alone.'

'No need to whisper,' Mrs. Baker said. 'She can't hear you. Anyway, Jessie's dealing with it damned well. Except that it's been quite a blow to her vanity. She was a beautiful woman when she was younger. And even in her later years, she was handsome. But she's lost an awful lot of weight, and the cancer's eaten at her until she looks haggard. She was always a tad vain about her appearance, so the disfiguring part of the disease is a lot worse for her than the knowledge that she's dying. She has a great many friends in town, but she specifically asked them not to come visit her in the hospital this time. She wants them to remember her as the woman she was. Doesn't want anyone but doctors and nurses to see her. That's why I drew the curtain around her bed. She's sedated, but if she woke up even for a few seconds and saw the curtain wasn't drawn, she'd be terribly upset.'

'Poor soul,' Susan said.

'Yes,' Mrs. Baker said, 'but don't feel too badly about it. That time comes for all of us, sooner or later, and she's held it off longer than a lot of folks.'

They retraced their path around the bed, and then Susan got up into it and leaned back gratefully against the pillows.

'Hungry?' Mrs. Baker asked.

'Now that you mention it, yes. Famished.'

'Good. You've got to put some flesh on your bones. I'll bring you a snack.'

Raising her bed into a sitting position, Susan said, 'Do you think it would bother Mrs. Seiffert if I switched on the television?'

'Not at all. She won't even know it's on. And if she does wake up and hear it, maybe she'll want to watch, too. Maybe it'll draw her out of her shell.'

As Mrs. Baker left the room, Susan used the remote-control box to turn on the TV. She checked several channels until she found an old movie that was just beginning: *Adam's Rib* with Spencer Tracy and Katherine Hepburn. She had seen it before, but it was one of those sophisticated, witty films that you could see again and again without becoming bored. She put the remote-control box aside and settled back to enjoy herself.

However, she found it difficult to pay attention

to the opening scenes of the movie. Her eyes repeatedly drifted to the other bed. The drawn curtain made her uneasy.

It was no different from the privacy curtain that could be drawn around her own bed. It was hooked into a U-shaped metal track in the ceiling, and it fell to within a foot of the floor, blocking all but the wheels of the bed from view. Her own curtain had been pulled shut on a couple of occasions during the past two days – when it had been necessary for her to use a bedpan, and when she had changed pajamas.

Nevertheless, Jessica Seiffert's closed curtain disturbed Susan.

It's really nothing to do with the curtain itself, she thought. It's just being in the same room with someone who's dying. That's bound to make anyone feel a bit strange.

She stared at the curtain.

No. No, it wasn't the presence of death that bothered her. Something else. Something that she couldn't put her finger on.

The curtain hung straight, white, as perfectly still as if it were only a painting of a curtain.

The movie was interrupted for a commercial break, and Susan used the remote-control box to turn the sound all the way down.

Like a fly in amber, the room was suspended in silence.

The curtain was motionless; not even the slightest draft disturbed it.

Susan said, 'Mrs. Seiffert?'

Nothing.

Mrs. Baker came in with a large dish of vanilla ice cream covered with canned blueberries. 'How's *that* look?' she asked as she put it down on the bed table and swung the table in front of Susan.

'Enormous,' Susan said, pulling her eyes away from the curtain. 'I'll never finish all of it.'

'Oh, yes, you will. You're on the road back now; that's plain to see. You'll be surprised what an appetite you'll have for the next week or two.' She patted her gray hair and said, 'Well, my shift just ended. Got to get home and make myself especially pretty. I've got a big date tonight – if you can call bowling, a hamburger dinner, and drinks a "big date." But you should get a gander at the man I've been dating lately. He's a fine specimen. If I was thirty years younger, I'd say he was a real hunk. He's been a lumberman all his life. He's got shoulders to measure a doorway. And you should see his hands! He's got the biggest, hardest, most calloused hands you've ever seen, but he's as gentle as a lamb.'

Susan smiled. 'Sounds like you might have a memorable night ahead of you.'

'It's virtually guaranteed,' Mrs. Baker said, turning toward the door.

'Uh . . . before you go.'

The nurse turned to her. 'Yes, honey, what do you need?'

'Would you . . . uh . . . check on Mrs. Seiffert?'

Mrs. Baker looked puzzled.

'Well,' Susan said uneasily, 'it's just . . . she's been so silent . . . and even though she's sleeping, it seems as if she's *too* silent . . . and I wondered if maybe . . .'

Mrs. Baker went straight to the second bed, pulled back the end of the curtain, and slipped behind it.

Susan tried to see beyond the curtain before it fell back into place, but she wasn't able to get a glimpse of Jessica Seiffert or of anything else other than the nurse's back.

She looked up at Tracy and Hepburn gesticulating and arguing in silence on the TV screen. She ate a spoonful of ice cream, which tasted wonderful and hurt her teeth. She looked at the curtain again.

Mrs. Baker reappeared, and the curtain shimmered into place behind her, and again Susan didn't have a chance to see anything beyond.

'Relax,' Mrs. Baker said. 'She hasn't passed away. She's sleeping like a baby.'

'Oh.'

'Listen, kid, don't let it prey on your mind. Okay? She's not going to die in this room. She'll be here for a couple of days, maybe a week, until her condition's deteriorated enough for her to be transferred to the intensive care unit. That's where it'll happen, there among all the beeping and clicking life support machines that finally won't be able to support her worth a damn. Okay?'

Susan nodded. 'Okay.'

'Good girl. Now eat your ice cream, and I'll see you in the morning.'

After Thelma Baker left, Susan turned up the sound on the TV set and ate all of her ice cream and tried not to look at Mrs. Seiffert's shrouded bed.

The exercise and the large serving of ice cream eventually conspired to make her drowsy. She fell asleep watching *Adam's Rib*.

In the dream, she was on a TV game show, in an audience of people who were wearing funny costumes. She herself was dressed as a hospital patient, wearing pajamas and a bandage around her head. She realized she was on 'Let's Make a Deal.' The host of the show, Monty Hall, was standing beside her. 'All right, Susan!' he said with syrupy enthusiasm. 'Do you want to keep the thousand dollars you've already won, or do you want to trade it for whatever's behind curtain number one!' Susan looked at the stage and saw that there were not three curtains, as usual; there were, instead, three hospital beds concealed by privacy curtains. 'I'll keep the thousand dollars,' she said. And Monty Hall said, 'Oh, Susan, do you *really* think that's wise? Are you *really* sure you're making the right decision?' And she said, 'I'll keep the thousand dollars, Monty.' And Monty Hall looked around at the studio audience, flashing his white-white teeth in a big smile. 'What do you think, audience? Should she keep the thousand, considering how little a thousand dollars will buy in these times of high inflation, or should she trade it for what's behind curtain number one?' The audience roared in unison: *'Trade it! Trade it!'* Susan shook her head adamantly and said, 'I don't want what's behind the curtain. Please, I don't want it.' Monty Hall – who had ceased to look anything like Monty Hall and now looked distinctly satanic, with arched eyebrows and terrible dark eyes and a wicked mouth – snatched the thousand dollars out of her hand and said, 'You'll take the curtain, Susan, because it's really what you deserve. You have it coming to you, Susan. The curtain! Let's see what's behind curtain number one!' On the stage, the curtain encircling the first hospital bed was whisked aside, and two men dressed as patients were sitting on the edge of the bed: Harch and Quince. They were both holding scalpels, and the stage lights glinted on the razor-sharp cutting edges of the instruments. Harch and Quince rose off the bed and started across the stage, heading toward the audience, toward Susan, their scalpels held out in front of them. The audience roared with delight and applauded.

* * *

A few minutes after Susan woke from her nap, the bedside phone rang. She picked up the receiver. 'Hello?'

'Susan?'

'Yes.'

'My God, I was so relieved to hear you were out

108

of the coma. Burt and I have been worried half to death!'

'I'm sorry. Uh . . . I . . . I'm not really sure who this is.'

'It's *me*. Franny.'

'Franny?'

'Franny Pascarelli, your next-door neighbor.'

'Oh, Franny. Sure. I'm sorry.'

Franny hesitated, then said, 'You . . . uh . . . you do remember me, don't you?'

'Of course. I just didn't recognize your voice at first.'

'I heard there was some . . . amnesia.'

'I've gotten over most of that.'

'Thank God.'

'How are you, Franny?'

'Never mind about me. I waddle along from day to day, fighting the dreaded double chin and the insidious, ever-expanding waistline, but nothing ever really gets me down. You know me. But my God, what you've been through! How are *you*?'

'Getting better by the hour.'

'The people where you work . . . they said you might not come out of the coma. We were worried *sick*. Then this morning Mr. Gomez called and said you were going to be okay. I was so happy that I sat down and ate a whole Sara Lee coffee cake.'

Susan laughed.

'Listen,' Franny said, 'don't worry about your house or anything like that. We're taking care of things for you.'

'I'm sure you are. It's a relief having you for a neighbor, Franny.'

'Well, you'd do the same for us.'

They talked for a couple of minutes, not about anything important, just catching up on neighborhood gossip.

When Susan hung up, she felt as if she had at last established contact with the past that she had almost lost forever. She hadn't felt that way when she had spoken with Phil Gomez, for he had been merely a voice without a face, a cipher. But she remembered pudgy Franny Pascarelli, and remembering made all the difference. She and Franny were not really close friends; nevertheless, just talking to the woman made Susan feel that there truly was another world beyond Willawauk County Hospital and that she would eventually return to it. Curiously, talking to Franny also made Susan feel more isolated and alone than ever before.

* * *

Dr. McGee made his evening rounds shortly before dinnertime. He was wearing blue slacks, a red plaid shirt, a blue vee-neck sweater, and an open lab coat. Chest hairs, as black as those on his head, curled out of the open neck of his shirt. He was so slim and handsome that he looked as if he had stepped out of a men's fashion advertisement in a slick magazine.

He brought her a large, prettily wrapped box of chocolates and a few paperback books.

110

'You shouldn't have done this,' Susan said, reluctantly accepting the gifts.

'It's not much. I wanted to.'

'Well . . . thank you.'

'Besides, it's all therapeutic. The candy will help you put on the weight you need. And the books will keep your mind off your troubles. I wasn't sure what kind of thing you liked to read, but since you mentioned Philip Marlowe and Raymond Chandler yesterday, I thought you might like mysteries.'

'These are perfect,' she said.

He pulled up a chair beside her bed, and they talked for almost twenty minutes, partly about her exercise sessions, partly about her appetite, partly about the two remaining blank spots in her memory, but mostly about personal things like favorite books, favorite foods, favorite movies.

They *didn't* talk about Peter Johnson, the Quince look-alike she had seen this morning. She was afraid of sounding hysterical or even irrational. *Two* dead ringers? McGee would have to wonder if the problem wasn't in her own perceptions. She didn't want him to think she was at all . . . unbalanced.

Besides, in truth, she wasn't entirely sure that her perceptions *weren't* affected by her head injury. Her doubts about herself were small, niggling, but they were doubts nonetheless.

Finally, as McGee was getting up to leave, she said, 'I don't see how you have any time for a private life, considering how much time you spend with your patients.'

'Well, I don't spend as much time with other patients as I spend with you. You're special.'

'I guess you don't often get a chance to treat an amnesiac,' she said.

He smiled, and the smile was not conveyed solely by the curve of his finely formed lips; his eyes were a part of it, too – so clear, so blue, filled with what seemed to be affection. 'It's not your amnesia that makes you so special. And I'm sure you're very well aware of that.'

She wasn't quite sure of him. She didn't know if he was just being nice, just trying to lift her spirits, or whether he really found her attractive. But how could he find her appealing in her current condition? Every time she looked in the mirror, she thought of a drowned rat. Surely, his flirting was just a standard part of his professional bedside manner.

'How's your roommate been behaving?' he asked in a very soft, conspiratorial voice.

Susan glanced at the curtain. 'Quiet as a mouse,' she whispered.

'Good. That means she's not in pain. There isn't much I can do for her, but at least I can make her last days relatively painless.'

'Oh, is she your patient?'

'Yes. Delightful woman. It's a shame that dying has to be such a long, slow process for her. She deserved a much better, cleaner exit.'

112

He went to the other bed and stepped behind the curtain.

Yet again, Susan failed to get a glimpse of Mrs. Seiffert.

Behind the curtain, McGee said, 'Hello, Jessie. How are you feeling today?'

There was a murmured response, nearly inaudible, a dry and brittle rasp, too low for Susan to make out any of the woman's words, even too low to be positively identifiable as a human voice.

She listened to McGee's side of the conversation for a minute or two, and then there was a minute of silence. When he came out from behind the curtain, she craned her neck, trying to see the old woman. But the curtain was drawn aside just enough for McGee to pass, not an inch more, and he let it fall shut immediately in his wake.

'She's a tough lady,' he said with obvious admiration. Then he blinked at Susan and said, 'In fact she's more than a little bit like you.'

'Nonsense,' Susan said. 'I'm not tough. For heaven's sake, you should have seen me hobbling around this bed today, leaning on poor Mrs. Baker so hard that it's a miracle I didn't drag both of us down.'

'I mean tough inside,' McGee said.

'I'm a marshmallow.' She was embarrassed by his compliments because she still couldn't decide in what spirit they were offered. Was he courting her? Or merely being nice? She changed the subject: 'If you drew back the curtain, Mrs. Seiffert could watch some TV with me this evening.'

'She's asleep,' McGee said. 'Fell asleep while I was talking to her. She'll probably sleep sixteen hours a day or more from here on out.'

'Well, she might wake up later,' Susan persisted.

'Thing is – she doesn't *want* the curtain left open. She's somewhat vain about her appearance.'

'Mrs. Baker told me about that. But I'm sure I could make her feel at ease. She might be self-conscious at first, but I know I could make her feel comfortable.'

'I'm sure you could,' he said, 'but I – '

'It can be excruciatingly boring just lying in bed all day. Some TV might make the time pass more quickly for her.'

McGee took her hand. 'Susan, I know you mean well, but I think it's best we leave the curtain closed, as Jessie prefers. You forget she's *dying*. She might not *want* the time to pass more quickly. Or she may find quiet contemplation infinitely preferable to watching an episode of "Dallas" or "The Jeffersons." '

Although he hadn't spoken sharply, Susan was stung by what he had said. Because he was right, of course. No TV sitcom was going to cheer up a dying woman who was teetering between drug-heavy sleep and intolerable pain.

'I didn't mean to be insensitive,' she said.

'Of course you didn't. And you weren't. Just let Jessie sleep, and stop worrying about her.' He squeezed Susan's hand, patted it, and finally let it go. 'I'll see you in the morning for a few minutes.'

She sensed that he was trying to decide whether or not to bend down and kiss her on the cheek. He started to do it, then drew back, as if he were as unsure of her feelings as she was of his. Or maybe she was only imagining those intentions and reactions; she couldn't make up her mind which it had been.

'Sleep well.'

'I will,' she said.

He went to the door, stopped, turned to her again. 'By the way, I've scheduled some therapy for you in the morning.'

'What kind of therapy?'

'PT – physical therapy. Exercise, muscle training. For your legs, mostly. And a session in the whirl-pool. An orderly will be around to take you down-stairs to the PT unit sometime after breakfast.'

* * *

Mrs. Seiffert couldn't feed herself, so a nurse fed dinner to her. Even that task was performed with the curtains drawn.

Susan ate dinner and read a mystery novel, which she enjoyed because it kept her mind off the Harch and Quince look-alikes.

Later, after a snack of milk and cookies, she shuffled to the bathroom, supporting herself against the wall, then shuffled back. The return trip seemed twice as long as the original journey.

When the night nurse brought a sedative, Susan

knew she didn't need it, but she took it anyway, and in a short time she was sound asleep—

'Susan . . . Susan . . . Susan . . .'

—until a voice softly calling her name penetrated her sleep and caused her to sit suddenly upright in bed.

'Susan . . .'

Her heart was hammering because, even as groggy as she was, she detected something sinister in that voice.

The night lamp provided little light, but the room was not entirely dark. As far as she could see, no one was there.

She waited to hear her name again.

The night remained silent.

'Who's there?' she asked at last, squinting into the purple-black shadows in the corners of the room.

No one answered.

Shaking off the last clinging threads of sleep, she realized that the voice had come from her left, from the curtained bed. And it had been a man's voice.

The curtain still encircled the bed. In spite of the gloom, she could see it. The white material reflected and seemed even to amplify the meager glow of the night light. The curtain appeared to shimmer like a cloud of phosphorus.

'Is someone there?' she asked.

Silence.

'Mrs. Seiffert?'

The curtain didn't move.

Nothing moved.

According to the radiant face of the nightstand clock, it was 3:42 in the morning.

Susan hesitated, then snapped on the bedside lamp. The bright light stung her eyes, and she left it on only long enough to be sure there was no one lurking where the shadows had been. Jessica Seiffert's shrouded bed looked far less threatening in full light than it had in darkness.

She clicked off the lamp.

The shadows scurried back to their nests, and their nests were everywhere.

Maybe I was dreaming, she thought. Maybe it was only a voice calling to me in a dream.

But she was pretty sure that tonight had provided the first dreamless sleep she'd had since coming out of her coma.

She fumbled for the bed controls and raised herself halfway up into a sitting position. For a while she listened to the darkness, waited.

She didn't think she would be able to get back to sleep. The strange voice had reminded her of the Harch and Quince look-alikes, and that seemed like a perfect prescription for insomnia. But the sedative she had been given was evidently still doing its work, for in time she dozed.

6

All day yesterday a storm had been pending. The sky had looked beaten, bruised, and swollen.

Now, Tuesday morning, the storm broke with no warning other than a single clap of thunder so loud that it seemed to shake the entire hospital. Rain fell suddenly and heavily like a giant tent collapsing with a *whoosh* and a roar.

Susan couldn't see the storm because the curtain around the other bed blocked her view of the window. But she could hear the thunder and see the brilliant flashes of lightning. The fat raindrops pounded on the unseen windowpane with the force of drumbeats.

She ate a filling breakfast of hot cereal, toast, juice, and a sweet roll, shuffled to and from the bathroom with more assurance and with less pain than she'd had last evening, then settled down in bed with another mystery novel.

She had read only a few pages when two orderlies arrived with a wheeled stretcher. The first one through the door said, 'We're here to take you down to the physical therapy department, Miss Thorton.'

She put her book aside, looked up – and felt as if February had just breathed down the back of her neck.

They were dressed in hospital whites, and the blue stitched lettering on their shirt pockets said *Willawauk County Hospital*, but they weren't merely two orderlies. They weren't anything as simple as that, nothing as ordinary as that.

The first man, the one who had spoken, was about five feet seven, pudgy, with dirty blond hair, a round face, dimpled chin, pug nose, and the small quick eyes of a pig. The other was taller, perhaps six feet, with red hair, hazel eyes, and a fair complexion spattered with freckles under the eyes and across the bridge of the nose; he was not handsome, but certainly good looking, and his open face, his soft-edged features, were distinctly Irish.

The pudgy one was Carl Jellicoe.

The redhead was Herbert Parker.

They were the last of the four fraternity brothers from the House of Thunder, friends of Harch and Quince.

Impossible. Nightmare creatures. They were meant to inhabit only the land of sleep.

But she was awake. And they were here. Real.

'Some storm, isn't it?' Jellicoe asked conversationally as a cannonade of thunder shot through the sky.

Parker pushed the wheeled stretcher all the way

120

into the room and parked it parallel to Susan's bed.

Both men were smiling.

She realized that they were young, twenty or twenty-one. Like the others, they had been utterly untouched by the passing of thirteen years.

Two *more* look-alikes? Showing up here at the same time? Both of them employed as orderlies by the Willawauk County Hospital? No. Ridiculous. Preposterous. The odds against such an incredible coincidence were astronomical.

They had to be the real thing, Jellicoe and Parker themselves, not dead ringers.

But then, with stomach-wrenching suddenness, she remembered that Jellicoe and Parker were dead.

Dammit, they were *dead*.

Yet they were here, too, smiling at her.

Madness.

'No,' Susan said, shrinking back from them, moving to the opposite edge of the bed, tight up against the tubular metal railing, which burned coldly through her thin pajamas. 'No, I'm not going downstairs with you. Not me.'

Jellicoe feigned puzzlement. Pretending not to see that she was terrified, pretending not to understand what she really meant, he glanced at Parker and said, 'Have we fouled up? I thought we were supposed to bring down Thorton in two fifty-eight.'

Parker fished in his shirt pocket, pulled out a folded slip of paper, opened it, read it. 'Says right here. Thorton in two-five-eight.'

121

Susan wouldn't have thought she'd known Jellicoe and Parker well enough to recognize their voices after thirteen years. She had met both of them for the first time on the night that they and the two others had beaten and murdered Jerry Stein. At the trial, Jellicoe had not spoken a word on the witness stand, had never even taken the stand, for he had exercised his rights under the Fifth Amendment to avoid incriminating himself; Parker had testified but not at length. Indeed, she *didn't* recognize Carl Jellicoe's voice. But when Herbert Parker spoke, reading from the slip of paper he had taken from his shirt pocket, Susan jerked in surprise, for he spoke with a Boston accent, which was something she had nearly forgotten.

He looked like Parker. He spoke like Parker. He had to *be* Parker.

But Herbert Parker was dead, buried and rotting away in a grave somewhere!

They were both looking at her strangely.

She wanted to look at the nightstand, behind her, to see if there was anything she could conceivably use as a weapon, but she didn't dare take her eyes off them.

Jellicoe said, 'Didn't your doctor tell you we'd be taking you downstairs for therapy this morning?'

'Get out of here,' she said, her voiced strained, tremulous. 'Go away.'

The two men glanced at each other.

A series of preternaturally brilliant lightning bolts

122

pierced the cloud-dark day, shimmered on the unseen rain-washed windowpane, and cast stroboscopic patterns of light and shadow on the wall opposite the foot of Susan's bed. The eerie light briefly transformed Carl Jellicoe's face, distorted it, so that for an instant his eyes were sunken caverns with a bead of hot white light far down at the bottom of each.

To Susan, Parker said, 'Hey, listen, there's really nothing to worry about. It's only therapy, you know. It's not painful or anything like that.'

'Yeah,' Jellicoe said, now that the incredible barrage of lightning was over. He wrinkled his piggish face in an unnaturally broad smile. 'You'll really like it down in the PT department, Miss Thorton.' He stepped up to the bed and started to put down the railing on that side. 'You'll *love* the whirlpool.'

'I said, get out!' Susan screamed. 'Get out! Get the *hell* out of here!'

Jellicoe flinched, stepped back.

Susan shook violently. Each beat of her heart was like the concrete-busting impact of a trip-hammer.

If she got on the stretcher and let them take her downstairs, she would never be brought back again. That would be the end of her. She knew it. She *knew* it.

'I'll claw your eyes out if you try to take me from this room,' she said, struggling to keep the tremor out of her voice. 'I mean it.'

Jellicoe looked at Parker. 'Better get a nurse.'

Parker hurried out of the room.

The hospital's lights dimmed, went off, and for a moment there was only the funereal light of the storm-gray day, and then the power came on again.

Jellicoe turned his small, close-set eyes on Susan and favored her with an utterly empty smile that made her chilled blood even colder. 'Just take it easy, huh? Look, lady, just relax. Will you do that for me?'

'Stay away.'

'Nobody's going to come near you. So just stay calm,' he said in a soft, singsong voice, making a placating gesture with his hands. 'Nobody wants to hurt you. We're all your friends here.'

'Dammit, don't pretend that you think I'm crazy,' she said. She was both terrified and furious. 'You know damned well I'm not nuts. You know what's going on here. *I* don't know, but *you* sure as hell do.'

He stared at her, saying nothing. But there was mockery in his eyes and in the smug half-smile that turned up only one corner of his mouth.

'Get back,' Susan said. 'Get away from the bed. *Now!*'

Jellicoe retreated to the open door, but he didn't leave the room.

The sound of Susan's own heartbeat was so loud in her ears that it challenged the rain-wind-thunder-lightning chorus of the autumn storm.

Each breath caught in her dry, jagged throat and had to be torn loose with conscious effort.

124

Jellicoe watched her.

This can't be happening, she told herself frantically. I'm a rational woman. I'm a scientist. I don't believe in miraculous coincidences, and as sure as the sun will rise tomorrow, I don't believe in the supernatural. There aren't such things as ghosts. Dead men don't come back. *They don't!*

Jellicoe watched her.

Susan cursed her weak, emaciated body. Even if she had a chance to run, she wouldn't get more than a few steps. And if they forced her to fight for her life, she wouldn't last very long.

Finally, Herbert Parker returned with a nurse, a severe looking blonde who was a stranger to Susan.

'What's wrong here?' the nurse asked. 'Miss Thorton, why are you upset?'

'These men,' she said.

'What about them?' the nurse asked, coming to the bed.

'They want to hurt me,' Susan said.

'No, they only want to take you down to the physical therapy department on the first floor,' the nurse said. She was at the bed now, at the side where Carl Jellicoe had lowered the safety railing.

'You don't understand,' Susan said, wondering how in the name of God she could explain the situation to this woman without sounding like a raving lunatic.

Parker was standing at the open door. He said, 'She threatened to claw our eyes out.'

Jellicoe had drifted closer and was near the foot of the bed; too near.

'Back off, you bastard,' Susan said, virtually spitting the words at him.

He ignored her.

To the nurse, Susan said, 'Tell him to back off. You don't understand. I've got good reason to be afraid of him. Tell him!'

'Now, there's no reason on earth for you to be upset,' the nurse said.

'We're all your friends here,' Jellicoe said.

'Susan, do you know where you are?' the nurse asked in a tone of voice usually reserved for very young children, very old people, and the mentally disturbed.

Frustrated, angry, Susan shouted at her. 'Hell, yes, I know where I am. I'm in the Willawauk County Hospital. I suffered a head injury, and I was in a coma for three weeks, but I'm not suffering any kind of relapse. I'm not having hallucinations or delusions. I'm not hysterical. These men are – '

'Susan, would you do something for me?' the nurse asked, still using that excessively reasonable, syrupy, patronizing tone of voice. 'Would you not shout? Would you please lower your voice? If you would just lower your voice and take a minute to catch your breath, I'm sure you'll feel calmer. Just take a few deep breaths and try to relax. Nothing can be accomplished until we're all relaxed and at ease with one another, until we're all polite to one another.'

'Christ!' Susan said, burning with frustration.

'Susan, I want to give you this,' the nurse said. She raised one hand; she was holding a damp cotton pad and a hypodermic syringe that she had already filled with an amber fluid.

'No,' Susan said, shaking her head.

'It'll help you relax.'

'No.'

'Don't you want to relax?'

'I want to keep my guard up.'

'It won't hurt, Susan.'

'Get away from me.'

The nurse leaned across the bed toward her.

Susan snatched up the paperback book that she'd been reading and threw it in the woman's face.

The nurse took a step backwards, but she was unhurt. She looked at Jellicoe. 'Can you help me?'

'Sure,' he said.

'Stay away,' Susan warned him.

Jellicoe started around the side of the bed.

She twisted to her left, scooped a drinking glass off the nightstand, and pitched it at Jellicoe's head.

He ducked, and the glass missed, shattering explosively against the wall beyond him.

Susan looked for something else to throw.

He moved in fast, and she tried to claw his face, and he seized her wrists in his viselike hands. He was stronger than he looked. She couldn't have wrenched free of him even if she'd been in better condition.

'Don't struggle,' the nurse said.

'We're all your friends here,' Carl Jellicoe said for the third time.

Susan fought back but without effect. Jellicoe forced her back against the mattress. She slid down on the bed until she was stretched out flat, helpless.

Jellicoe pinned her arms at her sides.

The nurse pushed up the sleeve of her green pajamas.

Susan thrashed and drummed her feet on the bed and cried out for help.

'Hold her still,' the nurse said.

'Not easy,' Jellicoe said. 'She's got a lot of fire in her.'

What he said was true. She was surprised that she could resist at all. Panic had brought new energy with it.

The nurse said, 'Well, at least, the way she's straining, I can see the vein. It's popped up real nice.'

Susan screamed.

The nurse quickly swabbed her arm with the cotton pad. It was wet and cold.

Susan smelled alcohol and screamed again.

A freight train of thunder roared in and derailed with a hard, sharp crash. The hospital lights flickered out, on, out, on.

'Susan, if you don't hold perfectly still, I might accidentally break off the needle in your arm. Now, you don't want that to happen, do you?'

She refused to go peacefully. She writhed and

128

twisted and tried to snake her way out of Jellicoe's grip.

Then a familiar voice said, 'What in heaven's name is going on here? What're you doing to her?'

The blond nurse drew the needle back just as it was about to prick Susan's bare skin.

Jellicoe's grip relaxed as he turned to see who had spoken.

Susan strained to lift her head from the mattress.

Mrs. Baker was at the foot of the bed.

'Hysteria,' the blond nurse said.

'She was violent,' Jellicoe said.

'Violent?' Mrs. Baker said, clearly not believing it. She looked at Susan. 'Honey, what's the matter?'

Susan looked up at Carl Jellicoe, who was still holding her. His eyes cut into her. He subtly increased the pressure he was applying with his fingers, and for the first time she realized that his flesh was warm, not cold and clammy like the flesh of the dead. She looked back at Mrs. Baker, and in a calm voice she said, 'Do you remember what happened to me thirteen years ago? Yesterday, I told you and Dr. McGee all about it.'

'Yes,' Mrs. Baker said, lifting her chain-hung glasses off her bosom and putting them on her face. 'Of course I remember. A terrible thing.'

'Well, I was just having a nightmare about it when these two orderlies came into the room.'

'All this is just because of a nightmare?' Mrs. Baker asked.

'Yes,' Susan lied. She just wanted to get Jellicoe, Parker, and the blond nurse out of the room. When they were gone, perhaps then she could explain the true situation to Thelma Baker. If she tried to explain it now, Mrs. Baker might well agree with the blond nurse's diagnosis: hysteria.

'Let her go,' Mrs. Baker said. 'I'll handle this.'

'She was violent,' Jellicoe said.

'She was having a nightmare,' Mrs. Baker said. 'She's fully awake now. Let her go.'

'Thelma,' the blond nurse said, 'it didn't seem like she was asleep when she threw that book at me.'

'She's had a tough time, poor kid,' Mrs. Baker said, pushing in to the side of the bed, nudging the other nurse away. 'Go on, the rest of you, go on. Susan and I will talk this out.'

'In my judgment—' the blond nurse began.

'Millie,' Mrs. Baker said, 'you know I trust your judgment implicitly. But this is a special case. I can handle it. I really can.'

Reluctantly, Jellicoe let go of Susan.

Susan went limp with relief, then sat up in bed. She massaged one wrist, then the other. She could still feel where Jellicoe's fingers had dug into her.

The two orderlies drifted out of the room, taking the wheeled stretcher with them.

The blond nurse hesitated, biting her thin lower lip, but at last she left, too, still carrying the damp cotton pad and the syringe.

Mrs. Baker walked around the bed, being careful

not to step on any shards of the broken drinking glass. She looked in on Mrs. Seiffert, came back to Susan, and said. 'The old dear slept right through all the ruckus.' She got another tumbler out of the nightstand and filled it with water from the dew-beaded metal pitcher that stood on a plastic tray atop the stand.

'Thank you,' Susan said, accepting the water. She drank thirstily. Her throat was slightly sore from screaming, and the water soothed it.

'More?'

'No, that was enough,' she said, putting the glass on the nightstand.

'Now,' Mrs. Baker said, 'for Pete's sake, what was all that about?'

Susan's relief quickly gave way to tension, to dread, for she realized that the terror wasn't over yet. In fact it had probably just begun.

PART TWO

Opening the
Curtain . . .

7

The lightning and thunder had moved off toward the next county, but the gray rain continued to fall, an ocean of it, and the day was dreary, still.

Susan sat in bed, feeling small and washed out, as if the rain, though never touching her, were nonetheless somehow sluicing away her very substance.

Standing beside the bed, hands thrust into the pockets of his lab coat, Jeffrey McGee said, 'So now you're saying that look-alikes for *three* of those fraternity men have shown up here.'

'Four.'

'What?'

'I didn't tell you about the one I saw yesterday.'

'That would be . . . Quince?'

'Yes.'

'You saw him here? Or someone who looked like him?'

'In the hall, while I was in the wheelchair. He's a patient, just like Harch. Room two-sixteen. His name's supposed to be Peter Johnson.' She hesitated, then said, 'He looks nineteen.'

McGee studied her in silence for a moment.

Although he had not yet been judgmental, although he seemed to be trying hard to find a way to believe her story, she could not meet his eyes. The things she had told him were so outlandish that the scientist in her was embarrassed merely by the need to speak of them. She looked down at her hands, which were knotted together in her lap.

McGee said, 'Is that how old Randy Lee Quince was when he helped kill Jerry Stein? Was he just nineteen?'

'Yes. He was the youngest of the four.'

And I know what's going through your mind right now, she thought.

You're thinking about my head injury, about the coma, about the possibility of minor brain damage that didn't show up on any of your X rays or other tests, a tiny embolism, or perhaps an exceedingly small hemorrhage in a threadlike cerebral capillary. You're wondering if I've received a brain injury that just, by sheerest chance, happens to affect that infinitesimal lump of gray tissue in which the memories of the House of Thunder are stored; you're wondering if such an injury – a sand-grain blood clot or a minuscule, ruptured vessel – could cause those memories to become excessively vivid, resulting in my preoccupation with that one event in my life. Am I fixated on Jerry's murder for the simple reason that some abnormal pressure in my brain is focusing my attention relentlessly upon the House of Thunder? Is that pressure causing me to fantasize new developments in that old nightmare? Is that nearly microscopic rotten spot in my head altering my perceptions so that I believe I see dead ringers for Harch and the others, when, in reality, neither Bill Richmond nor Peter Johnson nor the two orderlies bear any resemblance whatsoever to the quartet of fraternity brothers? Well, maybe that *is* what's happening to me. But then again, maybe not. One minute, I think that is the explanation. The next minute, I know it must be something else altogether. They're *not* dead ringers. They *are* dead ringers. They're *not* the real Harch, Quince, Jellicoe, and Parker. They *are* the real Harch, Quince, Jellicoe, and Parker. I just don't know. God help me, I just don't know what's happening to me, so dear Dr. McGee, I can't blame you for your confusion and your doubts.

'So now there are four of them,' he said. 'Four dead ringers, all here in the hospital.'

'Well . . . I don't know exactly.'

'But didn't you just tell me—'

'I mean, yes, they look identical to the men who killed Jerry. But I don't know if they're nothing more than dead ringers or if they're . . .'

'Yes?'

'Well, maybe they're . . . something else.'

'Such as?'

'In the case of Parker and Jellicoe . . .'

'Go on,' he urged.

Susan simply couldn't bring herself to speculate

137

aloud on the existence of ghosts. When Carl Jellicoe had been holding her down against the mattress, his hands clamped tightly on her arms, supernatural explanations had not been beyond consideration. But now it seemed like sheer lunacy to talk seriously about dead men returning from their graves to extract bloody vengeance from the living.

'Susan?'

She met his eyes at last.

'Go on,' he urged again. 'If the two orderlies aren't just look-alikes for Jellicoe and Parker, if they're something else, as you say, then what did you have in mind?'

Wearily, she said, 'Oh, Jeez, I just don't know. I don't know what to say to you, how to explain it to you – or to myself, as far as that goes. I don't know what to think about it. I can only tell you what I saw with my own eyes – or what I thought I saw.'

'Listen, I didn't mean to pressure you,' he said quickly. 'I know this can't be easy for you.'

She saw pity in his lovely blue eyes, and she immediately looked away from him. She didn't want to be an object of pity to anyone, especially not to Jeffrey McGee. She loathed the very thought of it.

He was silent for a while, staring at the floor, apparently lost in thought.

She wiped her damp palms on the sheets and leaned back against the pillow. She closed her eyes.

Outside, the marching *tramp-tramp-tramp* of the rain transformed the entire Willawauk Valley into a parade ground.

He said, 'Suggestion.'

'I'm sure ready for one.'

'You might not like it.'

She opened her eyes. 'Try me.'

'Let me bring Bradley and O'Hara in here right now.'

'Jellicoe and Parker.'

'Their names are really Bradley and O'Hara.'

'So Mrs. Baker told me.'

'Let me bring them in here. I'll ask each of them to tell you a little something about himself: where he was born and raised, where he went to school, how he came to be working at this hospital. Then you can ask them any questions you want, anything at all. Maybe if you talk to them for a while, maybe if you get to know them a bit . . .'

'Maybe then I'll decide they don't look so much like Parker and Jellicoe after all,' she said, completing the thought for him.

He moved closer, putting a hand on her shoulder, leaving her no choice but to look up at him and see the pity again. 'Isn't it at least a *possibility* that, once you know them, you might see them differently?'

'Oh, yes,' she said. 'It's not only possible or probable; it's almost a certainty.'

Clearly, her awareness and her objectivity surprised him.

She said, 'I'm fully aware that my problem is most likely either psychological or the result of some organically rooted brain dysfunction related to the auto accident, or possibly not to the accident directly but to the effects of spending three weeks in a coma.'

McGee shook his head and smiled; it was his turn to look embarrassed. 'I keep forgetting you're a scientist.'

'You don't have to coddle me, Dr. McGee.'

Virtually glowing with relief, he put his hands behind him, palms flat on the mattress, and boosted himself up; he sat on the edge of the bed, beside her. That casual and unaffected act, such a spontaneous physical expression of the pleasure he took from her no-nonsense response, made him seem ten years younger than he was – and even more appealing than he had been. 'You know, I was going crazy trying to think of some nice, gentle way to tell you that this whole look-alike business was probably in your head, and here you knew it all the time. Which means we can probably rule out one of the two diagnoses that you just outlined; I mean, it's probably *not* a psychological boogeyman that's riding you. You're too stable for that. You're amazing!'

'So my best hope is brain dysfunction,' Susan said with heavy irony.

He sobered. 'Well, listen, it can't be anything really life-threatening. It's certainly not a major hemorrhage or anything like that. If it was, you

140

wouldn't be as fit and aware as you are. Besides, it wasn't serious enough to show up on the brain scan that we did while you were in the coma. It's something small, Susan, something treatable.'

She nodded.

'But you're still scared of Bradley and O'Hara and the other two,' he said.

'Yes.'

'Even though you know it's most likely all in your head.'

'The operative words are "most likely." '

'I'd go so far as to say it's *definitely* a perceptual problem resulting from brain dysfunction.'

'I imagine you're right.'

'But you're still scared of them.'

'Very.'

'Your recovery mustn't be set back by stress or depression,' he said, frowning.

'I can cope, I guess. My middle name is Pollyanna.'

He smiled again. 'Good. That's the spirit.'

Except that, in my heart, Susan thought, I don't for a minute believe that I've got either a psychological problem or any kind of brain dysfunction. Those answers just don't *feel* right. Intellectually, I can accept them, but on a gut level they seem wrong. What *feels* right is the answer that is no answer, the answer that makes no sense: These men *are* dead ringers for Harch, Quince, Jellicoe, and Parker, not just in my eyes but in reality; and they want something from me – probably my life.

141

Wiping one hand across her face as if she could slough off her weariness and cast it aside, Susan said, 'Well . . . let's get this over with. Bring in Jellicoe and Parker, and let's see what happens.'

'Bradley and O'Hara.'

'Yeah, them.'

'Listen, if you *think* of them as Jellicoe and Parker, then you're bound to *see* them as Jellicoe and Parker; you're playing right into your perceptual problem. Think of them as Denny Bradley and Pat O'Hara, and that might help you keep your perceptions clear; it might help you see them as they *are*.'

'Okay. I'll think of them as Bradley and O'Hara. But if they *still* look like Jellicoe and Parker, I might want to see an exorcist instead of a neurologist.'

He laughed.

She didn't.

* * *

McGee had briefly explained the situation to Bradley and O'Hara before he had brought them back to her room. They appeared to be concerned about Susan's condition, and they seemed eager to help in any way they could.

She tried not to let them see how much their presence still disturbed her. Although her stomach was clenched and although her heart was racing, she forced a smile for their benefit and tried to appear relaxed. She wanted to give McGee a fair

142

chance to prove that these two men, on closer inspection, would turn out to be nothing but a pair of ordinary, innocuous young fellows without an ounce of meanness between them.

McGee stood beside the bed, one hand on the rail, occasionally touching her shoulder, offering moral support.

The orderlies stood at the foot of the bed. Initially, they were stiff, like a couple of schoolboys reciting a lesson in front of a stern teacher. But gradually they loosened up.

Dennis Bradley spoke first. He was the one who had held her down on the bed while the nurse had prepared to give her an injection.

'First of all,' Bradley said, 'I want to apologize if I was maybe a little too rough with you. I didn't mean to be. It's just that I was kind of scared, you know.' He shifted his weight awkwardly from one foot to the other. 'I mean, considering what you said . . . you know . . . about what you'd do . . . well, what you'd do to our *eyes* . . .'

'It's all right,' Susan said, though she could still feel his fierce grip, his fingers pressing cruelly into her thin arms. 'I was scared, too. Actually, I guess I owe *you* an apology. Both of you.'

At McGee's urging, Bradley talked about himself. He had been born in Tucson, Arizona, twenty years ago last July. His parents had moved to Portland, Oregon, when he was nine. He had no brothers, one older sister. He had attended a two-year junior college and had taken special courses to prepare for a career as a paramedic. One year ago, he had accepted this job in Willawauk as a combination orderly and ambulance superintendent. He answered all of Susan's questions. He was unfailingly candid, outgoing, and helpful.

So was Patrick O'Hara, the redhead. He had been born and raised, he said, in Boston. His family was Irish Catholic. No, he'd never known anyone named Herbert Parker. In fact he'd never known anybody in Boston named Parker, Herbert or otherwise. Yes, he had an older brother, but, no, his brother didn't really look much like him. No, he'd never been to Briarstead College in Pennsylvania; never even heard of it before this minute. He had come West when he was eighteen, three years ago. He'd been in Willawauk for, let's see, sixteen, no, more like seventeen months.

Susan had to admit that both Dennis Bradley and Pat O'Hara were friendly. Now that she had gotten to know a little about them, she could cite no logical reason why she should any longer regard them as a threat to herself.

Neither of them appeared to be lying.

Neither of them seemed to be hiding anything.

Yet to her eyes, confused perception or not, Bradley still looked exactly like Carl Jellicoe.

Exactly.

O'Hara was still a dead ringer for Herbert Parker.

And Susan had the feeling, unsupported by anything that the two young men had just said or done, that they were not what they presented themselves to be, that they *were* lying and *were* hiding something. Intuitively, in spite of all the solid evidence to the contrary, she sensed that this show-and-tell had been nothing more than a well-wrought performance, an act which they had brought off with consummate skill.

Of course maybe I'm just a raving paranoid, completely starkers, she thought grimly.

When the two orderlies had left the room, McGee said, 'Well?'

'It didn't work. I thought of them as Bradley and O'Hara, but they still looked like Jellicoe and Parker.'

'You realize that doesn't prove or disprove the theory that you've got brain-injury-related perceptual problems.'

'I know.'

'We'll begin another series of tests first thing tomorrow, starting with new X rays.'

She nodded.

He sighed. 'Damn, I was hoping that a talk with Bradley and O'Hara would set your mind at ease, make you feel more comfortable and less anxious until we can pinpoint the cause of your condition and correct this perceptual confusion.'

'I'm about as comfortable as a cat on a hot stove.'

'I don't want you to be overwhelmed with stress or anxiety. That's going to slow your recuperation. I guess it wouldn't help to reason with you?'

'No. As I said, intellectually, I accept your explanation. But emotionally, instinctually, on a gut level, I still feel that the four fraternity men are coming back . . . ganging up on me.'

She was cold. She put her hands and arms under the covers.

'Look,' McGee said, deciding to attempt to reason with her even though she'd said it was no use. 'Look, maybe you have good cause to be suspicious of Richmond and Johnson. It's not probable, but it is possible, *remotely* possible, that they're Harch and Quince living under new names.'

'Hey, you're supposed to be making me feel more comfortable, less anxious. Remember?'

'My point is that you have absolutely *no* cause to be suspicious of Bradley and O'Hara. They can't be Jellicoe and Parker because those men are dead.'

'I know. Dead.'

'So you should feel better about Bradley and O'Hara.'

'But I don't.'

'Furthermore, Bradley and O'Hara can't have been brought here as part of some complicated, nefarious plot to get even with you for your testimony in that trial. They were here long before you ever arrived, before you even planned to take your vacation in Oregon, before you'd ever even heard of the Viewtop Inn. Are you saying someone knew, in some fantastic, magical, clairvoyant fashion – that you would have an accident here one day and

146

wind up in Willawauk Hospital? Are you saying someone foresaw this and that he then set out to plant O'Hara here seventeen months ago – and then Dennis Bradley, a year ago?'

Her face was hot, for he was making her feel ridiculous. 'Of course I don't believe that.'

'Good.'

'It's silly.'

'Yes, it is. So you should feel perfectly safe with Bradley and O'Hara.'

She could only speak the truth: 'But I *don't* feel safe with them.'

'But you *should*.'

The building pressure in her passed the critical point. She exploded: 'Dammit, do you think I *like* being a prisoner of my emotions, the helpless victim of fear? I *hate* it. It's not like me. I'm not this way. I feel . . . out of control. Never in my life, *never* have I made decisions or in any other way operated primarily on emotion. I'm a *scientist*, for Christ's sake. I've been a woman of science, a woman of reason, all of my adult life. And I've been proud of that. In a world that sometimes seems like a madhouse, I've been proud of my rationality, my unfailing stability. Don't you see? Don't you see what this is doing to me? I had a scientific, mathematical mind even as a child. I wasn't given to tantrums even back then, not even as a little girl. Sometimes, it seems as if I never really had a childhood.'

Suddenly, to her surprise, a torrent of regrets,

frustrations, and private pains, long held, long hidden, came pouring out of her, a deluge greater than that which had been released by the storm outside.

In a voice she hardly recognized as her own, a voice distorted by anguish, she said, 'There've been times – usually late at night when I'm alone, which is most nights, most *days*, most always, God help me – times when I've thought there's something missing in me, some tiny piece that's an essential part of being human. I've felt different from other people, almost as if I'm a member of another species. I mean, God, the rest of the world seems driven at least as much by emotion as by intellect, as much by sentiment as by truth. I see others giving in to their emotions, abandoning reason, doing absurd things just for the hell of it. *Just for the hell of it!* I've never done anything in my life just for the hell of it. And the thing is, when I see friends or acquaintances just giving themselves over to their emotions, just *flowing* with their emotions . . . the thing of it is, they seem to *enjoy* it. And I can't. Never could. Too uptight. Too controlled. Always controlled. The iron maiden. I mean, I never cried over my mother's death. Okay, so maybe at seven I was too young to understand that I should cry. But I didn't cry at my father's funeral, either. I dealt with the mortician and ordered flowers and arranged for the grave to be dug and handled all the details with commendable efficiency, but I didn't *cry* for him. I loved him, in

spite of his standoffish manner, and I missed him –
God, how I missed him – but I didn't cry. *Shit*. I
didn't *cry* for him. And so I told myself that it was
good that I was different from other people. I told
myself I was a better person than they were,
superior to most of the rabble. I took tremendous
pride in my unshakable self-control, and I built a
life on that pride.' She was shaking. Violently. She
hugged herself. She looked at McGee. He seemed
shocked. And she couldn't stop talking. 'I built a
life on that pride, dammit. Maybe not a very exciting life by most standards. But a life. I was at peace
with myself. And now *this* has to happen to me. I
know it isn't rational to fear Richmond, Johnson,
Bradley, O'Hara . . . But I *do* fear them. I can't
help myself. I have this intellectually stupid but
emotionally powerful conviction that something
extraordinary, something indescribably bizarre,
maybe even something occult is happening here.
I've lost control. I've given in to my emotions. I've
become what I thought I wasn't. I've thrown over
what I was, tipped it over and rolled it down a long
hill. I'm no longer the Susan Thorton I was . . .
and . . . it's . . . tearing . . . me . . . apart.'

She shuddered, choked, doubled over on the
bed, sitting with her head to her knees, and gasped
for breath, and wept, wept.

McGee was speechless at first. Then he got her
some Kleenex. Then some more Kleenex.

He said, 'Susan, I'm sorry.'

He said, 'Are you all right?'

149

He got her a glass of water.

Which she didn't want.

He put it back on the nightstand.

He seemed confused.

He said, 'What can I do?'

He said, 'Jesus.'

He touched her.

He held her.

That was what he could do.

She put her head against his shoulder and sobbed convulsively. Gradually, she became aware that her tears did not make her feel even more miserable, as she had expected they would when she had been trying so hard to repress them. Instead, they made her feel cleaner and better, as if they were flushing out the pain and misery that had caused them.

He said, 'It's all right, Susan.'

He said, 'You're going to be fine.'

He said, 'You're not alone.'

He comforted her, and that was something that no one had ever done for her before – perhaps because she had never allowed it.

* * *

A few minutes later.

'More Kleenex?' he asked.

'No, thank you.'

'How do you feel?'

'Wrung out.'

'I'm sorry.'

'It wasn't anything you did.'

150

'I kept browbeating you about Bradley and O'Hara.'

'No, you didn't. You were only trying to help.'

'Some help.'

'You *did* help. You forced me to face up to something that I didn't want to face up to, something I desperately needed to face up to. I'm not as tough as I thought I was. I'm a different person than I thought I was. And maybe that's a good thing.'

'All those things you said about yourself, all that stuff about how you thought you were different from other people – did you really believe that?'

'Yes.'

'All those years?'

'Yes.'

'But everyone has a breaking point.'

'I know that now.'

'And there's nothing wrong with being unable to cope now and then,' he said.

'I've sure been unable recently. In spades.'

He put one hand under her chin, lifted her head, and looked at her. His marvelous eyes were the bluest that she had yet seen them.

He said, 'Whatever's wrong with you, no matter how subtle it might be, no matter how difficult it is to uncover the root of the problem, I'll find it. And I'll make you well again. Do you believe me, Susan?'

'Yes,' she said, realizing that for the first time in her life she was, at least to some extent, willingly placing her fate in the hands of another person.

'We will discover what's causing this perceptual confusion, this quirky fixation on the House of Thunder, and we'll correct it. You won't have to go through the rest of your life seeing Ernest Harch and those other three men in the faces of total strangers.'

'If that's what's happening.'

'That *is* what's happening,' he said.

'Okay. Until you've found the cause of my condition, until you've made me well, I'll try to cope with this craziness, with dead men who suddenly come back to life as hospital orderlies. I'll do my best to handle it.'

'You can. I know it.'

'But that doesn't mean I won't be scared.'

'You're allowed to be scared now,' he said. 'You're no longer the iron maiden.'

She smiled and blew her nose.

He sat there on the edge of the bed for a minute, thinking, and then he finally said, 'The next time you think you see Harch or Jellicoe or Quince or Parker, there's something you can do to keep from panicking.'

'I'd like to hear it.'

'Well, when I was completing my residency at a hospital in Seattle – more years ago than I like to remember – we had a lot of cases of drug overdose. People were always coming into the emergency ward – or being brought in by police – suffering from bad drug trips, uncontrollable hallucinations

152

that had them either climbing walls or shooting at phantoms with a real shotgun. No matter whether it was LSD, PCP, or some other substance, we didn't treat the patient with just counteractive drugs. We also talked him down. Encouraged him to loosen up. We held his hand and soothed him. Told him the big bad boogeymen he was seeing weren't real. And you know something? Usually, the talk did the trick, had a tremendous calming effect. I mean, frequently the talking down seemed more effective than the counteractive drugs that we administered.'

'And that's what you want me to do when I see Harch or one of the others. You want me to talk myself down.'

'Yes.'

'Just tell myself they aren't real?'

'Yes. Tell yourself they're not real and they can't hurt you.'

'Like saying a prayer to ward off vampires.'

'In fact if you feel that praying would ward them off, don't hesitate. Don't be embarrassed to pray.'

'I've never been a particularly religious person.'

'Doesn't matter. If you want to pray, do it. Do whatever works for you. Do whatever you need to do to keep yourself calm until I've had a chance to come up with a permanent, medical solution for your condition.'

'All right. Whatever you say.'

'Ah, I'm pleased to see that you've finally got the proper subservient attitude toward your doctor.'

She smiled.

He glanced at his wristwatch.

Susan said, 'I've made you late to the office.'

'Only a few minutes.'

'I'm sorry.'

'Don't worry about it. The only patients who had appointments this morning were all just hypochondriacs anyway.'

She laughed, surprised that she still *could* laugh.

He kissed her cheek. It was just a peck, a quick buss, and it was over before she realized it was happening. Yesterday, she had thought that he was going to kiss her on the cheek, but he had backed off at the last second. Now he had done it – and she still didn't know what it meant. Was it merely an expression of sympathy, pity? Was it just affection? Just friendship? Or was it something more than that?

As soon as he had kissed her, he stood up, straightened his rumpled lab coat. 'Spend the rest of the morning relaxing as best you can. Read, watch TV, anything to keep your mind off the House of Thunder.'

'I'll call in the four look-alikes and get a poker game going,' she said.

McGee blinked, then shook his head and grinned. 'You sure spring back fast.'

'Just obeying doctor's orders. He wants me to keep a positive attitude, no matter what.'

'Mrs. Baker's right.'

'About what?'

'About you. She says you've got plenty of moxie.'

'She's too easily impressed.'

'Mrs. Baker? She wouldn't be impressed if the Pope and the President walked through that door arm-in-arm.'

Self-conscious, feeling that she didn't really deserve this praise after having broken down and wept, Susan straightened the blanket and the sheets around her and avoided responding to his compliment.

'Eat everything they give you for lunch,' McGee said. 'Then this afternoon, I want you to take the physical therapy you were scheduled for this morning.'

Susan stiffened.

McGee must have seen the sudden change in her, for he said. 'It's important, Susan. You need to have physical therapy. It'll get you back on your feet considerably faster. And if we discover some physical cause for your perceptual problems, something that necessitates major surgery, you'll withstand the stress and strain of the operation a great deal better if you're in good physical condition.'

Resigned, she said, 'All right.'

'Excellent.'

'But please . . .'

'What is it?'

'Don't send Jelli—' She cleared her throat. 'Don't send Bradley and O'Hara to take me downstairs.'

'No problem. We've got plenty of other orderlies.'

'Thank you.'

'And remember – chin up.'

Susan put one fist under her chin, as if propping up her head, and she assumed a theatrical expression of heroic, iron-hard determination.

'That's the spirit,' he said. 'Think of yourself as Sylvester Stallone in *Rocky*.'

'You think I look like Sylvester Stallone?'

'Well . . . more than you look like Marlon Brando.'

'Gee, you sure know how to flatter a girl, Dr. McGee.'

'Yeah. I'm a regular lady-killer.' He winked at her, and it was the right kind of wink, very different from that which Bill Richmond had given her in the hall yesterday. 'I'll see you later, when I make my evening rounds.'

And then he was gone.

She was alone. Except for Jessica Seiffert. Which was the same as being alone.

She still hadn't seen the woman.

Susan looked at the curtained bed. There was not even the slightest movement or noise from behind it.

At the moment, she did not want to be alone, so she said, 'Mrs. Seiffert?'

There was no response.

She considered getting out of bed, going over there, and seeing if Mrs. Seiffert was all right. For reasons she could not explain, however, she was afraid to open that curtain.

8

Susan tried to follow doctor's orders. She picked up a book and read for a few minutes, but she couldn't get interested in the story. She switched on the TV, but she couldn't find a program that held her attention. The only thing that engaged her interest was the mystery of the four look-alikes, the puzzle of their purpose. What did they intend to do to her? In spite of McGee's advice, she spent a large part of the morning thinking about Harch and the other three, worrying.

Clear evidence of an unnatural fixation, obsession, psychological illness or brain dysfunction, she thought. I say I don't believe in elaborate fantasies. I say I don't believe in the occult. And yet I believe these four are real, including the two who are dead. It makes no sense.

But she worried anyway, and she looked forward with unalloyed dread to the prospect of being taken from her room for therapy. Not that she felt safe in her room. She didn't. But at least her room was known territory. She didn't want to go downstairs.

She recalled the way Jellicoe . . . the way *Dennis Bradley* had said it: '*We're here to take you downstairs.*' It had an ominous sound.

Downstairs.

Feeling guilty about ignoring much of McGee's advice, Susan made a point of eating everything she was served for lunch, which was what he had told her to do.

The condemned woman ate a hearty last meal, she thought with gallows humor. Then, angry with herself, she thought: Dammit, stop this! Get your act together, Thorton.

Just as she finished eating, the phone rang. It was a call from a couple of her fellow workers at Milestone. She didn't remember them, but she tried to be pleasant, tried to think of them as friends. It was nevertheless an awkward and disturbing conversation, and she was relieved when they finally hung up.

An hour after lunch, two orderlies came with a wheeled stretcher. Neither of them even faintly resembled any of the four fraternity men.

The first was a burly, fiftyish man with a beer gut. He had thick graying hair and a gray mustache. 'Hi ya, gorgeous. You ordered a taxi?'

The second man was about thirty-five. He was bald and had a smooth, open, almost childlike face. He said, 'We're here to take you away from all this.'

'I was expecting a limousine,' she said.

'Hey, sweetheart, what d'ya think *this* is?' the

160

older one asked. He swept his open hand across the wheeled stretcher as if he were presenting an elegant motor coach. 'Look at those classic lines!' He slapped the stretcher's three-inch foam mattress. 'Look at that upholstery. Nothing but the best, the finest.'

The bald one said, 'Is there any other mode of transportation, other than a limousine, in which you could ride lying down?'

'With a chauffeur,' said the older one, putting down the rail on her bed.

'With *two* chauffeurs,' the bald one said, pushing the stretcher against the side of her bed. 'I'm Phil. The other gent is Elmer Murphy.'

'They call me Murf.'

'They call him worse than that.'

Although she was still afraid of being taken downstairs, into unknown territory, Susan was amused by their patter. Their friendliness, their efforts to make her feel at ease, and her determination not to disappoint McGee gave her sufficient courage to slide off the bed and onto the stretcher. Looking up at them, she said, 'Are you two always like this?'

'Like what?' Murf asked.

'She means charming,' Phil said, slipping a small, somewhat hard pillow under her head.

'Oh, yeah,' Murf said. 'We're always charming.'

'Cary Grant has nothing on us.'

'It's just something we were born with.'

161

Phil said, 'If you look under "charm" in the dictionary—'

'—you'll see our faces,' Murf finished for him.

They put a thin blanket over her, put one strap across her to keep the blanket in place, and wheeled her into the hall.

Downstairs.

To keep from thinking about where she was going, Susan said, 'Why this contraption? Why not a wheelchair?'

'We can't deal with patients in wheelchairs,' Phil said.

'They're too mobile,' Murf said.

'Americans love mobility.'

'They hate to sit still.'

Phil said, 'If we leave a patient alone in a wheelchair for just ten seconds—'

'—he's halfway to Mesopotamia by the time we get back,' Murf finished.

They were at the elevators. Murf pushed the white button labeled *Down*.

'Lovely place,' Phil said as the doors opened wide.

'What?' Murf said. 'This elevator? Lovely?'

'No,' Phil said. 'Mesopotamia.'

'You been there, huh?'

'That's where I spend my winters.'

'Ya know, I don't think there *is* a Mesopotamia any more.'

'Better not let the Mesopotamians hear you say that,' Phil warned him.

They kept up their chatter in the elevator and all the way along the first-floor hall into the Physical Therapy Department, which was in one of the building's short wings. There, they turned her over to Mrs. Florence Atkinson, the specially trained therapist who was in charge of the hospital's PT program.

Florence Atkinson was a small, dark, birdlike woman, brimming with energy and enthusiasm. She guided Susan through half an hour of exercises, using a variety of machines and modified gym equipment that gave a workout to every muscle group. There was nothing in the least strenuous about it; a healthy person would have found it all laughably easy. 'For your first couple of visits,' Mrs. Atkinson said, 'we'll concentrate primarily on passive exercise.' But at the end of the half hour, Susan was exhausted and achy. Following the exercise period, she was given a massage that made her feel as if she were a loose collection of disjointed bones and ligaments that God had neglected to assemble into human form. After the massage, there was a session in the whirlpool. The hot, swirling water leeched the remaining tension out of her, so that she felt not just loose but *liquid*. Best of all, she was allowed to take a shower in a stall that was equipped with a seat and handrails for invalids. The glorious feeling and scent of soap, hot water, and steam was so wonderful, so *exquisite*, that merely taking a bath seemed deliciously sinful.

Florence Atkinson dried Susan's shaggy blond

hair with an electric blower while she sat in front of a dressing table mirror. It was the first time she had looked in a mirror in more than a day, and she was delighted to see that the bags under her eyes were entirely gone. The skin around her eyes was still a bit on the bluish side, but not much, and she actually had a touch of rosy color in her cheeks. The thin scar on her forehead was less red and swollen than it had been yesterday morning, when the bandages had come off, and she had no difficulty believing that it really would be all but invisible when it was entirely healed.

In her green pajamas again, she got onto the wheeled stretcher, and Mrs. Atkinson pushed her into the PT Department's waiting room. 'Phil and Murf will be around for you in a few minutes.'

'They can take their time. I feel like I'm floating on a warm, blue ocean. I could lay here forever,' she said, wondering how on earth she could ever have been so afraid of being brought downstairs to PT.

She stared at the acoustic-tile ceiling for a minute or two, finding outlines of objects in the pattern of dots: a giraffe, a sailboat, a palm tree. Drowsy, she closed her eyes and yawned.

'She looks too satisfied, Phil.'

'Yes, she does, Murf.'

She opened her eyes and smiled up at them.

'Got to be careful about pampering the patients too much,' Phil said.

'Massages, whirlpools, chauffeurs . . .'

164

'Pretty soon, she'll be wanting breakfast in bed.'

'What is this, Phil, a hospital or a country club?'

'Sometimes I wonder, Murf.'

'Well, if it isn't the Laurel and Hardy of Willa-wauk Hospital,' Susan said.

They wheeled her out of the PT waiting room.

Murf said, 'Laurel and Hardy? No, we think of ourselves more as the Bob and Ray of Willawauk.'

They turned the corner into the long main hall. The hard pillow raised Susan's head just enough so that she could see that the corridor was deserted. It was the first time she'd seen an empty hallway in the bustling hospital.

'Bob and Ray?' Phil said to Murf. 'Speak for yourself. Me, I think I'm the Robert Redford of Willawauk.'

'Robert Redford doesn't need a toupee.'

'Neither do I.'

'Right. You need an entire bearskin rug to cover that dome.'

They had reached the elevators.

'You're being cruel, Murf.'

'Just helping you face reality, Phil.'

Murf pushed the white button labeled *Up*.

Phil said, 'Well, Miss Thorton, I hope you've enjoyed your little trip.'

'Immensely,' she said.

'Good,' Murf said. 'And we guarantee you that the next part of it will be interesting.'

'Very interesting,' Phil agreed.

The elevator doors opened behind her.

They pushed her inside but didn't follow.

There were other people already in there. Four of them. Harch, Quince, Jellicoe, Parker. Harch and Quince were wearing pajamas and robes; they were standing at her left side. Jellicoe and Parker, in hospital whites, were at her right.

Shocked, disbelieving, she raised her head, looked out at Murf and Phil who were standing in the elevator alcove on the first floor, staring in at her, smiling. They waved goodbye.

The doors closed. The lift started up.

Ernest Harch punched a button on the control panel, and they stopped between floors. He looked down at her. His frosty gray eyes were like circles of dirty ice, and they transmitted a chill to the heart of her.

Harch said, 'Hello, bitch. Imagine meeting you here.'

Jellicoe giggled. It was a burbling, chortling, piggish sound that matched his piggish face.

'No,' she said numbly.

'Not going to scream?' Parker asked, grinning like a naughty, freckle-faced altar boy.

'We *had* hoped for a scream,' Quince said, his long face looking even longer from her perspective.

'Too surprised to scream,' Jellicoe said, and he giggled again.

She closed her eyes and did what Jeffrey McGee had suggested. She told herself that they were not real. She told herself that they couldn't hurt her. She told herself that they were just phantoms, the stuff of daydreams or, rather, daymares. *Not real*.

Someone put a hand on her throat.

Heart pounding, she opened her eyes.

It was Harch. He squeezed lightly, and the feel of her flesh in his grip apparently pleased him, for he laughed softly.

Susan put both of her hands on his, tried to pull it away. Couldn't. He was strong.

'Don't worry, bitch,' he said. 'I won't kill you.'

He sounded *exactly* like Harch had sounded at the trial and in the House of Thunder. That was one voice she would never forget. It was deep, with a gravelly edge to it, a cold and merciless voice.

'No, we won't kill you yet,' Quince said. 'Not yet.'

'When the time is right,' Harch said.

She dropped her hands. She felt increasingly numb in her extremities. Her feet and hands were cold. She was shaking like an old car whose engine was badly out of tune; her rattling, banging heart was shaking her to pieces.

Harch stroked her throat softly, tenderly, as if he were admiring the graceful curve of it.

She shuddered with revulsion and turned her head away from him, looked at Jellicoe.

His pig eyes glinted. 'How did you like our little song and dance in your room this morning?'

'Your name's Bradley,' she said, willing it to be so, willing reality to return.

'No,' he said. 'Jellicoe.'

'And I'm Parker, not O'Hara,' the redhead said.

167

'You're both dead,' she said shakily.

'All four of us are dead,' Quince said.

She looked at the hawk-faced man, bewildered by his statement.

He said, 'After I was kicked out of Briarstead, I went home to Virginia. My family wasn't very supportive. In fact they didn't want much contact with me at all. Very proper, very old-line Virginia hunt-country family, you understand. No breath of scandal must ever sully the family name.' His face grew dark with anger. 'I was given a modest income to tide me over until I could find work, and I was sent away. *Sent away!* My father – the self-righteous, sanctimonious, fucking *bastard* – cut me off as if I was a dead limb on a tree. What work was I to find that wasn't beneath me? I mean, I was from a privileged family. I wasn't bred to be a common laborer.' He was virtually speaking through clenched teeth now. 'I didn't get a chance to go to law school, as I'd wanted. Because of you, your testimony at the trial. Jesus, I hate your guts. It was because of you that I ended up in that dismal motel in Newport News. It was because of you that I slashed my wrists in that grubby little bathroom.'

She closed her eyes. She thought: They aren't real. They can't hurt me.

'I was killed in prison,' Harch said.

She kept her eyes tightly closed.

'Thirty-two days before I was scheduled to be paroled,' he said. 'Christ, I'd served almost *five* years, and with one month to go, I had the bad luck

168

to cross a nigger who'd had a knife smuggled into his cell.'

They're not real. They can't hurt me.

'And now I've finally come after you,' Harch said. 'I swore I would. In prison, a thousand times, ten thousand times, I swore I'd come after you some day. And you know what this Friday is, bitch? It's the anniversary of my death, that's what it is. This Friday makes seven years since that nigger shoved me up against the wall and cut my throat. Friday. That's when we're going to do it to you. Friday night. You've got about three days left, bitch. Just wanted to let you know. Just wanted you to sweat for a while first. Friday. We've got something really special planned for you on Friday.'

'We're all dead because of you,' Jellicoe said.

They're not real.

Their voices slashed at her.

'—if we could have found where she was hiding— '

'—would've kicked her head in, too— '

'—cut her pretty throat— '

'—hell, cut her heart out— '

'—bitch doesn't have a heart— '

They can't hurt me.

'—nothing but a stinking Jew-lover anyway— '

'—not bad looking— '

'—ought to screw her before we kill her— '

'—little on the scrawny side— '

'—she'll fatten up a bit by Friday— '

'—ever been screwed by a dead man?— '

169

She refused to open her eyes.

They're not real.

'—we'll all get on you— '

'—get *in* you— '

They can't hurt me.

'—all of that dead meat— '

'—shoved up in you— '

They can't hurt me, can't hurt me, can't hurt . . .

'—Friday— '

'—Friday— '

A hand touched her breasts, and another hand clamped over her eyes.

She screamed.

Someone put a hard, rough hand over her mouth.

Harch said, 'Bitch.' And it must have been Harch who pinched her right arm; hard; harder still.

And then she passed out.

9

The dark dissolved. It was replaced by milky fluorescent light, waltzing shadows that spun lazily in time to some unheard music, and blurred shapes that bobbled above her and spoke to her in fuzzy but familiar voices.

'Look who we've got here, Murf.'

'Who's that, Phil?'

'Sleeping Beauty.'

Her vision cleared. She was lying on the stretcher. She blinked at the two orderlies who were looking down at her.

'And you think you're the handsome prince?' Murf said to Phil.

'Well, *you're* certainly no prince,' Phil said.

Susan saw an accoustic-tile ceiling above the two men.

'He thinks he's a prince,' Murf said to Susan. 'Actually, he's one of the dwarfs.'

'Dwarfs?' Phil said.

'Dwarfs,' Murf said. 'Either Ugly or Grumpy.'

'There wasn't one named Ugly.'

'Then Grumpy.'

Susan turned her head left and right, bewildered. She was in the Physical Therapy Department's waiting room.

'Besides,' Phil said, 'Sleeping Beauty wasn't mixed up with any dwarfs. That was Snow White.'

'Snow White?'

'Snow White,' Phil said, gripping the bar at the foot of the stretcher and pushing as Murf guided from the other end.

They started moving toward the double doors that opened onto the first-floor corridor.

Her bewilderment was suddenly overlaid with fear. She tried to sit up, but she was restrained by the single strap across her middle. She said, 'No, wait. Wait. Wait a minute, dammit!'

They stopped moving. Both men appeared to be startled by her outburst. Murf's bushy gray eyebrows were drawn together in a frown. Phil's round, childlike face was a definition of puzzlement.

'Where are you taking me?' she demanded.

'Well . . . back to your room,' Murf said.

'What's wrong?' Phil asked.

She ran her hands over the fabric belt that held her down, felt desperately for the means by which it could be released. She found the buckle, but before she could tug at it, Murf put his hand on hers and gently moved it away from the strap.

'Wait,' he said. 'Just calm down, Miss Thorton. What's wrong?'

She glared up at them. 'You already took me out of here once, took me as far as the elevators— '

'We didn't— '

'—then just pushed me in there with *them*, just abandoned me to them. I'm not going to let you do anything like that again.'

'Miss Thorton, we— '

'How could you do that to me? Why in the name of God would you *want* to do that to me? What could you possibly have against me? You don't know me, really; I've never done anything to either of you.'

Murf glanced at Phil.

Phil shrugged.

To Susan, Murf said, 'Who's *them*?'

'You know,' she said bitterly, angrily. 'Don't pretend with me. Don't treat me like a fool.'

'No, really,' Murf said. 'I really don't know who you're talking about.'

'Me either,' Phil said.

'Them!' she said exasperatedly. 'Harch and the others. The four dead men, dammit!'

'Dead men?' Phil said.

Murf looked down at her as if she had lost her mind; then he abruptly broke into a smile. 'Ah, I understand. You must've been dreaming.'

She looked from one man to the other, and they appeared to be genuinely perplexed by her accusations.

Murf said to Phil, 'I guess she dreamed that we

173

took her out of here and put her in the elevator with some other patients who were . . . deceased.' He looked down at Susan. 'Is that it? Is that what you dreamed?'

'I can't have been dreaming. I wasn't even asleep,' she said sharply.

'Of course you were asleep,' Phil said, his voice every bit as patient and understanding as hers was sharp and angry. 'We just now watched you wake up.'

'A regular Sleeping Beauty,' Murf said.

She shook her head violently, side to side, 'No, no, no. I mean, I wasn't sleeping the *first* time you came in,' she said, trying to explain but realizing that she sounded irrational. 'I . . . I just closed my eyes for a second or two after Mrs. Atkinson left me here, and before I could possibly have had a chance to doze off, you came and took me out to the elevator and— '

'But that was all a dream, don't you see?' Murf said gently, smiling encouragingly.

'Sure,' Phil said. 'It had to be a dream because we don't ever move the deceased patients to the morgue by way of the public elevators.'

'Not ever,' Murf said.

'The deceased are transported in the service elevators,' Phil explained.

'That's more discreet,' Murf said.

'Discreet,' Phil agreed.

She wanted to scream at them: *That's not the kind of dead men I'm talking about, you conniving*

174

bastards! I mean the dead men who've come back from the grave, the ones who walk and talk and somehow manage to pass for the living, the ones who want to kill me.

But she didn't scream a word of that because she knew it would sound like the ravings of a lunatic.

'A dream,' Murf said placatingly.

Phil said, 'Just a bad dream.'

She studied their faces, which loomed over her and appeared disproportionately huge from her awkward perspective. The gray-haired, fatherly Murf had kind eyes. And could Phil's smooth, round, childlike countenance successfully conceal vicious, hateful thoughts? No, she didn't believe that it could. His wide-eyed innocence was surely as genuine as her own fear and confusion.

'But how could it have been a dream?' she asked. 'It was so real . . . so vivid.'

'I've had a couple of dreams so vivid that they hung on for a minute or so after I woke up,' Phil said.

'Yeah,' Murf said. 'Me, too.'

She thought of Quince's speech about his suicide. She thought of the hand on her breasts, the other hand over her eyes, the third hand sealing shut her mouth when she tried to scream for help.

'But this was . . . *real*,' she said, though she was increasingly coming to doubt that. 'At least . . . it *seemed* real . . . frighteningly real . . .'

'I swear to you, it wasn't more than five minutes ago that we got the call from Mrs. Atkinson, asking us to come and pick you up,' Murf said.

'And we came straight down,' Phil said.

'And here we are. But we weren't here before.'
She licked her dry lips. 'I guess . . .'

'A dream,' Murf said.

'Had to've been a bad dream,' Phil said.

At last, grudgingly, Susan nodded. 'Yeah. I suppose so. Listen . . . I'm sorry.'

'Oh, don't worry your pretty head,' Murf told her. 'There's no need for you to be sorry.'

'I shouldn't have snapped at you the way I did,' she said.

'Did she hurt your feelings, Phil?'

'Not in the least. Did she hurt your feelings, Murf?'

'Not one bit.'

'There, you see,' Phil said to Susan. 'Absolutely no reason for you to apologize.'

'No reason at all,' Murf concurred.

'Now, do you feel up to traveling?' Phil asked her.

'We'll make it a nice, gentle ride,' Murf promised.

Phil said. 'We'll take the scenic route.'

'First-class accommodations all the way,' Murf said.

'Gourmet meals at the captain's table.'

'Dancing in the ship's ballroom every night.'

'Free deck chairs and shuffleboard, plus a complimentary happy-hour cocktail,' Murf said.

She wished they would stop their bantering; it

no longer amused her. She was somewhat dizzy, queasy, still considerably confused, as if she had drunk too much or had been drugged. Their swift patter was like a ball bouncing frenetically back and forth inside her head; it made her dizzier by the minute. But she didn't know how to tell them to be quiet without hurting their feelings; and if the terror in the elevator *had* been just a dream, she had already been unjustifiably rude.

She said, 'Well . . . okay. Let's pull up anchor and get this ship out of the harbor.'

'Bon voyage,' Phil said.

'Lifeboat drill at sixteen hundred hours,' Murf said.

They rolled the stretcher through the swing-hinged double doors, into the first-floor hallway.

'You're *sure* Sleeping Beauty wasn't mixed up with a bunch of dwarfs?' Murf asked Phil.

'I told you, it was Snow White. Murf, I'm beginning to think you're a hopeless illiterate.'

'What a vile thing to say, Phil. I'm an educated man.'

They turned into the long main hall and wheeled Susan toward the elevators.

Murf said, 'It's just that I don't read children's fairy tales any more. I'm sure such stuff is adequate for you, but I prefer more complex literature.'

'You mean the *Racing Form*?' Phil asked.

'Charles Dickens is more like it, Phil.'

'And the *National Enquirer*?'

They reached the elevators.

Susan felt watchspring tense.

'I'll have you know that I've read all the published works of Louis L'Amour,' Murf said, pressing the white button that was marked *Up*.

'Dickens to L'Amour,' Phil said. 'That's quite a spread, Murf.'

'I'm a man of wide interests,' Murf said.

Susan held her breath, waiting for the doors to open. A scream crouched in her chest, ready to leap up into her throat and out.

Please, God, she thought, not again.

'And what about you, Phil? Have you read any good cereal boxes lately?'

The elevator doors opened with a soft hum. They were behind Susan's head; she couldn't see into the cab.

Murf and Phil rolled her inside and came with her this time. There were no dead men waiting.

She let out her breath in a rush and closed her eyes. Relief brought with it a headache.

The trip back to her room was uneventful, but when she was transferring herself from the stretcher to her bed, she felt a twinge of pain in her right arm, just above the inner crook of the elbow. She abruptly remembered that Harch – or maybe one of the others – had pinched that arm hard, very hard, just before she had passed out in the elevator.

After the two orderlies left, Susan sat for a while with her hands in her lap, afraid to look at her arm. At last, however, she pushed up the right sleeve of her green pajamas. There was a bruise on her frail biceps, a darker oval on the pale skin, two inches above the elbow joint. It was a light bruise, but it was getting darker. About the size of a nickel. The color of a strawberry birthmark. Quite sore to the touch. A *fresh* bruise: no doubt about that.

But what did it mean? Was it proof that the encounter with Harch and the other three men had actually taken place, proof that it had not been merely a bad dream during a short nap? Or had she acquired the bruise while exercising in the PT department, and – not consciously but subconsciously aware of it – had she then cleverly incorporated the injury into the dream about the dead men in the elevator?

She tried to remember if she had bumped her arm at any time during the therapy session. She couldn't be sure. She thought back to the shower that she had taken in the PT Department. Had her arm shown any discoloration then? Had there been a small spot of tenderness on the biceps? She didn't recall that there had been either a mark or any soreness whatsoever. However, it might have been so slight that it had escaped her notice then; after all, most bruises developed slowly.

I *must* have gotten it when I was exercising, she told herself. That's the only explanation that isn't . . . insane. Ernest Harch and the other fraternity brothers aren't real. They can't hurt me. They're only phantoms generated by some peculiar form of brain dysfunction. If I regain my strength,

179

if McGee finds out what's wrong with me, if I get well again, that will be the last I'll ever see of these walking, talking dead men. In the meantime, they simply cannot hurt me.

* * *

Jeff McGee showed up for his evening rounds at half past five, dressed as if he were going to a fancy dinner party. He was wearing a dark blue suit that was well-tailored to his tall, trim frame, a pearl-gray shirt, a blue- and gray-striped necktie, and a sky-blue display handkerchief in the breast pocket of his suit jacket.

He looked so elegant and moved with such exceptional grace that Susan found herself suddenly responding to him sexually. From the moment she had seen him Sunday morning, she thought he was an extremely attractive man, but this was the very first time since waking from her long coma that she had experienced the warm, welcome, delicious fluttering-tingling-melting of sexual desire.

My God, she thought with amusement, I *must* be getting well: I'm horny!

McGee came directly to her bedside, and without hesitation this time, he leaned down and kissed her on the cheek, near the corner of her mouth. He was wearing a subtle after-shave lotion that smelled vaguely of lemons and even more vaguely of several unidentifiable herbs, but beneath that crisp fragrance, Susan detected the even more appealing, freshly scrubbed scent of his own skin.

180

She wanted to throw her arms around his neck and hold on to him, cling to him; she wanted to draw him close and take strength from him, strength she needed, strength he seemed to possess in such abundance. But however far their personal relationship had come in these past few days, it most certainly had not come *that* far. McGee felt considerable affection for her; she was sure of that. But given the natural restraints of the doctor-patient relationship, to which any romantic feelings had to remain strictly secondary, she could not cast aside all reserve. And given the fact that she couldn't entirely trust her perceptions – which told her that Jeff McGee felt a great deal more than mere affection for her – she dared risk nothing other than a swift, chaste kiss planted lightly on his cheek in return for the kiss that he had bestowed upon her.

'I'm in a bit of a hurry tonight,' he said, drawing away from her too soon. 'Let me have a quick look at Jessie Seiffert, see how she's coming along, and then I'll be back for a few minutes.'

He went to the other bed and slipped behind the curtain.

A whip of jealousy lashed through Susan. She wondered for whom he had put on his best suit. With whom was he having dinner tonight? A woman? Well, of course it would be a woman, and a pretty woman, too. A man didn't dress up like that, pocket handkerchief and all, just to grab a bite and have a few beers with the boys. Jeffrey

McGee was a most desirable man, and there was never any shortage of women for desirable men. And he certainly didn't have the air of a celibate; good heavens, no! He had enjoyed a private life, a romantic life – all right, face up to it, a *sex* life – long before one Susan Kathleen Thorton had arrived on the scene. She could claim absolutely no right to be jealous of his relations with other women. Absolutely no right whatsoever. There was nothing serious between her and him; he was under no obligation to remain faithful to her. The very idea of that was patently ridiculous. Still, she *was* jealous; terribly, surprisingly jealous.

He stepped out from behind the curtain and returned to Susan's bedside. He took her hand and smiled at her; his hand was strong and warm, and his teeth were very white and even. 'So tell me how it went down in PT. Did you have a good afternoon with Flo Atkinson?'

Susan had intended to recount the terror of that strikingly vivid dream in which she had been trapped in the elevator with Ernest Harch and the other fraternity men. But now she decided against telling McGee anything about it. She didn't want him to see her as just a weak, frightened, dependent woman. She didn't want him to pity her.

'It was a terrific afternoon in every detail,' she lied.

'That's great. I'm glad to hear it.'

'Yeah. The physical therapy is exactly what I need,' she said, and at least that much was true.

'You've got some color in your face now.'

'Washed my hair, too.'

'Yes, it looks very nice.'

'You're a terrible liar, Dr. McGee, It won't look nice for another six weeks or two months, thanks to your emergency room hairdresser, who apparently trims the incoming patients with a chain saw. At least now it's clean.'

'I think it looks clean *and* nice,' he insisted. 'It's cute. Shaggy like that, it reminds me of . . . Peter Pan.'

'Thanks a lot. Peter Pan was a boy.'

'Well, you certainly can't be mistaken for a boy. Forget I said Peter Pan. It makes you look like . . .'

'An English sheepdog?'

'Are you determined to fend off any compliment I give you?'

'Come on, admit it. English sheepdog, right?'

He pretended to scrutinize her for canine qualities. 'Well, now that you mention it . . . Do you know how to fetch a pair of slippers?'

'Arf, arf,' she said.

'Seriously,' he said, 'you look good. I think your cheeks are already starting to fill out a bit.'

'*You're* the one who's looking good. Sharp outfit.'

'Thanks,' he said, but he didn't tell her why he was wearing his best suit, which was the information she had been probing for when she'd complimented him. 'See Harch or the others today?'

'Not a glimpse,' she lied.

183

'That's a positive sign. I've scheduled tests for tomorrow morning. Blood samples, urinalysis, X-rays . . . a spinal tap if necessary.'

'Ouch.'

'It won't be too bad.'

'Easy for you to say. It's not *your* spine they'll be tapping.'

'True. But if a tap is necessary, I'll do it myself, and I'm known for my gentle touch.' He glanced at his watch. 'I've got to run, I'm afraid.'

'Heavy date?'

'I wish it were! Unfortunately, it's only the monthly meeting of the Tri-County Medical Association. I'm the dinner speaker tonight, and I've got stage fright.'

She almost sighed aloud with relief. 'Stage fright?' she said, hoping he wouldn't see how much she had feared the possibility of a hot romance in his life. 'Not you. I can't imagine you being afraid of anything.'

'Among other things,' he said, 'I'm afraid of snakes, and I have a mild case of claustrophobia, and I dread public speaking.'

'What about English sheepdogs?'

'I adore English sheepdogs,' he said, and he kissed her on the cheek again.

'They'll love your speech,' she assured him.

'Well, anyway, it won't be the worst part of the evening,' he said. 'No matter how bad the speech is, it's sure to be better than the banquet food at the Holiday Inn.'

She smiled. 'See you in the morning.'

He hesitated. 'Are you sure you're all right?'

'I'm fine.'

'Remember, if you see any of them again, just tell yourself they aren't real and— '

' —they can't hurt me.'

'Remember that.'

'I will.'

'And listen, all the nurses on this floor have been apprised of your condition. If you have any attacks . . . hallucinations, just call for a nurse, and she'll help you. She'll talk you down.'

'That's good to know.'

'You aren't alone.'

'I'm aware of that – and I'm grateful.'

He left, turning at the door to smile and wave.

He had been gone for several minutes before Susan's sweet, warm, liquid feeling of sexual arousal faded, before her body heat subsided to a mere 98.6 degrees.

God, she thought wonderingly, he makes me feel like a young girl. A sex-crazy teenager.

She laughed softly at herself.

Then, although she wasn't alone, she *felt* alone.

Later, as she was eating dinner, she remembered what McGee had said about her inability to accept any of his compliments graciously. It was true. And odd. She thought about it for a while. She had never wanted compliments from a man half as much as she wanted them from Jeff McGee. Maybe she repeatedly turned aside his compliments as a

185

means of forcing him to repeat them and elaborate upon them. No . . . The more she thought about it, the more she suspected that she ducked any praise from him because, deep down inside, she was afraid of the strong pull that he exerted on her, was afraid of the tremendous attraction she felt for him. Over the years, she'd had a few lovers, not many, but a few, and in every case she had been very much in control of the relationship. With each man, when the time had finally come to say goodbye, she had broken off the romance with regret but always without serious emotional trauma. She had been as thoroughly in command of her heart as she had been in command of her career as a physicist. But she sensed that it couldn't be like that with Jeff McGee. This would be a more intense relationship, more emotional, more entangling. Maybe it scared her a bit – even as she longed for it.

She knew she wanted Jeff McGee. His effect on her was undeniable. But aside from wanting him, did she also *love* him? That was a question which she had never needed to ask herself before.

Love?

It's impossible, dammit, she told herself. I can't be in love with a man I met only three short days ago. I hardly know anything about him. I haven't even given him a *real* kiss. Or received one from him. Just pecks on the cheek. For God's sake, I can't say for sure that his feelings for me are even remotely passionate. No one falls in love overnight.

It simply doesn't happen that way.

Yet she knew it *had* happened to her. Just like in the movies.

All right, she thought, if it *is* love, then *why* is it? Have I fallen in love with him only because I'm sick and weak and helpless, only because I'm grateful to have a strong, reliable man on my side? If that's it, then it could hardly be called love; it's merely gratitude and a shameless, headlong flight from responsibility for my own life.

However, the more she thought about it, the more she came to feel that the love had been there first. Or at the very least, the love and the desperate need for McGee's strength had come to her simultaneously.

Which came first, she thought, the chicken or the egg? And does it matter anyway? What matters is how I feel about him – and I really want him.

Since, for the time being, romance had to take second place to recuperation, she tried to put the subject out of her mind. After dinner, she read several chapters of a good mystery novel and ate three or four chocolates. The night nurse, a perky brunette named Tina Scolari, brought ginger ale. Susan read more of the mystery, and it got even better. Outside, the rain stopped falling, and the irritatingly monotonous drumming of water on the windowpane ceased at last. She asked for and was given a second glass of ginger ale. The evening was relatively pleasant. For a while.

10

Nurse Scolari came in at 9:15. 'You've got an early day tomorrow. Lots of tests.' She gave Susan a small pill cup that contained a single pink tablet, the mild sedative that McGee had prescribed for her. While Susan washed the pill down with the last of her second glass of ginger ale, Nurse Scolari checked on Jessica Seiffert in the next bed, drawing back the curtain just far enough to ease behind it. When she reappeared, she said to Susan, 'Lights out as soon as you feel drowsy.'

'Sooner than that, even. I just want to finish this chapter,' Susan said, indicating the book she had been reading. 'Just two more paragraphs.'

'Want me to help you to the bathroom then?'

'Oh, no. I can make it on my own.'

'You're sure?'

'Yes, positive.'

The nurse stopped by the door and flipped up the switch that turned on the small night light at the far end of the room, so that Susan wouldn't have to cross the room to do it later. The swinging

189

door had been propped open all day; on her way out, Nurse Scolari pushed up the rubber-tipped prop that was fixed to the base of the door, and she pulled the door shut behind her.

After Susan had read two more paragraphs, she got out of bed and went into the bathroom, trailing one hand lightly along the wall, so that she could lean on it for support if that were suddenly necessary. After she brushed her teeth, she returned to bed. Her legs were weak and sore, especially the calves and the backs of her thighs, but she was no longer dangerously shaky. She walked without fear of falling, even though she was not yet entirely sure-footed, and even though she knew she still couldn't travel any great distance under her own steam.

In bed, she fluffed her pillows and used the power controls to lower the upper end of the mattress. She switched off the lamp that stood on her nightstand.

The moon-soft beams of the night light fell upon the curtain that enclosed Jessica Seiffert's bed and, as it had done last night, the white fabric seemed to absorb the light, magnify it, and cast back a phosphoric glow all of its own, making it by far the most prominent object in the shadowy room. Susan stared at it for a minute or two and felt a renewal of the curiosity and uneasiness that had plagued her ever since the unseen Seiffert woman had been brought into the room.

'Susan . . .'

She nearly exploded off the bed in surprise, sat straight up, quivering, the covers thrown back, her breath quick-frozen in her lungs, her heart briefly stilled.

'Susan . . .'

The voice was thin, dry, brittle, a voice of dust and ashes and time-ravaged vocal cords. It possessed a disturbing, bone-chilling quality that seemed, to Susan, to be inexplicably yet undeniably sinister.

'Susan . . . Susan . . .'

Even as low as it was, even as raspy and tortured as it was, that ruined voice was nevertheless clearly, indisputably masculine. And it was coming from behind the luminous curtain, from Jessica Seiffert's shrouded bed.

Susan finally managed to draw a breath, with a shudder and a gasp. Her heart started again with a *thud*.

'Susan . . .'

Last night, waking in the dead and lonely hours of the morning, she had thought she'd heard a voice calling to her from behind the curtain, but she had convinced herself that it had been only part of a dream, and she had gone back to sleep. Her senses had been dulled by sedatives, and she had not been sufficiently clear-headed to recognize that the voice was, indeed, real. Tonight, however, she was not asleep nor even sleepy yet; the sedative hadn't begun to take effect. Wide-eyed, not the least bit drowsy, she had no doubt

191

whatsoever that the voice was real.

'*Susan* . . .'

It was the pleading cry of some grim and grisly siren, and it exerted an emotional, visceral pull that was almost physical in its intensity. Although she was afraid of that bizarre voice and was afraid, too, of whatever man – whatever *creature* – owned that voice, she had the urge to get up and go to Mrs. Seiffert's bed; she felt strangely compelled to draw back the white curtain and confront the being who was summoning her. She gripped a wad of sheets in one hand, seized the cold bed rail with the other hand, and resisted that crazy urge with all her might.

'*Susan* . . .'

She fumbled for the switch on the bedside lamp, found it after too many seconds had ticked by in darkness, clicked it. Light drove back the shadows, which seemed to retreat only with the greatest reluctance, as if they were hungry wolves that were slinking grudgingly away from prey that had at first appeared to be easy pickings.

Susan stared at the curtained bed. Waited.

There wasn't a sound.

Ten seconds passed. Twenty. Half a minute.

Nothing. Silence.

At last she said, 'Who's there?'

No response.

More than twenty-four hours had passed since Susan had returned from her wheelchair constitutional to discover that a roommate had been

192

installed in the other bed. Mrs. Baker had told her that it was Jessica Seiffert; otherwise, she wouldn't have known with whom she was sharing her room. More than twenty-four hours, and *still* she hadn't gotten a glimpse of Mrs. Seiffert. Nor had she heard the old woman speak a single word: she'd heard only that vague, wordless murmur that had answered Jeff McGee's questions, that soft mumbled response to the various nurses who had gone behind the curtain. People had come and gone and come again, attending to Mrs. Seiffert with commendable concern and diligence – emptying the old woman's bedpan, taking her temperature and her blood pressure, timing her pulse, feeding her meals, giving her medicine, changing her bed linens, offering her encouragement – but in spite of all that activity, Susan had not gotten even one brief peek at the mysterious occupant of the other bed.

And now she was troubled by the unsettling notion that Jessie Seiffert had never been in that bed to begin with. It was someone else. Ernest Harch. One of the other three fraternity men? Or something even worse than that?

This is insane.

It *had* to be Jessica Seiffert in that bed, for if it was not her, then everyone in the hospital was involved in some grotesque conspiracy. Which was impossible. Thoughts like those – paranoid fantasies of complicated conspiracies – were only additional proof of her brain dysfunction. Mrs. Baker hadn't lied to her. She knew that as surely as she knew her own name. Yet she couldn't stop considering the possibility that Jessica Seiffert didn't exist, that the unseen roommate was someone far less innocent and far less harmless than an old woman dying of cancer.

'Who's there?' she demanded again.

Again, there was no reply.

'Dammit,' she said, 'I know I didn't just imagine you!'

Or *did* I?

'I heard you call me,' she said.

Or did I only *think* I heard it?

'Who are you? What are you doing here? What do you want from me?'

'*Susan* . . .'

She jerked as if she had been slapped, for the voice was even eerier in bright light than it had been in darkness. It belonged to darkness; it seemed impossible, twice as monstrous, when heard in the light.

Stay calm, she told herself. Stay cool. Stay collected. If I've got a brain injury that causes me to see things that are not really there, then it's entirely logical that it also causes me to hear sounds that were never made. Auditory hallucinations. There are such things.

'*Susan* . . .'

She had to regain control of herself before this episode progressed any further; she had to quickly squelch this incipient hysteria. She had to prove to herself that there was no voice coming from behind

194

the curtain, that it was only an imagined voice. The best way to prove it was to go straight over there and draw back the curtain. The only thing she would find in Jessica Seiffert's bed was an old woman who was dying of cancer.

'Susan . . .'

'Shut up,' she said.

Her hands were cold and damp. She wiped the icy sweat on the sheets. She took a deep breath, as if she thought that courage was merely a vapor that could be siphoned out of the air.

'Susan . . . Susan . . .'

Stop procrastinating, she told herself. Get up, get moving, get it over with.

She put down the safety rail and pushed back the covers and sat on the edge of the bed, legs dangling. She stood up, holding on to the mattress. She had gotten out of the bed on the side nearest Jessica Seiffert. Her slippers were on the other side, out of reach, and the green tile floor was cold against her bare feet. The distance between the two beds was only nine or ten feet. She could cover it in three shuffling steps, four at the most. She took the first one.

'Sssuuuuusssaaaaannn . . .'

The thing in the bed – and in spite of her brave and oh-so-rational thoughts about auditory hallucinations, she could only think of it now as a *thing* – seemed to sense both her approach and her timidity. Its voice became even more hoarse, even more insistent and sinister than it had been; it did not speak her name so much as moan it.

'Sssuuuuusssaaaaannn . . .'

She considered returning to the bed and pushing the call button that would summon a nurse. But what if the nurse came and heard nothing? What if the nurse pulled back the curtain and found only an old, pathetic, dying woman who was murmuring senselessly in a drug-induced stupor? Which was almost certainly what she *would* find, of course. What then?

She took a second step toward the other bed, and the cold floor seemed to be getting colder.

The curtain fluttered as if something had brushed against the other side of it.

Susan's ice-water blood grew colder and moved sluggishly through her veins in spite of the rapid beating of her heart.

'Sssssuuuuusssaaaaannn . . .'

She retreated one step.

The curtain fluttered again, and she saw a dark shape behind it.

The voice called her again, and this time there was definitely a threatening tone to it.

The curtain rustled, then flapped violently. It rattled the hooks by which it was suspended from the ceiling track. A dark form, shapeless but surely much too large to be a cancer-withered woman, groped clumsily against the far side of the white fabric, as if searching for a place to part it.

Susan was stricken by a premonition of death. Perhaps that was a sure sign of her mental imbalance; perhaps it was irrefutable proof that she was irrational and was imagining everything, yet the premonition was too powerful to be ignored. *Death*. Death was very near. Suddenly, the last thing on earth she wanted was to see what lay beyond the curtain.

She turned and fled. She stumbled around the foot of her own bed, then glanced back.

The curtain appeared to be caught in a turbulent whirlpool of cross-drafts – though she could feel no air moving in the room. It trembled and fluttered and rustled and billowed. And it was beginning to slide open.

She shuffled quickly into the bathroom – the door to the hall seemed too far away – and her legs protested at the speed that she demanded from them. In the bathroom, she closed the door and leaned against it, breathless.

It isn't real. It can't hurt me.

The bathroom was dark, and she could not tolerate being alone in the dark now. She felt for the switch and finally located it; the white walls, the white sink and commode, and the white ceramic-tile floor all gleamed brightly.

It can't hurt me.

She was still holding the doorknob. It moved in her hand. Someone was turning it from the other side.

She twisted the latch. It was loose, broken.

'No,' she said. 'No.'

She held the knob as tightly as she could, and

she put her shoulder to the door, digging her heels into the tile floor of the bathroom. For interminably long seconds, seconds that seemed like minutes, the person on the other side continued to try the knob, working it back and forth; it strained against Susan's hand, but she gritted her teeth and tensed her wasted muscles and refused to let herself be budged. After a while the knob stopped moving. She thought the surrender might be only a trick, so she maintained a firm grip.

Something scratched on the other side of the door. The sound, so near her face, startled her. It was a stealthy noise at first, but it quickly grew louder. Fingernails. Clawing at the wood.

'Who's there?'

She received no answer.

The nails scratched furiously for perhaps half a minute. Then paused. Then scratched again, but languidly this time. Now – steadily and relentlessly. Now – desultorily.

'What do you want?'

The only response was a new fit of scratching.

'Listen, if you'll just please tell me who you are, I'll open the door.'

That promise accomplished nothing, either.

She listened worriedly to the fingernails that picked determinedly along the edges of the door, exploring the cracks between the door and the frame, as if purchase and leverage might be found there, sufficient to tear the door open or rip it from its hinges with one mighty heave.

Finally, after two or three more minutes of fruitless but busy scraping and probing, the noise stopped abruptly.

Susan tensed herself and prepared to recommence the struggle with the doorknob, but, much to her surprise and relief, the battle did not begin again.

She waited hopefully, hardly daring to breathe.

The bathroom gleamed in the hard fluorescent light, and a drop of water made a soft, soft *tink* as it fell from the faucet onto the metal stopper in the sink.

Gradually, Susan's panic subsided. A trickle of doubt found its way into her mind; the trickle became a stream, a flood. Slowly, reason reasserted itself. She began to consider, once more, the possibility that she had been hallucinating. After all, if there really had been a man – or something else – behind the curtain, and if he really had wanted to get his hands on her, she would not have been able to hold the door against him. Not in her enfeebled condition. If someone actually *had* been twisting the doorknob – and now she was virtually awash in doubt, floundering in it – then the person on the other side had been markedly weaker than she was. And no one in such poor health could have posed a serious threat to her.

She waited. Leaned hard against the door.

Her breath came to her more easily now.

Time passed at a measured, plodding pace, and

her heart slowed, and the silence continued without interruption.

But as yet she was unable to relax her grip on the doorknob. She stared at her hand. Her knuckles were sharp and bloodless. Her fingers looked like talons curled around the metal knob.

She realized that Mrs. Seiffert was the only one around who was weaker than she herself. Had Mrs. Seiffert tried to get out of bed on her own? Is that what all the thrashing behind the curtain had been about? And had the old woman somehow crossed the room in drugged confusion or in desperate pain? Had it been Mrs. Seiffert clawing at the door, unable to speak, seeking help, scratching and scratching at the wood in a frantic bid to gain attention?

Good God, Susan thought, was I defending the door against a dying woman who was seeking nothing but my help?

But she didn't open the door. Couldn't. Not yet.

Eventually, she thought: No. No, Mrs. Seiffert, *if* she exists, is too debilitated to get out of bed and cross the room all by herself. She's an invalid, a limp bag of flesh and bones. It couldn't possibly have been Mrs. Seiffert. Besides, the threatening form that had risen up behind the curtain couldn't have been Mrs. Seiffert, either. It was too big.

In the sink, a drop of water fell.

On the other hand, maybe there hadn't been a rising form behind the curtain to begin with. Maybe the curtain had never really moved, either. Maybe there had been no mysterious voice, no hand turning the knob, no persistent scratching at the door. All in her head.

Brain dysfunction.

A sand-grain blood clot.

A tiny cerebral capillary with an even tinier hemorrhage.

A chemicoelectrical imbalance of some kind.

The more she thought about it, the easier it was to rule out supernatural and conspiratorial explanations. After a lot of consideration, she seemed to be left with only two possibilities: either she had imagined the entire thing . . . or Mrs. Seiffert now lay dead just the other side of the bathroom door, a victim of Susan's mental problems.

In either case, there was no one after her, no reason to continue to guard the door. At last she leaned away from it; her shoulder ached, and her entire left side was stiff. She relaxed her iron-tight grip on the knob, which was now slick and shiny with her sour sweat.

She opened the door. Just a crack.

No one tried to force his way into the bathroom.

Still frightened, prepared to slam the door shut at the slightest sign of movement, she opened it wider: two inches, three. She looked down, expecting the worst, but there was no elderly dead woman sprawled on the floor, no gray face contorted in an eternal expression of contempt and accusation.

The hospital room looked normal. The lamp burned beside her bed, and her covers were heaped in a tangled mess, as she had left them. The night light was still on, too. The curtain around Jessica Seiffert's bed was in place, hanging straight from the ceiling to the floor, stirred neither by a draft nor by a malevolent hand.

Susan slowly opened the door all the way.

No one leaped at her.

No dust-choked, half-human voice called to her.

So . . . every bit of it was the product of my imagination, she thought dismally. My runaway imagination, galloping merrily off on another journey through temporary madness. My damned, sick, *traitorous* brain.

All of her life, Susan had limited her drinking to infrequent social occasions, and even then she had allowed herself no more than two cocktails in one evening, for she had always hated being drunk. She had been booze-blasted once, just once, when she was a senior in high school, and that had been a memorable and extremely nasty experience. No artificially induced high, no matter how pleasant it might be, had ever seemed worth the loss of control that went along with it.

Now, without taking a single sip of alcohol, she could lose control in an instant and not even be aware that she had lost it. At least when you got drunk, you relinquished the reins of reason slowly, in stages, and you knew that you were no longer in the driver's seat. Drunk, you knew that your senses could not be trusted. But brain dysfunction was more insidious than that.

It scared her.

What if Jeff McGee couldn't find the problem?

What if there was no cure?

What if she were forced to spend the rest of her life teetering on the razor-edge of insanity, frequently toppling over the brink for short but devastating travels in the shadowy land of Never-Was?

She knew she couldn't live that way. Death would be far preferable to such a tortured existence.

She snapped off the bathroom light and fancied that she could feel the weight of the darkness on her back.

She followed the wall to her bed, wincing at the pain in the backs of her legs.

When she reached the bed, she used the power controls to lower it, and she put down the safety railing as she had done on the other side when she'd gotten out, and she started to sit down on the mattress, but then she hesitated. She raised up again and stood for a long while, staring at the curtain. Eventually, she accepted the fact that she could not simply go to sleep now; not yet. She had to find the courage to do what she had been unable to do earlier. She had to go over there, pull back the curtain, and prove to herself that her roommate was only an old, sick woman. Because if she did not do it now, the hallucinations might start again the moment that she turned out the light and put her head down on her pillow. Because if she didn't fight this sickness every step of the way, it would probably overwhelm her much sooner than if she resisted. Because she was Susan Kathleen Thorton, and Susan Kathleen Thorton never ran away from trouble.

She was standing beside her slippers. She put her cold feet in them.

She moved creakily around the bottom of her bed, holding on to it as she went. She shuffled across the space between the two beds and, standing in the open with nothing to hold on to, she raised one hand and touched the curtain.

The room seemed extraordinarily quiet – as if she were not the only one holding her breath.

The air was as still as the air in a crypt.

She closed her hand, clenching a wad of drapery material in her fist.

Open it, for heaven's sake! she told herself when she realized that she had been hesitating for almost a minute. There's nothing threatening behind here, nothing but one old lady who's sleeping through the last few days of her life.

Susan pulled the curtain aside. Overhead, the dozens of small metal hooks rattle-clattered along the stainless-steel track in the ceiling.

As she swept the curtain out of the way, Susan stepped closer to the bed, right up to the safety railing, and she looked down. In that gut-wrenching moment, she knew that there was a Hell and that she was trapped in it.

Mrs. Seiffert wasn't in the bed, as she should have been. Something else. Something hideous. A corpse. Jerry Stein's corpse.

No. It was just imagination.

Confused perceptions.

Brain dysfunction.

A minuscule hemorrhage in a tiny capillary.

And . . . oh yes . . . the well-known, oft-discussed, mischievous, sand-grain blood clot.

Susan went through the entire litany of medical explanations, but the corpse did not vanish or magically metamorphose into Mrs. Seiffert.

Nevertheless, Susan did not scream. She did not run. She was determined to sweat this one out; she would *force* herself back to reality. She clung to the safety railing to keep from collapsing.

She closed her eyes.

Counted to ten.

It isn't real.

She opened her eyes.

The corpse was still there.

The dead man was lying on his back, the covers drawn up to the middle of his chest, as if he were merely sleeping. One side of his skull had a crumpled look; it was indented, matted with dark, dry blood, where Ernest Harch had kicked him three times. The body's bare arms were atop the covers, stretched straight out at its sides; the hands were turned palms-up, and the fingers were bent into rigid curves, as if the dead man had made one last, futile grasp at life.

The corpse didn't look *exactly* like Jerry Stein, but that was only because it wasn't in very good condition; death had corrupted it somewhat. The skin was gray with greenish-black patches around the sunken eyes and at the corners of the purple, swollen, suppurating lips. The eyelids were mottled and crusty. Dark, peeling, oozing blisters extended out of the nostrils and across the upper lip. On both sides of the bloated, misshapen nose, other blisters glistened with some foul, brown fluid. In spite of the swelling and the discoloration and the disgusting disfigurement, the dead man was clearly Jerry Stein.

But Jerry had been dead for thirteen years. In that time, death would have visited upon him considerably more corruption than this. His flesh should have completely decomposed years ago. By now he should have been little more than a skeleton with a few strands of brittle hair clinging to its fleshless skull, the bleached bones bound together loosely by scraps of mummified skin and leathery ligaments. Yet he appeared to have been dead for only about ten days or a week, perhaps less.

Which is proof that this is a hallucination, Susan told herself, squeezing the bed's safety railing so hard that she wondered why it didn't bend in her hands. Only a hallucination. It doesn't conform to reality, to the laws of nature, or to logic; not in any detail. So it's only a vision, a horror that exists nowhere else but in my mind.

More proof of the corpse's nonexistence was the fact that Susan couldn't detect even the mildest odor of decay. If the dead man actually were here, even in this inexplicably early stage of decomposition, the stench would be overpowering. But the air, while not exactly sweet, was hospital clean, tainted only by Lysol.

Touch it, she told herself. That would dispel it. No one can touch and feel a mirage. Embracing a mirage is like embracing empty air: your arms come together around yourself. Go ahead. Touch it and prove it isn't really there.

She couldn't do it. She tried hard to pry her hand off the railing in order to reach out to the dead man's cold gray arm, but she didn't have the courage.

Instead, she said aloud, as if chanting magical words that would banish the vision: 'It's not here. It's not real. It's all in my mind.'

The crusted eyelids of the corpse fluttered.

No!

They opened.

No, she thought desperately. No, no, no, this is not happening to me.

Even open, these were not the eyes of a living man: they were rolled far back in the head, so that only the whites were visible; however, the whites were not white at all, but yellow and smeared with streaks of red-brown blood. Then those terrible eyes moved, rolled, *bulged*, and the brown irises were visible, though coated by milky cataracts. The eyes jittered for a moment, seeing nothing, and then they focused on Susan.

She screamed but didn't make a sound. The noise of the scream fell back inside of her, like a rubber ball bouncing down a long, long set of dark cellar stairs, until it came to the bottom and was still. She shook her head violently, and she gagged with revulsion, choked on her own sour saliva.

The corpse raised one stiff, gray hand. The rigor-mortised fingers gradually uncurled. It reached toward her.

She tore her hands off the bed's safety railing as if the metal had suddenly become red hot.

The corpse opened its filthy, oozing mouth. With rotting tongue and lips, it formed her name: '*Sssuuuuusssaaaaannn . . .*'

She stumbled backwards one step.

It isn't real, it isn't real, it isn't, isn't . . .

Jerkily, as if animated by a sputtering electrical current, the dead man sat up in bed.

It's all in my mind, she told herself, trying very hard to talk herself down, as McGee had advised.

The dead man called her name again and smiled.

Susan swung away from the apparition and bolted for the door to the hall, her slippered feet slapping flatly against the tile floor, and she (*I'm out of control*) reached the door after what seemed like hours, grabbed the big handle, tugged on it, but the door (*I've got to stop, get calm*) seemed to weigh a thousand tons, and she cursed her weakness, which was costing her precious seconds, and she heard a wet gurgling noise behind her (*Imagination!*), and she grunted and put her back into the should-have-been-simple task of opening the damned door, and finally she did drag it open, and she (*I'm running from a mirage*) plunged into the corridor, not daring to glance behind her to see if the corpse was in pursuit (*Just a mirage*), then she staggered, nearly fell, turned left, weaved down the hall, unable to progress in a straight line, her leg muscles afire, her knees and ankles melting more rapidly with each step she took, and she careened into the wall, put her hands against it, gasping, and shuffled forward, didn't think she could go on, then felt (*Imagined!*) the dead man's bitterly cold breath against the bare nape of her neck, and somehow she *did* go on, and she reached the main corridor, saw the nurses' station down by the elevators, tried to cry out, still couldn't produce a sound, and pushed away from the wall, hurrying as best she could along the dark green floor, beneath the pale yellow ceiling, hurrying toward the nurses' station. Toward help. Safety.

* * *

Nurse Scolari and a chunky, red-faced nurse named Beth Howe both did for Susan what she had been unable to do for herself: They talked her down, just as Jeff McGee had talked down the raving, hallucinating acid freaks in that Seattle hospital where he had served his residency. They brought her around behind the counter at the nurses' station and settled her into a spring-backed office chair. They gave her a glass of water. They reasoned with her, soothed her, listened to her, cajoled her, calmed her.

But they couldn't entirely convince her that it was safe to go back to room 258. She wanted another bed for the night, a different room.

'That's not possible, I'm afraid,' Tina Scolari said. 'You see, there's been an upturn in admissions the last day or so. The hospital's nearly full tonight. Besides, there's really nothing wrong with two fifty-eight. It's just a room like any other room. You know that's true, don't you, Susan? You know that what happened to you was just another of your attacks. It was just another dysfunctional episode.'

Susan nodded, although she wasn't sure what she believed any more. 'I still . . . I . . . don't want . . . to go back there,' she said, her teeth chattering.

While Tina Scolari continued to talk to Susan, Beth Howe went to have a look in 258. She was gone only a couple of minutes, and upon her return, she reported that all was well.

'Mrs. Seiffert?' Susan asked.

'She's in bed where she belongs,' Beth said.

'You're sure it's her?'

'Positive. Sleeping like a rock.'

'And you didn't find . . . ?'

'Nothing else,' Beth assured her.

'You looked where it might have hidden?'

'Not many places to hide in that room.'

'But you did look?'

'Yes. Nothing was there.'

They coaxed Susan into a wheelchair, and both of them took her back to 258. The closer they got to the room, the more violently Susan shivered.

The curtain was drawn tightly shut around the second bed.

They pushed her wheelchair past the first bed and kept going.

'Wait!' Susan said, sensing their intention.

'I want you to have a look for yourself,' said Beth Howe.

'No, I shouldn't.'

'Of course you should,' Beth said.

'You must,' Tina Scolari said.

'But . . . I don't think . . . I can.'

'I'm sure you can,' Tina Scolari said encouragingly.

They wheeled her right up to Jessica Seiffert's bed.

Beth Howe pulled the curtain aside.

Susan snapped her eyes shut.

Clutched the arms of the wheelchair.

'Susan, look,' Tina said.

'Look,' Beth said. 'It's only Jessie.'

'You see?'

'Only Jessie.'

With her eyes closed, Susan could see the dead man – a man she had perhaps loved a long time ago, a man she now feared because the quick were meant to fear the dead – could see him on the inside of her eyelids as he sat up in the bed and smiled at her with soft lips that were like bursting pieces of spoiled fruit. The horror show behind her eyes was worse than what might lie in front of them, so she blinked; she looked.

211

An old woman lay in the bed, so small, so shrunken, so badly withered by disease that she looked, ironically, like a wrinkle-faced baby mistakenly placed in an adult's bed. Except – her skin was waxy and mottled, not smooth like a baby's skin, and her complexion was yellow, not newborn-pink. Her hair was yellow-gray. Her wrinkled mouth resembled a drawstring purse that had been pulled as tight as only a miser could pull it. An IV drip seeped into her through a gleaming needle that punctured her left arm, an arm that was far skinnier than Susan's.

'So that's Jessica Seiffert,' Susan said, greatly relieved that such a person actually existed, but shocked that her befuddled brain could so easily – and more to the point, so *convincingly* – transform the old woman into a supernaturally animated male corpse.

'The poor old dear,' said Beth.

'She's been the most popular citizen of Willawauk since I was a toddler,' Tina said.

'Since before you were even around to toddle,' Beth said.

'Everybody loves her,' Tina said.

Jessica continued to sleep, her nostrils flaring almost imperceptibly with each shallow breath.

'I know two hundred people who'd be here to visit if Jessie would accept visitors,' Beth said.

'But she doesn't want anyone seeing her like this,' Tina said. 'As if anyone would think less of her just because of what the cancer's done to her.'

212

'Its always been the *inner* Jessie that Willawauk loves,' Beth said.

'Exactly,' Tina said.

'Feel better now?' Beth asked Susan.

'I guess so.'

Beth closed the curtain.

Susan said, 'You looked in the bathroom?'

'Oh, yes,' Beth said. 'It's empty.'

'I'd like to have a look myself, if you don't mind,' Susan said. She felt like a fool, but she was still a prisoner to her fear.

'Sure,' Beth said obligingly. 'Let's have a look and set your mind at ease.'

Tina pushed the wheelchair to the open bathroom door, and Beth switched on the light in there.

No dead man waited in the white-on-white room.

'I feel like a perfect idiot,' Susan said, feeling a blush creep into her cheeks.

'It's not your fault,' Beth said.

Tina Scolari said, 'Dr. McGee circulated a fairly long memo about your condition. He made it perfectly clear.'

'We're all on your side,' Beth said.

'We're all pulling for you,' Tina agreed.

'You'll be well in no time. Really you will. McGee's a whiz. The best doctor we've got.'

They helped Susan get into bed.

'Now,' Tina Scolari said, 'at the discretion of the night nurse, you are permitted to have a second sedative if the first one doesn't do the trick. They're

213

mild enough. And in my judgment, you sure do need another one.'

'I'll never get to sleep without it,' Susan said. 'And I was wondering . . . could you . . .'

'What is it?'

'Do you think . . . could someone stay with me . . . just until I fall asleep?'

Susan felt like a child for making that pathetic request: a dependent, emotionally immature, thumb-sucking, goblin-fearing, thirty-two-year-old child. She was disgusted with herself. But she couldn't help it. No matter how often she told herself about the bizarre effects of temporal-lobe brain lesions and sand-grain blood clots, regardless of how earnestly she argued to convince herself that one of those – or perhaps one of a dozen other – medical maladies was the cause of her *imaginary*, entirely imaginary, encounters with dead men, she was nonetheless terrified of being awake and alone in room 258 – or anywhere else, in fact.

Tina Scolari looked at Beth Howe and raised her eyebrows inquiringly.

Beth considered it for a moment, then said, 'Well, we aren't short-handed tonight, are we?'

'Nope,' Tina said. 'Everyone who was scheduled for duty showed up this evening. And so far there haven't been any big crises.'

Beth smiled at Susan. 'Slow night. No three-car crashes or barroom brawls or anything. I think one of us can spare an hour to sit with you until the sedative works.'

214

'It probably won't even take an hour,' Tina said. 'You've overtaxed yourself, Susan. It'll catch up with you in a few minutes, and you'll go out like a light.'

'I'll stay here,' Beth said.

'I'd really appreciate it,' Susan said, loathing herself for her inability to face the night alone.

Tina left but returned shortly with the second sedative in a pill cup.

When Susan took the pink tablet, she poured only a half-measure of water for herself because her hands were shaking too badly for her to safely manage a full tumbler. When she drank, the glass rattled against her teeth, and for a moment the pill stuck in her throat.

'I'm sure you'll have a good night now,' Nurse Scolari said before she left.

Beth pulled up a chair beside the bed, smoothed her uniform skirt over her round knees, and sat quietly, reading a magazine.

Susan stared at the ceiling for a while, then glanced at Jessica Seiffert's curtained bed.

She looked the other way, too, at the darkness beyond the half-opened bathroom door.

She thought of the corpse scratching insistently at the closed bathroom door against which she had been leaning. She remembered the *click-snickety-click* of his fingernails as he probed the cracks around the door frame.

Of course that had never happened. Purely imaginary.

She closed her eyes.

Jerry, she thought, I loved you once. At least it was as close to love as an inexperienced, nineteen-year-old girl could ever get. And you said that you loved me. So why in the name of God would you come back now to terrorize me?

Of course it had never happened. Purely imaginary.

Please, Jerry, stay in the cemetery there in Philadelphia, where we put you so long ago. Please stay there. Don't come back here again. Please stay there. Please.

Without realizing that she was approaching sleep, she stepped over the rim of it and was gone.

11

A nurse woke Susan at six o'clock Wednesday morning. It was another gray day, but no rain was falling.

Jeffrey McGee arrived before six-thirty. He kissed her on the cheek again, but his lips lingered there for a couple of seconds longer than they had before.

'I didn't realize you'd be here so early,' Susan said.

'I want to personally oversee most of the tests.'

'But weren't you up late last night?'

'Nope. I inflicted my after-dinner speech on the Medical Association, and then I quickly slipped away before they had time to organize a lynching party.'

'Seriously, how did it go?'

'Well, no one threw his dessert at me.'

'I *told* you that you'd be a big success.'

'Of course, maybe no one threw his dessert at me because it was the only edible part of the meal, and no one wanted to give it up.'

'I'm sure you were wonderful.'

'Well, I don't think I should plan to have a career on the lecture circuit. Anyway, enough about me. I understand there was some excitement here last night.'

'Jeez, did they have to tell you about that?'

'Of course. And so do you. In detail.'

'Why?'

'Because I said so.'

'And the doctor must be obeyed.'

'Right. So tell me.'

Embarrassed, she told him everything about the corpse behind the curtain. Now, after a good night's sleep, the whole affair sounded ludicrous, and she wondered how she could ever have been convinced that any part of it was real.

When Susan finished talking, McGee said, 'God, that's a hair-raising little tale!'

'You should've been there.'

'But now that you've had time to think, you *do* realize it was just another episode.'

'Of the Susan Thorton Soap Opera?'

'I mean, another attack, another hallucination,' he said. 'You do see that now?'

'Yes,' she said miserably.

He blinked at her. 'What's wrong?'

'Nothing.'

He scowled at her and put his hand against her forehead to see if she was running a noticeable temperature. 'Do you feel all right?'

218

'As right as I can feel under the circumstances,' she said morosely.

'Cold?'

'No.'

'You're shaking.'

'A little.'

'A lot.'

She hugged herself and said nothing.

'What's wrong?' he asked again.

'I'm . . . scared.'

'Don't be scared.'

'Jesus, what's wrong with me?'

'We'll find out.'

She couldn't stop shaking.

Yesterday morning, after she had broken down in front of McGee, after she wept against his shoulder, she had thought that she'd reached the bottom for sure. She had been ready and eager to believe that the future could only be brighter. For the first time in her life, she had admitted that she needed other people; she had confronted and accepted the unpleasant truth of her own vulnerability. That had been a shocking discovery for a woman who had built her life upon the erroneous but fiercely held assumption that she was strictly a creature of intellect, immune to emotional excess. But now she faced another realization that was even more shocking than the one whose impact she had already, somehow, absorbed. Having placed her fate in the hands of McGee and the Willawauk County Hospital's medical staff, having relinquished to them the responsibility for her survival, she now realized that the people upon whom she depended might fail her. Not intentionally, of course. But they were only human, too. *They* couldn't always control events, either. And if they failed to make her well, it wouldn't matter whether their failure was intentional or accidental or inevitable; in any case, she would be condemned to a chaotic existence, unable to distinguish reality from fantasy, and in time she would be driven completely mad.

And so she couldn't stop shaking.

'What's going to happen to me?'

'You'll be all right,' McGee said.

'But . . . it's getting worse,' she said, her voice quavering in spite of her determination to keep it steady.

'No. No, it isn't getting worse.'

'Much worse,' she insisted.

'Listen, Susan, last night's hallucination might have been more gruesome than the others— '

'*Might* have been?'

'Okay, it was more gruesome than the others— '

'And more vivid, more *real*.'

'—and more real. But it was the first one you've had since early yesterday morning, when you thought the two orderlies were Jellicoe and Parker. You're not in a *constant* state of flux between reality and— '

Susan shook her head and interrupted him. 'No. The business with the orderlies . . . and the apparition later, here in the room . . . they weren't the only things I saw yesterday. There was an . . . an attack in between those two.'

He frowned. 'When?'

'Yesterday afternoon.'

'You were with Mrs. Atkinson, downstairs in PT, yesterday afternoon.'

'That's right. It happened shortly after I'd completed the therapy session, before I was brought back up here.'

She told him how Murf and Phil had shoved her into the elevator with the four fraternity men.

'Why didn't you report all of this last evening when I was here?' McGee asked, a reprimanding tone to his voice.

'You were in such a hurry . . .'

'Not *that* much of a hurry. Am I a good doctor? I think I am. And a good doctor always has time for a patient in distress.'

'I wasn't *in* distress by the time you made your evening rounds,' she protested.

'Like hell you weren't. You had it all bottled up inside of you, but you were in distress sure enough.'

'I didn't want to make you late for the Medical Association meeting.'

'Susan, that's no excuse. I'm your *doctor*. You've got to level with your doctor at all times.'

'I'm sorry,' she said, looking down at her hands, unable to meet his forthright, blue-blue-eyes. She couldn't bring herself to explain why she hadn't told him about the elevator vision. She had been

221

worried that she would appear hysterical, that he would think less of her because she had panicked yet again. Worse, she had been afraid that he would pity her. And now that she was beginning to think that she was falling in love with him, the very *last* thing she wanted was for him to pity her.

'You don't dare hide things from me. You've got to tell me everything that happens, everything you feel. And I mean *everything*. If you *don't* tell me everything, then I might not be aware of an important symptom that would explain the root cause of all your troubles. I need every piece of information I can gather in order to make an informed diagnosis.'

She nodded. 'You're right. From now on, I won't hide anything from you.'

'Promise?'

'Promise.'

'Good.'

'But you see,' she said, still staring at her hands, which she was flexing and unflexing in nervous agitation, 'it *is* getting a lot worse.'

He put a hand against the side of her face, caressed her cheek.

She looked up at him.

'Listen,' he said softly, reassuringly, 'even if you *are* having more frequent attacks, at least you come out of them. And when one of these episodes passes, you're able to see it for what it was. After the fact, you're always aware that you were only hallucinating. Now, if you still believed that a dead

222

man had come to get you last night, if you still thought that it had *really happened*, then you'd be in very deep trouble. If that's the way it was, then maybe I'd be sweating. But I'm not sweating yet. Am I? Do you see rivers of sweat streaming down my face? Are there dark, damp circles under my arms? Do I look as if I belong in a TV ad for Right Guard? Huh? Do I?'

She smiled. 'You look as dry as toast.'

'As dry as a sandbox,' he said. 'As dry as a stick of chalk. As dry as chicken cordon bleu when I try to cook it myself. Can you cook chicken cordon bleu, by the way?'

'I've made it a few times,' she said.

'Does yours come out dry?'

She smiled again. 'No.'

'Good. I was *hoping* you could cook.'

And what does he mean by that? she thought. His blue eyes seemed to say that he meant just what she thought he meant: He was as interested in her as she was in him. But still she couldn't trust her perceptions; she couldn't be positive of his intentions.

'Now,' he said, 'will you *please* think positive?'

'I'll try,' she said.

But she couldn't stop shaking.

'Do more than try. Keep your chin up. That's doctor's orders. Now, I'll go find a couple of orderlies and a stretcher, and we'll go downstairs to diagnostic and get these tests out of the way. Are you ready to go?'

'I'm ready,' she said.

'Smile?'

She did.

So did he. And he said, 'Okay, now keep it on your face until further notice.' He headed toward the door, and over his shoulder he said, 'I'll be right back.'

He left, and her smile slipped off.

She glanced at the curtained bed.

She wished it wasn't there.

She longed for a glimpse of the sky, even if it was as gray and somber as it had been yesterday. Perhaps if she could see the sky, she wouldn't feel quite so trapped.

She had never before been this miserable; she felt wrung out and useless, even though her physical recuperation was coming along well. Depression. That was the enemy now. She was depressed not merely because other people had taken some control of her life, but because they had taken over *all* control of it. She was helpless. She could do absolutely nothing to shake off her illness. She could only lie on an examining table as if she were a mindless hunk of meat, letting them poke and prod her in their search for answers.

She looked at Mrs. Seiffert's bed again. The white curtain hung straight and still.

Last night, she had not merely opened a privacy curtain that had enclosed a hospital bed. She had opened another curtain, too, a curtain beyond which lay madness. For a few nightmarish minutes, she had stepped beyond the veil of sanity, into a shadowy and moldering place from which few people ever returned.

She wondered what would have happened if she hadn't run away from her hallucination last night. What would have happened if she had bravely and foolishly refused to back off from Jerry Stein's decomposing corpse? She was afraid she knew the answer. If she had held her ground, and if her long-dead lover had clambered out of his bed and had touched her, if he had embraced her, if he had pressed his rotting lips against her lips, stealing a warm kiss and giving her a cold one in return, she would have snapped. Real or not, hallucination or not, she would have snapped like a taut rubber band, and after that she would have been forever beyond repair. They would have found her curled up on the floor, gibbering and chuckling, lost far down inside herself, and they would have transferred her from Willawauk County Hospital to some quiet sanitarium, where she would have been assigned to a nice room with soft, quilted walls.

She couldn't take much more of this. Not even for McGee. Not even for whatever future they might have together if she got well again. She was stretched taut.

Please, God, she thought, let the tests reveal something. Let McGee find the problem. *Please*.

* * *

The walls and ceiling were the same shade of

robin's-egg blue. Lying flat on her back on the wheeled stretcher, her head raised just a few inches by a firm little pillow, looking up, Susan almost felt as if she were suspended in the middle of a summer sky.

Jeff McGee appeared beside her. 'We're going to start with an EEG.'

'Electroencephalograph,' she said. 'I never had one of those.'

'Yes, you did,' he said. 'While you were in the coma. But of course you weren't aware of it; you wouldn't remember it. Now, don't be afraid. It doesn't hurt at all.'

'I know.'

'It'll give us a look at the pattern of your brain waves. If you've got abnormal brain function of any kind, it's almost sure to show up on an EEG.'

'Almost?'

'It's not perfect.'

A nurse rolled the EEG machine out of the corner where it had been standing, and she positioned it beside Susan.

'This works best if you're relaxed,' McGee told Susan.

'I'm relaxed.'

'It won't be very reliable at all or easily interpreted if you're in an emotional turmoil.'

'I'm relaxed,' she assured him.

'Let's see your hand.'

She lifted her right hand off the stretcher's three-inch-thick matress.

'Hold it straight out in front of you, keeping the

fingers together. Okay. Now spread the fingers wide apart.' He watched closely for a few seconds, then nodded with satisfaction. 'Good. You're not trying to fake me out. You *are* calmer. You aren't trembling any more.'

As soon as they had brought her downstairs, Susan became relatively calm, for she felt that progress, however limited, was finally being made. After all, as a first-rate physicist, she could understand, appreciate, and approve of what was happening now: tests, laboratories, the scientific method, a carefully planned search for answers conducted by eliminating possibilities until the solution stood alone, exposed. She was comfortable with that process and trusted it.

She trusted Jeffrey McGee, too. She had a lot of faith in his medical abilities and confidence in his intellect. He would know what to look for, and, more importantly, he would know how to recognize it when he saw it.

The tests would provide an answer, perhaps not quickly but eventually. McGee was now taking the first tentative steps toward putting an end to her ordeal.

She was sure of it.

'Calm as a clam,' she said.

'Oyster,' he said.

'Why oyster?'

'It seems to fit you better.'

'Oh, you think I look more like an oyster than like a clam?'

'No. *Pearls* are found in oysters.'

She laughed. 'I'll bet you're a shameless come-on artist in a singles' bar.'

'I'm a shark,' he said.

McGee attached eight saline-coated electrodes to Susan's scalp, four on each side of her head.

'We'll take readings from both the left and the right side of the brain,' he said, 'then compare them. That'll be the first step in pinpointing the trauma.'

The nurse switched on the EEG apparatus.

'Keep your head just as you have it,' McGee told Susan. 'Any sudden movement will interfere.'

She stared at the ceiling.

McGee watched the green, fluorescent screen of the EEG monitor, which was not in Susan's line of sight.

'Looks good,' he said, sounding somewhat disappointed. 'No spikes. No flats. A nice, steady pattern. All within normal parameters.'

Susan kept very still.

'Negative,' he said, more to himself than to either her or the nurse.

Susan heard him click a switch.

'Now I'm taking a look at the comparative readings,' McGee told her.

He was silent for a while.

The nurse moved off to another corner, readying another piece of equipment either for Susan or for a patient who had not yet been brought into the room.

After a while, McGee shut off the machine.

'Well?' Susan asked.

'Nothing.'

'Nothing at all?'

'Well, the electroencephalograph is a useful device, but the data it provides isn't one hundred percent definitive. Some patients with serious intracranial diseases have been known to exhibit normal patterns during an EEG. And some people with no demonstrable disease have abnormal EEGs. It's a helpful diagnostic tool, but it isn't where we stop. It's where we begin.'

Disappointed, but still certain that one or more of these tests would pinpoint her malady, Susan said, 'What's next?'

As McGee removed the electrodes from Susan's scalp, he said, 'Well, radiology's right next door. I want new X rays taken of your skull.'

'Sounds like fun.'

'Oh, it's a genuine laugh riot.'

* * *

The Radiology Lab was an off-white room filled with lots of cumbersome, shiny, black and white equipment that looked somewhat dated to Susan. Of course she wasn't an expert on X-ray technology. Besides, she couldn't expect a hospital in rural Oregon to have all the very latest diagnostic tools. Though they might be a bit dated, Willawauk's machines looked more than adequate.

The radiologist was a young man named Ken Piper. He developed the plates while they waited, then pinned the sheets of X-ray film to a pair of light boxes. He and McGee studied the pictures, murmuring to each other, pointing at shadows and areas of brightness on the film.

Susan watched from the wheeled stretcher to which she had returned from the X-ray table.

They took down the first X rays, pinned up others, murmured and pointed again.

Eventually, McGee turned away from the light boxes, looking thoughtful.

Susan said, 'What'd you find?'

He sighed and said, 'What we *didn't* find are signs of brain lesions.'

'We couldn't detect any collections of fluid, either,' Ken Piper said.

'And there's been no shifting of the pineal gland, which you sometimes find in cases where the patient suffers from really vivid hallucinations,' McGee said. 'No depressions in the skull; not the slightest indication of intracranial pressure.'

'It's just a perfectly clean set of pictures,' Ken Piper said brightly, smiling down at her. 'You've got nothing to worry about, Miss Thorton.'

Susan looked at McGee and saw her own feelings mirrored in his eyes. Unfortunately, Ken Piper was wrong; she had *plenty* to worry about.

'Now what?' she asked.

'I want to do an LP,' McGee said.

'What's that?'

'A lumbar puncture.'

'Spinal tap?'

'Yeah. We might have missed something with the EEG and the X rays, something that'll show up in the spinal. And there are some conditions that can be identified only through spinal fluid analysis.'

McGee used radiology's phone to ring the hospital's lab. He told the answering technician to get set up for a complete spinal workup on the samples he was about to take from Susan.

When he put the phone down, she said, 'Let's get this over with.'

* * *

In spite of the fact that McGee anesthetized Susan's lower spinal area with Novocain, the lumbar puncture wasn't painless, but neither was it remotely as bad as she had expected it to be. It brought quick, sharp tears to her eyes, and she winced and bit her lip; but the worst part was having to remain perfectly still, worrying about the needle breaking off in her if she twitched or jerked suddenly.

McGee kept one eye on the manometer as he extracted the fluid, and he said, 'Normal pressure.'

A couple of minutes later, when the final sample had been taken, Susan whimpered with relief and wiped at the stinging tears that had beaded on her eyelids.

McGee held up one glass tube full of spinal fluid and stared at it against the light. 'Well, at least it's clear,' he said.

231

'How long until we get the results?' Susan asked.

'It'll take a little while,' McGee said. 'In the meantime, we've still got a few minor tests to run. Feel up to giving some blood?'

'Anything for the cause.'

* * *

Shortly before ten o'clock, while McGee went to the lab to see how the spinal workup was coming along, Murf and Phil arrived in diagnostic to escort Susan back to room 258. Although she knew that yesterday's terror in the elevator had not been real, although she knew that the orderlies were innocent of the malicious behaviour that she had attributed to them in her hallucinations, she felt somewhat ill at ease with them.

'Everyone's missed you up on the second floor,' Phil told Susan as they wheeled her stretcher into the hall.

'Lots of glum faces up there,' Murf said.

'Oh, I'll bet,' she said.

'It's true,' Phil said.

'The place seems so grim without you,' Murf said.

'Like a dungeon,' Phil said.

'Like a cemetery,' said Murf.

'Like a hospital,' said Phil.

'It *is* a hospital,' she said, playing along with them in an effort to keep her spirits up as they approached the elevators.

'You're absolutely right,' Murf told her.

'It *is* a hospital, of course,' Phil said.

'But with you around, fair lady— '

' —it seems warmer, brighter— '

' —like a resort hotel— '

' —in some country where it's always sunny— '

' —someplace exciting, exotic— '

' —like Mesopotamia.'

They reached the elevators, and Susan held her breath.

'Phil, I told you yesterday – there isn't a Mesopotamia any more.'

One of them pushed the elevator call button.

'Then where have I been going every winter, Murf? My travel agent always told me it was Mesopotamia.'

'I'm afraid you've got a crooked travel agent, Phil. You've probably been going to New Jersey.'

The elevator doors opened, and Susan stiffened, but there were no dead men waiting.

'No, I'm sure I've never been to New Jersey, Murf.'

'Lucky for New Jersey, Phil.'

Dammit, I can't live like this! Susan thought grimly as they rolled her out of the elevator and into the second-floor corridor. I just can't go through life being suspicious and frightened of everyone I meet. I can't cope with this constant expectation that one horror or another will pop out at me from behind every door and from around every corner.

How could *anyone* possibly get through an entire

233

life that was like a continuous, exhausting ride through an especially nasty, gruesome, carnival funhouse?

Why would anyone *want* to get through such a life?

* * *

Jessica Seiffert was gone.

The curtain was open.

An orderly was stripping off the last of the soiled sheets and dropping them into a laundry cart. In answer to Susan's question, he said, 'Mrs. Seiffert took a turn for the worse. They had to rush her down to intensive care.'

'I'm sorry to hear that.'

'Well, everyone expected it,' the orderly said. 'But it's still a shame. She's such a nice lady.'

Susan *was* sorry for Jessica Seiffert, but she was also relieved that her roommate was gone.

It was nice to be able to see the window, even though the day was gray and misty and teetering on the edge of another storm.

* * *

Ten minutes after Susan had been delivered to her room by Phil and Murf, as she was sitting in bed, adjusting the covers around her, Mrs. Baker came in with a tray of food.

'You missed breakfast this morning. And honey, you just can't afford to skip a single meal. You're

234

not well padded like I am. I could afford to skip a whole week of meals!'

'I'm starved.'

'I don't doubt it for a minute,' the nurse said, putting the tray down on the bed table. 'How do you feel, kid?'

'Like a pincushion,' Susan said, aware of a dull pain in her back, a souvenir of the spinal tap.

'Did Dr. McGee handle most things himself?'

'Yes.'

'Then it could have been worse,' Mrs. Baker said, removing the lid from the tray. 'There are some around here who're not as gentle as McGee.'

'Yes, but I'm afraid he's going to be late to his office.'

'He doesn't have office hours Wednesday mornings,' the nurse said. 'Just five hours in the afternoon.'

'Oh, and by the way,' Susan said, 'I saw so little of you yesterday that I forgot to ask you how everything went on Monday night.'

Mrs. Baker blinked, and her forehead creased in perplexity. 'Monday night?'

'How was your date? You know – the bowling and the hamburger dinner?'

For a couple of seconds, the nurse appeared to have no idea what Susan was talking about. Then her eyes suddenly brightened. 'Oh! The date. Of course. My jolly big lumberman.'

'The one with the shoulders to measure a doorway,' Susan said, quoting what Mrs. Baker herself had said on Monday when describing her beau.

'And those big, hard, *gentle* hands,' the nurse said rather wistfully.

Susan grinned. 'That's better. I didn't think you could've forgotten *him*.'

'It was a night to remember.'

'I'm glad to hear it.'

A mischievous expression came over Mrs. Baker's face. She said, 'We knocked down all the pins. And I don't just mean at the bowling alley, either.'

Susan laughed. 'Why, Mrs. Baker, you've got a randy streak in you wider than I'd have thought.'

The nurse's merry eyes gleamed behind her white-framed glasses. 'Life's not very tasty if you don't add just a dash of spice now and then.'

Unfolding her paper napkin and tucking it into the collar of her pajamas – she had changed into her recently laundered blue pair after returning from downstairs – Susan said, 'I suspect you flavor it with more than just a *dash* of spice.'

'Whole tablespoons sometimes.'

'I knew it. Mrs. Baker, you're a regular Sybarite.'

'No. I'm a Methodist, but Methodists know how to have fun, too. Now, you eat everything on that tray, honey. It's really good to see you starting to fill out in the face a little. We don't want any backsliding.'

For the next half hour, Susan ate her late breakfast and watched the turbulent sky that roiled beyond the window. Masses of clouds, painted a dozen shades of gray, raced from horizon to horizon.

A few minutes after eleven o'clock, Jeff McGee came by. 'Sorry I've been so long. We had the lab results some time ago, but I've been up in the intensive-care ward with Jessie Seiffert.'

'How's she doing?'

'Fading fast.'

'That's a shame.'

'Yeah. It's a shame she has to die. But since there wasn't anything we could do for her, I'm glad she's finally going downhill in a hurry. She was always an active woman, and it was hard on her to be bedridden, harder than it might have been on a lot of other people. I hated to see her lingering and suffering these past few weeks.' He shook his head sadly, then snapped his fingers as a thought struck him. 'Say, something occurred to me when I was with Jessie, upstairs in intensive care. You know why you might have hallucinated Jerry Stein's corpse when you were actually looking at Jessie? I think there was a trigger that did it for you, that set you off.'

'Trigger?'

'Yes. Initials.'

'Initials,' Susan echoed, not sure what he was talking about.

'That's right. Don't you see? Jerry Stein and Jessica Seiffert – both JS.'

'Oh. I hadn't noticed that.'

'Maybe you didn't notice it on a *conscious* level. But nothing escapes the subconscious; it's too damned observant. I'll bet you were aware of it subconsciously. It might have been the coincidence of their initials that fixated you on the curtain and made you so afraid of it. If that's the case, then perhaps none of your attacks is merely a random, spontaneous event. Maybe all of them were triggered by one thing or another, unimportant little events and observations that harkened back to some memory connected with the House of Thunder; and once that connection was made on an unconscious level, maybe the hallucinatory episode followed like clockwork.'

He was visibly excited by the theory, and Susan said, 'If what you say is true, what difference does it make?'

'I'm not entirely sure. I haven't had much time to think about all the ramifications. But I suspect it could be important in helping me decide whether or not the official diagnosis should come down on the side of a physical cause.'

She didn't like what she was hearing.

Frowning, she said, 'If my hallucinations aren't merely random, spontaneous sparks thrown off by an injured brain, then perhaps the root cause of them isn't physical at all. Is that what you're saying? If the visions are triggered by some subtle psychological mechanism, then possibly the entire problem is best left to a psychiatrist.'

'No, no, no,' McGee said quickly, making a placating gesture with his hands. 'We don't have enough data to leap to conclusions like that. We still have to pursue a physical explanation because that seems by far the most likely possibility, considering that you *did* suffer a head injury and were in a coma for more than three weeks.'

Susan wanted very much to believe that her problem was entirely physical, nothing more than the expected consequences of vital tissue damage. If it was a tiny blood clot in the brain, a lesion, or some other malady of the flesh, medical science would take care of it posthaste. She trusted medical science precisely because it *was* a science. She *distrusted* psychiatry because, to her way of thinking, which had been shaped by her education as a physicist, psychiatry was not really a science at all; she thought of it as little more than voodoo.

She shook her head adamantly. 'You're wrong about the trigger effect of the initials. JS. It wasn't that. This isn't a psychological condition.'

'I tend to agree with you,' he said. 'But we can't rule out any possibilities at this stage.'

'*I* can. I've ruled it out.'

'But I *can't*. I'm a doctor. And a doctor's got to remain objective.'

For the first time since entering the room, he took her hand, and his touch was wonderfully soothing.

Squeezing his hand, she said, 'What were the results of the spinal?'

With his free hand, McGee pulled thoughtfully

on his ear. 'The protein analysis showed no abnormalities. Then we did a blood count. If there had been too many red cells, that would've told us that there was bleeding either inside the skull, at the base of the brain, or somewhere along the spine.'

'But the red count was normal,' Susan said, anticipating him.

'Yes. Now, if there was an abundance of white cells, we'd know there was a cerebral or spinal infection.'

'But the white count was normal, too.'

'Yes.'

Susan felt as if she were being backed into a corner by an advancing army of cold, hard facts. You're as healthy as a teenager, the facts seemed to be shouting at her. *Your body hasn't betrayed you. Your brain hasn't betrayed you, either. It's your* mind *that has gone rotten. You're not physically ill, Susan. There's no organic problem. You're just plain crazy; that's all. Nuts. You're as nutty as a jumbo-size can of Planter's Party Mix.*

She tried very hard not to listen to those invidious inner voices, tried to tune out the increasingly loud chorus of self-doubt, self-loathing, and confusion.

Plaintively, she said, 'Didn't the spinal show *anything* out of the ordinary?'

'Not a thing. We even analyzed the sugar content of your spinal fluid. There are some diseases in which bacteria eat that particular sugar, so a low count would have set off alarms. But your spinal sugar is two-thirds the level of your blood sugar, and that's also normal.'

'Sounds as if I'm a textbook example of a thirty-two-year-old woman in perfect health,' she said with heavy irony.

McGee was clearly troubled by the difficulty he was having in pinpointing her illness. 'No. *Something* is wrong somewhere.'

'What?'

'I don't know.'

'That's not terribly reassuring.'

'We'll just keep looking.'

'I have a feeling I'm going to be here a long time.'

'No. We'll find it soon. We have to.'

'But how?'

'Well, first of all, I'm taking the EEG printouts, the X rays, and all the lab data home with me. I'm going to go over everything one more time, with a magnifying glass if I have to. Maybe we didn't look carefully this morning. Maybe the answer was there and we just failed to spot it. Some little thing that was easily overlooked . . . some subtle anomaly . . .'

'And what if you still don't find anything?'

He hesitated, and he looked worried as he finally said, 'Well, then . . . there's another test we can run.'

'Tell me,' she said.

'It's not a simple procedure.'

'I could figure that much just by taking a look at your face,' she said.

'A cerebral angiogram. It's a diagnostic technique that we usually reserve for functionally impaired stroke victims who've got to undergo brain surgery for clot removal or for the repair of a hemorrhaged blood vessel.'

'What's it entail?'

'We'd inject a radiopague substance into your bloodstream, into an artery between the heart and the brain, which means in the neck, and that isn't pleasant.'

'I guess not.'

'There's pain involved.'

Susan put one hand to the side of her neck and rubbed the tender flesh uneasily.

McGee said, 'And the procedure isn't entirely risk-free. A small percentage of patients suffer complications leading to death subsequent to an angiogram. Notice that I didn't say it was a "tiny" percentage or an "infinitesimal" percentage.'

'You said it was a "small" percentage, and I gather that means it's not large, but that it's also not small enough to be considered insignificant.'

'Exactly.'

'What we're talking about is a more sophisticated series of cranial X rays,' she said. 'Is that right?'

'Yes. As soon as the radiopague tracer reaches the blood vessels in the brain, we take a long, rapid sequence of X rays, following its dispersal. That gives us the most detailed look at your cerebral circulatory system that we could hope to get. We're able to clearly define the size and shape of all the veins and arteries. We can pinpoint a clot, a hemorrhage, a bulge in an arterial wall, virtually anything, no matter how small it might be.'

'Sounds like just the thing for getting to the bottom of my problem,' Susan said.

'Ordinarily, I wouldn't even resort to an angiogram unless the patient had serious functional impairment – loss of speech, loss of motor control, partial paralysis – or was suffering from apopletic stroke-related mental confusion of such severity that not even a hope of leading a normal life existed.'

'Sounds like me,' she said glumly.

'Oh, no. Not at all. There's an enormous difference between stroke-related mental disorientation and the kind of hallucinations you've been having. Believe it or not, your condition is the less life-disrupting of the two.'

For a long moment, neither of them said anything. McGee stood beside the bed, and Susan sat there in it, feeling small and weak, and they just held hands in silence.

Then she said, 'Suppose you still don't find anything when you look over the X rays and lab reports again this evening.'

'Suppose.'

'Would you order an angiogram for me then?'

He closed his eyes and thought about it for a moment.

Susan saw that there was a nervous tic in his left eyelid.

Finally he said, 'I just don't know. It depends on so many things. I'd have to consider the old, physician's credo: "If you can't do any good, at least don't do any harm." I mean, if there's not the slightest indication that your problem is physical, then scheduling an angiogram would be— '

'It *is* physical,' Susan insisted.

'Even if there was evidence of a physical cause, sufficient evidence to justify putting you through an angiogram, I'd want to wait a few days until you were a little stronger.'

She licked her lips, which felt dry and rough. 'And if we did go through with an angiogram, and if it didn't reveal any physical damage to the brain, and if the hallucinations continued anyway – what then?' she asked.

'We'd have exhausted every avenue offered by traditional medicine.'

'Surely not.'

'We'd have to rule out a diagnosis of physical cause and start looking elsewhere.'

'No.'

'Susan, we'd simply have to.'

'No.'

'Consulting a psychiatrist is nothing that you should be ashamed of. It's only an— '

'I'm not ashamed of it,' she said. 'I just don't

believe it would do any good.'

'Modern psychiatry has achieved— '

'No,' she said, cutting him off, afraid even to consider the possibility of submitting to years of therapy, years and years of continuing hallucinations. 'No. There must be something wrong that you can locate, something you can *do*. There must be. There *has* to be.'

He dropped the subject of psychiatry. 'I'll do my best.'

'That's all I'm asking.'

'I'm not licked yet.'

'Didn't think you were.'

Apparently he saw that her lips were dry, for he said, 'Like a drink of water?'

'Yes, please.'

He poured it for her, and she drank all of it in several long, greedy swallows; then he returned the empty glass to the tray on the nightstand.

'Have you remembered anything at all about your job?' McGee asked.

His question startled her. The last time she had given a thought to the Milestone Corporation or to her job there was when she had telephoned Philip Gomez in Newport Beach on Monday morning. More than two days ago. Since then, she had pushed the entire subject to the back of her mind, had thrown a dark cloth over it – as if she were frightened of it. And she *was* frightened. Now, the mere mention of Milestone sent a chill through her. Furthermore, she was suddenly stricken by the strange and unnerving conviction that her bizarre hallucinations – the encounters with dead men – were all somehow directly related to her work at Milestone.

McGee evidently sensed her fear, for he leaned closer to her and said, 'Susan? What's wrong?'

She told him what she had been thinking: that there was a link between the Milestone Corporation and her hallucinations.

'Link?' McGee asked. He was clearly perplexed. 'What sort of link?'

'I haven't the faintest idea. But I *feel* it.'

'Are you suggesting that you were having similar hallucinations *prior* to your auto accident?'

'No, no. How could that be?'

'You mean that you aren't sure if you were or weren't having them prior to the accident.'

'I wasn't. Definitely not.'

'You don't sound certain enough to please me.'

So she thought about it for a minute.

He watched her with keen anticipation.

At last she said, 'Yes. Yes, I'm sure. These attacks have come only since the accident. If I'd had them before, I wouldn't have forgotten them. Not something like this.'

McGee cocked his head and regarded her at an angle. 'If there's a physical cause of your condition – which is what both you and I want very much to believe – then it must be an injury arising out of the car crash.'

'I know.'

'It can't be something that was sparked by your work at Milestone. Because if it's caused by the pressure of your work or something like that— '

' —then we'd be talking about a psychological condition,' she finished for him. 'A nervous breakdown.'

'Yes.'

'Which it isn't.'

'Then how can there be a link to Milestone?'

She frowned. 'I don't know.'

'So you must be wrong.'

'I guess so. But I still . . .'

'Feel frightened?'

'Yes.'

'That's easily explained,' McGee said. 'You're afraid of the Milestone Corporation for pretty much the same reason that you were afraid of the drawn curtain around Jessie's bed. You couldn't see what was on the other side of that curtain, which gave your imagination a chance to run wild. And your job has that same quality of the unknown about it. There's a curtain drawn around that part of your life, and because you can't see what lays beyond it, your imagination is given an opportunity to supply you with frightening possibilities. Perhaps because of an almost immeasurably small amount of brain damage, you're fixated on the House of Thunder and on what happened to you in that cavern; so it follows that your imagination, whenever it *does* have a chance to run wild, invariably harkens back to those events of thirteen years ago.

247

Your hallucinations have nothing to do with your job; they can't have anything to do with it; because Milestone has nothing to do with the House of Thunder. You're just trying to tie them all together because . . . well, that's what it means to be psychologically *obsessed* with a single event in your life. Do you understand?'

'Yes.'

'Yet the Milestone Corporation still frightens you.'

'Every time you mention the name, a cold wave passes through me,' she admitted.

She could see goose bumps on her arm where the sleeve of her pajamas had slid back.

McGee had been leaning against the bed all this time. Now he boosted himself up and sat on the edge of it, still holding her hand.

'I know it scares you,' he said sympathetically. 'Your hand is freezing. It wasn't cold at all when I first took hold of it, but the moment we started talking about your job, it just turned to ice.'

'You see?'

'Yes, but those cold waves, those feelings of suspicion directed toward Milestone, all of those things are just facets of your obsession. This fear is like a miniature episode, a very small version of the kind of attack in which you thought you saw Jerry Stein's corpse. You have no logical reason to be afraid of Milestone or of anyone who works there.'

She nodded, dismayed by the ever-complicating nature of her condition. 'I guess I don't.'

'You *know* you don't.'

Susan sighed. 'You know what I wish? I wish there were such things as ghosts. I wish this *were* a case of dead men returning from the grave to take revenge on me, like something out of one of those EC Horror Comics. I mean, Jeez, how much *easier* it would be to deal with *that*. No spinal taps. No angiograms. No sharply clawed little self-doubts tearing me apart from inside. All I'd have to do is call up a priest and ask him, please, to come over here and chase these nasty demonic spirits all the way back to Hell, where they belong.'

McGee frowned at her, and there was a troubled expression in his eyes when he said, 'Hey, I don't think I like to hear you talking that way.'

'Oh, don't worry,' Susan quickly assured him, 'I'm not going to go mystical on you. I'm perfectly aware that there ain't no such things as ghosts. Besides, if there were ghosts, and if that's what these things were that've been bothering me lately, then they'd be transparent, wouldn't they? Or they'd look like a bunch of bed sheets with eye holes cut out of them. *That's* a ghost. They wouldn't be warm-skinned and solid like the things I've been running into and away from lately.' She smiled at him. 'Hey, I know why you're so worried all of a sudden! You're afraid that if it *did* turn out to be ghosts, then I wouldn't need you any more. Doctors don't perform exorcisms, right?'

He smiled, too. 'Right.'

'You're afraid that I'd cast you aside, just throw

you over in favor of some priest with a prayer book in one hand and a golden crucifix in the other.'

'Would you do that to me?' he asked.

'Never. For heaven's sake, too many things could go wrong if I relied on a priest. Like . . . what if I entrusted myself to a priest who'd lost his faith? Or what if I went to a Catholic priest for help – and then the ghosts all turned out to be Protestants? What good would an exorcism do me then?'

She was certain that McGee hadn't been conned by her forced good humor; he knew that she was still depressed and scared. But he played along with her anyway, for he apparently sensed, as she had done, that she'd dwelt on her problems far too much this morning and that chewing them over any longer would be harmful to her. She needed a change of subject, needed to kid around for a while, and McGee obliged.

'Well,' he said, 'as I understand it, the exorcism is supposed to work regardless of the spirit's religious affiliation in any prior life it might have lived. After all, what kind of mess would the supernatural world be in if it had to take logic into account? I mean, if Catholic exorcisms didn't work against Protestant ghosts, then a crucifix wouldn't repel a Jewish vampire.'

'In that case, how *would* you repel a Jewish vampire?'

'You'd probably have to brandish a mezuzah at him instead of a crucifix.'

250

'Or maybe you could just offer him a ham dinner,' Susan said.

'That would only repel him if he was a devout, practicing Jewish vampire. And then what about Moslem vampires?'

'See?' she said. 'It's all too complicated. I can't possibly fire you and hire a priest.'

'Ah, it's so nice to know I'm needed.'

'Oh, you're definitely needed,' she assured him. 'I need you. I *do* need you.' She heard her voice change abruptly as she was speaking, heard the bantering tone evaporate in the intense heat of her true feelings for him. 'There's no doubt about *that*.' She was as startled by her own boldness as McGee appeared to be, but she couldn't stop herself. She could only plunge ahead recklessly, speaking too fast, in too much of a rush to express what had been on her mind and in her heart for the past day or two. 'I need you, Jeff McGee. And if you want me to, I'll sit here all day, saying it over and over again, until my voice wears out.'

He stared at her, his beautiful blue eyes a darker and more intense blue than she had ever seen them before.

She tried to read those eyes, but she couldn't tell a thing about the thoughts behind them.

As she waited for him to respond to her, Susan wondered if she had done something stupid. Had she misinterpreted his treatment of her and his reactions to her during the past few days? Where she had thought she'd seen romantic interest – was

251

there really only doctorly concern? If she had mistaken his usual bedside manner for special interest, the next few minutes were going to be among the most socially awkward in her life.

She wished desperately that she could call back the words she had spoken, roll back the clock just one minute.

Then McGee kissed her.

It was not like any of the kisses that he had planted on her cheek or on the corner of her mouth during the past couple of days. There was nothing chaste or timid about it this time. He kissed her full upon the lips, tenderly yet forcefully, both giving and taking, seeking and demanding. She responded to him with an instancy and with a heat that were not at all like her; this time, there was no trace of the ice maiden in her, nothing whatsoever held in reserve, no part of her that stopped to think about keeping control of the situation and of the relationship that might follow. This would be different from all other love affairs she'd ever known. This time she, too, was being swept away. This kiss involved not only lips and teeth and tongues, but passion, hunger, need. He put his hands on her face, one on each side of her face, holding her gently but firmly, as if he was afraid that she would reconsider her commitment and would pull back from him – as if he could not bear the thought of her doing so.

When at last the kiss ended and they drew apart a few inches to look at each other, to decide how the kiss had changed them, Susan saw a mixture of emotions in McGee's face: happiness, surprise, awe, confusion, embarrassment, and more.

His breathing was fast.

Hers was faster.

For a moment she thought she saw something else in his eyes, too; something . . . darker. For only a second or two, she thought she saw fear in his eyes, just a flicker of it, a fluttering bat-wing apprehension.

Fear?

Before she could decide what that might mean, before she could even be sure that she had actually seen fear in his eyes, the silence was broken, and the spell, too.

'You surprised me,' Jeff said. 'I didn't . . .'

'I was afraid I'd offended you or . . .'

'No, no. I just . . . didn't realize . . .'

'. . . that both of us . . .'

'. . . the feeling was mutual.'

'I thought I understood and . . . Well, the signals you were sending out seemed . . .'

'. . . the kiss put an end to any doubts that you . . .'

'God, yes!'

'What a kiss,' he said.

'Some kiss.'

He kissed her again, but only briefly, glancing at the door with evident uneasiness. She couldn't blame him for holding back. He was a doctor, after all, and she was a patient; and necking with the patient was a couple of thousand miles below the level of decorum that was expected of a physician. She wanted to throw her arms around him and draw him tight against her; she wanted to possess him and be possessed by him. But she knew this was neither the right time nor the right place, and she let him draw back from her.

She said, 'How long have you . . .'

'I don't know. Maybe even before you came out of the coma.'

'Before that? Loved me . . . ?'

'You were so beautiful.'

'But you didn't even know me then.'

'So it probably really wasn't love at that point. But something. Even then, I felt *something*.'

'I'm glad.'

'And after you came out of the coma . . .'

'You found out what a charmer I am, and you were hooked.'

He smiled. 'Exactly. And I found out that you had what Mrs. Baker calls "moxie." I like a woman with moxie.'

For a few seconds they were silent again, just staring at each other.

Then she said. 'Can it really happen this fast?'

'It has.'

'There's so much to talk about.'

'A million things,' he said.

'A billion,' she said. 'I hardly know a thing about your background.'

'It's shady.'

'I want to know everything there is to know about you,' she said, holding one of his hands in both of hers. 'Everything. But I guess . . . here, in this place . . .'

'It's too awkward here.'

'Yes. It's hardly the right place for new lovers to become better acquainted with each other.'

'I think we ought to keep our relationship on a strictly doctor-patient basis as long as you've got to be here. Later, when you're feeling better, when you've been discharged and our time together isn't so public . . .'

'That's probably wise,' she said, although she wanted to touch him and to be touched by him in ways that doctors and patients didn't touch each other. 'But does it have to be *strictly* doctor-patient? Can't we bend a little? Can't you at least kiss me on the cheek now and then?'

Jeff smiled and pretended to think hard about it. 'Well . . . uh . . . let's see now . . . so far as I remember, the Hippocratic Oath doesn't contain any admonishment against kissing patients on the cheek.'

'So how about right now?'

He kissed her on the cheek.

'Seriously,' he said, 'I think the most important thing now is for both of us to concentrate our energies on getting you well. If we can make you well again, then everything else – everything else there might be between us – will follow.'

255

'You've given me a new motivation for beating this thing,' Susan said.

'And you *will* beat it, too,' he said in a tone of voice that admitted to no doubt. '*We'll* beat it. Together.'

Looking at him now, Susan realized that she *had* seen fear in his eyes a couple of minutes ago. Although he would not express any pessimistic thoughts to her, there had to be a part of him that wondered if they really could find a way to put an end to her terrifying hallucinations. He wasn't a fool; he knew that failure was a lurking possibility. Fear? Yes. Yes, he had every right to be afraid. He was afraid that he had fallen in love with a woman who was on a fast train to a nervous breakdown or, worse, to the madhouse at the end of the line.

'Don't worry,' she said.

'I'm not worried.'

'I'm strong.'

'I know.'

'Strong enough to make it – with your help.'

He kissed her on the cheek again.

Susan thought of what she'd said earlier about ghosts. She really did wish there were such things. If only her problem were that simple. Just ghosts. Just walking dead men who could be harried back to their graves by the recital of the proper prayers and by the liberal sprinkling of holy water. How nice it would be to discover that the problem was not within her, that the source lay outside of her.

Knowing it was impossible, she nonetheless wished that they would find proof that the phantom Harch and the other phantoms were all real, that ghosts were real, and that she had never been sick at all.

A short while later, she got her wish – or something rather like it.

12

Lunch came so soon after her late breakfast that Susan couldn't finish everything, but she ate enough to win Mrs. Baker's approval.

An hour and a half later, she was taken downstairs for her second physical therapy session with Mrs. Atkinson. A new pair of orderlies came for her, but, happily, neither of them had a face from out of her past.

At the elevators, she expected the worst. Nothing happened.

She had not hallucinated since last night, when she had seen Jerry Stein's corpse in Jessica Seiffert's bed. As the orderlies wheeled her along the first-floor corridor toward the PT Department, she counted up the hours since that attack: almost sixteen.

Almost sixteen hours of peace.

Maybe there would never be another attack. Maybe the visions would stop as suddenly as they had begun.

The therapy session with Florence Atkinson was

slightly more strenuous than the one Susan had been through yesterday, but the massage felt even better this time, and the shower was no less of a treat than it had been yesterday.

At the elevators once more, on the way back upstairs, Susan held her breath.

Again, nothing bad happened to her.

More than seventeen hours had passed now.

She had the feeling that she would be forever free of the hallucinations if she could only get through one entire day without them; one ghost-free day might be all she needed to cleanse her mind and her soul.

Less than seven hours to go.

When she got back to her room from the PT Department, two bouquets of fresh flowers were waiting for her; crysanthemums, carnations, roses, and sprays of baby's breath. There were cards attached to both arrangements. The first card urged her to get well soon, and was signed, 'As ever, Phil Gomez.' The second one said, 'We all miss you here at the slave pit.' It was signed by a number of people. Susan recognized some of their names, but only because Phil Gomez had mentioned them on the telephone Monday morning. She stared at the list: Ella Haversby, Eddie Gilroy, Anson Brecken-ridge, Tom Kavinsky . . . Nine names altogether. She couldn't summon up a face to go with any one of them.

As on every other occasion when the Milestone Corporation had come to mind, the mere thought of it was sufficient to send a chill through her.

And she didn't know why.

She was determined to keep a positive attitude and let nothing disturb her, so she turned her mind away from Milestone. At least the flowers were pretty. She could enjoy them without thinking about where they had come from.

In bed again, she tried to read a book but discovered that the therapy session and the hot shower had made her sleepy. She napped. She didn't dream.

When she awoke, the room was playing host to a large party of shadows. Outside, the sun had just crested the mountains; although true sunset was still some time away, the cloud-darkened day was already slouching toward evening. She yawned, sat up, wiped at her matted eyes with the back of one hand.

The second bed was still empty.

According to the nightstand clock, it was four-thirty. Now nineteen hours since her most recent attack.

She wondered if the blossoming of her relationship with Jeff McGee was responsible for keeping the ghosts at bay. Having someone to love and *being* loved: that couldn't hurt. She hadn't wanted to believe that her problem was psychological, but now it looked as if her troubles might be behind her, she was more willing to consider psychological explanations. Perhaps Jeff's love was all the medicine she had needed.

She got out of bed, stepped into her slippers, and made her way to the bathroom. Snapped on the light.

Jerry Stein's decapitated head was resting on the closed commode seat.

Susan stood on the white ceramic tiles, in the harsh white fluorescent light, her face equally as white as anything in the snow-white bathroom; she didn't want to believe her eyes.

It's not real.

The head was in the same terrible state of decomposition that it had been in last night, when Jerry had risen out of Jessica Seiffert's bed, moaning Susan's name through lips that glistened with corruption. The skin was still gray and gray-green. Both corners of the mouth were clotted with thick suppuration. Hideous blisters on the upper lip. And around the swollen nose. Dark, bubbled spots of decay at the corners of the eyes. Eyes open wide. Bulging from their sockets. They were opaque, sheathed in pearly cataracts, as they had been last night, and the whites of them were badly discolored, yellowish and streaked with blood. But at least these were unseeing eyes, as the eyes of a dead man ought to be: inanimate, blind. The head had been severed from the rest of the corpse with savage glee; a ragged mantle of flesh lay like a rumpled, frilly collar at the termination of the neck. Something small and bright lay twisted in a fold of that gray neck-skin, something that caught the light and gleamed. A pendant. A religious pendant. It was the small, gold-plated mezuzah that Jerry Stein had always worn.

It's not real, it's not real, it's not real . . .

That three-word charm seemed even less effective than usual; if anything, the grisly head became more vivid, more *real*, the longer that she stared at it.

Rigid with horror, yet determined to dispel the vision, Susan shuffled one step closer to the commode.

The dead eyes stared through her, unaware of her, fixed on something in another world.

It isn't real.

She reached out to touch the gray face. Hesitated.

What if the face came alive just as she put her hand against it? What if those graveyard eyes rolled and focused on her? What if that gaping, ruined mouth suddenly snapped at her, bit her fingers, and wouldn't let go? What if—

Stop it! she told herself angrily.

She heard a strange wheezing noise – and realized that it was the sound of her own labored breathing.

Relax, she said to herself. Dammit, Susan Kathleen Thorton, you're too old to believe in this nonsense.

But the head didn't fade away like a mirage.

Finally she pushed her trembling hand forward, through the air that seemed as thick and resistant as water. She touched the dead man's cheek.

It felt solid.

It felt real.

Cold and greasy.

She jerked her hand back, shuddering and gagging.

The cataract-sheathed eyes didn't move.

Susan looked at the fingertips with which she had touched the head, and she saw that they were wet with silvery slime. The scum of decomposition.

Sickened almost to the point of vomiting, Susan frantically wiped her sticky fingers on one leg of her blue pajamas, and she saw that the disgusting slime was staining the fabric.

It isn't real, isn't real, isn't, isn't . . .

Although she dutifully repeated that incantation, which was supposed to summon sanity, she had lost the courage required to continue with this confrontation. She wanted only to get the hell out of the bathroom, into the hospital room, into the corridor, down to the nurses' station by the elevators, where there was help. She turned—

—and froze.

Ernest Harch was standing in the open bathroom doorway, blocking her escape.

'No,' she said thickly.

Harch grinned. He stepped into the bathroom with her and closed the door behind him.

He isn't real.

'Surprise,' he said in that familiar, low, gravelly voice.

He can't hurt me.

'Bitch,' he said.

Harch was no longer masquerading as William Richmond, the hospital patient. The pajamas and bathrobe had been discarded. Now he was wearing the clothes that he had worn in the House of Thunder on the night he had murdered Jerry Stein, thirteen years ago. Black shoes, black socks. Black jeans. A very dark blue shirt, almost black. She remembered that outfit because, in the House of Thunder, in the sputtering candlelight and the glow of the flashlights, he had reminded her of a Nazi in an old war movie. An SS man. Gestapo. Whatever the ones were who dressed all in black. His square face, his perfectly square features, pale yellow hair, ice-colored eyes – all of those things contributed to the image of a cold-blooded storm trooper, an image which, in life, he had always seemed to cultivate not only consciously but with care, with attention to detail, with a certain perverse pleasure.

'Do you like my little gift?' Harch asked, pointing to the head on the commode seat.

She couldn't speak.

'I know how much you loved your Jewboy,' Harch said, his cold voice filled with an ice-hard hatred. 'So I thought I'd bring a piece of him back to you. Something for you to remember him by. Wasn't that thoughtful of me?' He laughed softly.

The power of speech returned to Susan with a jolt, and words burst from her: 'You're dead, damn you, dead! You told me so yourself. You're dead.'

Don't play along with this, she told herself des-

265

perately. For God's sake, listen to what you just said. Don't step into the hallucination willingly; back away from it.

'Yes,' he said. 'Of course I'm dead.'

She shook her head. 'I won't listen to this. You're not here. You're not real.'

He stepped forward, farther into the small room.

She was backed against the wall, with the sink on her left side, the commode on her right. Nowhere to run.

Jerry Stein's dead eyes stared into space, oblivious of Harch's arrival.

One of Harch's strong hands snapped out, quick as a lashing whip, and seized Susan's left wrist before she knew what he was doing.

She tried to pull loose; couldn't.

Her mouth had gone as dry as ashes. Her tongue cleaved to the roof of her burned-out mouth.

Harch held her hand in a viciously tight grip. Grinning down at her, he dragged her to him – her slippers scraping on the tile – and he pressed her captive hand firmly against his slab-solid, rock-muscled chest.

'Do I *feel* real enough to suit you?' he demanded.

She sucked air. The weight of the indrawn breath seemed tremendous, sufficient to bring her crashing to the floor and on down, down into darkness.

No! she thought, terrified of surrendering to unconsciousness, afraid that she would wake up a madwoman. Mustn't pass out, for God's sake. Got to fight this. Got to fight it with all my heart.

266

'Do I *feel* real, you bitch? Do I? How do you like the way I feel?'

In the fluorescent light, his gray eyes, usually the color of dirty ice, looked almost white now, bright and utterly alien – just as they had looked that night in the House of Thunder, in the glow of the candles.

He rubbed Susan's hand back and forth across his big chest. The fabric had a coarse feel, and the buttons on the shirt were cold against Susan's skin.

Buttons? Would she actually imagine that she could feel the buttons – a tiny detail of that kind – in a *vision*? Would hallucinatory images be this vivid, this concrete, this thoroughly detailed?

'*Now* do you think I'm here?' Harch asked, grinning broadly but mirthlessly.

Somehow she found the strength to speak and to deny him one more time. Her dry tongue peeled off the powdery roof of her mouth with a sound she could almost hear, and she said, 'No. Not here. Not here.'

'*No?*'

'You aren't real.'

'What a complete bitch!'

'You can't hurt me.'

'We'll see about that, you little bitch. Oh, yeah, we'll sure see about *that*.'

Still gripping her left hand, he slid it over his chest, up to his shoulder, down his arm, made her feel his hard, flexed biceps.

Again, she tried to pull loose. And again, she

failed. He was hurting her; his hand was like a steel pincer clenched around her fragile wrist.

He moved her captive hand back to his chest, then down to his flat, muscular belly.

'Am I real? Huh? What do you think? What's your considered opinion, Susan? Am I real?'

Susan felt something crumbling inside her. Hope. Or maybe the last vestiges of her self-control. Or both.

It's only a vision, a sick fantasy generated by a damaged brain. Just an evil vision. Just a vision. It'll be over soon. Very soon. After all, how long can a vision last?

She thought of a frightening answer to her own question: It could last forever; it could last for the rest of her life, until she drew her last breath in some padded room. Why not?

Harch forced her hand onto his crotch.

He was very aroused. Even through his jeans, she could feel the great heat of him. The stiff, thick, pulsing shape of his maleness.

But he's dead.

'Feel *that*?' he demanded lasciviously, with a little laugh, a sneer. 'Is *that* real?'

In the dark turmoil that whirled within her, a mad hilarity began to rise like a feeding shark in a night sea, streaking up toward the precious fragments of her sanity that still bobbled on the surface.

'Friday night, I'll shove this old poker right into you. Do you know what Friday night is? Tenth anniversary of my untimely demise. Ten years ago

268

Friday, that nigger shoved a knife in my throat. So *this* Friday, I'll shove my poker all the way up into you, and then I'll use a knife on *you*.'

A high, silvery giggle tinkled deep within her, and she knew that she dared not let it escape. It was the whooping, bell-clear sickly sweet laughter of madness. If she gave voice to it just once, there would never be an end to it; she would pass the years in a corner, cackling to herself.

Harch let go of her hand.

She snatched it away from his crotch.

He slammed her back against the wall, jarring her bones. Pressed his body against hers. Ground his hips against her. And grinned.

She tried to squirm free of him. She was pinned by his weight, trapped.

'Should've banged that pretty little ass of yours thirteen years ago,' Harch said. 'A nice little gang-bang right there in the goddamned cave. Then we should've slit your throat and dumped you into a sinkhole with the Jewboy.'

He's not real, he can't hurt me, he's not—

No. It wasn't doing a bit of good to chant that stupid litany. He was real, all right. He was *here*.

And, of course, that was impossible.

He was real; he was here; he could hurt her; and he *would* hurt her.

She gave up the struggle to control the situation. She threw her head back and screamed.

Harch leaned away from her, taking his weight off her. He tilted his head, watching her with unconcealed amusement. He was enjoying this, as if her screams were music to him.

No one came to find out why she was screaming. Where were the nurses? The orderlies, the doctors? Why couldn't they hear her? Even with the bathroom door shut, they should be able to hear her screaming.

Harch bent toward her, bringing his face close to hers. His gray eyes were shining like a wild animal's eyes in the beams of a car's headlights.

'Give me a little sample of what I'm going to get from you Friday night,' he said in a sandpapery, wheedling voice. 'Just a kiss. Give me a nice little kiss. Huh? Give your old Uncle Ernie a little kiss.'

Whether or not this was really happening to her, she could not surrender entirely. She couldn't bring herself to kiss him even if it was all a dream. She twisted her head violently to one side, avoiding his lips, then to the other side, as he pursued her mouth with his own.

'You stinking bitch,' he said angrily, finally giving up. 'Saving all your kisses for your Jewboy?' He stepped back from her. He glanced at the head that rested on the commode; he looked at Susan again; at the head; at Susan. His smile was unholy. His voice became sarcastic, tinged with a black glee. 'Saving your kisses for poor old Jerry Stein, are you? Isn't that touching? Such lovely, old-fashioned constancy. Oh, such admirable fidelity. I'm deeply moved. I truly, truly am. Oh, yes, by all means, you must give your virgin kisses only to Jerry.'

Harch turned theatrically toward the moldering head, which was facing partly away from Susan.

No.

He reached for the head.

Susan thought of that rotting countenance and tasted bile in the back of her mouth.

Still yammering about Susan's fidelity, Harch gripped a handful of the lank, brown hair on the grisly head.

Shaking with dread, Susan knew he was going to force her to kiss those cold, oozing lips.

Heart exploding, she saw an opportunity to escape, a slim chance, and she took it without hesitation; screamed; bolted. Harch was turned away from her, lifting the head off the commode. She pushed past him, squeezed between him and the sink, fumbled with the doorknob, expecting a hand to fall upon her neck, tore the door open, and burst into the hospital room, from the bright fluorescent light into the dim grayness of late afternoon, throwing the bathroom door shut behind her.

At first she headed for the bed, for the call button that would summon a nurse, but she realized she wouldn't be able to reach it before Harch was upon her, so she whirled the other way, her legs rubbery, almost buckling beneath her, and she stumbled toward the outer door, which was standing open, and beyond which lay the corridor.

Screaming, she reached the doorway just as Mrs. Baker came in from the hall at a trot. They collided; Susan nearly fell; the nurse steadied her.

271

'Honey, what's wrong?'

'In the bathroom.'

'You're soaked with sweat.'

'*In the bathroom!*'

Mrs. Baker slipped a supportive arm around her. Susan sagged against the generously padded woman, welcoming her strength.

'What's in the bathroom, kid?'

'Him.'

'Who?'

'That b-b-bastard.'

Susan shuddered.

'Who?' Mrs. Baker asked again.

'Harch.'

'Oh, no, no, no.'

'Yes.'

'Honey, you're only having a— '

'He's *there*.'

'He isn't real.'

'He *is*.'

'Come on.'

'Where—?'

'Come with me.'

'Oh, no.'

'Come along.'

'Let's get out of here.'

'Come along with me.'

She half coaxed, half carried Susan back into the room.

'But Jerry's head— '

'Jesus, you poor kid.'

272

'—his decapitated head— '

'Nothing's really there.'

'It *is*.'

'This was a bad one, huh?'

'He was going to m-make me k-k-kiss that thing.'

'Here now.'

They were at the closed bathroom door.

'What are you doing?' Susan asked, panicky.

'Let's take a look.'

'*For Christ's sake, what're you doing?*'

Mrs. Baker reached for the doorknob.

'Just showing you there's nothing to be afraid of.'

Susan grabbed the woman's hand. 'No!'

'Nothing to be afraid of,' the nurse repeated soothingly.

'If it was just an hallucination— '

'It was.'

'—then would I have been able to feel the goddamned buttons on his goddamned *shirt*?'

'Susan— '

'And would his disgusting erection have felt so big, so hot, so *real*?'

Mrs. Baker looked baffled.

I'm not making sense to her, Susan thought. To her, I sound and look like a babbling lunatic. For that matter, am I making any sense to *me*?

Suddenly she felt foolish. Defeated.

'Have a look, Susan.'

'Please don't do this to me.'

'It's for your own good.'

273

'Please don't.'

'You'll see it's okay.'

Whimpering now: 'Please . . .'

Mrs. Baker started to open the door.

Susan snapped her eyes shut.

'Look, Susan.'

She squeezed her eyes tightly shut.

'Susan, it's all right.'

'He's still there.'

'No.'

'I can *feel* him.'

'There's no one here but you and me.'

'But . . .'

'Would I lie to you, honey?'

A drop of cold sweat trickled down the back of Susan's neck and slithered like a centipede along her spine.

'Susan, look.'

Afraid to look but equally afraid to keep her eyes closed, she finally did as Mrs. Baker asked.

She looked.

She was standing at the threshold of the bathroom. Bleak fluorescent light. White walls. White sink. White ceramic tile. No sign of Ernest Harch. No staring, rotting head perched on the white commode.

'You see?' Mrs. Baker said cheerily.

'Nothing.'

'Never was.'

'Oh.'

'Now do you feel better?'

274

She felt numb. And very cold.

'Susan?'

'Yeah. Better.'

'You poor kid.'

Depression settled over Susan, as if someone had draped a cloak of lead upon her shoulders.

'Good heavens,' Mrs. Baker said, 'your pajamas are *soaked* with sweat.'

'Cold.'

'I imagine you are.'

'No. The head. Cold and greasy.'

'There was no head.'

'On the commode.'

'No, Susan. There wasn't a head on the commode. That was part of the hallucination.'

'Oh.'

'You *do* realize that?'

'Yeah. Of course.'

'Susan?'

'Hmmm?'

'Are you all right, honey?'

'Sure. I'll be all right. I'll be fine.'

She allowed herself to be led away from the bathroom and back to her bed.

Mrs. Baker switched on the nightstand lamp. The huddling, late-afternoon shadows crept into the corners.

'First of all,' Mrs. Baker said, 'we've got to get you into something dry.'

Susan's spare pajamas, the green pair, had been washed just that morning and were not ready to be worn. Mrs. Baker helped her strip out of the damp blue pair – they really were heavy with perspiration; you could almost wring them out as you would a washcloth – and helped her into a standard-issue hospital gown that laced up the back.

'Isn't that better?' Mrs. Baker asked.

'Isn't it?'

'Susan?'

'Hmmm?'

'I'm worried about you, honey.'

'Don't worry. I just want to rest. I just want to go away for a while.'

'Go away?'

'Just for a little while. Away.'

13

'Susan?'

She opened her eyes and saw Jeff McGee looking down at her, his brow lined with concern.

She smiled and said, 'Hi.'

He smiled, too.

It was funny. The slow reshaping of his face from a frown into a smile seemed to take an incredibly long time. She watched the lines in his flesh rearrange themselves as if she were viewing a slow-motion film.

'How are you feeling?'

His voice was funny, too. It sounded distant, heavy, deeper than it had been before. Each word was drawn out as if she were listening to a phonograph record played at the wrong speed; too slow.

'I'm not feeling too bad,' she said.

'I hear you had another episode.'

'Yeah.'

'Want to tell me about it?'

'No. Boring.'

'I'm sure I wouldn't be bored.'

'Maybe not. But *I* would.'

'It'll help to talk about it.'

'Sleep is what helps.'

'You've been sleeping?'

'A little . . . on and off.'

Jeff turned to someone on the other side of the bed and said, 'Has she been sleeping ever since?'

It was a nurse. Mrs. Baker. She said, 'Dozing. And kind of disassociated like you see.'

'Just tired,' Susan assured them.

Jeff McGee looked down at her again, frowning again.

She smiled at him and closed her eyes.

'Susan,' he said.

'Hmmm?'

'I don't want you to sleep right now.'

'Just for a while.'

She felt as if she were adrift on a warm sea. It was so nice to be relaxed again; lazy.

'No,' Jeff said. 'I want you to talk to me. Don't sleep. Talk to me.'

He touched her shoulder, shook her gently.

She opened her eyes, smiled.

'This isn't good,' he said. 'You mustn't try to escape like this. You know it isn't good.'

She was perplexed. 'Sleep isn't good?'

'Not right now.'

' "Sleep ravels up the knitted sleeve of care," ' she misquoted in a thick voice.

And closed her eyes.

'Susan?'

'In a while,' she murmured. 'In a while . . .'

* * *

'Susan?'

'Hmmm?'

'I'm going to give you an injection.'

'Okay.'

Something clinked softly.

'To make you feel better.'

'I feel okay,' she said drowsily.

'To make you more alert.'

'Okay.'

Coolness on her arm. The odor of alcohol.

'It'll sting but only for a second.'

'Okay,' she said.

The needle pierced her skin. She flinched.

'There you go, all finished.'

'Okay,' she said.

'You'll feel better soon.'

'Okay.'

* * *

Susan was sitting up in bed.

Her eyes were grainy, hot, and itchy. She rubbed at them with the back of one hand. Jeff McGee rang for a nurse and ordered some Murine, which he applied to Susan's eyes himself. The drops were cool and soothing.

She had a sour, metallic taste in her mouth. Jeff poured a glass of water for her. She drank all of it, but that didn't do much good.

279

Drowsiness still clung to her, but she was shaking it off minute by minute. She felt a bit cross at Jeff for spoiling her nice sleep.

'What did you give me?' she asked, rubbing one finger over the spot where he had administered the injection into her arm.

'Methylphenidate,' he said.

'What's that?'

'A stimulant. It's good for bringing someone out of a severe depression.'

She scowled. 'I wasn't depressed. Just sleepy.'

'Susan, you were heading toward total withdrawal.'

'Just sleepy,' she said querulously.

'Extreme, narcoleptic-phase depression,' he insisted. He sat on the edge of the bed. 'Now, I want you to tell me what happened to you in the bathroom.'

She sighed. 'Do I have to?'

'Yes.'

'All of it?'

'All of it.'

She was almost completely awake. If she had been suffering from a form of depression that caused her to seek escape in sleep, she certainly wasn't suffering from it any longer. If anything, she felt unnaturally energetic, even a bit edgy.

She thought about Ernest Harch in the bathroom. The severed head on the commode.

She shivered. She looked at Jeff and was warmed by his encouraging smile.

She forced a thin smile of her own. Trying hard to make light of what she'd been through, she said, 'Gather 'round the old campfire, children, and I'll tell you a scary story.'

* * *

She had dinner an hour later than usual. She didn't want anything; she wasn't hungry. However, Jeff insisted that she eat, and he sat with her, making sure that she finished most of the food on her tray.

They talked for more than an hour. His presence calmed her.

She didn't want him to leave, but he couldn't stay all night, of course. For one thing, he intended to go home and spend a couple of hours with her EEG printouts, her cranial X rays, and the lab reports on the spinal workup.

At last the time came for him to go. He said, 'You'll be all right.'

Wanting to be brave for him, braver than she felt, Susan said, 'I know. Don't worry about me. Hey, I've got a lot of moxie, remember?'

He smiled. 'The methylphenidate will start wearing off just about by bedtime. Then you'll get a sedative, a stronger one than you've been getting.'

'I thought you didn't want me to sleep.'

'That was different. That was unnatural sleep, psychological withdrawal. Tonight, I want you to sleep soundly.'

Because when I'm sleeping soundly, Susan thought, I can't have one of my hallucinations, one

281

of my little expeditions into the jungle of insanity. And if I have one more of them . . . one more safari into madness . . . I very likely won't come back. Just be swallowed up by the lions and tigers. One gulp. Gone.

'The nurses will stop in and out all evening,' Jeff said. 'About every fifteen minutes or so. Just to say hello and to let you know you aren't alone.'

'All right.'

'Don't just sit here in silence.'

'I won't.'

'Turn on your TV. Keep your mind active.'

'I will,' she promised.

He kissed her. It was a very nice kiss, tender and sweet. That helped, too.

Then he left, glancing back as he went out the door.

And she was alone.

* * *

She was tense for the rest of the evening, but the time passed without incident. She watched television. She even ate two pieces of candy from the box of chocolates that Jeff had brought her a couple of days ago. Two night-shift nurses – Tina Scolari and Beth Howe – took turns checking in on her, and Susan found that she was even able to joke with them a little.

Later, just after she took the sedative that Jeff had prescribed for her, she felt the need to go to the bathroom. She looked at the closed door with trepidation and considered ringing the nurse to ask for a bedpan. She hesitated for a few minutes, but she grew increasingly ashamed of her timidity. What had happened to the stiff backbone on which she had always prided herself? Where was the famous Thorton pluck? She reached for the call button. Stopped herself. Finally, reluctantly, driven more by her protesting bladder than by her humiliation, she threw back the covers, got out of bed, and went to the bathroom.

Opened the door.

Turned on the light.

No dead men. No severed heads.

'Thank God,' she said, her breath whooshing out of her in relief.

She went inside, closed the door, and went about her business. By the time she had finished and was washing her hands, her heart had slowed to a normal beat.

Nothing was going to happen.

She pulled a paper towel from the wall dispenser and started to dry her hands.

Her eye was suddenly caught by something gleaming on the bathroom floor. It was in the corner, against the wall. Something small and shiny.

She dropped the paper towel in the waste can.

She stepped away from the sink. Bent down. Picked up the glittering object.

She stared at it in disbelief.

Earlier, she had wished that ghosts were real.

And now it appeared as if she'd been granted her wish.

She held the proof in her hand. The thing she had picked up from the floor. A thin gold chain and a gold-plated pendant. Jerry Stein's mezuzah. The same one that she had seen tangled around the ruined throat of his severed head.

PART THREE

Going Into Town . . .

14

Susan went to bed that night without showing the gold mezuzah to anyone.

When she had found it on the bathroom floor, her first impulse had been to run with it straight to the nurses' station. She wanted to show it to as many people as she could find, for initially it seemed to be proof that she wasn't merely a victim of brain injury, and that the dead men's visitations were something considerably stranger than hallucinations.

On second thought, however, she decided to be cautious. If she clutched the mezuzah and ran breathlessly to show it to someone else, was it possible that she would open her hand in revelation – only to discover that she wasn't really clutching a mezuzah? She couldn't be sure that her brain was properly interpreting the images that her senses were transmitting to it. She might be having another attack right now, a miniepisode of brain dysfunction; when the fit passed, she might find that the gold mezuzah was only a small ball of scrap paper or a bent nail or a screw that had popped loose from the wall-mounted towel dispenser – or any of a hundred other mundane items. Better to wait, put the mezuzah aside, give herself time to recover from this attack – if it *was* another attack – and look at the object again, later, to see if it then appeared to be what it *now* appeared to be.

Furthermore, she suddenly wasn't very eager to consider the existence of walking dead men and the possibility of vengeance being taken from beyond the grave. When she'd been talking with Jeff McGee, she had jokingly wished that there really were such things as ghosts, so that her problems could be blamed on an external cause, rather than on her own loss of mental control. But she had not given any thought to what it would mean to her if her wish were granted. What it meant, she now saw with chilling clarity, was an even deeper descent into the cellars of insanity. She simply wasn't prepared to believe that dead men could come back from their tombs. She was a scientist, a woman of logic and reason. Whenever she saw gross superstition at work in other people, she was either amused or appalled by it. There wasn't room for the supernatural in her philosophy or, more importantly, in her self-image. This far, she had retained possession of her sanity primarily because a small part of her had clung tenaciously to the knowledge that her tormentors were only figments of her sick mind, nothing but imaginary creatures, phantoms. But if they were *real* . . .

What then?

What next?

She looked at her face in the mirror and could see the stark, haunted look in her own gray-green eyes.

Now there were new insanities, new terrors, new horrors to contemplate.

What next?

She didn't want to think about that. Indeed, there was no point in thinking about it until she knew whether the mezuzah was real or not.

Besides, the strong sedative she'd been given was beginning to take effect. Her eyes were rapidly becoming heavy, and her thoughts were getting fuzzy at the edges.

She carefully wrapped the gold pendant in a strip of toilet paper. She made a small, square, tidy bundle of it.

She left the bathroom, turning off the overhead fluorescents as she went. She got into bed and put the wad of toilet tissue in the top drawer of the nightstand, beside her wallet; closed the drawer; her little secret.

The sedative was like a great wave in the sea, rolling inexorably over her, pulling her down, down.

She reached out to snap off the bedside lamp, but she noticed that no one had turned on the night light. If she switched off her lamp, she would be in total darkness, except for what little indirect

289

illumination the hall lights provided. She didn't like the prospect of lying alone in darkness, not even for the few minutes she would need to fall soundly asleep. She pulled her hand back from the lamp.

Staring at the ceiling, trying not to think, she lay in light – until, a minute later, she herself went out with the suddenness of a clicking switch.

* * *

Thursday morning. Clouds again. Also some torn strips of blue sky, like bright banners in the gloom.

Susan lay motionless for a minute or two, blinking at the window, before she remembered the treasure that she had secreted in the nightstand.

She raised the bed, sat up, quickly combed her shaggy hair with her fingers, then opened the nightstand drawer. The toilet tissue was there, where she remembered having put it. At least that much was real. She took it out and held it in the palm of her hand for a while, just staring at it. Finally, she opened it with as much care as she had employed in the wrapping of it.

The religious pendant lay in the center of the tissue. Its gold chain was tangled; it gleamed.

Susan picked it up, fingered it wonderingly. The mezuzah was real; there was no doubt about that.

As impossible as it seemed, it must follow that the dead men were real, too.

Ghosts?

She turned the pendant over and over in her fingers, the chain trailing out of her hand and along

290

her arm, while she tried to make up her mind whether or not she wanted to believe in ghosts. And even if she wanted to believe in them, *could* she? Her ingrained level-headedness, her lifelong skepticism in such matters, and her preference for neatly packaged scientific answers made it difficult for her to turn abruptly away from logic and just blithely embrace superstition.

Even if she had been predisposed to supernatural explanations, there was one thing that would nevertheless have made it hard for her to accept the ghost theory. That one hitch was the mezuzah. If the dead men were malevolent spirits who were capable of vanishing in the blink of an eye – as Harch had seemed to vanish from the bathroom yesterday afternoon, taking Jerry Stein's severed head with him – then the mezuzah should have vanished, too. After all, if it was a part of the apparition, it couldn't also be a part of the real world. Yet here it was, in her hand.

Last night when her mind had been clouded by a sedative, it had seemed to her that the mezuzah was proof that there *were* such things as ghosts. However, now she realized that the pendant's existence proved only that the dead men were not merely hallucinations. In fact it didn't even prove that much; it only *indicated* that such was the case.

Ghosts? That seemed unlikely.

And with the mezuzah in her hand, blaming everything on brain dysfunction seemed too simplistic.

291

She couldn't completely forget about either of those theories, of course. But for the time being, she could relegate them to a back room in her mind.

So what explanations were left?

She stared at the mezuzah, frowning.

She seemed to have come full circle, back to the look-alike theory. But that was no good to her, either, because she had never been able to explain why four perfect look-alikes for the four fraternity brothers would show up in Willawauk County Hospital – of all places – intent upon tormenting and perhaps killing her. If a theory made absolutely no sense, then it was a worthless theory.

Besides, even the conspiracy theory didn't explain how Harch had disappeared from the windowless bathroom yesterday. It didn't explain how he could have recovered so completely and so quickly from the back surgery that he'd undergone on Monday. Or how Jerry Stein's corpse could have turned up in Jessica Seiffert's sickbed. Or why the corpse was not completely decomposed, reduced by now to a mere collection of bones.

Ghosts?

Brain dysfunction?

Bizarre conspiracies?

None of the available theories answered all of the questions – or even most of them. Every avenue of inquiry seemed to lead only to further confusion.

Susan felt light-headed.

She clenched her hand tightly around the

mezuzah, as if she could squeeze the truth from it.

A nurse entered the room from the hall. It was Millie, the thin, fox-faced blonde. On Tuesday morning, when Susan had become hysterical at the appearance of the Jellicoe and Parker duplicates – the orderlies named Bradley and O'Hara – it had been Millie who had attempted to give Susan an injection against her will, while Carl Jellicoe held her down on the bed.

'The breakfast cart's just right down the hall,' Millie said as she passed the bed, heading toward the bathroom. 'Ought to be here in a minute,' she added, slipping into the bathroom before Susan had an opportunity to respond.

Through the half-open door, Susan saw the nurse crouch down and peer behind the commode; first, around one side of it; then, around the other side. She squinted at the shadowy spots back there, where the overhead fluorescent lights didn't reach.

After the nurse had carefully inspected all around the toilet, she turned her back to it, still hunkering down. She swung her head left, right, keeping her eyes down toward the baseboard. She peeked behind the door. Under the sink.

Susan's eyes turned inexorably down to her own hand. The mezuzah, now hidden in her fist, seemed to grow icy, leeching the warmth from the flesh that encircled it.

The gold chain trailed from between her clenched fingers. Without fully understanding why she did it, operating solely on a hunch, Susan opened her fingers just long enough to quickly, surreptitiously push the chain in to keep company with the pendant. She made a fist again. Put the fist in her lap. Covered it with her other, open hand. Tried to look relaxed. Just sitting there in bed, yawning, blinking at the morning light, hands folded oh-so-casually in her lap.

Millie came out of the bathroom and over to the side of the bed. She hesitated for only a second or two, then said, 'Say, did you find any jewelry in there yesterday?'

'Jewelry?'

'Yeah.'

'In where?' Susan asked, feigning surprise, yawning. 'You mean in the bathroom?'

'Yeah.'

'You mean like pearl necklaces and diamond brooches?' Susan asked lightly, as if she thought the nurse was leading up to a joke.

'No. Nothing like that. It's mine. I lost it somewhere yesterday, and I can't find it.'

'What kind of jewelry?'

Millie hesitated only an instant, then said, 'A mezuzah. It was on a gold chain.'

Susan could see the tension, the lies, the deception in the nurse's foxlike face and in her hard, watchful eyes.

It isn't yours, Susan thought. You didn't leave it here. You're a damned liar.

The mezuzah had been left behind by mistake. Obviously, it had dropped unnoticed from the sev-

294

ered head. And now they were trying to cover up and keep the charade going.

'Sorry,' Susan said. 'I didn't find anything.'

The nurse stared at her.

Susan could see what they wanted her to believe. They wanted her to think that she had seen Millie's mezuzah on the bathroom floor and had linked it subconsciously to Jerry Stein's mezuzah, and thereby triggered another attack of nasty hallucinations.

But Millie's behavior had made Susan suspicious. And now she was sure that her problem was not merely psychological. They were running her through some kind of . . . test or program . . . a charade, the purpose of which she could not begin to understand. She was sure of that now.

But who were *they*?

'I hope you find it,' she said to Millie, smiling sweetly.

'The chain must have broke,' Millie said. 'It could have fallen off anywhere, I guess.'

The nurse wasn't a good liar. Neither her eyes nor her voice contained any conviction.

An orderly entered, pushing a cafeteria cart. Millie put Susan's breakfast tray on the bed table. Then both she and the orderly left.

Alone again, Susan opened her hand. The mezuzah was damp with perspiration.

* * *

Susan went into the bathroom, snapped on the fluorescent lights, and closed the door, leaving her untouched breakfast to get cold on the tray.

She began to examine the walls, starting behind the commode. It was drywall construction, not plaster; it was a pebbly surface, white, freshly painted, without a visible crack. At the corner, she examined the drywall joint with special care, but she didn't find anything out of the ordinary. The second wall bore no cracks, either, and the second corner was as smooth and seamless as the first one had been. The sink stood in the middle of the third wall; above the sink, the mirror filled in from the backsplash to the ceiling. On both sides of the sink and the mirror, the wall was perfectly even in texture, unmarked, normal.

Three-quarters of the way around the small room, in the third corner, behind the door, she found what she was looking for. The drywall joint was marred by an unnaturally straight hairline crack that extended all the way from the mitered junction of the three-inch-high base molding to the ceiling.

This is madness.

She raised her hands to her face, rubbed her eyes gently with her fingertips, blinked, looked at the corner again. The crack was still there, a knife-edge line that clearly had not been caused by the settling of the building over the years. It was a deliberate feature of the wall.

She went to the sink again, stared at the mirror, looking at the surface of it, not at her own reflection. It was a single sheet of glass; there was no division down the middle of it, nothing as obvious as that. Apparently, it served as an unconnected flange; it was probably fixed to the wall only on the left side, neatly concealing the pivot point behind it.

She knelt on the cold tile floor and peered beneath the sink. All of the plumbing, both the drain and the two water lines, came up out of the floor; nothing came out of the wall. She squirmed under the sink as far as she could and peered at the shadowed drywall back there. It was scarred by another crack that evidently came down from the ceiling, for the most part hidden by the mirror and the sink, appearing here and running all the way to the baseboard; this crack was as straight as a plumb line, just as the one in the corner was. The base molding had been cut through; the cut aligned with the crack in the wall. Susan was able to insert a fingernail into the crevice where the two sections of molding met; it had never been filled with putty.

She could feel a faint, cold draft puffing through that narrow gap, a vague but icy breath against her fingertips.

She retreated from beneath the sink and stood up, brushing her dusty hands together.

She stared thoughtfully at the six-foot-wide expanse of drywall between the corner by the door and the middle of the sink. Apparently, that entire section of the wall swung inward, away from the bathroom.

This was how Ernest Harch had exited, the severed head tucked under his arm, unaware that the mezuzah had fallen to the floor behind him.

What lay on the other side?

Madness.

* * *

Behind the second bed, the one in which Jessica Seiffert had lain until yesterday afternoon, Susan inspected the wall. It was marked by another hairline, ruler-straight crack that extended from the floor to the ceiling. From a distance of more than six or eight feet, the line was invisible. A similar seam was hidden in the corner.

Susan put one hand flat against the wall and pressed hard at several points on both sides of both cracks, hoping that the hidden doorway was operated by a pressure latch of some kind. But the wall remained in place in spite of her careful prodding.

She knelt down and squinted at the baseboard. Felt along it with one hand.

Again, there was a draft coming out of the gaps; faint but detectable, and cold.

Near the left-hand crack, she found a trace of grease. Lubricant for the swinging partition's secret hinges?

She pressed every couple of inches along the molding, but she could find no pressure latch there, either.

Secret doors? It seemed too bizarre to be true.

Shadowy conspirators moving clandestinely

through the walls? That was a classic paranoid fantasy.

But what about the seams in the drywall?

Imagination.

And the drafts seeping through from hidden rooms?

Perceptual confusion.

And the grease?

Misinterpretation of visual and tactile stimuli due to brain dysfunction. A tiny cerebral hemorrhage. Or a sand-grain blood clot. Or a brain lesion. Or a—

'Like hell it is,' she muttered.

* * *

Her oatmeal had gotten cold and gummy. She ate it anyway; more than ever, she needed to keep up her strength.

While she ate, she tried to figure out what the hell was going on. She seemed stuck with the conspiracy theory, though it made no sense at all.

Who could possibly have the resources and the determination to organize such an elaborate plot, such an incredible masquerade, involving four dead ringers that must have been located with only the most titanic effort? And for what purpose? Why all this expenditure of time and money and energy? What could be gained? Was some relative of one of the dead fraternity men – a father, mother, sister, brother – seeking revenge on Susan for her testimony at the trial, even though she had told only the truth? Seeking revenge – after thirteen years? By trying to drive her out of her mind? No. Good heavens, that was absurd! That was a scenario straight out of a comic book. People didn't seek revenge by means of such complicated – and *expensive* – conspiracies. If you were dead set on getting revenge for something like this, then you did it with a knife or a gun or poison. And you didn't wait thirteen years, either. Surely, a raging hatred – a hatred sufficiently powerful to inspire a vengeance killing – could not be sustained for thirteen years.

But what kind of hospital had hidden rooms and secret doors in its walls?

In a madhouse clinic, in a sanitarium for the hopelessly insane, there might be such secret doors – but only in the fevered minds of the most severely disturbed patients. Yet these doors were not merely figments of her demented imagination; she wasn't just a disassociated schizophrenic sitting in a padded cell, fantasizing that she was in some ordinary hospital in a town called Willawauk. She was *here*, damn it all. This was really happening. The secret doors *did* exist.

As she thought back over the past four days, she remembered a few strange incidents that hadn't seemed important at the time but which seemed vitally important now. They were incidents that should have alerted her to the fact that this place and the people in it were not what they pretended to be.

Viteski. The first indication that something was

amiss had come from him.

Saturday night, when Susan had awakened from her coma, Dr. Viteski had been stiff, ill at ease, noticeably uncomfortable with her. When he had told her about her accident and about Willawauk County Hospital, his voice had been so stilted, so wooden, that each word had seemed like a cast-off splinter. At times he had sounded as if he were reciting lines from a well-memorized script. Perhaps that was precisely what he *had* been doing.

Mrs. Baker had made a mistake, too. On Monday, as the nurse was finishing up her shift and preparing to go home for the day, she had spoken of having a hot date that night with a man whose shoulders were big enough 'to measure a doorway.' Two days later, when Susan had asked belatedly whether the date was a success or not, Mrs. Baker had been lost for a moment, utterly baffled. For a *long* moment. Too long. Now, it seemed perfectly clear to Susan that the story about the lumberman and the bowling date and the hamburger dinner had been nothing but a spur-of-the-moment ad-lib, the kind of sharp and colorful detail that a good actor frequently invents in order to contribute to the verisimilitude of a role. In actuality, there had been no aging, virile lumberman. No bowling date. Poor pudgy, graying Thelma Baker had not enjoyed a wild night of unrestrained passion, after all. The nurse merely improvized that romantic tale to flesh out her characterization, then later forgot what she had improvized – until Susan reminded her.

Susan finished eating the cold, gummy oatmeal. She started on the hardened whole-wheat toast, upon which the butter had congealed in milky-looking swirls, and she washed it down with swigs of orange juice.

The bruise, she thought as she continued to eat.

The bruise was another thing that should have made her suspicious. On Tuesday afternoon, when she had been trapped in the elevator with the four dead fraternity men, Harch had pinched her arm very hard. Later, there had been a small bruise on her biceps, two inches above the crook of her arm. She had told herself that she had unwittingly sustained the bruise during the exercise period in the therapy room, and that her subconscious mind had incorporated that injury into the hallucination. But that had not been the case. The bruise had been proof that Harch and the others were real; it had been like the mezuzah in the sense that both the bruise and the religious pendant were fragments of supposed hallucinations that had survived the dissipation of the rest of those nightmares.

Suddenly, Susan thought she knew *why* Harch had pinched her. He hadn't just been delighting in the opportunity to torture her. He had pinched her a moment or two before she had grown dizzy, seconds before she had swooned and passed out on the wheeled stretcher. She now understood that the cruel pinch was intended to cover the sting of a hypodermic needle. Harch had pinched her hard enough to make her cry, and then one of the other three men had quickly administered an injection before the first pain subsided, before she could distinguish the second pain as a separate event. Once the four men had thoroughly terrorized her, there had been, of course, no way for them to bring a dramatic and credible conclusion to the scene, unless she conveniently passed out – *because they were neither ghosts who could simply vanish in a puff of supernatural light and smoke, nor hallucinated images that would fade away as she finally regained her senses.* When she had failed to oblige them by fainting, they had been forced to knock her unconscious with a drug. And they had covered the injection with a pinch because, after all, no self-respecting ghost would require the assistance of sodium pentathol or some like substance in order to effect a suitably mysterious exit.

Susan paused as she was about to start eating a sweet roll with lemon icing, and she pushed up the sleeve of her hospital gown. The bruise was still there on her biceps, yellowing now. She peered closely at it, but too much time had elapsed for her to be able to find the tiny point at which the needle had pierced her skin.

Undoubtedly, her tormentors had made other mistakes which she had failed to notice. Indeed, she wouldn't have made anything of the mistakes that she *had* noticed, not if the Harch look-alike hadn't accidentally left the mezuzah behind in the bathroom, for the mezuzah had set her imagination ablaze and had cast a bright light of healthy suspicion upon her memories of other curious incidents.

All things considered, the conspirators had brought it off exceptionally well thus far; brilliantly, in fact.

But who *were* these people? Who had put so much money and energy and time into the painstakingly detailed creation of this three-dimensional drama? And for what purpose?

What in God's name do they want from me?

More than vengeance. No question about that. Something more than vengeance; something infinitely stranger – and worse.

In spite of the quiver of fear that shimmered through her and caused her stomach to yaw and pitch, Susan took a bite of the sweet roll. Fuel for the engine. Vital energy for the fight that lay ahead.

Reluctantly, she considered the role of Jeff McGee in all of this, and the pastry turned chalky and bitter in her mouth. She swallowed only with considerable effort, and that first bite of pastry went down as if it were a wet lump of clay. She nearly choked on it.

There was no chance whatsoever that Jeff was unaware of what was being done to her.

He was a part of it.

He was one of *them* – whoever they were.

Although she knew that she ought to eat to keep her strength up, especially now that illness was not her only or even her primary enemy, Susan was unable to take another bite. The very thought of food was repellent. With the sweet roll still tasting like clay in her mouth, she pushed her breakfast tray aside.

She had trusted McGee.

He had betrayed her.

She had loved him.

He had taken advantage of her love.

Worst of all, she had willingly relinquished control to him, had given to him the responsibility for her life, for her *survival*, something she had never given to anyone before, something she would never even have considered doing with anyone else she had ever known – except, perhaps, for her father, who had never *wanted* responsibility for her, anyway. And now that she had forsaken her lifelong principle of self-reliance, now that she had allowed Jeff McGee to bring her out of her shell, now that she had allowed him to take control with his warm assurances of concern and his tender statements of devotion, *now* he had failed her. Intentionally.

Like all the others, he was playing his part in a conspiracy that seemed to have no other goal but to drive her out of her mind.

She felt used.

She felt like a fool.

She hated him.

* * *

The Milestone Corporation.

Somehow, the events of the past few days were directly related to the Milestone Corporation.

For several minutes she concentrated very hard on pushing back the black veil of amnesia that obscured all recollections of Milestone, but she found, as before, that the barrier was not a veil but a formidable shield, a veritable wall of lead, impenetrable.

The harder she struggled to remember, the greater and darker her fear became. Intuitively, she knew that she dared not remember what work she had done at Milestone. To remember was to die. She felt the truth of that in her bones, but she didn't understand it. For God's sake, what was so evil about Milestone?

* * *

She wondered about the automobile accident. Had it actually happened? Or was it a lie, too?

She closed her eyes and tried to relive the few minutes on the highway immediately prior to the crash that (supposedly) had taken place four weeks ago. The curve in the road . . . rounding it . . . slowly . . . slowly around . . . then blackness. She strained against the unyielding amnesia, but she could not seize the memory. She was reasonably sure that it had never happened.

Something frightening had transpired on that mountain road, just around that blind curve, but it hadn't been an accident. They had been waiting for her there – whoever *they* were – and they had taken her by force, and they had brought her to this place. *That* was how she had acquired her head injury. She had no proof of it, no memory of the kidnapping, but she also had no doubt, either.

* * *

Twenty minutes after Susan finished her cold breakfast, Jeff McGee stopped by on his morning rounds.

He kissed her on the cheek, and she returned the kiss, although she would have preferred not to be touched by him. She smiled and pretended to be glad to see him because she didn't want him to know that she suspected anything.

'How do you feel this morning?' he asked, leaning casually against the bed, smiling, supremely confident about his ability to keep her bamboozled.

'I feel marvelous,' she said, wanting to hit him in the face with all her might. 'Invigorated.'

'Sleep soundly?'

'Like a hibernating bear. That was some sedative.'

'I'm glad it worked. Speaking of medication, I've scheduled you for a tablet of methylphenidate at nine o'clock and another one at five this afternoon.'

'I don't need it.'

'Oh? Diagnosing yourself now? Did you sneak out and acquire a medical degree during the night?'

'Didn't have to. I just sent for it in the mail.'

'How much did it cost?'

'Fifty bucks.'

'Cheaper than mine,' he said.

'God, I *hope* so,' she said and smiled a smile she didn't feel. 'Look, I don't need methylphenidate

307

for the simple reason that I'm not suffering from depression any more.'

'Not right at this moment, maybe. But another wave of deep narcoleptic depression might come at any time, especially if you have another one of your hallucinations. I believe in preventive medicine.'

And I believe that you're a goddamned fraud, Dr. McGee, she thought.

She said, 'But I don't need any pills. Really. I tell you, I'm *up*!'

'And I tell you, *I'm* the doctor.'

'Who must be obeyed.'

'Always.'

'Okay, okay. One pill at nine and one at five.'

'Good girl.'

Why don't you just pat me on the head and scratch me behind the ears like you would a favorite dog? she thought bitterly, even as she kept her true emotions hidden.

She said, 'Did you have a chance to look over my tests again last night?'

'Yeah. I spent almost five hours with them.'

You damned liar, she thought. You didn't spend ten lousy minutes with them because you know I don't have a medical problem of any kind.

She said, 'Five hours? That was above and beyond the call of duty. Thank you. Did you find anything?'

'I'm afraid not. The EEG graphs didn't turn up anything more than what I saw on the CRT readout yesterday. And your X rays are like a set of textbook illustrations labeled "full cranial sequence of a healthy human female." '

'I'm glad to know I'm human, anyway.'

'Perfect specimen.'

'And female.'

'*Perfect* specimen,' he said, grinning.

'What about the spinal tests?' Susan asked, playing along with him, softening her voice and permitting a trace of nervous strain to color it, carefully projecting exactly the proper amount of worry and self-concern. She beetled her brow to a carefully calculated degree, letting McGee read fear and doubt in the furrows of her creased forehead.

'I couldn't find any mistakes in the lab's procedures,' McGee said. 'There wasn't anything the pathologist overlooked, nothing he misread in the data.'

Susan sighed wearily and let her shoulders sag.

McGee responded to the sigh, took her hand in his in an effort to comfort her.

She resisted the powerful urge to pull loose of him and to slap his face.

She said, 'Well . . . now what? Do we move on to the cerebral angiogram you talked about yesterday?'

'No, no. Not yet. I still need to do a lot of thinking about the advisability of that. And you need to regain more of your strength before we can give it serious consideration. For the next couple of days, I guess we're just in a holding pattern. I'm sorry, Susan, I know this is frustrating for you.'

They talked for another five minutes, mostly about personal things, and McGee never appeared to realize that she was looking at him from a different and considerably less flattering perspective than that from which she had viewed him previously. She was surprised by her own acting ability and even rather pleased by it; she was as good as Mrs. Baker.

I'll beat these bastards at their own game, if I can only find out what the devil it *is*, she thought with more than a little satisfaction.

But no one in this vicious charade was half as good an actor as McGee. He had style and control and panache. Although Susan knew he was a fraud, just five minutes of personal chitchat with him was nearly sufficient to convince her of his sincerity. He was so kind and considerate. His blue eyes were achingly sensitive and utterly unclouded by any sign of deception. His concern for her well-being seemed genuine. He was charming, always charming. His laugh was natural, never forced.

But the most impressive thing about McGee's act was the love that he radiated. In his company, Susan felt as if she were cradled in love, swathed in it, afloat in a sea of it, protected by it. Over the years, there had been at least two other men who had loved her – men for whom she had felt only affection – but in neither case had she been so intensely aware of the love given to her. McGee's love was almost a visible radiance.

Yet it was fake.

It *had* to be fake.

He had to know what was going on here.

But when McGee left her room to continue his morning rounds, Susan was filled with doubt again. The possibility of her own madness rose in her mind for reconsideration. Hidden rooms, secret doors, a hospital full of conspirators? For what purpose? Seeking what gain? It seemed almost easier to believe herself insane than to believe that Jeff McGee was a liar and a fraud.

She even put her head down on the pillow and wept quietly for a few minutes, shaken, not sure whether she was weeping about his perfidy or about her lack of faith in him. She was miserable. She'd had within her grasp the kind of relationship with a man that she had long desired, with the kind of man she had always dreamed about. Now it was slipping away, or perhaps she was throwing it away. Confused, she didn't know which it was, didn't know what she ought to believe or exactly what she ought to feel.

Eventually, she reached under the pillow and pulled out the gold mezuzah.

She stared at it.

She turned it over and over again in her hand.

Gradually, the solidity of that object, the stark reality of it, brought her to her senses. Doubt evaporated.

She was not losing her mind. She wasn't mad – but she was very angry.

* * *

At nine o'clock, Millie brought the day's first dose of methylphenidate.

Susan took the capsule out of the small paper pill cup and said, 'Where's Mrs. Baker this morning?'

'Thursday's her day off,' Millie said, pouring a glass of water from the metal carafe. 'She said something about washing and waxing her car this morning, then going on a last autumn picnic with some friends this afternoon. But wouldn't you know it: They say we're going to get a pretty good rain later this afternoon.'

Oh, very nice. Very nice detail, Susan thought with a combination of sarcasm and genuine admiration for the planning that had gone into this production. *Thursday's her day off.* My, what a thoughtful, realistic touch that is! Even though this isn't an ordinary hospital, and even though Mrs. Baker isn't an ordinary nurse, and even though we're all involved in some unimaginably bizarre charade, she gets a day off for the sake of realism. Washing and waxing her car. A late autumn picnic. Oh, very nice indeed. A splendid bit of detail for authenticity's sake. My compliments to the scenarist.

Millie put down the metal carafe and handed the glass to Susan.

Susan pretended to put the capsule of methyl-phenidate in her mouth, palmed it instead, and drank two long swallows of ice water.

Henceforth, she wasn't going to take any of the medications that she was given. For all she knew, these people were slowly poisoning her.

* * *

Because she was a scientist, it naturally occurred to her that she might be the subject of an experiment. She might even have willingly agreed to take part in it. An experiment having to do with sensory manipulation or with mind control.

There was sufficient precedent to inspire such a theory. In the 1960s and 1970s, some scientists had voluntarily subjected themselves to sensory deprivation experiments, settling into dark, warm, watery SD tanks for such extended lengths of time that they temporarily lost all touch with reality and began to hallucinate.

Susan was sure she wasn't hallucinating, but she wondered if the second floor of the hospital had been adapted for an experiment in mind control or brainwashing techniques. Brainwashing sounded like a good bet. Was that the kind of research the Milestone Corporation was engaged in?

She considered the possibility very seriously for a while, but at last she discarded it. She couldn't believe that she would have permitted herself to be used and abused in this fashion, not even to further the cause of science, not even if it was a requirement of her job. She would have quit any job that demanded her to test her sanity to the breaking point.

Who would engage upon that sort of immoral research, anyway? It sounded like something that

313

the Nazis might have done with their prisoners of war. But no reputable scientist would become involved with it.

Furthermore, she was a physicist, and her field in no way touched upon the behavioral sciences. Brainwashing was so far outside her field that she could imagine no circumstances under which she would have become associated with such an experiment.

No, she hadn't walked into this with her eyes open; she hadn't come to this place willingly.

* * *

McGee had scheduled Susan for a physical therapy session at ten o'clock Thursday morning.

Murf and Phil came for her at a few minutes before ten. As usual, they kept up a steady line of amusing patter all the way downstairs to the PT Department. Susan wanted to tell them that, in her humble opinion, they were definitely Academy Award material, but she didn't break her cover. She only smiled and laughed and responded when it seemed appropriate.

During the first part of the therapy session, Susan did all of the exercises that Florence Atkinson suggested, but at the halfway point, she complained of painful muscle cramps in her legs. She winced and groaned convincingly, though she actually had no cramps. She just didn't want to exhaust herself in a therapy session. She was saving her strength now, for she would have desperate need of it later.

She intended to escape tonight.

Mrs. Atkinson seemed genuinely concerned about the cramps. She cut short the exercise part of the session and gave Susan a longer massage than usual, plus ten extra minutes in the whirlpool. By the time Susan had taken a hot shower and had dried her hair, she felt much better than she had felt at any time since she had come out of her coma.

On the way back to her room, in the care of Phil and Murf once more, Susan grew tense at the elevators, wondering if another 'hallucination' was planned for this moment. But the elevator was empty; the ride upstairs was uneventful.

She hadn't decided exactly how she should handle the next apparition.

She knew how she *wanted* to handle it. She wanted to respond with blind rage, with a furious assault that would drive them back in surprise. She wanted to claw their faces and draw their blood, lots of blood, which would be more proof that they weren't ghosts or hallucinations. She wanted to hurt them, and then she wanted to defiantly accuse them.

But she knew she couldn't do what she wanted. As long as they weren't aware that she was wise to their games, she had the advantage. But the moment she revealed her knowledge, she would lose what little freedom to maneuver that she now had. The charade would end abruptly. They would stop trying to drive her insane – which seemed to be their single-minded intention – and they would do something even worse than that to her. She was sure of it.

* * *

She ate every bite of her lunch.

When Millie came to take the tray away, Susan yawned and said, 'Boy, am I ready for a nap.'

'I'll close the door so the hall noise won't bother you,' the sharp-faced blonde said.

As soon as the nurse had gone, pulling the door shut behind her, Susan got out of bed and went to the closet, slid the door open. Blankets and pillows for the room's other bed were stored on the closet shelf. On the floor were Susan's battered suitcases, which supposedly had been salvaged from her wrecked car.

She dragged the suitcases into the room and opened them on the floor, praying that no one would walk in on her during the next few minutes. She rummaged quickly through the contents of the bags, putting together an outfit that was suitable for a jailbreak. A pair of jeans. A dark blue sweater. Thick, white athletic socks and a pair of Adidas running shoes. She shoved that bundle to the back of the shallow closet, then stood the suitcases in front to conceal it.

She shut the closet door and hurried back to the bed, got in, put up the safety railing, lowered the mattress, put her head down on her pillow, and closed her eyes.

She felt good. She felt as if she were in charge of her life again.

Then she had another unsettling thought; lately, she seemed to have an endless supply of them, and this one was especially unsettling. She wondered if she was being watched by concealed, closed-circuit television cameras. After all, if they went to the trouble of hidden rooms and secret doors, wouldn't they also put her under twenty-four-hour observation? And wouldn't they now know that she had found the mezuzah and that she was preparing to escape?

She opened her eyes and looked around the room, seeking places where cameras might be concealed. The heating vents in the walls, up near the ceiling, offered the only logical hiding places. There were two vents in two different walls. If cameras were placed in the heating ducts – a few inches behind the vent grilles in order to avoid detection from the glint of light on their lenses – and if they were properly positioned, fully motor-driven for the widest possible lateral view, aimed downward, and equipped with remote-control zoom lenses, then they would be able to cover most if not all of the hospital room.

For a few minutes Susan was sick with despair. She hugged herself and shuddered.

Gradually, however, her spirits rose somewhat, for she decided that there mustn't be any cameras. If there *were* cameras, she would have been observed handling the mezuzah this morning. It wouldn't have been necessary for Millie to question her about lost jewelry. If they had seen her with the mezuzah, they would have been afraid that she was aware of their charade, and they would have called a halt to it.

Wouldn't they?

Probably. There didn't seem to be any point to staging more 'hallucinations' if she could no longer be fooled by them.

Yet, although she was pretty sure they wouldn't go on toying with her this way, she couldn't be absolutely positive about it, for she didn't know what motivated them.

She would just have to wait and see.

If she managed to get out of the hospital tonight, she would know that there hadn't been any TV cameras in her room.

On the other hand, if she started to sneak out of the place and got as far as the stairs and discovered the four dead men were waiting for her there, smiling . . .

Although she now knew they *weren't* dead men, she nevertheless shuddered again.

She would just have to wait.

And see.

15

Later Thursday afternoon, a fast-weaving loom of wind brought new gray cloth for the rents in the clouds, patching over every last glimpse of blue September sky. The hospital room darkened early again.

A crash, a roll, and an echo of thunder preceded a violent fall of rain. For a while, fat droplets of water snapped bullet-hard against the window in great profusion and with the sound of a dozen submachine guns. The wind hummed, then moaned, then howled like a wild thing in pain, then roared. In time, the storm abated somewhat, but only temporarily; it settled into a rhythmic pattern that alternated between fury and docility, between a torrential downpour and a pleasant drizzle. Cloudbursts were followed by the soothing pitter-patter of light autumn showers.

Although the storm waxed and waned, the day grew steadily darker, not brightening for even a moment, and Susan looked forward to the coming nightfall with barely containable excitement – and with fear, too.

For nearly an hour, she pretended to nap, her back turned to the closed door, while she watched the raging storm. She need not have continued with the ruse, for during that time no one came around to check on her.

Later, she sat up in bed and switched on the television set, in front of which she passed the rest of the afternoon. She didn't pay much attention to the programs that flickered across the screen. Her mind was elsewhere, preoccupied with plans and schemes and dreams of escape.

At five o'clock sharp, Nurse Scolari, who had come on duty at four, brought another dose of methylphenidate and a fresh carafe of ice water. Susan faked the taking of the capsule, palmed it as she had done with the first dose this morning.

At suppertime, McGee came in with two trays and announced that he was having dinner with her. 'No candles. No champagne,' he said. 'But there are some delicious-looking stuffed pork chops and apple-nut cake for dessert.'

'Sounds terrific to me,' she said. 'I never liked the taste of candles, anyway.'

He also brought several magazines and two more paperback novels. 'I thought maybe you might be running out of reading material.'

He stayed for more than two hours, and they talked of many things. Eventually, the strain of playing the innocent, the stress of pretending to love him when she actually despised him –

it all became almost too much for Susan to bear. She had found that she was a pretty good actress, but she had also learned that deception exacted a high toll from her. She was relieved and exhausted when McGee finally kissed her good night and left.

She was relieved, yes, but she was also curiously sorry to see him go. Until he was walking out of the door, she wouldn't have believed that she could be sorry to see him go; but when he crossed the threshold and disappeared into the corridor, Susan felt a sudden and unexpected loss, an emptiness. She knew she might never seen him again – except in a court of law, where he would stand trial for his part in her kidnapping and peculiar torture. In spite of the fact that she knew him to be a fraud, she still found him to be good company. He was as charming as he had ever been. He was still a good conversationalist. He still had an excellent sense of humor and an appealing, infectious laugh. Worst of all, he still seemed to glow with love for her. She had tried hard to see through him, to discern the duplicitous bastard beneath the surface saint, and she had tried with all her might to hear the lies in his love talk, but she had failed.

If you know what's good for you, forget him, she told herself angrily. Just put him out of your mind. All the way out. Think about getting out of here. *That's* what's important. Getting out.

She looked at the bedside clock.

8:03.

Outside, lightning briefly drove back the darkness.

Rain fell and fell.

At nine o'clock, Tina Scolari brought the sedative that McGee had prescribed. Putting her cupped hand to her mouth, she pantomimed taking the sedative; she quickly washed down the nonexistent pill with the swallow of water that the nurse offered her.

'Have a good night,' Tina Scolari said.

'I'm sure I will.'

A few minutes after the nurse had gone, Susan switched off the bedside lamp. The night light cast its phosphoric luminescence across the room, leeching all color from the chamber, so that everything appeared to be either ash-gray or the ghost-white of moonglow. The night light was no threat to the crowd of shadows, but it was good enough for what Susan had to do.

She waited another few minutes, lying in bed, staring at the dark ceiling, which flickered now and then with the reflected flash of lightning that bounced off the water-filmed windows. She wanted to be certain that the nurse wasn't going to come back with some forgotten medication or with a warning about an early wake-up call for new tests.

At last she got up and went to the closet. She took two pillows and two blankets from the top shelf, carried them back to the bed. She arranged them under the covers in a series of lumps that she hoped would pass for a huddled, sleeping woman.

The dummy was crude, but she didn't waste any more time with it; there were no awards for art and craftsmanship.

She returned to the closet. She reached behind the suitcases and located the bundle of clothes that she had put there earlier in the day. By the time she had pulled off her pajamas and had dressed in the jeans, sweater, heavy socks, and running shoes, and by the time she had retrieved her wallet from the nightstand, the bedside clock read 9:34.

She tucked the mezuzah in a pocket of her jeans, even though it was proof of nothing to anyone except to her.

She went to the door and put her head against it, listening. She couldn't hear anything from the other side.

After a moment of nervous hesitation, after she wiped her sweaty palms on her jeans, she pushed the door open. Just a crack. Peered into the well-lighted hallway. Opened the door a few inches farther. Stuck her head out. Looked right. Looked left. There was no one in sight.

The corridor was silent. It was so silent, in fact, that in spite of the highly polished tile floor and the spotless yellow walls and the dust-free fluorescent ceiling lights, it seemed as if the building had been abandoned and had not known the sound of human activity for ages.

Susan left the room, easing the door shut behind her. She stood for a breathless moment with her

323

back pressed flat against the door, afraid to step away from it, prepared to turn and open it and scurry inside again, into her bed and under the covers, dispossessing the crudely formed dummy, at the slightest sound of an approaching nurse.

To her left lay the junction of the corridors, where the two short wings connected with the long main hall. If there was going to be any trouble, it would most likely come from that direction, for the nurses' station was around the corner and halfway down the longest corridor.

The silence continued, however, disturbed only by the low, distant rumble of the storm.

Convinced that further hesitation was more dangerous than any action she could take, Susan moved cautiously to the right, away from the confluence of corridors, directly toward the large fire door at the end of the short wing, where there was a red EXIT sign. She stayed close to the wall and kept glancing back toward the center of the building.

She was acutely aware of the squeaking noise made by her rubber-soled shoes on the highly polished tile floor. It wasn't really a loud sound, but it had the same nerve-grating quality as did the sound of fingernails scraped across a blackboard.

She reached the metal fire door without incident and opened it. She winced as the push-bar handle rattled under her hand and as the big hinges rasped, creaked. Quickly, she stepped across the threshold, onto a stairwell landing, and shut the heavy door behind her as quietly as possible, which wasn't nearly quietly enough to suit her.

The stairs were bare concrete and were dimly lighted. There was only one small bulb on each landing. Here and there between the landings, the concrete walls were draped with shadows like webs of dust and soot.

Susan stood perfectly still and listened. The stairwell was even more silent than the second-floor hallway had been. Of course she had made so much noise with the door that any guard who might have been stationed on the stairs would now be frozen, listening, just as she was.

Nevertheless, she was sure that she was alone. They probably hadn't posted guards because they didn't expect her to try to escape; they didn't know that she was aware of their trickery. And the hospital staff – or the staff of *whatever* kind of institution this was – most likely used only the public and the service elevators, leaving the stairs for emergencies when the power failed.

She stepped to the black iron railing and leaned over it, looked up, then down. Four more flights of steps and four more landings lay above her. Two flights, one landing, and the bottom of the stairwell lay below.

She went down to the bottom, where there were two fire doors, one set in the inner wall of the stairwell and apparently opening onto a first-floor corridor, the other set in the outer wall. Susan put her hands on the push-bar and creaked open the outer door two or three inches.

Cold wind forced its way into the rough concrete vestibule and capered around Susan's legs. It seemed to be sniffing at her as if it were a large, excited dog trying to make up its mind whether to wag its tail or bite.

Beyond the door, a small rain-swept parking lot lay in the yellowish glow of a pair of tall sodium-vapor lamps, each of which bore two globes like luminescent fruit. It didn't look nearly large enough to be the public parking area. But if it was the staff's lot, where were all the cars? Now that visiting hours were over, the public lot would be virtually deserted, but there should still be quite a few cars in the staff's parking area, even at night. There were only four vehicles: a Pontiac, a Ford, and two other makes with which she was not familiar.

There was no one in the parking lot, so she stepped outside and let the fire door close behind her.

The rain had nearly stopped falling now, as the storm entered one of its quieter moments. Only a thin mist floated down from the night sky.

The wind, however, was fierce. It stood Susan's shaggy blond hair on end, made her eyes water, and forced her to squint. When it gusted, howling banshee-like, Susan had to stand with her head tucked down and her shoulders drawn up. It was surprisingly cold, too; it stung her exposed face and cut through the sweater she was wearing. She wished she had a jacket. She thought it seemed much *too* cold for September in Oregon. It was more like a late-November wind. Or even December.

Had they lied to her about the date? Why on earth would they have lied about that, too? But then again – why not? It made no less sense than anything else they had done.

She moved away from the emergency exit, into the shadows by a bristling evergreen shrub, where she crouched for a minute while she decided which way to go from here. She could head toward the front of the hospital and follow the road that led directly downhill into Willawauk. Or she could go overland and into town by a more cautious, circuitous route, to avoid being spotted by anyone at the hospital.

Lightning pulsed softly, and thunder crashed like a train derailing in the darkness.

No matter which way she went, she was going to get very wet. Already, the light mist had begun to paste her hair to her skull. Soon, the rain would be coming down hard again, and she would be soaked to the skin.

Then a frighteningly bold course of action occurred to her, and she launched herself upon it before she had time to think about it and lose her nerve. She ran out into the parking lot, toward the nearest car, the green Pontiac.

There were four cars in the lot, four chances that someone had left a set of keys in an ignition or under a seat, or tucked up behind a sun visor. In rural towns like Willawauk, where almost everyone knew everyone else, people weren't worried about car thieves nearly so much as were people in the cities and suburbs. Trust thy neighbor: That was still a rule that people lived by in a few favored places. Four cars; four chances. She probably wouldn't have any luck, but it was worth taking a look.

She reached the Pontiac and tried the door on the driver's side. It was unlocked.

When she pulled the door open, the ceiling light came on inside the car. It seemed as bright as a lighthouse beacon, and she was sure that she had given herself away and that alarms would begin ringing at any moment.

'*Damn!*'

She slipped into the car, behind the steering wheel, and quickly closed the door, not concerned about the sound it made, just worried about shutting off that damned light.

'Stupid,' she said, cursing herself.

She scanned the parking lot through the blurry, water-spotted windshield. She saw no one. She looked at the lighted windows of the four-story hospital; there was no one standing in any of them, no one watching her.

She sighed with relief and took a deep breath. The car reeked of stale tobacco smoke. Susan wasn't a smoker herself and was usually offended and sometimes even sickened by such odors. But this time the stench seemed like a sweet perfume to her, for at least it was not a *hospital* odor.

Increasingly confident that she was going to make good her escape, Susan leaned forward, thrusting one hand under the seat, feeling along the floor for the car keys—

—and froze.

The keys were in the ignition.

They glinted in the yellowish sodium-vapor glow that came through the car windows.

The sight of them rocked Susan. She stared at them with a mixture of elation and apprehension, and she found herself arguing with herself.

—*Something's wrong.*

—*No, things are just finally going my way for a change.*

—*It's too easy.*

—*This is what I hoped to find.*

—*And it's too easy.*

—*In small towns, some people* do *leave keys in their cars.*

—*In the very first car you checked?*

—*What's it matter whether it's the first or the fourth or the three hundredth car?*

—*It matters because it's too easy.*

—*Just luck. I'm overdue for some good luck.*

—*It's too easy.*

Sharp ax blades of lightning chopped up the pitch-black sky, and there was a bellow of thunder. Rain fell in spurts at first, then in a sudden, terrible flood.

Susan listened to the rain pounding on the car,

watched it streaming down the windshield in rippling ribbons of sodium light, watched it as it continuously shattered the mirrored surface of the puddles on the pavement, and she knew that she wasn't going to walk all the way into town, which was as much as a mile away, longer if she went in a roundabout fashion. Why struggle through a cloudburst when she had a perfectly good automobile at her disposal? Okay, so maybe it was a little too easy – all right, so there wasn't any 'maybe' about it; too easy by far – but there wasn't any law against things going smoothly and easily now and then. It was easy, this finding a key straight off, but it was also just a stroke of good fortune, nothing more than that.

What else *could* it be?

She twisted the key in the ignition. The engine came to life instantly.

She switched on the headlights and the windshield wipers, put the car in gear, and released the emergency brake. She drove out of the parking lot and around to the front of the hospital. She came to a one-lane, one-way drive, and turned the wrong way into it because the right way out would first take her beneath the brightly lit portico, where someone at the front doors might spot her. She reached the end of the short accessway without encountering any oncoming traffic, and she paused at a stop sign where the drive intersected the two-lane county road.

Glancing back at the four-story building from

which she had just escaped, she saw a large sign on the well-manicured, rolling lawn. It was eight feet long and four or five feet high, set on a stone base, flanked by low shrubbery. Four small floodlights were evenly spaced along the top of the sign, their beams directed down upon the bold white lettering, which was set against a royal-blue background. Even through the heavy, wind-driven rain, Susan could read the sign without any difficulty:

THE MILESTONE CORPORATION

Susan stared at those three words in disbelief.

Then she raised her eyes to the building again, regarding it with confusion, cold fear, and anger. It wasn't a hospital at all.

But what in God's name was it?

And wasn't the Milestone Corporation supposed to be located in Newport Beach, California? That was where she lived. That was where she was supposed to work.

Get the hell out of here, she told herself urgently.

She turned left and drove downhill, away from the Milestone Corporation.

Through the rain and through the thin fog that blanketed the lowlands, Willawauk was visible as a collection of soft, fuzzy lights, none of which had clear points of origin, many of which bled together into yellow and white and pale pink blobs.

Susan remembered that Dr. Viteski had said the town boasted a population of eight thousand. It had to be exactly that: a boast. It just didn't look that big. At best, it appeared to be half that size.

Past the midpoint of the long hill, leaning over the steering wheel while she drove, squinting between the thumping windshield wipers, Susan watched a change come over the lights of Willawauk. Now they seemed to shimmer and wink and ripple and blink as if the entire town was an enormous, intricate neon sign. Of course that was only an effect of the weather.

One thing that did not change was the impression of size that the lights imparted. The town still appeared to be considerably smaller than eight thousand souls. Maybe even smaller than four thousand.

The county road took a hard turn to the right and descended a last slope, past the first houses in town. In some of them, lights shone at the windows; others were dark; all were obscured by the rain and by the eddying fog.

The county road became Main Street. They couldn't have picked a more bland or more apt name for their primary avenue. The heart of Willawauk was like ten thousand other towns scattered across the country. There was a pocket-size park with a war memorial statue at the entrance of it. There was a bar and grill named the Dew Drop Inn; its sign was fashioned out of orange neon, and the *D* in Drop was flickering on the edge of burnout; the windows were decorated with other neon advertisements, all for various brands of beer. The town supported a lot of small businesses, some local enterprises, some minor outlets of major national chains: Jenkin's Hardware; Laura Lee's Flowers; a Sears storefront that dealt solely in catalogue orders; the Plenty Good Coffee Shop, where Susan could see about a dozen customers seated in booths beyond the huge plate-glass windows; two dress shops; a men's store; the First National Bank of Willawauk; the Main Street Cinema, which was currently playing a double feature comprised of two of last summer's comedies, *Arthur* and *Continental Divide*; Thrift Savings and Loan, with its big electronic time-and-temperature sign; an intersection with three service stations – Arco, Union 76, and Mobil – and with a computer games arcade, Rocketblast, on the fourth corner; Giullini Brothers, TV and Appliances; a small bookstore and another bar and grill on the left; a drugstore and a G. C. Murphy's five-and-dime on the right; a funeral home, Hathaway and Sons, set back from the street on a big chunk of property; an empty storefront, a hamburger joint, a furniture store . . .

Although Willawauk was like ten thousand other towns in so many details, a couple of things seemed . . . *wrong*. It seemed to Susan that everything in town was too neat. Every one of the stores looked as if it had been painted within the last month. Even the Arco, Union 76, and Mobil stations sparkled pristinely in the rain, gasoline pumps gleaming, service bay doors raised to proudly reveal brightly lighted, neatly ordered garages. There was not a single piece of litter in the gutters. Trees were planted in regularly spaced cutouts in the sidewalks on both sides of the street, and these were not merely well pruned, but meticulously shaped into two long lines of perfect clones. In all of the many street lamps, not one bulb was burned out. Not one. The only advertising sign with a fluttering neon letter was the one at the Dew Drop Inn, and that seemed to be the town's worst example of blight.

Perhaps Willawauk had an exceptionally strong and widely shared civic pride and an especially energetic citizenry. Or perhaps the rain and the thin veil of fog were softening the scene, concealing the frayed and tattered edges of everything. Except that rain usually made a town look drearier and shabbier than it actually was, not better. And could civic pride really explain a town that looked almost as if robots inhabited it?

Another strange thing was the small number of cars in view. In three blocks, she had passed only three cars and a camper van parked at the curb. In the lot beside the Main Street Cinema, there had been only two cars, and at the Dew Drop Inn, there had been only one other and one pickup truck. So far, she hadn't passed another car in motion; she was the only one driving tonight.

Well, the weather *was* wretched. People were wise to stay home on a night like this.

On the other hand, how many people did she know who usually did the wise thing?

Not very damned many.

Not *this* many.

The Dew Drop Inn was the kind of place that did good business in the middle of a blizzard. A simple rain wouldn't stop the serious drinkers from making their way to their favorite hangout, and most of them would come in cars, the better to kill each other as they weaved blearily home at two o'clock in the morning.

Keep driving, Susan told herself. Drive all the way through this burg and keep on going. Don't stop here. Something is wrong with this place.

But she didn't have a map, and she wasn't familiar with the countryside around these parts, and she didn't know how far it was to the nearest town, and she was also afraid that what had happened to her in the hospital – in *Milestone* – was turning her into a paranoid after all. Then, at the beginning of the fourth block, she saw a place where she was sure to find help, and she pulled her car into the parking lot.

WILLAWAUK COUNTY SHERIFF HEADQUARTERS

WILLAWAUK, OREGON

It was a squat, stone building with a slate roof and all-glass front doors, just south of the considerably more stately county courthouse.

Susan parked the stolen Pontiac near the entrance. She was glad to be getting out of the car; already the odor of stale tobacco smoke had ceased to be the least bit appealing, even if it didn't remind her of the hospital.

She ran through the hammering rain. She ducked under a mammoth spruce tree, through which the cold wind soughed in an enormous chorus of whispers. From there she dashed to the shelter of a white aluminum awning, and thus to the glass doors, through which she pushed.

She found herself in a typically drab, institutional room with gray walls, fluorescent lights and a speckled, multicolored Armstrong tile floor designed to conceal wear. A U-shaped counter separated the largest part of the main room from a waiting area just inside the doors. Susan walked past several uncomfortable-looking metal chairs, past two small tables on which were stacked a variety of public service pamphlets, and went straight to the counter.

On the other side, there were several desks, file cabinets, a large work table, a bottled-water dispenser, a photocopier, a giant wall map of the county, and a huge bulletin board that was covered with tacked-on bulletins and photographs and wanted notices and odd scraps of paper.

In an adjacent alcove, out of sight, a woman dispatcher was talking to a patrol officer on a short-

336

wave radio. The storm was throwing in bursts of static.

In the main room there was only one man. He was sitting at a desk, typing on an IBM Selectric, his back turned to the counter and to Susan.

'Excuse me,' Susan said, brushing at her rain-beaded eyelashes with the back of one hand. 'Can you help me?'

He swung around on his swivel chair, smiled, and said, 'I'm Officer Whitlock. What can I do for you?'

He was young, perhaps twenty or twenty-one.

He was a bit on the pudgy side.

He had dirty blond hair, a round face, a dimpled chin, a pug nose, and the small quick eyes of a pig.

He had a twisted, nasty smile.

He was Carl Jellicoe.

Susan sucked in a breath that seemed to pierce her lungs as if it were a nail, and she wasn't able to expel it.

When he had been wearing a hospital orderly's uniform, he had called himself Dennis Bradley. Now he was wearing a brown uniform with the County Sheriff's Department seal stitched to his left sleeve and to the breast pocket of his shirt, and he carried a .45-caliber revolver in a black leather holster on his hip, and he called himself Officer Whitlock.

Susan couldn't speak. Shock had seared her vocal cords as thoroughly as a gas flame could have; her throat was parched, cracking; her mouth was

337

suddenly hot, dry, and filled with a burnt-out taste.

She couldn't move.

She finally let out her breath with a sob, and she gasped for more air, but she still couldn't move.

'Surprise, surprise,' Jellicoe said, giggling, getting up from his swivel chair.

Susan shook her head, slowly at first, then vehemently, trying to deny his existence.

'Did you really think you could get away from us that easily? Did you really?' he asked, standing with his legs spread, hitching up his holster.

Susan stared at him, transfixed, her feet fused to the floor. Her hands were clenched tightly around the edge of the wooden counter, as if that were her only grip on reality.

Not taking his piggish little eyes off Susan, Jellicoe called out to someone in an adjoining room. 'Hey, come look at what we've got here!'

Another deputy appeared. He was twenty or twenty-one, tall, with red hair and hazel eyes and a fair complexion that was spattered with freckles. In his hospital orderly's uniform, he had called himself Patrick O'Hara. Susan didn't know what he called himself now, but she knew what he had called himself thirteen years ago, when he had been a student at Briarstead College, when he had helped kill Jerry Stein in the House of Thunder: Herbert Parker.

'My, my,' Parker said. 'The lady looks distressed.'

'Well, you see, the poor thing thought she'd

338

gotten away from us,' Jellicoe said.

'Did she really?' Parker said.

'Really.'

'Doesn't she know she can never get away from us? Doesn't she know we're dead?'

Jellicoe grinned at her. 'Don't you know we're dead, you silly little bitch?'

'You read about it in the newspapers,' Parker reminded her. 'Don't you recall?'

'The car accident?' Jellicoe prodded.

'About eleven years ago, it was.'

In the communications alcove, the unseen dispatcher continued to talk with cruising patrol officers over the shortwave radio, as if nothing unusual were happening out here in the main room. But the woman *must* know.

'We rolled that damned car over like it was just a little toy,' Jellicoe said.

'Rolled it twice,' Parker said.

'What a mess it was.'

'What a mess *we* were.'

'All because of this slut.'

They both started toward the counter, neither of them in a hurry, ambling between the desks, smiling.

'And now she thinks it'll be easy to run away from us,' Carl Jellicoe said.

Parker said, 'We're dead, you stupid bitch. Don't you understand what that means? You can't *hide* from dead men.'

'Because we can be anywhere— '

'—everywhere— '

'—all at the same time.'

'That's one of the advantages of being dead.'

'Which doesn't *have* many advantages.'

Jellicoe giggled again.

They were almost to the counter.

Susan was gasping now, breathing as frantically as a pumping bellows in a blazing forge.

'You aren't dead, damn you,' she said, abruptly finding her voice.

'Oh, yes. We're dead— '

'—and buried— '

'—and gone to Hell— '

'—and come back again.'

'And now this place is Hell.'

'For you, it is, Susan. For you, for a little while, this is Hell.'

Jellicoe was moving around to the gate, where a section of the counter top lifted to allow passage between the waiting area and the bullpen.

A heavy glass ashtray was on the counter, within Susan's reach. She finally moved, snatched up the ashtray, and threw it at Jellicoe's head.

He didn't just stand there and let the missile pass magically through his body to prove that he was, indeed, a ghost. For a dead man, Jellicoe exhibited a surprisingly healthy fear of being hurt. He ducked behind the counter.

The ashtray missed him, struck the metal desk, cracked apart, and clattered in pieces to the floor.

A long-handled, police-issue flashlight also stood

on the counter, and Susan seized that, too. She swung it back over her shoulder, prepared to let it fly at Jellicoe, but out of the corner of her eye, she saw that Herbert Parker was drawing his revolver, so she fled across the waiting area, through the glass doors, into the night.

The boughs of the giant spruce flailed at one another, and the tree's tens of thousands of green needles were briefly colored silver by a flash of lightning.

Susan ran to the stolen Pontiac and jerked open the door. She got in and reached for the keys, which she had left dangling in the ignition.

The keys were gone.

For you, for a little while, this is Hell.

She glanced toward the glass doors.

Jellicoe and Parker were just coming out of the slumpstone building. They weren't in a hurry.

Susan slid across the seat, frantically pushed open the door on the passenger's side, and got out of the car, putting it between her and the two men.

She looked around her, determining the best route of escape, hoping that her legs would hold up. Thank God for those physical therapy sessions with Mrs. Atkinson! Otherwise, she wouldn't have gotten this far. But four days of exercise and good food didn't mean she was back to full power. Eventually, she would collapse, and that moment would come for her long before it would come for either Jellicoe or Parker.

Above the roar of the rain, above the trumpeting

of the wind, Jellicoe called to her. 'There's no use running, Susan.'

'There's no place to hide!' Parker shouted.

'Fuck you,' she said, and she ran.

16

The house had a welcoming look to it. There was a white picket fence, a shrub-bordered walkway, and a wide front porch with an ornate wooden railing and an old-fashioned porch swing suspended from the rafters. Warm yellow light shone through the lace curtains that covered the downstairs windows.

For a few minutes, Susan stood at the gate in the fence, studying the house, wondering if it was a safe place. She was cold, thoroughly wet, and miserable, and the rain was still coming down hard. She was eager to get inside where it was warm and dry, but she didn't intend to walk into another trap if she could avoid it; she wanted to feel *right* about the house before she went up to the door, rang the bell, and asked for help.

Go on, she urged herself. Do it. Don't just stand there. The whole damned town can't be part of the conspiracy, for God's sake!

Everyone at the hospital was a part of it, of course, but then it wasn't a *real* hospital. It was the Milestone Corporation, whatever the hell *that* was.

The police were involved, too, which was outrageous and scary, constituting a stunning setback for her, but she understood how such a thing was possible. Sometimes, in a small town like Willawauk, if one major company totally dominated the economic life of the community – through the jobs it provided and the taxes it paid – then it wielded tremendous power over the local authorities, even to the extent of being able to use the police as a sub rosa enforcement arm for the company's own purposes and protection. Susan didn't know for sure that Milestone was *the* employer of note in town, but it clearly had used its influence and a lot of money to corrupt the sheriff's department. The situation was outlandish, although not unbelievable.

But that was where the conspiracy ended, surely. Milestone, all of its employees, and the police were part of it; all right, she could accept that much. Already, however, the size of the conspiracy was unwieldy. It couldn't possibly encompass anyone else without starting to unravel at the seams. By their very nature, conspiracies could not include *thousands* of people.

Nevertheless, she stood in the rain by the gate, studying the house, envying the people who were warm and dry inside – and fearing them, too.

She was three blocks from the sheriff's offices. She had gotten away from Jellicoe and Parker with little trouble, running down alleyways, staying in the shadows, darting from tree to tree across several lawns.

In fact, now that she thought about it, avoiding Jellicoe and Parker had been too easy. Like finding the keys in the Pontiac when she needed a car. With good reason, she had come to distrust easy escapes.

An exceptionally brilliant flash of lightning briefly transformed the night into day. Rain began falling harder than ever, and it seemed colder, too.

That was enough to propel Susan through the gate and up the walk to the front porch. She rang the bell.

She didn't see what else she could do. She had nowhere else to go, no one to turn to except strangers chosen at random from all the houses full of strangers on all these strange, rain-scoured streets.

The porch light came on.

Susan smiled and tried to appear harmless. She knew that she must look wild: waterlogged, her hair curled into tight ringlets and tangled in knots by the rain and the wind, her face still somewhat emaciated, her eyes stark and haunted. She was afraid of presenting such a bad image that people would be discouraged from opening their doors to her. A tremulous smile was not enough to make her look like the Welcome Wagon lady, but it was all she could offer.

Happily, the door opened, and a woman peered

out, blinking in surprise. She was in her middle or late forties, a cherub-faced brunette with a pixie-style haircut. She didn't even wait for Susan to speak, but said, 'Good gracious, whatever are you doing out on a night like this, without an umbrella or a raincoat? Is something wrong?'

'I've had some trouble,' Susan said. 'I was— '

'Car trouble?' the brunette asked, but she didn't wait for an answer. She was a bubbly, outgoing woman, and she seemed to have been waiting for someone who had an ear that needed talking off. 'Oh, don't they just always break down in weather like this! Never on a sunny day in June. Always at night and always in a storm. And never when you can find a mechanic or when you have change for a pay phone. You'll be wanting to know if you can use our phone. That's it, isn't it? Well, of course, of course. Come in here where it's warm, call whoever you want. And I think I'll make you some hot coffee. By the look of you, you'll need something hot if you're going to stave off pneumonia.' She stepped aside so that Susan could enter.

Startled by the woman's unreserved hospitality and by her nonstop chatter, Susan said, 'Well . . . uh . . . I'm dripping.'

'Won't hurt a thing. We've got a dark carpet – have to with the kids; just imagine what they'd do to a *white* carpet – and it's an Antron Plus fiber, which means it just *won't* take a stain no matter how hard the little devils try. Besides, you're only dripping rainwater, not spaghetti sauce or chocolate syrup. A little rain isn't going to hurt it. Come in, come in.'

Susan went inside, and the woman closed the door.

They were standing in a cozy foyer. The flower-patterned wallpaper was too busy for Susan's taste, but it wasn't unattractive. A small table stood against one wall of the foyer; a brass-framed mirror hung above the table; an arrangement of dried flowers stood on the table, in front of the mirror.

A television set was playing in another room. It was tuned to an action show: tires squealed; people shouted; guns blazed; dramatic music swelled.

'My name's Enid,' the brunette said. 'Enid Shipstat.'

'I'm Susan Thorton.'

'You know, Susan, you should always carry an umbrella in your car, even when it doesn't look like it's going to rain, just in case something like this happens. An umbrella and a flashlight and a first-aid kit. Ed – that's my hubby – he also keeps a little tire pump in the trunk, a little electric model that plugs right into the cigarette lighter, so if you get a flat that's caused by a slow leak or a puncture, then you can reinflate it long enough to get to a gas station. That way you don't have to change the tire yourself, out on the road, in bad weather, maybe in the middle of a storm like this. But good heavens, this isn't the time to talk about being a good Girl Scout, is it? What in the world is wrong with me? Here I am offering you all sorts of

347

unsolicited advice, when you're standing there shaking like a leaf. Sometimes I think my mouth isn't wired up to my brain. Come on back to the kitchen. That's probably the warmest room in the house, and I can brew you up some good hot coffee. There's a phone in the kitchen, too.'

Susan decided to wait until she'd had a few sips of coffee before explaining that her plight didn't involve car trouble. She followed Enid Shipstat into a narrow hall, where the only light was that which spilled in from the foyer and a bluish TV glow that came from the living room, on the right.

As they passed the living room archway, Susan almost stopped and gaped in surprise at the sight beyond the arch. It was a relatively normal American living room, arranged around the TV as most American living rooms were, but it was over-furnished with chairs and sofas – and with children. A dozen kids ringed the television, sitting on the furniture and on the floor, all intently watching the softly glowing screen, which provided, along with one small lamp, the only light in the room. A dozen heads turned as if they were all part of a single organism, and a dozen young faces looked expressionlessly at Susan for a moment, eyes shining with reflected TV light, then turned to the screen again when their attention was drawn by a burst of gunfire and the wail of a police siren. Their rapt silence and their blank expressions were eerie.

'I only have Hills Brothers,' Enid said as she led Susan down the hall toward the kitchen. 'That's the only kind of coffee Ed will drink. Personally, I like Folger's just as well, but Ed thinks it's not as mellow as Hills Brothers, and he just can't *stand* that Mrs. Olsen on the commercials. He says she reminds him of a busybody old schoolteacher he once had.'

'Anything you've got is fine,' Susan said.

'Well, like I told you, all we have is just Hills Brothers, I'm afraid, so I hope you like Hills Brothers.'

'That'll be fine.'

Susan wondered how the Shipstats managed to raise a dozen children in this simple, two-story house. It was a fairly large place, but not *that* large. The bedrooms would have to be organized like army barracks, with sets of bunk beds, at least four kids to a room.

As Enid Shipstat pushed open the swinging kitchen door, Susan said, 'You've got quite a family.'

'You *see* why we don't have white carpet?' Enid said, and she laughed.

They stepped into the kitchen, a brightly lit room with clean yellow ceramic-tile counters and white cabinets with yellow porcelain knobs on the doors and drawers.

A young man was sitting sideways to the door, his elbows propped on the kitchen table, his head buried in his hands, bent over a large textbook.

'That's Tom, my oldest boy,' Enid said with pride. 'He's in his senior year at college, always

349

studying. He's going to be a rich lawyer some day, and then he's going to support his poor old mom and dad in luxury. Isn't that right, Tom?' She winked at Susan to show that she was only kidding.

Tom took his hands down from his face, raised his head, and looked at Susan.

It was Ernest Harch.

Madness, Susan thought, her heart lurching into high gear. *Sheer madness*.

'This lady's had some trouble with her car,' Enid told her son. 'She needs to use our phone.'

Harch smiled and said, 'Hello, Susan.'

Enid blinked. 'Oh, you *know* each other.'

'Yeah,' Harch said. 'We know each other real well.'

The room seemed to tilt beneath Susan's feet.

Harch stood up.

Susan backed up, bumped against the refrigerator.

'Mom,' Harch said to Enid, 'I can help Susan, if you want to get back to your TV show.'

'Well,' Enid said, looking back and forth between Susan and Harch, 'I was going to make some coffee . . .'

'I've already brewed up a pot,' Harch said. 'I always need coffee when I've got a long night of studying ahead of me. You know that, Mom.'

'Well,' Enid said to Susan, pretending not to notice the sudden tension in the room, 'you see, it *is* one of my favorite shows, and I hate to miss it even one week because the story kind of continues episode to episode— '

'*Shut up, shut up, shut up!*' Susan said in a voice that was half whimper, half snarl. 'Just cut the crap.'

Enid's mouth fell open, and she blinked stupidly, as if she was genuinely amazed by Susan's outburst and was utterly unable to imagine the reason for it.

Harch laughed.

Susan took a step toward the swinging door through which she and Enid had entered the kitchen. 'Don't try to stop me. I swear to God, I'll claw your eyes out and I'll try my damnedest to bite your jugular open. I *swear* I will.'

'Are you *crazy*?' Enid Shipstat said.

Still laughing, Harch started around the table.

Enid said, 'Tom, is your friend joking, or what?'

'Don't try to stop me,' Susan warned him as she edged away from the refrigerator.

'If this is a joke, it doesn't seem the least bit funny to me,' Enid said.

Harch said, 'Susan, Susan, it's no use. Don't you know that by now?'

Susan turned, slammed through the kitchen door, bolted into the hall. She half expected to find the children blocking her exit, but the hallway was deserted. The kids were still sitting in the living room when she ran past the archway. Bathed in blue light and the flickering reflections of the images on the screen, they appeared to be oblivious

351

to the shouting in the kitchen.

What kind of house *is* this? Susan wondered desperately as she hurried down the shadowy hall. What kind of kids *are* they? Little zombies in front of that TV.

She reached the front door, tried it, and found that it was locked.

Harch entered the hall from the kitchen. He was pursuing her but without urgency, just as Jellicoe and Parker had done. 'Listen, you stupid bitch, we'll get you whether you run or not.'

Susan twisted the doorknob back and forth.

Harch approached leisurely along the shadowy hall. 'Tomorrow night you'll pay for what you did to us. Tomorrow night, I'll have been dead for seven years, and you'll pay for that. We'll screw you, all four of us, every which way we can, turn you inside out and upside down, screw your damned brains out—'

The door shuddered as she pulled frantically on it, but it would not open.

'—screw you like we should have that night in the cave, and then we'll slit you wide open, all the way up the middle, and cut your pretty head off, just exactly the way we should have handled you, just like I *wanted* to do thirteen years ago.'

Susan wished that she had the courage to spin around and face him, strike him, and go for his throat with her teeth. She could do something like that if she were sure it would hurt him; it wouldn't turn her stomach. She had the nerve and the rage to feel his blood bubbling in her mouth without gagging on it. But she was afraid that she would cut him and find that he *didn't* bleed, that he was dead, after all. She knew that was impossible. But now that she had encountered Harch again, now that she had seen those peculiar gray eyes once more, had seen them filled with an arctic hatred, she could no longer hold on to her carefully reasoned refutation of the supernatural. Her faith in the scientific method and in logic was crumbling again; she was being reduced to babbling fear once more, losing control, hating it, despising herself, but losing control nevertheless.

Jellicoe's words came back to her: *For you, for a little while, this is Hell.*

She wrenched at the door in blind panic, and it opened with a scraping sound. It hadn't been locked, just warped by the damp weather.

'You're wasting your energy, baby,' Harch called after her. 'Save it for Friday. I'd be angry if you were too worn out to be any fun on Friday.'

She stumbled through the door, onto the porch, and down the three steps to the walk. She ran to the gate in the picket fence, into the rain and wind.

As she pelted along the dark street, splashing through deep puddles that came over the tops of her shoes, she heard Harch calling to her from back at the house.

'. . . pointless . . . no use . . . nowhere to hide . . .'

* * *

353

Susan approached the Main Street Cinema by way of alleys and parking lots. Before rounding the corner of the theater, onto the well-lighted Main Street sidewalk, she looked both ways, studying the rain-slashed night for signs of the police.

The ticket booth was closed. The last show for the night was already underway; no more tickets could be sold.

She pushed through the outer doors, into the lobby. It was deserted.

But it was warm, gloriously warm.

The lights had been turned off behind the refreshment counter, which seemed odd. Since theaters made more money from selling food and beverages than they did from their share of the ticket sales, they usually kept the refreshment stand open until the last patron had gone home after seeing the last scene of the final show of the night.

From inside the theater auditorium, music swelled, and Dudley Moore's voice was raised in drunken laughter. Obviously, the movie currently unreeling was *Arthur*.

She had come to the theater because she needed to get warm and dry; but more than that, she had to have a chance to sit and think, think, think – before she lost her mind altogether. From the moment she had walked into the sheriff's offices and had encountered Jellicoe, she had been *react*-ing rather than acting, and she knew she must stop drifting wherever they pushed her. She had to regain control of events.

She had considered going up the street to the Plenty Good Coffee Shop instead of to the theater, but she had worried about the police cruising by and spotting her through the restaurant's big plate-glass windows. By contrast, the movie theater was a dark and private sanctuary.

She crossed the clean, plushly carpeted lobby to the padded inner doors, opened one of them just far enough to slip through, and closed it quickly behind her.

On the big screen, Arthur had just awakened in bed after a night of debauchery. It was John Gielgud's first scene. Susan had seen the film when it had first been released, early last summer. In fact she had liked it so much that she had gone to see it twice. She knew that the scene now playing was fairly early in the movie. There must be at least an hour to go before the end credits, an hour of dry, warm time during which she could attempt to make some sense of what had happened to her tonight.

Susan's eyes hadn't yet adjusted to the pitch-black theater. She couldn't see if there was a crowd or only a few patrons. Then she remembered that there were only two cars in the parking lot. Mustn't be a crowd; not many people would *walk* to the theater on a night like this.

She was standing beside the left-hand aisle seat in the last row, which was the only seat she could see clearly, and it was empty. She took it, rather than search for something more private and risk drawing attention to herself. Her wet clothes squished as she sat down, and they clung to her, cold and sticky.

She tuned the movie out.

She thought about ghosts.

Demons.

Walking dead men.

Again, she decided that she couldn't accept a supernatural explanation. At least not for the time being. For one thing, there wasn't anything to be gained by dwelling on the occult possibilities, for if that *was* the explanation, there was absolutely nothing she could do to save herself. If all the forces of Hell were aligned against her, then she was lost for sure, so she might just as well rule out the very possibility of it.

She ruled out madness, too. She might actually *be* mad, but there was nothing whatsoever she could do to change that if it were the case, so it was better not even to think about it.

Which left her with the conspiracy theory.

That wasn't much of a theory, either. She didn't have the slightest idea who, how, or why.

As she puzzled over those three essential questions, her thoughts were briefly disturbed by a wave of laughter that swept the theater. Although it came in reaction to a very funny scene in *Arthur* and wasn't at all out of place, there was something about the laughter which seemed distinctly *odd* to Susan.

Of course, the volume of laughter indicated that there were quite a few people in the theater, at least a hundred, maybe more, and that was certainly a surprise, considering the fact that there were only two cars in the parking lot. But that wasn't what was odd about it.

Something else.

Something about the sound of it.

The laughter subsided, and Susan's thoughts returned to her escape plans.

When had it begun to go wrong?

As soon as she had left the hospital – or, rather, as soon as she'd left Milestone – *that* was when it had begun to go wrong. The keys in the Pontiac. Too easy. Which meant they had known she would try to escape, and they had actually *wanted* her to try. The Pontiac had been left there expressly for her use.

But how had they known that she would think to look in the car for the keys? And how could they have been so certain that she would stop at the sheriff's station?

How could they have known she would go to the Shipstat house for help? Willawauk contained hundreds of other houses, other people to whom she might have turned. Why had the Harch lookalike been waiting with such perfect confidence at the Shipstat place?

She knew the most likely answer to her own question, but she didn't want to believe it. Didn't even want to consider it. Maybe they always knew where she was going to go next because they had *programmed* her to go there. Maybe they had planted a few crucial directives in her subconscious while she'd been in the coma. That would explain why they never seriously pursued her when she ran from them; they knew she would walk into their arms later, at a prearranged place.

Maybe she had no free will whatsoever. That possibility made her feel sick to her stomach – and in her soul, as well.

Who *were* these shadowy manipulators with god-like power over her?

Her train of thought was derailed by another wave of loud laughter that rolled through the theater, and this time she realized what was odd about the sound. It was the laughter of young people: higher pitched than that of a general audience, quicker and more eager and more shrill than the laughter of adults.

Her eyes had adapted somewhat to the darkness in the theater, and she raised her head, looked around. At least two hundred people were present. No, it was more like three hundred. Of those nearest to Susan, of those she could see, all appeared to be kids. Not young children. Teenagers. Thirteen to eighteen, or thereabouts. High school and junior high kids. As far as she could tell, she was the only adult in the crowd.

Why had three hundred kids walked through a fierce storm to see a movie that was almost six months old? And what kind of uncaring parents would have permitted them to risk pneumonia and possibly even electrocution by lightning just to come to a movie?

She thought of the dozen children at the Shipstat house, their faces glazed by the bluish light from the TV.

Willawauk seemed to have more than its share of children.

And what the devil did all these children have to do with her own situation?

Something. There was some connection, but she couldn't figure it out.

While Susan was puzzling over the oddity of Willawauk's youthful population, she saw a door open at the front of the theater, to the left of the screen. A pale blue light shone in a room beyond the door. A tall man came out into the auditorium and closed the door behind him. He switched on a flashlight, one with a very narrow beam, and pointed it at the floor immediately in front of him.

An usher?

He started up the aisle.

Toward Susan.

The theater was fairly large, three times longer than it was wide. The usher took at least half a dozen steps up the sloping aisle before Susan became aware, through some sixth sense, that he was a threat to her.

She stood up. Her wet clothes stuck to her. She had been in the theater only fifteen minutes, not nearly long enough to dry out, and she was reluctant to leave.

The usher kept coming.

The narrow flashlight beam bobbled up and down a bit with each step the man took.

Susan edged away from her seat, into the aisle. She squinted into the gloom ahead, trying to perceive the usher's face.

He was forty feet away, coming slowly toward her, invisible behind his flashlight, suddenly silhouetted but unrevealed by a bright scene on the movie screen.

Dudley Moore said something funny.

The audience laughed.

Susan began to shake.

John Gielgud said something funny, and Liza Minelli said something funny right back at him, and the audience laughed again.

If I was programmed to steal the Pontiac, Susan thought, and if I was programmed to go to the sheriff's station and to the Shipstat house, then perhaps I was also programmed to come here instead of going up the street to the Plenty Good Coffee Shop or somewhere else.

The usher was no more than thirty feet away now.

Susan took three sliding steps backwards to the padded doors that opened onto the lobby. She reached behind her and put one hand against the door.

The usher raised the flashlight, no longer directing it toward the sloping floor in front of him, and shone it straight into Susan's face.

360

The beam wasn't terribly bright, but it blinded her because her eyes had adjusted to the darkness.

He's one of *them*, she thought. One of the dead men. Probably Quince because Quince hasn't yet put in an appearance tonight.

Or maybe it was Jerry Stein, his face rotting away from his bones, pus oozing from his swollen, purple lips. Jerry Stein, all dressed up in a neat usher's uniform, coming to say hello, coming to get a kiss.

There's nothing supernatural about this, she told herself in a desperate attempt to stave off panic.

But maybe it *was* Jerry, his face gray, a little green around the eyes, with brown-black blisters of corruption extending from his nostrils. Maybe it was Jerry, coming to give her a hug, coming to take her in his arms. Maybe he would lower his face to hers and put his lips to hers and thrust his cold, slimy tongue into her mouth in a grotesque kiss of graveyard passion.

For you, for a little while, this is Hell.

Susan flung open the door and raced out of the theater, into the lobby, across the plush carpeting, through the outer doors, not daring to look back. She turned right at the corner of the building, into the parking lot, and headed toward the dark alley. She sucked the humid air deep into her heaving lungs, and she felt as if she were breathing wet cotton.

In seconds, her clothes were as thoroughly

soaked as they had been when she'd gone into the theater.

Hot flashes of pain shot through her legs, but she tried to ignore them. She told herself she could run all night if that were necessary.

But she knew she was lying to herself. She was quickly using up what little strength she had managed to store away during the past five days. Not much was left. Dregs.

* * *

The Arco service station was closed for the night. Rain lashed the gasoline pumps and rattled against the big windows and drummed on the metal garage doors.

Beside the station, a public telephone booth stood in shadows. Susan stepped into it but didn't close the door because closing it would turn on the booth light.

She had gotten change for a dollar from a change machine in a coin-operated laundromat. She dropped a dime in the phone and dialed the operator.

She was shivering uncontrollably now, miserably cold and exhausted.

'Operator.'

'Operator, I'd like to place a long-distance call and charge it to my home number.'

'And what is the number you're calling, please?'

Susan gave her Sam Walker's number in Newport Beach. She had dated Sam for over a year, and he had been more serious about their relationship than she had been. They had broken off last spring, not without pain, but they were still friends; they talked once in a while on the phone, and they occasionally encountered each other by accident at restaurants they both favored, in which case they weren't so estranged that they couldn't have dinner together.

It was perhaps a condemnation of her excessively solitary, self-reliant, go-it-alone nature that she had no really close girl friends from whom she could seek help. She had no one closer than Sam, and she had last seen him nearly five weeks before she had left on her vacation to Oregon.

'What is the number to which you wish to bill the call?' the operator asked.

Susan recited her home number in Newport Beach.

After fleeing from the Main Street Cinema, she had decided that she couldn't be sure of escaping from Willawauk unless she had help from someone outside of town. She didn't know if she could convince Sam that she was in danger and that the Willawauk police couldn't be trusted. Even though he knew she didn't take drugs or drink to excess, he'd have to wonder if she was stoned. She could not possibly tell him the whole story or even most of it; for sure, he'd think she had slipped a mental gear. The trick was to tell him only enough to make him come running or to convince him to call the FBI for her.

The FBI, for God's sake! It all sounded so ludicrous. But who else did you call when you couldn't trust the local police? Who else did you turn to? Besides, there was kidnapping involved here, and that was a federal offense, within the FBI's jurisdiction.

She would have called the Bureau's Oregon office herself, except she didn't think she'd be able to convince a total stranger that she was really in trouble. She wasn't even certain that she could convince Sam, who knew her very well.

Down in Newport Beach, Sam's phone began to ring.

Please be there, please, she thought.

A gust of icy wind rammed through the open door of the phone booth. It pummeled her back with hard-driven rain.

Sam's phone rang three times.

Four times.

Please, please, please . . .

A fifth time.

Then someone picked it up. 'Hello?'

'Sam?'

'Hello?'

There was a lot of static on the line.

'Sam?'

'Yeah. Who's this?'

His voice was faint.

'Sam, it's me, Susan.'

A hesitation. Then: 'Suzie?'

'Yes.'

'Suzie Thorton?'

'Yes,' she said, relieved that at last she had

touched someone beyond Willawauk.

'Where are you?' he asked.

'Willawauk, Oregon.'

'Will *who* walk to Oregon?'

'No, no. Willawauk.' She spelled it.

'Sounds like you're calling from Tahiti or something,' he said as the static temporarily abated.

Listening to him, Susan felt a terrible suspicion
uncoiling like a snake in her mind. A new chill
slithered through her, a tongue of ice flickering on
her spine.

She said, 'I can hardly hear you.'

He said, 'I said, it sounds like you're calling from
Tahiti or something.'

Susan pressed the receiver tightly to her ear, put
her hand over her other ear, and said, 'Sam, you
don't . . .'

'What? Suzie, are you there?'

'Sam . . . you don't . . . sound like yourself.'

'Suzie, what's this all about?'

She opened her mouth, but she couldn't bring
herself to speak the dreadful truth.

'Suzie?'

Even the goddamned *telephone company* couldn't
be trusted in Willawauk.

'Suzie, are you there?'

Her voice cracked with fury and anger, but she
spat out the unthinkable thought: 'You aren't Sam
Walker.'

Static.

Silence.

More static.

At last he giggled and said, 'Of course I'm not Walker, you stupid bitch.'

It was Carl Jellicoe's giggle.

Susan felt a thousand years old, older than that, ancient, wasted, shriveled, hollow.

The wind changed direction, slammed against the side of the phone booth, rattled the glass.

Jellicoe said, 'Why do you insist on thinking it's going to be easy to get away from us?'

Susan said nothing.

'There's no place to hide. Nowhere to run.'

'Bastard,' she said.

'You're finished. You're through,' Jellicoe said. 'Welcome to Hell, you dumb slut.'

She slammed the phone down.

Susan stepped out of the booth and looked around at the rain-drenched service station and at the street beyond. Nothing moved. There was no one in sight. No one was coming after her. Yet.

She was still free.

No, not free. She was still on a very long leash, but she was not free. On a leash – and she had the strong feeling that they were about to begin reeling it in.

* * *

For a little while, she walked, hardly aware of the rain and the cold wind any more, stubbornly disregarding the pain in her legs, unable to formulate any new escape plans. She was merely passing time now, waiting for them to come for her.

She paused in front of St. John's Lutheran Church.

There was a light inside. It filtered out through the large, arched, stained-glass windows; it colored the rain red, blue, green, and yellow for a distance of three or four feet, and it imparted a rainbow glow to the thin veil of wind-whirled fog.

A parsonage was attached to the church, a Victorian-style structure: two full stories plus a gabled attic, bay windows on the second floor. The neatly tended lawn was illuminated by an ornate iron lamppost at the outer end of the walk, and two smaller, matching iron lamps on the porch posts, one on each side of the steps. A sign on the gate read, REV. POTTER B. KINFIELD.

Susan stood in front of Reverend Kinfield's house for a couple of minutes, one hand on the gate, leaning against it. She was too weary to go on, but she was too proud to lie down in the street and just give up as if she were a whipped dog.

Without hope, but also without anything else to do and without anywhere else to go, she finally went up the walk and climbed the steps to the parsonage porch. You were supposed to be able to count on clergymen. You were supposed to be able to go to them with any kind of problem and get help. Would that be true of clergymen in Willawauk? Probably not.

She rang the bell.

Although the outside lights were burning

brightly, the house itself was dark. That didn't necessarily mean the preacher wasn't home. He might have gone to bed. It was late, after all. She didn't know exactly how late it was; she had lost track of time. But it must be somewhere between eleven o'clock and midnight.

She rang the bell again.

And again.

No lights came on inside. No one answered.

In anticipation of the minister's response to the bell, Susan had summoned up images of warmth and comfort; a toasty parlor; a big, soft easy chair; pajamas, a heavy robe, and slippers borrowed from the preacher's wife; maybe some nice buttered toast and hot chocolate; sympathy, outrage at what had been done to her; promises of protection and assistance; a bed with a firm mattress; crisp, clean sheets and heavy woolen blankets; two pillows; and a lovely, lovely feeling of being safe.

Now, when no one answered the door, Susan couldn't get those images out of her mind. She simply could not forget them and just walk away. The loss hurt too much, even though it was the loss of something she'd never really possessed in the first place. She stood on the porch, quivering on the verge of tears, desperately wanting those damned dry pajamas and that hot chocolate, wanting them with such fierce intensity that the wanting drove out all other emotions, including all fear of Ernest Harch and the walking dead men and the people behind Milestone.

She tried the door. It was locked.

She moved along the porch, trying the dash-hung windows. The three to the left of the door were all locked. The first one to the right was also locked, but the second one was not. It was swollen by the damp air, and it didn't move easily, but finally she raised it far enough to squeeze through, into the parsonage.

She had just committed an illegal act. But she was a desperate woman, and the Reverend Kinfield would surely understand once he heard all the facts. Besides, this was Willawauk, Oregon, where the normal rules of society didn't apply.

The interior of the house was utterly black. She couldn't see more than two or three inches in front of her face.

Curiously, the house wasn't warm, either. It seemed almost as cold as the night outside.

Susan felt her way along the wall, moving left, past the first window on that side of the door, then to the door itself. She located the switch on the wall, flicked it.

She blinked at the sudden flood of light – then blinked in surprise when she saw that the Lutheran parsonage was not what it appeared to be from the outside. It wasn't a gracious old Victorian house. It was a *ware*house: one room as large as a barn, more than two stories high, with no partitions, and a bare concrete floor. Life-size papier-mâché figures for a nativity scene, plus a large red sleigh complete with reindeer were suspended from the ceiling on wires, stored away until the holidays. The room itself was filled with cardboard cartons, hundreds upon hundreds of them stacked four and five high; there were also trunks, chests, enormous wooden crates and a couple of dozen metal cabinets, each about seven feet high, four feet deep and eight feet long. Everything was arranged in neat rows that extended the length of the building, with access aisles in between.

Baffled, Susan ventured away from the wall and went exploring through the stacks. In the first couple of cabinets, she found black choir robes hanging from metal bars, each robe sealed tightly in a clear plastic bag. In the third cabinet, she uncovered several Santa Claus outfits, two Easter Bunny costumes, and four sets of Pilgrims' clothes that apparently were used in Thanksgiving celebrations. The first of the cardboard cartons – according to the labels on them – contained religious pamphlets, Bibles, and church songbooks.

All of those things, including the Christmas figures that were suspended from the ceiling, were objects that any church might wish to store. Not, of course, in a fake parsonage; that part of it didn't make any sense at all. But those goods were perfectly legitimate.

Then she found other things that seemed out of place and more than a little strange.

Three entire, sixty-foot-long walls of boxes and crates – as many as two or three thousand containers – were filled with clothes. The labels told a curious story. The first hundred or so were all marked the same:

U.S. FASHIONS
WOMEN'S DRESSES
1960–1964
(KENNEDY ERA)

A smaller number of containers were labeled:

U.S. FASHIONS
MEN'S SUITS AND TIES
1960–1964
(KENNEDY ERA)

There were a lot of women's clothes, some men's clothes, and a few boxes of children's clothes from every subsequent fashion era through the late Seventies. There were even clusters of boxes in which the clothing of various subcultures was stored:

U.S. FASHIONS
MALE ATTIRE – MIXED
HIPPIE SUBCULTURE

All of this was not simply evidence of an ambitious clothing drive to benefit the church's overseas missions. It was clearly a long-term storage program.

Susan was also convinced that it wasn't merely

some ambitious historical preservation project. These weren't museum samples of American clothing styles; these were entire wardrobes, sufficient to clothe hundreds upon hundreds of people in virtually any fashion period from the past twenty years.

It appeared as if the people of Willawauk were so extraordinarily thrifty – every man, woman, and child of them – that they had joined en masse to preserve their out-of-date clothing, just in case old styles came back into fashion some day and could be used again. It was wise and admirable to attempt to circumvent the expensive tyranny of fashion designers. But in a throwaway culture like America's, where virtually everything was designed to be disposable, what kind of people, what kind of community, could organize and so perfectly execute an enormous storage program like this one?

A community of robots, perhaps.

A community of ants.

Susan continued to prowl through the stacks, her confusion increasing. She found scores of boxes labeled INFORMAL HOLIDAYS: HALLOWEEN. She peeled the tape off one of those boxes and opened it. It was crammed full of masks: goblins, witches, gnomes, vampires, the Frankenstein monster, werewolves, alien creatures, and assorted ghouls. She opened another box and found Halloween party decorations: orange and black paper streamers, plastic jack-o'-lanterns, bundles of real Indian corn, black paper cutouts of cats and ghosts. This huge collection of Halloween gear was not just for parties at St. John's Church; there was enough stuff here to decorate the entire town and to costume all of its children.

She moved along the aisles, reading labels on some of the hundreds of other containers:

INFORMAL HOLIDAYS: VALENTINE'S DAY
FORMAL HOLIDAYS: CHRISTMAS
FORMAL HOLIDAYS: NEW YEAR'S EVE
FORMAL HOLIDAYS: INDEPENDENCE DAY
FORMAL HOLIDAYS: THANKSGIVING
PRIVATE PARTIES: BABY SHOWER
PRIVATE PARTIES: BIRTHDAY
PRIVATE PARTIES: WEDDING ANNIVERSARY
PRIVATE PARTIES: BAR MITZVAH
PRIVATE PARTIES: BACHELOR/STAG

Susan finally stopped examining the boxes and the cabinets because she realized there were no answers to be found among them. They only raised new questions about Willawauk. In fact, the more she probed through this place, the more confused and disoriented and depressed she became. She felt as if she had chased a white rabbit and had fallen down a hole into a bizarre and considerably less than friendly Wonderland. Why were bar mitzvah decorations stored in St. John's Lutheran Church?

And wasn't it strange for a church to store supplies for a stag party? Dirty movies, posters of naked women, party napkins bearing obscene cartoons – that sort of stuff kept in a *church*? Why wasn't the parsonage really a parsonage? Was there a Reverend B. Kinfield, or was he only a fictitious character, a name on a gate plaque? If he existed, where did he live, if not in the parsonage? Was Willawauk inhabited by four thousand or more pack rats who never threw *anything* away? What was going on in this town? At a glance, everything appeared to be normal. But on closer inspection, there hadn't been a single thing about Willawauk that hadn't turned out to be strange.

How many other buildings in town were not what they appeared to be?

She walked wearily out of the storage aisles and returned to the front door. She was growing increasingly shaky. She wondered if there was any chance at all that she would eventually be able to climb out of the rabbit hole, back into the real world.

Probably not.

Outside again, she could barely stay on her feet. Her rain-sodden clothes felt as if they weighed a couple thousand pounds. The impact of the raindrops was incredible, and the wind struck with sledgehammer blows that threatened to drive her to her knees.

She knew that Harch and the others would come for her, sooner or later, and until they did, she just wanted to sit where it was warm. All hope of escape had left her.

The church might be warm. At least it would be dry, and she would be out of the cold wind. That is – if the church was real. If it wasn't just a facade, like a false-front set on a Hollywood back-lot.

There was light in the church, anyway. Maybe that was a good sign; maybe there would be heat, too.

She climbed the dozen brick steps toward the heavy, hand-carved oak doors, hoping they were unlocked.

The doors of a church were supposed to remain unlocked at all times, twenty-four hours a day, every day, so that you could go inside to pray or to be comforted whenever you needed to escape from the pain of life. That's the way it was *supposed* to be, but you could never be sure of anything in good old Willawauk, Oregon.

She reached the doors. There were four doors, two sets of two. She tried the one on the extreme right. It was unlocked.

At least *something* in Willawauk was as it should be.

Pulling open the door, about to step into the building, she heard an engine in the street behind her. The hiss of tires on the wet pavement. The squeal of brakes.

She turned and looked down the steps.

An ambulance had drawn up to the curb in front

of the church. Three words were painted on the side of it: WILLAWAUK COUNTY HOSPITAL.

'There is no such goddamned thing,' Susan said, surprised to find a drop of anger remaining in her vast pool of resignation and depression.

Jellicoe and Parker got out of the ambulance and looked up at her. They were no longer dressed as sheriff's deputies. They were wearing white raincoats and white rain hats, black boots. They were playing hospital orderlies again.

Susan didn't intend to run from them. She couldn't. Her strength and her will power were gone, used up.

On the other hand, she wasn't going to walk down the steps and into their arms, either. They would have to come and get her and carry her back to the ambulance.

Meanwhile, she would go inside where it was warm, go as far toward the front of the church as her legs would take her, so that Jellicoe and Parker would have to carry her that much farther when they took her out to the ambulance. It was a small, perhaps meaningless protest. Pathetic, really. But passive resistance was the only kind of which she was still capable.

The church *was* warm. It felt wonderful.

She shuffled through the vestibule. Into the church proper. Down the center aisle. Toward the altar.

It was a pretty church. Lots of wood, marble, and brass. During the day, when light was coming in through the stained-glass windows, painting everything in bright hues, it would be beautiful.

She heard Carl Jellicoe and Herbert Parker enter the church behind her.

Her aching, quivering legs supported her all the way to the front pew, but she knew they would crumple under her if she took another step.

'Hey, slut,' Jellicoe said from the back of the church.

She refused to turn and face them, refused to acknowledge her fear of them.

She sat down on the first, highly polished pew.

'Hey, bitch.'

Susan faced forward, staring at the large brass cross behind the altar. She wished she were a religious woman, wished she were able to take comfort from the sight of the cross.

At the front of the church, to the left of the altar, the door to the sacristy opened. Two men came out.

Ernest Harch.

Randy Lee Quince.

The extent to which she had been manipulated was clear now. Her escape hadn't been her own idea. It had been *their* idea, part of *their* game. They had been teasing her the way a cat will sometimes tease a captured mouse: letting it think there's a real hope of freedom, letting it squirm away, letting it run a few steps, then snatching it back again, brutally. The mezuzah hadn't been dropped accidentally in the bathroom. It had been left there on purpose, to nudge her toward an escape again, so that the cats could have their bit of fun.

She'd never really had a chance.

Harch and Quince descended the altar steps and moved to the communion railing.

Jellicoe and Parker appeared in the aisle at her side. They were both grinning.

She was limp. She couldn't even raise a hand to protect herself let alone to strike out against them.

'Has it been as much fun for you as it's been for us?' Carl Jellicoe asked her.

Parker laughed.

Susan said nothing. Stared straight ahead.

Harch and Quince opened a gate in the communion railing and walked up to the first pew, where Susan sat. They stared down at her, smiling. All of them smiling.

She stared between Quince and Harch, trying to keep her eyes fixed steadily on the cross. She didn't want them to see her quaking with fear; she was determined to deny them that pleasure, at least this one time.

Harch stooped down, squarely in front of her, forcing her to look at him.

'Poor baby,' he said, his raspy voice making a mockery of any attempt at sympathy. 'Is our poor little bitch tired? Did she run her little butt off tonight?'

Susan wanted to close her eyes and fall back into the darkness that waited within her. She wanted to go away inside herself for a long, long time.

But she fought that urge. She met Harch's hateful, frost-gray eyes, and her stomach churned, but she didn't look away.

'Cat got your tongue?'

'I hope not,' Quince said. 'I wanted to cut her tongue out myself!'

Jellicoe giggled.

To Susan, Harch said, 'You want to know what's going on?'

She didn't respond.

'Do you want to know what this is all about, Susan?'

She glared at him.

'Oh, you're so tough,' he said mockingly. 'The strong, silent type. I *love* the strong, silent type.'

The other three men laughed.

Harch said, 'I'm sure you want to know what's going on, Susan. In fact I'm sure you're *dying* to know.'

'Dying,' Jellicoe said, giggling.

The others laughed, sharing a secret joke.

'The car accident you had,' Harch said. 'Two miles south of the turnoff to the Viewtop Inn. That part was true.'

She refused to be prodded into speaking.

'You rolled the car over an embankment,' Harch said. 'Slammed it into a couple of big trees. We weren't lying about that. The rest of it, of course, was all untrue.'

'We're all shameless fibbers,' Jellicoe said, giggling.

'You didn't spend three weeks in a coma,' Harch told her. 'And the hospital was a fake, of course. All of it was lies, deceptions, a clever little game, a chance to have some fun with you.'

She waited, continuing to meet his cold gaze.

'You didn't have a chance to languish in a coma,' Harch said. 'You died instantly in the crash.'

Oh, shit, she thought wearily. What are they up to now?

'Instantly,' Parker said.

'Massive brain damage,' Jellicoe said.

'Not just a little cut on the forehead,' Quince said.

'You're dead, Susan,' Harch said.

'You're here with us now,' Jellicoe said.

No, no, no, she thought. This is crazy. This is madness.

'You're in Hell,' Harch said.

'With us,' Jellicoe said.

'And we've been assigned to entertain you,' Quince said.

'Which we're looking forward to,' Parker said.

Quince said, 'Very much.'

No!

'Never thought you'd wind up here,' Jellicoe said.

'Not a goody-goody bitch like you,' Parker said.

'Must have all sorts of secret vices,' Jellicoe said.

'We're really glad you could make it,' Quince said.

Harch just stared at her, stared hard, his cold eyes freezing her to the core.

'We'll have a party,' Jellicoe said.

Quince said, 'An endless party.'

'Just the five of us,' Jellicoe said.

'Old friends,' Parker said.

Susan closed her eyes. She knew it wasn't true. It *couldn't* be true. There wasn't such a place as Hell. No Hell or Heaven. That was what she had always believed.

And didn't nonbelievers go to Hell?

'Let's fuck her now, right here,' Jellicoe said.

'Yeah,' Quince said.

She opened her eyes.

Jellicoe was unzipping his pants.

Harch said, 'No. Tomorrow night. The seventh anniversary of my death. I want it to have that significance for her.'

Jellicoe hesitated, his fly half undone.

'Besides,' Parker said, 'we want to do it to her in the right place. This isn't the right place.'

'Exactly,' Harch said.

Please, God, please, Susan thought, let me find my way back up the rabbit hole . . . or let me just go to sleep. I could just lay back here against the pew . . . and go to sleep . . . forever.

'Let's get the bitch out of here,' Harch said. He stood, reached down, seized Susan by her sweater, dragged her to her feet. 'I've waited a long time for this,' he said, his face close to hers.

She tried to pull away from him.

He slapped her face.

Her teeth rattled; her vision blurred. She sagged, and other hands grabbed her.

They carried her out of the church. They weren't gentle about it.

In the ambulance, they strapped her down, and Harch began to prepare a syringe for her.

Finally, she rose out of her lethargy far enough to speak. 'If this is Hell, why do you need to give me an injection to knock me out? Why don't you just cast a spell on me?'

'Because *this* is so much more fun,' Harch said, grinning, and with savage glee he rammed the hypodermic needle into her arm.

She cried out in pain.

Then she slept.

17

Flickering light.

Dancing shadows.

A high, dark ceiling.

Susan was in bed. The hospital bed.

Her arm hurt where Harch had stabbed her viciously with the needle. Her entire body ached.

This wasn't her old room. This place was cool, too cool for a hospital room. Her body was warm underneath the blankets, but her shoulders and neck and face were quite cool. This place was damp, too, and musty. Very musty.

And familiar.

Her vision was blurry. She squinted, but she still couldn't see anything.

Squinting made her dizzy. She felt as if she were on a merry-go-round instead of a bed; she spun around, around, and down into sleep again.

* * *

Later.

Before she opened her eyes, she lay for a

moment, listening to the roar of falling water. Was it still raining outside? It sounded like a deluge, like Armageddon, another Great Flood.

She opened her eyes, and she was immediately dizzy again, although not as dizzy as before. There was flickering light and dancing shadows, as there had been the first time. But now she realized that it was candlelight, disturbed by crossdrafts.

She turned her head on the pillow and saw the candles. Ten thick cylinders of wax were arranged on the rocks and on the nearest limestone ledges and formations.

No!

She turned her head the other way, toward the roaring water, but she couldn't see anything. The candlelight drove the darkness back only a distance of about fifteen feet. The waterfall was much farther away than that, at least eighty or a hundred feet away, but there was no doubt that it was out there, tumbling and frothing in the blackest corner of the cave.

She was in the House of Thunder.

No, no, no, she told herself. No, this must be a dream. Or I'm delirious.

She closed her eyes, shutting out the candlelight. But she couldn't shut out the musty smell of the cavern or the thunderous noise of the underground waterfall.

She was three thousand miles away from the House of Thunder, dammit. She was in Oregon, not Pennsylvania.

Madness.

Or Hell.

Someone jerked the blankets off her, and she opened her eyes with a snap, gasping, crying out.

It was Ernest Harch. He put one hand on her leg, and she realized that she was naked. He slid his hand along her bare thigh, across her bristling pubic thatch, across her belly, to her breasts.

She went rigid at his touch.

He smiled. 'No, not yet. Not yet, you sweet bitch. Not for a while yet. Tonight. That's when I want it. Right at the hour I died in prison. Right at the minute that damned nigger stuck a knife in my throat, *that's* when I'm going to stick a knife in your throat, and I'm going to be up inside you at the same time, screwing you, spurting inside you just as I push the knife deep into your pretty neck. Tonight, not now.'

He took his hand off her breasts. He raised the other hand, and she saw that he was holding a hypodermic syringe.

She tried to sit up.

Jellicoe appeared and pushed her down.

'I want you to rest for a while,' Harch said. 'Rest up for the party tonight.'

Again, he was vicious with the needle.

As he finished administering the injection, he said, 'Carl, you know what I'm going to like most about killing her?'

'What's that?' Jellicoe asked.

'It's not the end. It's just the beginning. I get to kill her again and again.'

Jellicoe giggled.

Harch said, 'That's your fate, bitch. That's the way you're going to spend eternity. We're going to use you every night, and every night we're going to kill you. We'll do it a different way each time. There are thousands of ways, an infinite number of ways to die. You're going to experience all of them.'

Madness.

She sank down into a drugged sleep.

* * *

Underwater. She was underwater and drowning.

She opened her eyes, gasping for breath, and realized that she was only under the *sound* of water. The waterfall.

She was still in bed. She tried to sit up, and the covers slid off her; but she hadn't the strength to stay sitting up, and she collapsed back against the pillows, heart pounding.

She closed her eyes.

For just a minute.

Oh, maybe for an hour.

No way to tell for sure.

'*Susan . . .*'

She opened her eyes, and she was filled with dread. Her vision was smeary, but she saw a face in the flickering light.

'*Susan . . .*'

He drew nearer, and she saw him clearly. It was Jerry. The awful, rotting face. His lips were riper, more swollen than before, bursting with pus.

'*Susan* . . .'

She screamed. The harder she screamed, the faster the bed seemed to spin. She whirled off into deepest space.

* * *

And woke again.

The effects of the drug had almost worn off. She lay with her eyes closed, afraid to open them.

She wished she had not awakened. She didn't want to be awake ever again. She wanted to die.

'Susan?'

She lay perfectly still.

Harch thumbed one of her eyelids open, and she twitched in surprise.

He grinned. 'Don't try to fool me, you dumb bitch. I know you're there.'

She felt numb. Afraid but numb. Maybe, if she was lucky, the numbness would grow and grow until that was the *only* thing she could feel.

'It's almost time,' Harch said. 'Did you know that? In an hour or so, the party starts. In three hours, I'll cut your throat wide open. See, that gives us two hours for the party. Wouldn't want to disappoint the other guys, would we? Two hours ought to satisfy them, don't you think? You'll wear them out fast, a sexy girl like you.'

None of it seemed real. It was too crazy, too

senseless, too fuzzy at the edges to be real. A hospital bed in the middle of a cave? Not real at all. The terror, the violence, the implied violence, the purity of Harch's evil . . . all of that had the quality of a dream.

Yet she could feel the two separate pains of the two needles that he had jammed in her arms. *That* felt real enough.

Harch threw the covers aside, exposing her again.

'Bastard,' she said weakly, so weakly that she could barely hear her own voice.

'Just getting a preview,' Harch said. 'Say, baby, aren't you looking forward to it as much as I am? Hmmmmm?'

She closed her eyes, seeking oblivion, and she—

'*Harch!*'

—heard McGee shout her tormentor's name.

She opened her eyes and saw Harch turning away from her with a startled look on his face. He said, 'What are *you* doing here?'

Lacking the strength to sit all the way up in bed, Susan lifted her head as far off the pillow as she could, which wasn't very far, and she saw Jeff McGee. He was only a few feet from the end of the bed. The draft-blown candle flames cast wavering shadows over him, so that he appeared to be wearing a rippling black cape. He was holding a long-barreled pistol, and it was pointed at Harch.

Harch said, 'What in the hell are you— '

McGee shot him in the face. Harch pitched back-

388

wards, out of sight, and hit the floor with a sickening thud.

The pistol had made only a whispering sound, and Susan realized that part of the long barrel was a silencer.

That soft hiss, the sight of Harch's face exploding, the deadweight sound of him hitting the floor – all of that had the unmistakably gritty feeling of reality. It wasn't the stylized, exaggerated, endlessly extended, surreal violence to which she had been subjected during the last few days; there wasn't anything remotely dreamlike about this. It was death: cold, hard, quick.

McGee came around to the side of the bed.

Susan blinked at the pistol. She was no less confused by this strange turn of events. She felt herself teetering on the edge of a chasm. 'Am I next?'

He shoved the gun in a pocket of his overcoat.

He was carrying a bag in his other hand, and he dropped that on the bed beside her. No, not a bag. It was a pillowcase, stuffed full of something.

'We're getting out of here,' he said.

He began pulling clothes out of the pillowcase. Her clothes. Panties. A pair of dark slacks. A white sweater. A pair of penny loafers.

There was still a large, round object in the bottom of the pillowcase, and she regarded it with growing fear. The dreamlike feeling overtook her again; reality faded; and she was suddenly sure that the last thing in that pillowcase was Jerry Stein's severed, rotting head.

'No,' she said. 'Stop!'

He pulled out the last object. It was only her corduroy blazer, which had been rolled into a ball.

Not a dead man's head.

But she didn't feel any better. She was still adrift, unable to grab at the edge of reality and stabilize herself.

'No,' she said. 'No. I can't go through any more of this. Let's just get it over with.'

McGee looked at her oddly for a moment, then understanding came into his blue eyes. 'You think this is just a setup for another series of nasty little scenes.'

'I'm very, very tired,' she said.

'It's not,' he said. 'It's not a setup.'

'I just want to be finished with this.'

'Listen, half of your weariness is because of the drug they've been pumping into you. You'll perk up a bit in a little while.'

'Go away.'

She couldn't hold her head up any longer. She fell back on the pillow.

She didn't even care that she was naked before him. She didn't reach for the blankets. She wasn't sure she could pull them up, anyway. Besides, any attempt at modesty was ludicrous after what they'd already done to her, after what they had seen of her.

She was cold. That didn't matter, either. Nothing mattered.

'Look,' McGee said, 'I don't expect you to

understand what's going on. I'll explain later. Just trust me for now.'

'I did,' Susan said softly. 'I trusted you.'

'And here I am.'

'Yes. And here you are.'

'Here I am, *rescuing* you, dummy.' He said it with what seemed to be very real frustration and affection.

'Rescuing me from what?'

'From Hell,' he said. 'Wasn't that the latest line they were feeding you? Hell. That's what the program called for.'

'Program?'

He sighed and shook his head. 'We don't have time for this now. You've got to trust me.'

'Go away.'

He slipped an arm under her shoulders and lifted her into a sitting position. He snatched up the white sweater and tried to get her arms into the sleeves.

She resisted him as best she could. 'No more,' she said. 'No more sick games.'

'Christ!' he said. He dropped the sweater and eased her back onto the pillow. 'Stay here and listen. Can you *listen*?'

Before she could respond, he withdrew a penlight from his overcoat pocket, switched it on, and hurried away, into the darkness. The sound of the waterfall, toward which he was headed, soon masked the *tap-tap-tap* of his footsteps.

Maybe he would leave her alone now. Or finish her off. One or the other.

391

She closed her eyes.

The roar of the waterfall stopped abruptly.

In an instant, the House of Thunder became the House of Silence.

She opened her eyes, frowning. For a second, she thought she had gone deaf.

McGee shouted to her from the darkness. 'Hear that? Nothing but a tape recording of a waterfall.' He was drawing nearer as he spoke; there was no sound to mask his footsteps now. 'It was a tape recording, blasting through four big quadraphonic speakers.' He stepped into the glow of the candles and switched off his penlight. 'Driest waterfall you'll ever see. And this cave? It's a bunch of hollowed-out rocks, papier-mâché, cardboard and spit. A stage setting. That's why there's only a few candles; if you could see only a few feet farther, you'd know it was just a hoax. It's set in the middle of the high school gymnasium, so that you get a feeling of open space beyond the darkness. I'd turn the lights on and show you, except I don't dare draw any attention. The windows are blacked out, but if even a little light escaped, someone might notice – and come running. And that musty smell, in case you're wondering, is *canned* odor, guaranteed to make a spelunker feel right at home. Some of our people whipped it up in the lab. Aren't they handy?'

'What *is* Willawauk?' she asked, getting interested in spite of herself and in spite of her fear that she was being set up once more.

'I'll explain in the car,' McGee said. 'There isn't time now. You'll just *have* to trust me.'

She hesitated, head spinning.

He said, 'If you don't trust me, you might *never* find out what Willawauk is.'

She let her breath out slowly. 'All right.'

'I *knew* you had moxie,' he said, smiling.

'I'll need help.'

'I know.'

She let him dress her. She felt like a little girl as he put her sweater on for her, pulled her panties and then her jeans up her legs, and slipped her shoes on her feet.

'I don't think I can walk,' she said.

'I didn't intend to ask you to walk. Can you at least hold the flashlight?'

'I think I can do that.'

He picked her up. 'Light as a feather. A *big* feather. Hold tight to my neck with your free arm.'

She directed the light where he told her, and he carried her out of the phony cavern, across the floor of the gymnasium. The beam of the small flash bounced off the highly polished wood floor, and in that pale glow, she was aware that they passed under a basketball hoop. Then they went down a set of concrete steps, through a door that McGee had left ajar, and into a locker room.

The lights were on here, and three dead men were sprawled in the area between the coach's office and the lockers. Jellicoe and Parker were on the floor. Half of Jellicoe's face was gone. Parker had two holes in his chest. Quince was draped over a bench, still dripping blood onto the floor from a wound in his neck.

Beginning to huff a bit, McGee carried her between two rows of tall lockers, past the shower room, to another door that had been left ajar. He shouldered through it, into a well-lighted hallway.

Another dead man lay on the floor here.

'Who's he?' she asked.

'Guard,' McGee said.

They went a short distance down the hall, turned the corner into another hall, and went to a set of metal doors, beside which lay another corpse, apparently another guard.

'Kill the flash,' McGee said.

She switched it off, and he leaned against the pushbar handle on the metal doors, and then they were outside.

It was a clear, cool night. Almost an entire day had passed while she had slid in and out of a drugged stupor.

Two cars waited in the school lot. Breathing hard now, McGee took her to a blue Chevrolet and put her down beside it. She leaned against the car, for her legs were too limp to support her even for the few seconds he took to open the door and help her inside.

They drove boldly out of Willawauk by way of Main Street, which eventually turned into a county road. They were not only headed away from Willawauk, but also away from the building in which she had been hospitalized. Neither of them spoke until the last lights of town were out of sight, until only wild, green countryside lay around them.

Huddled in the passenger's seat, Susan looked over at McGee. His face was strange in the green luminescence of the dashboard gauges. Strange – but not threatening.

She still didn't entirely trust him. She didn't know what to believe.

'Tell me,' she said.

'It's hard to know where to begin.'

'Anywhere, dammit. Just begin.'

'The Milestone Corporation,' he said.

'Back there on the hill.'

'No, no. That sign you saw on the hospital lawn when you escaped in the Pontiac – that was just put up to confuse you, to add to your disorientation.'

'Then the place is really a hospital.'

'A hospital – and other things. The real Milestone Corporation is in Newport Beach.'

'And I work for them?'

'Oh, yes. That's all true. Although it wasn't Phil Gomez you spoke with on the phone. That was someone in Willawauk, pretending to be Gomez.'

'What do I *do* at Milestone?'

'It's a think tank, just like I told you. But it doesn't work with private industry. Milestone's a front for a super-secret U.S. military think tank that functions under the direct control of the Secretary of Defense and the President. Congress doesn't even know it exists; its appropriations are obtained in a *very* round-about fashion. At Milestone, two dozen of the finest scientific minds in the country have been brought together with perhaps the most sophisticated data library and computer system in the world. Every man and woman at Milestone is a brilliant specialist in his or her field, and every science is covered.'

'I'm one of the experts?' she asked, still not able to recall a thing about Milestone, still not even convinced that it actually existed.

'You're one of two particle physicists they have there.'

'I can't remember.'

'I know.'

As he drove through the dark, forested countryside, McGee told her everything he knew about Milestone – or at least, everything he *professed* to know.

Milestone (according to McGee) had one primary goal; to develop an ultimate weapon – a particle beam, some new kind of laser, a new biological weapon, *anything* – which would in one way or another render nuclear weaponry not just obsolete but useless. The U.S. government had for some time been convinced that the Soviet Union was seeking nuclear superiority with the express intention of launching a first-strike attack the moment that such a monstrous tactic was likely to result in a clean, painless Soviet victory. But it hadn't been possible, until recently, to sell the American public on the idea that rearmament was a desperate necessity. Therefore, in the middle Seventies, the President and the Secretary of Defense could see no hope except a miracle; a miracle weapon that would cancel out the Soviet arsenal and free mankind from the specter of an atomic holocaust. While it wasn't possible to launch a massive arms buildup costing hundreds of billions of dollars, it *was* possible to secretly establish a new research facility, better funded than any had ever been before, and hope that American ingenuity would pull the country's ass out of the fire. In a sense, Milestone became America's last best hope.

'But surely that kind of research was already being done,' Susan said. 'Why was there a need to establish a new program?'

'Anti-war elements within the research community – primarily student lab assistants – were stealing information and leaking it to anyone who would listen and who would join the battle against the Pentagon war machine. In the mid-Seventies, the university-based weapons research establishment was crumbling. The President wanted that kind of research to go forward strictly in the shadows, so that any breakthroughs would remain the exclusive property of the United States.

'For years, the very existence of Milestone was unknown to Soviet Intelligence. When agents of the KGB finally learned of it, they were afraid that the U.S. might be nearing – or might already have achieved – its goal of rendering the Soviet war machine impotent. They knew they had to get their hands on one of Milestone's scientists and engage in weeks of unrestrained interrogation.'

The Chevy began to accelerate too rapidly down a long, steep hill, and McGee tapped the brakes.

'The scientists at Milestone are encouraged to familiarize themselves with one another's fields of interest, in order to search for areas of overlap and to benefit from cross-fertilization of ideas. *Every one of the twenty-four department chiefs at Milestone knows a great deal about the workable ideas that have come out of the place so far*. It means that many of the Pentagon's future plans could be compromised by any *one* of the Milestone people.'

'So the Soviets decided to snatch me,' Susan said, gradually beginning to believe him, but still filled with doubts.

'Yeah. The KGB managed to find out who worked at Milestone, and it investigated everyone's background. You seemed the most likely target, for you were having serious doubts about the morality of weapons research. You had started on that road immediately after earning your doctorate, when you were only twenty-six, before you were really old enough to have developed a sophisticated system of values. As you grew older, you also grew concerned about your work and its impact on future generations. Doubts surfaced. You expressed them to your fellow workers, and you even took a month-long leave of absence to consider your position, during which time you apparently reached

398

no conclusions, because you returned to work, still doubting.'

'As far as I'm concerned, you might as well be talking about a total stranger,' Susan said, regarding him suspiciously. 'Why can't I remember any of this now that you're telling me about it?'

'I'll explain in a moment,' he said. 'We're about to be stopped.'

They reached the bottom of the long hill and turned a bend. There was a mile-long straightaway ahead, and there seemed to be a roadblock straddling the center of it.

'What's that?' Susan asked anxiously.

'A security checkpoint.'

'Is this where you turn me over to them? Is this where the game gets nasty again?' she asked, still having trouble believing that he was on her side.

He glanced at her, frowning. 'Give me a chance, okay? Just give me a chance. We're leaving a highly restricted military zone, and we have to pass through security.' He fished two sets of papers out of a coat pocket while he drove with one hand. 'Slouch down and pretend to be asleep.'

She did as he said, watching the brightly lighted checkpoint – two huts, a gate between them – through slitted eyes. Then she closed her eyes and let her mouth sag open as if she were sleeping deeply.

'Not a word out of you.'

'All right,' she said.

'No matter what happens – not a word.'

McGee slowed the car, stopped, and wound down the windows.

Susan heard booted feet approaching.

The guard spoke and McGee answered. Not in English.

Susan was so startled to hear them speaking in a foreign language that she almost opened her eyes. It hadn't occurred to her to ask him why she must feign sleep when he possessed papers that would get them through the checkpoint. He hadn't wanted her to be required to talk to the guards; one word of English, and they would both be finished.

The wait was interminable, but at last she heard the power-operated gate rolling out of the way. The car moved.

She opened her eyes but didn't dare glance back. 'Where are we?' she asked McGee.

'You didn't recognize the language?'

'I'm afraid maybe I did.'

'Russian,' he said.

She was speechless. She shook her head: *no, no*.

'Thirty-some miles from the Black Sea,' he said. 'That's where we're headed. To the sea.'

'*Inside the Soviet Union?* That's not possible. That's just crazy!'

'It's true.'

'No,' she said, huddling against the passenger door. 'It can't be true. This *is* another setup.'

'No,' he said. 'Hear me out.'

She had no choice but to hear him out. She wasn't going to throw herself from a speeding car.

And even if she could get out of the car without killing herself, she wouldn't be able to run. She wouldn't even be able to walk very far. The effect of the drugs had begun to fade, and she felt strength returning to her legs again, but she was nevertheless exhausted, virtually helpless.

Besides, maybe McGee was telling the truth this time. She wouldn't want to bet her life on it. But maybe.

He said, 'KGB agents kidnapped you while you were on your vacation in Oregon.'

'There never was a car accident then?'

'No. That was just part of the program we designed to support the Willawauk charade. In reality, you were snatched in Oregon and smuggled out of the U.S. on a diplomatic flight.'

She frowned. 'Why can't I remember that?'

'You were sedated throughout the trip to Moscow.'

'But I should at least remember being kidnapped,' she insisted.

'All memories of that event were carefully scrubbed from your mind with certain chemical and hypnotic techniques— '

'Brainwashing.'

'Yes. It was necessary to remove the memory of the kidnapping in order that the Willawauk program would seem like reality to you.'

She had dozens of questions about Willawauk and about this 'program' to which he repeatedly referred, but she restrained herself and allowed him to tell it in his own way.

'In Moscow, you were first taken to a KGB detention facility, a truly nasty place at Lubyianka Prison. When you failed to respond to questioning and to the standard array of psychological trickery, they got rougher with you. They didn't beat you or anything like that. No thumbscrews. But in some ways, it was worse than physical torture. They used a variety of unpleasant drugs on you, stuff with extremely dangerous side effects, very physically and mentally debilitating crap that should *never* be used on a human being for *any* reason. Of course, it was all just standard KGB procedure for extracting information from a stubborn source. But as soon as they employed those methods, as soon as they tried to *force* answers from you, a strange thing happened. You lost all conscious memory of your work at Milestone, every last scrap of it, and only a gaping hole was left where those memories had been.'

'There's still a gaping hole,' she said.

'Yes. Even drugged, even perfectly docile, you were unable to tell the KGB anything. They worked on you for five days, five very intense days, before they finally discovered what had happened.'

McGee stopped talking and cut the car's speed in half as they approached a small village of about a hundred houses. This tiny village didn't resemble Willawauk in any way whatsoever. It was very obviously not an American place. Except for a few scattered electric lights, it appeared as if it belonged in another century. Some of the houses had stone roofs, others had board and thatched roofs. All the structures were squat, with very small windows, drab and somber places. It looked medieval.

When they had passed through the town and were on the open road again, McGee put his foot down hard on the accelerator once more.

'You were about to tell me why I lost all my memories of Milestone,' Susan said.

'Yeah. Well, as it turns out, when anyone goes to work for the Milestone project, he must agree to undergo a series of highly sophisticated behavioral modification treatments that make it impossible for him to talk about his work with anyone outside of Milestone. If he won't agree to undergo the treatment, then he doesn't get the job. In addition, deep in their subconscious minds, all the employees of Milestone are fitted with cunningly engineered psychological mechanisms that can trigger memory blockages, memory blockages that prevent foreign agents from *forcing* vital information out of them. When someone tries to pry secret data out of a Milestone employee by means of torture or drugs or hypnosis, *all* of that employee's conscious knowledge of his work drops instantly far, far down into his deep subconscious mind, behind an impenetrable block, where it cannot be squeezed out.'

Now she knew why she couldn't even recall what her laboratory at Milestone had looked like. 'All the memories *are* still there, inside me, some-where.'

'Yes. When and if you get out of Russia, when you get back to the States, Milestone undoubtedly has some procedure for dissolving the block and bringing back your memory. And it's probably a procedure that can *only* be carried out at Mile-stone, something involving you and the computer, perhaps a series of block-releasing code words that the computer will reveal only to you, and only after you've been positively identified to it by letting it scan your fingerprints. Of course, this is merely conjecture. We don't really know *how* Milestone would restore your memory; if we knew, we'd have used the same technique. Instead, we had to resort to the Willawauk program in hopes of shattering the block with a brutal series of psychological shocks.'

The night flashed by them. The land was much flatter now than it had been back around Willa-wauk. There were fewer trees. A moon had risen, providing a ghostly radiance.

Susan slouched in her seat, both weary and tense, watching McGee's face as he spoke, trying hard to detect any sign of deception, desperately hoping that he wasn't just setting her up for *another* brutal psychological shock.

'A memory block can be based on any emotion – love, hate, fear – but the most effective is fear,' McGee said. 'That was the inhibitor that Milestone used when creating your block. *Fear*. On a deep

404

subconscious level, you are terrified of revealing anything whatsoever about Milestone, for they have used hypnotic suggestion and drugs to convince you that you will die horribly and painfully the moment that you make even the smallest revelation to foreign agents. A fear block is by far the most difficult to break; usually, getting through it is utterly impossible – especially when it's as well implanted as your block is.'

'But you found a way.'

'Not me, personally. The KGB employs hordes of scientists who specialize in behavioral modification techniques – brainwashing and so forth – and a few of them think that a fear block *can* be demolished if the subject – that's you, in this case – is confronted with a fear far greater than the one upon which the block is based. Now, it isn't easy to find a fear that's greater than the fear of death. With most of us, that's numero uno. But the KGB had very thoroughly researched your life before they'd decided to snatch you, and when they looked through your dossier, they thought they saw your weak spot. They were looking for an event in your past that could be resurrected and reshaped into a living, breathing nightmare, into something you would fear more than death.'

'The House of Thunder,' she said numbly. 'Ernest Harch.'

'Yes,' McGee said. 'That was the key to the plan they put together. After studying you for some time, the KGB determined that you were an unusually well-ordered, efficient, rational person; they knew you abhorred disorder and sloppy thinking. In fact you seemed to be almost compulsively, obsessively ordered in every aspect of your life.'

'Obsessive? Yes,' she said, 'I guess maybe I am. Or I *was*.'

'To the KGB, it appeared that the best way to make you come apart at the seams was to plunge you into a nightmare world in which *everything* gradually became more and more irrational, a world in which the dead could come back to life, in which nothing and no one was what it seemed to be. So they brought you to Willawauk, and they sealed off one wing of the behavioral research hospital located there, turned it into a stage for their elaborate charades. They intended to push you slowly toward a mental and/or an emotional collapse, culminating in a scene in the phony House of Thunder. They had a very nasty bit of business planned. Rape. Repeated rape and torture at the hands of the four "dead" men.'

Susan shook her head, bewildered. 'But forcing me into a mental and emotional collapse . . . What good would that do them? Even if the fear block was broken in the process, I wouldn't have been in any condition to provide them with the information they wanted. I'd have been a babbling fool . . . or catatonic.'

'Not forever. A mental and emotional breakdown brought on by extreme *short-term* pressure is the easiest form of mental illness to cure,' McGee said. 'As soon as they'd broken you, they would have removed your memory block by promising relief from terror in return for your total submission and cooperation. Then they'd have immediately begun to rehabilitate you, nursing you back to sanity, or at least to a semblance of it, to a state in which you could be questioned and in which you could be relied upon to provide accurate information.'

'But wait,' she said. 'Wait a minute. Getting together the look-alikes, writing the script for the whole damned thing, working out all the contingencies, converting the wing of the hospital . . . all of that must have taken a lot of time. I was only kidnapped a few weeks ago . . . wasn't I?'

He didn't answer right away.

'*Wasn't I?*' she demanded.

'You've been inside the Soviet Union for more than a year,' McGee said.

'No. Oh, no. No, no, I can't have been.'

'You have. Most of the time, you were on ice in Lubyianka, just sitting in a cell, waiting for something to happen. But you don't remember that part of it. They erased all of that before bringing you to Willawauk.'

Her confusion gave way to white-hot anger. '*Erased?*' She sat up straight in her seat, her hands squeezed into fists. 'You say it so casually. Erased. You talk as if I'm a goddamned tape recorder! Jesus Christ, I spent a year in a stinking prison, and then they stole that year from me, and then they put me through this thing with Harch and the others . . .' Rage choked off her voice.

But she realized that she now believed him. Almost. She had almost no doubt at all that *this* was the truth.

'You have a right to be furious,' McGee said, glancing at her, his eyes unreadable in the glow from the dashboard. 'But please don't be angry with me. I didn't have anything to do with what happened to you then. I didn't have anything to do with you until they finally brought you to Willawauk, and then I had to bide my time until there was a chance of breaking you out of there.'

They rode in silence for a minute, while Susan's anger cooled from a boil to a simmer.

They came to the edge of the moonlit sea and turned south on a highway where, at last, there was other traffic, though not much. The other vehicles were mostly trucks.

Susan said, 'Who the hell *are* you? How do you fit into this whole thing?'

'To understand that,' he said, 'you'll have to understand about Willawauk first.'

Confusion and suspicion roiled in her again. 'Even in a year, they couldn't possibly have built that entire town. Besides, don't tell me they'd go to all *that* trouble just to pump me about the work being done at Milestone.'

'You're right,' he said. 'Willawauk was built in the early 1950s. It was designed to be a perfect model of an average, American small town, and it's constantly being modernized and refined.'

'But why? Why a model American town here in the middle of the USSR?'

'Willawauk is a training facility,' McGee said. 'It's where Soviet deep-cover agents are trained to think like Americans, to *be* Americans.'

'What's a . . . deep-cover agent?' she asked as McGee swung the Chevy into the outer lane and passed a lumbering, exhaust-belching truck of stolid Soviet make.

'Every year,' McGee said, 'between three and four hundred children, exceptionally bright three- and four-year-olds, are chosen to come to Willawauk. They're taken from their parents, who are not told what the child has been chosen for and who will never see their child again. The kids are assigned new foster parents in Willawauk. From that moment on, two things happen to them. First, they go through intense, daily indoctrination sessions designed to turn them into fanatical Soviet Communists. And believe me. I don't use the word "fanatical" lightly. Most of those kids are transformed into fanatics who make the Ayatollah Khomeini's followers seem like sober, reasonable Oxford professors. There's a two-hour indoctrination session every morning of their lives; worse, subliminal indoctrination tapes are played during the night, while they sleep.'

'Sounds like they're creating a small army of child robots,' Susan said.

'That's precisely what they're doing. Child

robots, spy robots. Anyway, secondly, the kids are taught to live like Americans, to think like Americans, and to *be* Americans – at least on the surface. They must be able to pass for patriotic Americans without ever revealing their underlying, fanatical devotion to the Soviet cause. Only American English is spoken in Willawauk. These children grow up without knowing a word of Russian. All books are in English. All the movies are American movies. Television shows are taped from the three American networks and from various independent stations – all kinds of shows, including entertainment, sports, news – and are then replayed to every house in Willawauk on a closed-circuit TV system. These kids grow up with the same media backgrounds, with the same experiences as real American kids. Each group of trainees shares social touchstones with its corresponding generation of true Americans. Finally, after many years of this, when the Willawauk children are saturated with U.S. culture, when the day-to-day minutiae of U.S. life is deeply ingrained in them, they are infiltrated into the U.S. with impeccable documents – usually between the ages of eighteen and twenty-one. Some of them are placed in colleges and universities with the aid of superbly forged family histories and high school records that, when supported by a network of Soviet sympathizers within the U.S., cannot be disputed. The infiltrators find jobs in a variety of industries, many of them in government, and they spend ten, fifteen, twenty, or more years slowly working up into positions of power and authority. Some of them will never be called upon to do any dirty work for their Soviet superiors; they will live and die as patriotic Americans – even though in their hearts, where they truly exist, they *know* they are good Russians. Others will be used for sabotage and espionage. *Are* used, all the time.'

'My God,' Susan said, 'the expense of such a program! The maniacal effort it would take to establish and maintain it is almost beyond conception. Is it really worth the expenditures?'

'The Soviet government thinks so,' McGee said. 'And there have been some astonishing successes. They have people placed in sensitive positions within the U.S aerospace industry. They have Willawauk graduates in the Army, the Navy, and the Air Force; not more than a few hundred, of course, but several of those have become high-ranking officers over the years. There are Willawauk graduates in the U.S. media establishment, which provides them with a perfect platform from which to sow disinformation. From the Soviet point of view, the best thing of all is that one U.S. senator, two congressmen, one state governor, and a score of other influential American political figures are Willawauk people.'

'Good God!'

Her own anger and fear were temporarily forgotten as the enormity of the entire plot became clear to her.

'And it's rare that a Willawauk graduate can be

turned into a double agent, serving the Americans. Willawauk people are just too well programmed, too fanatical to become turncoats. The hospital at Willawauk, where you were kept, serves the town as a fully equipped medical center, much better than hospitals in many other parts of the USSR, but it's also a center for research into behavioral modification and mind control. Its discoveries in those areas have helped to make the Willawauk kids into the most tightly controlled, most devoted and reliable espionage web in the world.'

'And you. What about you, McGee? Where do you fit in? And is your name really McGee?'

'No,' he said. 'My name's Dimitri Nicolnikov. I was born a Russian, to parents in Kiev, thirty-seven years ago. Jeff McGee is my Willawauk name. You see, I was one of the first Willawauk kids, though that was in the early days of the program, when they took young teenagers and tried to make deep-cover agents out of them in three or four years of training. Before they started working solely with kids obtained at the age of three and four. And I'm one of the few who ever turned double agent on them. Although they don't know it as yet.'

'They will when they find all the bodies you left behind.'

'We'll be long gone by then.'

'You're so confident.'

'I've got to be,' he said, giving her a thin smile. 'The alternative is unthinkable.'

Again, Susan was aware of the man's singular

strength, which was one of the things that had made her fall in love with him.

Am I still in love with him? she wondered.

Yes.

No.

Maybe.

'How old were you when you underwent training in Willawauk?'

'Like I said, that was before they started taking them so young and spending so many years on them. The recruits then were twelve or thirteen. I was there from the age of thirteen to the age of eighteen.'

'So you finished the training almost twenty years ago. Why weren't you seeded into the U.S.? Why were you still in Willawauk when I showed up?'

Before he could answer her, the traffic ahead began to slow down on the dark road. Brake lights flashed on the trucks as they lumbered to a halt.

McGee tapped the Chevy's brakes.

'What's going on?' Susan asked, suddenly wary.

'It's the Batum checkpoint.'

'What's that?'

'A travel-pass inspection station just north of the city of Batum. That's where we're going to catch a boat out of the country.'

'You make it sound as simple as just going away on a holiday,' she said.

'It could turn out like that,' he said, 'if our luck holds just a little longer.'

The traffic was inching ahead now, as each

vehicle stopped at the checkpoint, each driver passing his papers to a uniformed guard. The guard was armed with a submachine gun that was slung over his left shoulder.

Another uniformed guard was opening the doors on the back of some of the trucks, shining a flashlight inside.

'What're they looking for?' Susan asked.

'I don't know. This isn't usually part of the procedure at the Batum checkpoint.'

'Are they looking for us?'

'I doubt it. I don't expect them to find out we're gone from Willawauk until closer to midnight. At least an hour from now. Whatever these men are searching for, it doesn't seem to be all that important. They're being casual about it.'

Another truck was passed. The line of traffic moved forward. There were now three trucks in front of the Chevy.

'They're probably just hoping to catch a black market operator with contraband goods,' McGee said. 'If it was *us* they were looking for, there'd be a hell of a lot more of them swarming around, and they'd be a lot more thorough with their searches.'

'We're that important?'

'You better believe it,' he said worriedly. 'If they lose you, they lose one of the potentially biggest intelligence coups of all time.'

Another truck was waved through the checkpoint.

McGee said, 'If they could break you and pick

414

your mind clean, they'd get enough information to tip the East-West balance of power permanently in the direction of the East. You're *very* important to them, dear lady. And as soon as they realize that I've gone double on them, they'll want me almost as bad as they'll want to get you back. Maybe they'll even want me worse, because they'll *have* to find out how many of their deep-cover agents in the U.S. have been compromised.'

'And how many of them *have* you compromised?'

'All of them,' he said, grinning.

Then it was their turn to face the checkpoint guard. McGee turned down the window and passed out two sets of papers. The inspection was perfunctory; the papers were coming back through the window almost as soon as they had been handed out.

McGee thanked the guard, whose attention was already turned to the truck behind them. Then they headed into Batum, and McGee rolled up his window as he drove.

'Black market sweep, like I thought,' he said.

As they drove into the outskirts of the small port city, Susan said, 'If you were a graduate of Willawauk at eighteen, why weren't you seeded into the U.S. nineteen years ago?'

'I was. I earned my college degrees there, a medical degree with a specialty in behavioral modification medicine. But by the time I had obtained an important job with connections to the U.S. defense establishment, I was no longer a faithful Russian.

415

Remember, in those days, recruits were chosen at the age of thirteen. They weren't yet putting three-year-olds into the Willawauk program. I had lived twelve years of ordinary life in Russia, before my training was begun, so I had a basis for comparing the U.S. and the Soviet systems. I had no trouble changing sides. I acquired a love for freedom. I went to the FBI and told them all about myself and all about Willawauk. At first, for a couple of years, they used me as a conduit for phony data which helped screw up Soviet planning. Then, five years ago, it was decided that I would go back to the USSR as a double agent. I was "arrested" by the FBI. There was a big trial, during which I refused to utter one word. The papers called me the "Silent Spy." '

'My God, I remember! It was a big story back then.'

'It was widely advertised that, even though caught red-handed in the transmission of classified information, I refused even to state what country I was from. Everyone *knew* it was Russia, of course, but I played this impressively stoic role. Pleased the hell out of the KGB.'

'Which was the idea.'

'Of course. After the trial, I received a long prison sentence, but I didn't serve much time. Less than a month. I was quickly traded to the USSR for an American agent whom they were holding. When I was brought back to Moscow, I was welcomed as a hero for maintaining the secret of the

Willawauk training programme and the deep-cover network. I was the famous Silent Spy. I was eventually sent back to work at my old alma mater, which was what the CIA had hoped would happen.'

'And ever since, you've been passing information the other way, to the U.S.'

'Yes,' he said. 'I've got two contacts in Batum, two fishermen who have limited-profit deals with the government, so they own their own boats. They're Georgians, of course. This is Georgian SSR that we're traveling through, and a lot of Georgians despise the central government in Moscow. I pass information to my fishermen, and they pass it along to Turkish fishermen with whom they rendezvous in the middle of the Black Sea. And thereafter, it somehow winds up with the CIA. One of those fishermen is going to pass us along to the Turks the same way he passes classified documents. At least, I *hope* he'll do it.'

* * *

Access to the Batum docks was restricted; all ships, including the fishing boats, could be reached only by passing through one of several checkpoints. There were guarded gates that accepted trucks loaded with cargo, and there was one gate that accepted only military vehicles and personnel, and there were gates to accommodate dock workers, sailors, and others who were obliged to approach on foot; Susan and McGee went to one of the latter.

At night the wharves were poorly lighted, gloomy, except around the security checkpoints, where floodlights simulated the glare of noon. The walk-through gate was overseen by two uniformed guards, both armed with Kalisnikovs; they were involved in an animated conversation that could be heard even outside the hut in which they sat. Neither guard bestirred himself from that small, warm place; neither wanted to bother conducting a close inspection. McGee passed both his and Susan's forged papers through the sliding window. The older of the two guards examined the documents perfunctorily and quickly passed them back, not once pausing in the discussion he was having with his compatriot.

The chainlike gate, crowned with wickedly pointed barbed wire, swung open automatically when one of the guards in the hut touched the proper button. McGee and Susan walked onto the docks, uncontested, and the gate swung shut behind them.

Susan held on to McGee's arm, and they walked into the gloom, toward rows of large dark buildings that blocked their view of the harbor.

'Now what?' Susan whispered.

'Now we go to the fishermen's wharf and look for a boat called the *Golden Net*,' McGee said.

'It seems so easy,' she said.

'Too easy,' he said worriedly.

He glanced back at the checkpoint through which

they had just passed, and his face was drawn with apprehension.

* * *

Leonid Golodkin was master of the *Golden Net*, a hundred-foot fishing trawler with immense cold-storage capacity. He was a ruddy, rough-hewn man with a hard-edged, leathery face and big hands.

Summoned by one of his crewmen, he came to the railing at the gangway, where McGee and Susan waited in the weak yellow glow of a dock lamp. Golodkin was scowling. He and Jeff McGee began to converse in rapid, emotional Russian.

Susan couldn't understand what they were saying, but she had no difficulty understanding Captain Golodkin's mood. The big man was angry and frightened.

Ordinarily, when McGee had information to pass to Golodkin for transfer to Turkish fishermen on the high seas, those documents were forwarded through a black market vodka dealer who operated in Batum, two blocks from the wharves. McGee and Golodkin rarely met face-to-face, and McGee *never* came to the boat. Until tonight.

Golodkin nervously scanned the docks, apparently searching for curious onlookers, agents of the secret police. For a long, dreadful moment, Susan thought he was going to refuse to let them come aboard. Then, reluctantly, Golodkin swung back the hinged section of railing at the top of the gangway and hurried them through the open boarding

419

gate. Now that he had grudgingly decided to take them in, he was clearly impatient to get them below-decks, out of sight.

They crossed the afterdeck to a spiral, metal staircase and went below. They followed Golodkin along a cold, musty, dimly lighted corridor, and Susan wondered if she would ever again be in a place that wasn't somehow alien and forbidding.

The captain's quarters at the end of the corridor were unquestionably foreign, even though the room was warm and well lighted by three lamps. There was a desk – on which stood a half-filled brandy snifter – a bookcase with glass doors, a liquor cabinet, and four chairs, including the one behind the desk. A sleeping alcove was separated from the main cabin by a drawn curtain.

Golodkin motioned them to two of the chairs, and McGee and Susan sat down.

Directing Susan's attention to the brandy, McGee said, 'Would you like a glass of that?'

She was shivering. The mere thought of brandy warmed her. 'Yeah,' she said. 'It would sure hit the spot right now.'

In Russian, McGee asked Golodkin for brandy, but before the captain could respond, the curtains rustled in front of the alcove, drawing everyone's attention. Rustled . . . and parted. Dr. Leon Viteski stepped into the main cabin. He was holding a silencer-equipped pistol, and he was smiling.

A shockwave passed through Susan. Angry about being betrayed again, furious about being manipulated through yet another charade, Susan looked at McGee, hating herself for having trusted him.

But McGee appeared to be just as surprised as she was. At the sight of Viteski, Jeff started to rise from his chair, reaching into his coat pocket for his own pistol.

Captain Golodkin stopped him from drawing the weapon and took it away from him.

'Leonid,' McGee said in an accusatory tone. Then he said something in Russian that Susan couldn't understand.

'Don't blame poor Leonid,' Dr. Viteski said. 'He had no choice but to play along with us. Now sit down, please.'

McGee hesitated, then sat. He glanced at Susan, saw doubt in her eyes, and said, 'I didn't know.'

She wanted to believe him. His face was ashen, and there was fear in his eyes, and he looked like a man who had suddenly come eye-to-eye with Death. *But he's a good actor*, she reminded herself. For days, he had deceived her; he might *still* be deceiving her.

Viteski walked around the desk and sat in the captain's chair.

Golodkin stood by the door, his face unreadable.

'We've known about you for two and a half years,' Viteski told McGee.

McGee's pale face reddened. His embarrassment appeared to be genuine.

'And we've known about your contact with Leonid almost as long as we've known about you,'

Viteski said. 'The good captain has been working with us ever since we discovered that he was one of your couriers.'

McGee looked at Golodkin.

The captain flushed and shuffled his feet.

'Leonid?' McGee said.

Golodkin frowned, shrugged, and said something in Russian.

Susan watched Jeff McGee as McGee watched the captain. He seemed truly abashed.

'Leonid had no choice but to betray you,' Viteski told McGee. 'We have a strong grip on him. His family, of course. He doesn't like the fact that we've turned him into a double agent, but he knows we hold the reins. He's been quite useful, and I'm sure he'll be useful unmasking other agents in the future.'

McGee said, 'For two years or more, every time I passed documents to Leonid— '

'—he passed them directly to us,' Viteski said. 'We tinkered with them, edited them, inserted false data to mislead the CIA, then returned your packages to Leonid. *Then* he passed them to the Turks.'

'Shit,' McGee said bitterly.

Viteski laughed. He picked up the brandy glass and sipped the amber liquid.

Susan watched both men, and she grew increasingly uneasy. She began to think this wasn't just another charade. She began to think that McGee really *had* meant to take her to safety and that he *had* been betrayed. Which meant that both of them

422

had lost their last best chance of gaining freedom.

To Viteski, McGee said, 'If you knew I was going to try to rescue Susan, why didn't you stop me before I took her out of that House of Thunder mock-up, before I shattered the illusion?'

Viteski tasted the brandy again. 'We'd already decided that she couldn't be broken. She just wasn't responding satisfactorily to the program. *You* saw that.'

'I was half out of my mind with fear,' Susan said.

Viteski looked at her and nodded. 'Yes. *Half* out of your mind. And that was as far as you were going to get, I believe. You weren't going to break down. You're too tough for that, my dear. At worst, you would have withdrawn into some semi-catatonic state. But not a breakdown. Not *you*. So we decided to scrap the program and go with the contingency plan.'

'*What* contingency plan?' McGee asked.

Viteski looked at Leonid Golodkin and spoke rapidly in Russian.

Golodkin nodded and left the room.

'What did you mean by that?' McGee asked.

Viteski didn't respond. He merely smiled and picked up the brandy snifter again.

To McGee, Susan said, 'What's going on?'

'I don't know,' McGee said.

He held out his hand, and after only a brief hesitation, Susan took it. He gave her a smile of encouragement, but it was tissue-thin, unconvincing. Behind the smile, she saw fear.

Viteski said, 'This is excellent brandy. Must be black market stuff. You can't buy anything this good over the counter – unless you can get into one of the stores reserved for high Party officials. I'll have to ask the good captain for the name of his dealer.'

The door opened, and Leonid Golodkin came in. Two people entered behind him.

One of the newcomers was Jeffrey McGee.

The other was Susan Thorton.

Two more look-alikes.

They were even dressed the same as Jeff and Susan.

Susan's veins seemed to crystallize into fragile tubes of ice as she stared at her own duplicate.

The fake Susan smiled. The resemblance was uncanny.

His face bloodless, his eyes haunted, the real Jeff McGee glared at Leon Viteski and said, 'What the hell is this?'

'The contingency plan,' Viteski said. 'We had it in reserve right from the start, though we didn't tell *you*, of course.'

The fake Susan spoke to the real Susan: 'It's absolutely fascinating to be in the same room with you at last.'

Shocked, Susan said, 'She sounds exactly like me!'

The fake McGee said, 'We've been working with tapes of your voices for nearly a year.' He sounded exactly like the real McGee.

Viteski smiled at the doppelgängers with what appeared to be paternal pride. Then, to the real McGee, he said, 'You'll be shot and dumped overboard in the middle of the Black Sea. These two will go back to the U.S. in your places. *Our* Susan will start working at Milestone again.' He turned to Susan and said, 'My dear, it would have been most helpful if we could have broken you. It would have given us a head start. Nevertheless, we'll still get most of what we wanted by placing your lookalike in your office at Milestone. It'll just take us a lot longer; that's all. In a year or so, we'll have found out everything you could've told us. And if our little ruse can last longer than a year, we'll wind up getting more data than we could've gotten from you.' He turned to Jeff. 'We expect your double will find a place in the American intelligence community, perhaps in their behavioral control research, and that'll give us *another* well-placed mole.'

'It won't work,' McGee said. 'They may sound like Susan and me. And your surgeons did a damned good job of making them look like us. But no surgeon can alter fingerprints.'

'True,' Viteski said. 'But you see, for people with very high security clearances, the U.S. has a special system of filing and retrieving fingerprints. It's called SIDEPS, Security ID Protection System. It's part of a Defense Department computer to which we've managed to gain access. We can simply pull the electronic representation of your fingerprints and replace them with electronic representations of the fingerprints of your look-alikes. In this age of centralized computer data storage, it isn't necessary to change the real prints; we need only change the computer's memory of what the real prints look like.'

'It'll work,' Susan said softly, plagued by a mental image of her own body being dumped over the side of the *Golden Net*, into the cold waters of the Black Sea.

'Of course it'll work,' Viteski said happily. 'In fact, we would have sent the duplicates back to the U.S. even if you had broken and had told us everything we wanted to know.' Viteski finished the brandy in his glass, sighed in appreciation of it, and got to his feet, holding the pistol. 'Captain, while I cover these two, please tie their hands securely.'

Golodkin already had the rope. He made McGee and Susan stand while he tied their hands behind their backs.

'Now,' Viteski said, 'take them someplace very private and secure.' To McGee and Susan, he said, 'Your twins will visit you later. They have a number of questions about your intimate habits, things that will help them perfect their imitations. I suggest that you answer them truthfully because several of the questions are meant to test your veracity; they already know the correct answers to those test questions, and if you don't respond properly, they'll slowly cut you to pieces until you're convinced that cooperation is in your best interests.'

Susan glanced at the McGee look-alike. The man was smiling; it was not a nice smile. He looked like McGee in every respect except one: He did not have McGee's compassion and sensitivity in his eyes. He appeared to be quite capable of torturing an adversary into bloody, agonized submission.

Susan shuddered.

'I'll say goodbye now,' Viteski said. 'I'll be leaving the ship before it gets underway.' He smiled smugly. 'Bon voyage.'

Golodkin ushered McGee and Susan into the corridor, while Viteski remained behind in the captain's cabin with the look-alikes. In cold silence, refusing to reply to anything that McGee said, Leonid Golodkin escorted them to another companionway and drove them down into the bowels of the trawler, to the bottom deck, into the compartments that serviced the cargo holds. The place reeked of fish.

He took them into a small storage locker at the foot of the companionway; it was no larger than four meters on a side. The walls were hung with spare coils of rope; thicker hawsers were coiled and braided in stacks upon the deck. The walls were also racked with tools, including gaffs and skewers. There were four block-and-tackle sets of varying sizes, and crates of spare machine parts.

Golodkin made them sit on the bare deck, which was ice-cold. He tied their feet together, then checked to be sure that the ropes on their hands

427

were tightly knotted. When he left, he turned off the lights and closed the door, plunging them into unrelieved blackness.

'I'm scared,' Susan said.

McGee didn't reply.

She heard him scuffling about, twisting, wrenching at something.

'Jeff?'

He grunted. He was straining against something in the darkness, beginning to breathe hard.

'What're you doing?' she asked.

'Ssshh!' he said sharply.

A moment later, hands groped over her, and she almost cried out in surprise before she realised it was McGee. He had freed himself, and now he was feeling for her bonds.

As he unknotted the ropes that bound her hands, he put his mouth against her ear and spoke in the softest whisper possible. 'I doubt that anyone's listening in on us, but we can't be too careful. Golodkin didn't tighten my knots that last time; he *loosened* them just a bit.'

Her hands came free of the ropes. She rubbed her chafed wrists. Putting her mouth to Jeff's ear in the darkness, she said, 'How much more will he do to help us?'

'Probably nothing,' McGee whispered. 'He's already taken an enormous risk. From here on, we can count only on ourselves. We won't be given another chance.'

He moved away from her as she got to her feet.

He fumbled in the darkness for a while before he finally found the light switch and flipped it on.

Even before McGee moved away from the switch, Susan knew what he would go after, and she shivered with revulsion.

As she had anticipated, he went straight to the long-handled, fishermen's gaffs that hung on the wall and pulled two of them out of the spring-clips that held them. The slightly curved hooks at the ends of the gaffs were wickedly sharp; the light glinted on the pointed tips.

Susan took one of the weapons when Jeff handed it to her, but she whispered, 'I can't.'

'You've got to.'

'Oh, God.'

'Your life or theirs,' he whispered urgently.

She nodded.

'You can do it,' he said. 'And if we're lucky, it'll be easy. They won't be expecting anything. I'm sure they aren't aware that Golodkin locked us in a room full of handy weapons.'

She watched while he decided upon the best positions from which to launch a surprise attack, and then she stood where he told her.

He turned out the lights again.

It was the deepest darkness she had ever known.

* * *

McGee heard a furtive, rustling noise in the dark. He stiffened, cocked his head, listened attentively. Then he realized what it was, and he relaxed. He called softly to Susan, 'Just a rat.'

She didn't answer.

'Susan?'

'I'm okay,' she said softly from her position on the other side of the small cabin. 'Rats don't worry me.'

In spite of their precarious situation, McGee smiled.

They waited for long, tiresome minutes.

The *Golden Net* suddenly shuddered, and the deck began to vibrate as the engines were started up. Later, bells clanged in other parts of the vessel. The quality of the deck vibrations changed when, at last, the boat's screws began to churn in the water.

More minutes. More waiting.

They had been underway at least ten minutes, perhaps for a quarter of an hour, long enough to be out of Batum harbor, before there was finally a sound at the door.

McGee tensed and raised the gaff.

The door swung inward, and light spilled through from the corridor. The doppelgängers entered, first the woman and then the man.

McGee was positioned to the left of the door, almost behind it. He stepped out, swung the gaff, and hooked the vicious point through the belly of his own twin, just as the man switched on the cabin lights. Revolted by the sudden gush of blood, sickened by what he had to do, nevertheless determined to do it, McGee wrenched the long-handled

430

hook, twisted it inside his twin, trying to tear the man wide open. The gored McGee collapsed at the feet of the real McGee, flopping as if he were a fish, too shocked and too shattered by the flood of pain to scream.

The woman had a gun. It was the same silencer-equipped pistol that Viteski had been holding in the captain's cabin. She stumbled back in surprise and then fired a nearly silent shot at McGee.

Missed.

Fired again.

McGee felt the bullet tug at his sleeve, but he had been spared a second time.

Behind the fake Susan, the real Susan stepped out from behind a stack of crates and swung the other gaff.

Blood exploded from the look-alike's throat, and her eyes bulged, and the gun dropped from her hand.

McGee's heart twisted inside of him. Although he knew that he was witnessing the death of the look-alike, he was shaken by the terrible sight of Susan's slender throat being pierced by the iron hook . . . Susan's sweet mouth dribbling blood . . .

The fake Susan fell to her knees, then toppled onto her side, eyes glazed, mouth open in a cry that would never be given voice.

McGee turned and looked down at the other one, at the carbon copy of himself. The man was

431

holding his ruined belly, trying to hold his intestines inside of him. His face was contorted in agony and, mercifully, the light of life abruptly went out of his eyes.

It was like seeing a preview of my own death, McGee thought as he stared down at the duplicate's face.

He felt cold and empty.

He had never enjoyed killing, though he had always been able to do it when it was necessary. He suspected he wouldn't be able to kill anymore, regardless of the need.

Susan turned away from the bodies, stumbled into a corner, leaned against the wall, and retched violently.

McGee closed the door.

* * *

Later in the night, in a cabin that had been reserved for the fake Susan and the fake McGee, Susan sat on the lower of two bunk beds and said, 'Does Golodkin know for sure which we are?'

Standing by the porthole, looking out at the dark sea, McGee said, 'He knows.'

'How can you be sure?'

'He didn't say a word to you – because he knows you couldn't answer him in Russian.'

'So now we go back and start feeding tricked-up data to the Russians, but they think it's the real dope, coming from their two look-alikes.'

'Yes,' McGee said. 'If we can figure out what

channels they were supposed to use to get their information out.'

They were both silent a while. McGee seemed fascinated with the ocean, even though he could see very little of it in the darkness.

Susan sat studying her hands, searching for any blood that she had failed to scrub away. After a while, she said, 'Was that a bottle of brandy Golodkin left?'

'Yes.'

'I need a shot.'

'I'll pour you a double,' McGee said.

* * *

At sea. Shortly after dawn.

Susan woke, a scream caught in her throat, gasping, gagging.

McGee switched on the light.

For a moment Susan couldn't remember where she was. Then it came back to her.

Although she knew where she was, she couldn't stop gasping, for her dream was still with her, and it was a dream that, she thought, might just possibly be a reality, too.

McGee had jumped down from the upper bunk. He knelt beside her bed. 'Susan, it's okay. It's really okay. We're at sea, and we're going to make it.'

'No,' she said.

'What do you mean?'

'The crew.'

'What about the crew?'

'Harch, Quince, Jellicoe, and Parker. They're all members of the crew.'

'No, no,' he said. 'You were dreaming.'

'*They're here!*' she insisted, panicky.

'The charade is over,' McGee assured her patiently. 'It's not going to start again.'

'They're *here*, dammit!'

He couldn't calm her. He had to take her through the entire boat as the crew began the day's trawling. He had to show her every room on board and let her see every crewman in order to prove to her, beyond all doubt, that Harch and the others were not aboard.

* * *

They had breakfast in their cabin, where they could talk without rubbing Golodkin's face in the fact that Susan couldn't speak Russian.

She said, 'Where *did* they locate the look-alikes of Harch and the other three?'

'Soviet agents in the U.S. obtained photographs of Harch and the others from newspapers and college files,' McGee said. 'A search was made for Russians who even vaguely resembled the four fraternity men, and then perfection was achieved with the help of plastic surgery and the judicious use of makeup.'

'Harch's eyes . . .'

'Special contact lenses.'

'Like a Hollywood film.'

'What?'

'Special effects.'

'Yes, I guess they were worthy of Hollywood, all right.'

'Jerry Stein's corpse.'

'A hideous piece of work, wasn't it?'

She began to shake uncontrollably.

'Hey,' he said. 'Easy, easy.'

She couldn't stop shaking.

He held her.

* * *

She felt better the next day on the Turkish boat after the transfer had been effected.

Their sleeping accommodations were more comfortable, cleaner, and the food was better, too.

Over a lunch of cold meats and cheeses, she said to McGee, 'I *must* be important for the U.S. to sacrifice your cover to get me out of there.'

He hesitated, then said, 'Well . . . that wasn't the original plan.'

'Huh?'

'I wasn't supposed to bring you out.'

She didn't understand.

McGee said, 'I was supposed to kill you before the Willawauk program had a chance to work on you. A bit of air in a hypodermic needle – *bang*, a lethal brain embolism. Something like that. Something that no one could trace to me. That way, I'd be kept in place, and there'd be no chance of the Soviets breaking you.'

The blood had gone from her face. She had suddenly lost her appetite. 'Why *didn't* you kill me?'

'Because I fell in love with you.'

She stared at him, blinking.

'It's true,' he said. 'During the weeks we were setting you up for the program, working with you, planting the hypnotic suggestions that sent you to the sheriff's station and the Shipstat house, I was impressed by your strength, your strong will. It wasn't easy to set you up and manipulate you. You had . . . moxie.'

'You fell in love with my moxie?'

He smiled. 'Something like that.'

'And couldn't kill me?'

'No.'

'They'll be mad at you back in the States.'

'To hell with them.'

* * *

Two nights later, in a bedroom in the United States Ambassador's residence in Istanbul, Susan woke, screaming.

The maid came at a run. A security man. The ambassador and McGee.

'The house staff,' Susan said, clutching at McGee. 'We can't trust the house staff.'

McGee said, 'None of them looks like Harch.'

'How do I know? I haven't seen them all,' she said.

'Susan, it's three o'clock in the morning,' the security man said.

'I *have* to see them,' she said frantically.

The ambassador looked at her for a moment, glanced at McGee. Then, to the security man, he said, 'Assemble the staff.'

Neither Harch nor Quince nor Jellicoe nor Parker was employed by the United States Ambassador to Turkey.

'I'm sorry,' Susan said.

'It's okay,' McGee assured her.

'It's going to take a while,' she said apologetically.

'Of course it will.'

'Maybe the rest of my life,' she said.

* * *

A week later, in Washington, D.C., in a hotel suite that was being paid for by the United States government, Susan went to bed with Jeff McGee for the first time. They were very good together. Their bodies fit together like pieces of a puzzle. They moved together fluidly, in perfect, silken rhythm. That night, for the first time since leaving Willawauk, sleeping naked with McGee, Susan did not dream.

* * *

The year was 1980 – an ancient time, so long ago and far away. Humanity was divided into armed camps, millions lived in chains, freedom was in jeopardy, and a town like Willawauk actually existed. But there is a new world order, and the

437

human heart has been purified. Has it not? A place like Willawauk is impossible now. Evil has been purged from the human soul. Has it not?

A selection of bestsellers from Headline

BURYING THE SHADOW	Storm Constantine	£4.99 □
SCHEHERAZADE'S NIGHT OUT	Craig Shaw Gardner	£4.99 □
WULF	Steve Harris	£4.99 □
EDGE OF VENGEANCE	Jenny Jones	£5.99 □
THE BAD PLACE	Dean Koontz	£5.99 □
HIDEAWAY	Dean Koontz	£5.99 □
BLOOD GAMES	Richard Laymon	£4.99 □
DARK MOUNTAIN	Richard Laymon	£4.99 □
SUMMER OF NIGHT	Dan Simmons	£4.99 □
FALL OF HYPERION	Dan Simmons	£5.99 □
DREAM FINDER	Roger Taylor	£5.99 □
WOLFKING	Bridget Wood	£4.99 □

All Headline books are available at your local bookshop or newsagent, or can be ordered direct from the publisher. Just tick the titles you want and fill in the form below. Prices and availability subject to change without notice.

Headline Book Publishing PLC, Cash Sales Department, Bookpoint, 39 Milton Park, Abingdon, OXON, OX14 4TD, UK. If you have a credit card you may order by telephone — 0235 831700.

Please enclose a cheque or postal order made payable to Bookpoint Ltd to the value of the cover price and allow the following for postage and packing:
UK & BFPO: £1.00 for the first book, 50p for the second book and 30p for each additional book ordered up to a maximum charge of £3.00.
OVERSEAS & EIRE: £2.00 for the first book, £1.00 for the second book and 50p for each additional book.

Name ....

Address ....

....

....

If you would prefer to pay by credit card, please complete:
Please debit my Visa/Access/Diner's Card/American Express (delete as applicable) card no:

Signature ....Expiry Date ....